Lick

Kylie Scott is a long-time fan of erotic love stories and B-grade horror films. She demands a happy ending and if blood and carnage occur along the way then all the better. Based in Queensland, Australia with her two children and one delightful husband, she reads, writes and never dithers around on the internet.

www.kylie-scott.com

@KylieScottbooks

Lick

Kylie Scott

PAN BOOKS

First published 2013 by Momentum,
an imprint of Pan Macmillan Australia as *Lick: Stage Dive #1*

This edition first published 2014 by St Martin's Press, New York

This edition first published in the UK 2014 by Pan Books
an imprint of Pan Macmillan, a division of Macmillan Publishers Limited
Pan Macmillan, 20 New Wharf Road, London N1 9RR
Basingstoke and Oxford
Associated companies throughout the world
www.panmacmillan.com

ISBN 978-1-4472-6052-3

1 3 5 7 9 8 6 4 2

A CIP catalogue record for this book is available from the British Library.

Designed by Steven Seighman
Printed and bound by CPI Group (UK) Ltd, Croydon, CR0 4YY

Visit **www.panmacmillan.com** to read more about all our books
and to buy them. You will also find features, author interviews and
news of any author events, and you can sign up for e-newsletters
so that you're always first to hear about our new releases.

For Hugh.

And also for Mish, who wanted something without zombies.

ACKNOWLEDGMENTS

First up, all lyrics (with the exception of the final song) are used courtesy of Soviet X-Ray Record Club. You can learn more about the band at www.sovietxrayrecordclub.com. The term "topless cuddles" comes courtesy of the writer Daniel Dalton.

Much love to my family, who suffered as always while I wandered around in a story daze working on this. Your patience is legendary, thank you so much. To my invaluable friends who give me feedback and support (in no particular order because you are all Queens in my eyes): Tracey O'Hara, Kendall Ryan, Mel Teshco, Joanna Wylde, Kylie Griffin, and Babette. A big thank-you to all book bloggers for doing what you do, especially my friends Angie from *Twinsie Talk,* Cath from *Book Chatter Cath,* Maryse from *Maryse's Book Blog,* and Katrina from *Page Flipperz.* Thanks to Joel, Anne, and Mark at Momentum for being so supportive. And special thanks to my editor, Sarah JH Fletcher.

Last but not least, to the lovely folk who chat with me on Twitter and Facebook, and send me e-mails saying kind things about my books. To the people who enjoy my stories and take the time to write a review, THANK YOU.

ACKNOWLEDGEMENTS

Lick

CHAPTER ONE

I woke up on the bathroom floor. Everything hurt. My mouth felt like garbage and tasted worse. What the hell had happened last night? The last thing I remembered was the countdown to midnight and the thrill of turning twenty-one—legal, at last. I'd been dancing with Lauren and talking to some guy. Then BANG!

Tequila.

A whole line of shot glasses with lemon and salt on the side.

Everything I'd heard about Vegas was true. Bad things happened here, terrible things. I just wanted to crawl into a ball and die. Sweet baby Jesus, what had I been thinking to drink so much? I groaned, and even that made my head pound. This pain had not been part of the plan.

"You okay?" a voice inquired, male, deep, and nice. Really nice. A shiver went through me despite my pain. My poor broken body stirred in the strangest of places.

"Are you going to be sick again?" he asked.

Oh, no.

I opened my eyes and sat up, pushing my greasy blond hair aside. His blurry face loomed closer. I slapped a hand over my mouth because my breath had to be hideous.

"Hi," I mumbled.

Slowly, he swam into focus. He was built and beautiful and strangely familiar. Impossible. I'd never met anyone like him.

He looked to be in his mid to late twenties—a man, not a boy. He had long, dark hair falling past his shoulders and sideburns. His eyes were the darkest blue. They couldn't be real. Frankly, those eyes were overkill. I'd have swooned perfectly fine without them. Even with the tired red tinge, they were a thing of beauty. Tattoos covered the entirety of one arm and half his bare chest. A black bird had been inked into the side of his neck, the tip of its wing reaching up behind his ear. I still had on the pretty, dirty white dress Lauren had talked me into. It had been a daring choice for me on account of the way it barely contained my abundance of boobage. But this beautiful man easily had me beat for skin on show. He wore just a pair of jeans, scuffed black boots, a couple of small silver earrings, and a loose white bandage on his forearm.

Those jeans . . . he wore them well. They sat invitingly low on his hips and fit in all the right ways. Even my monster hangover couldn't detract from the view.

"Aspirin?" he asked.

And I was ogling him. My gaze darted to his face and he gave me a sly, knowing smile. Wonderful. "Yes. Please."

He grabbed a battered black leather jacket off the floor, the one I'd apparently been using as a pillow. Thank God I hadn't puked on it. Clearly, this beautiful half-naked man had seen me in all my glory, hurling multiple times. I could have drowned in the shame.

One by one he emptied the contents of his pockets out onto the cold white tiles. A credit card, guitar picks, a phone, and a string of condoms. The condoms gave me pause, but I was soon distracted by what emerged next. A multitude of paper scraps tumbled out onto the floor. All had names and numbers scrawled across them. This guy was Mr. Popularity. Hey, I could definitely see why. But what on earth was he doing here with me?

Finally, he produced a small bottle of painkillers. Sweet relief. I loved him, whoever he was and whatever he'd seen.

"You need water," he said, and got busy filling a glass from the sink behind him.

The bathroom was tiny. We both barely fit. Given Lauren's and my money situation, the hotel had been the best we could afford. She'd been determined to celebrate my birthday in style. My goal had been a bit different. Despite the presence of my hot new friend, I was pretty sure I'd failed. The pertinent parts of my anatomy felt fine. I'd heard things hurt after the first couple of times. They sure as hell had after the first. But my vagina might have been the only part of my body not giving me grief.

Still, I took a quick peek down the front of my dress. The corner of a foil package could still be seen, tucked into the side of my bra. Because if it was sitting there, strapped to me, no way would I be caught unprepared. The condom remained whole and hearty. How disappointing. Or maybe not. Finally plucking up the courage to get back on the horse, so to speak, and then not remembering it would have been horrible.

The man handed me the glass of water and placed two pills into my hand. He then sat back on his haunches to watch me. He had an intensity to him that I was in no condition to deal with.

"Thanks," I said, then swallowed the aspirin. Noisy rumbles rose from my belly. Nice, very ladylike.

"Are you sure you're okay?" he asked. His glorious mouth twitched into a smile as if we shared a private joke between us.

The joke being me.

All I could do was stare. Given my current condition, he was just too much. The hair, face, body, ink, all of it. Someone needed to invent a word superlative enough to describe him.

After a long moment it dawned on me that he expected an answer to his question. I nodded, still unwilling to unleash my morning breath, and gave him a grim smile. The best I could do.

"Okay. That's good," he said.

He was certainly attentive. I didn't know what I'd done to deserve such kindness. If I'd picked up the poor guy with promises of sex and then proceeded to spend the night with my head in the toilet, by rights he should be a bit disgruntled. Maybe he hoped I'd make good on the offer this morning. It seemed the only plausible explanation for why he'd linger.

Under normal conditions, he was light-years out of my league and (for the sake of my pride) worlds away from my type. I liked clean-cut. Clean-cut was nice. Bad boys were highly overrated. God knows, I'd watched enough girls throw themselves at my brother over the years. He'd taken what they'd offered if it suited him, and then moved on. Bad boys weren't the stuff serious relationships were made of. Not that I'd been chasing forever last night, just a positive sexual experience. Something not involving Tommy Byrnes being mad at me for getting a smear of blood on the backseat of his parents' car. God, what a horrible memory. The next day the douche had dumped me for a girl on the track team half my size. He then added insult to injury by spreading rumors about me. I hadn't been made bitter or twisted by this event at all.

What had happened last night? My head remained a tangled, throbbing mess, the details hazy, incomplete.

"We should get something into you," he said. "You want me to order some dry toast or something?"

"No." The thought of food was not fun. Not even coffee appealed, and coffee always appealed. I was half tempted to check myself for a pulse, just in case. Instead, I pushed my hand through my crappy hair, getting it out of my eyes. "No . . . ow!" Strands caught on something, tugging hard at my scalp. "Crap."

"Hang on." He reached out and carefully disentangled my messy do from whatever was causing the trouble. "There we go."

"Thanks." Something winked at me from my left hand, snagging my attention. A ring, but not just any ring. An amazing ring, a stupendous one.

"Holy shit," I whispered.

It couldn't be real. It was so big it bordered on obscene. A stone that size would cost a fortune. I stared, bemused, turning my hand to catch the light. The band beneath was thick, solid, and the rock sure shone and sparkled like the real deal.

As if.

"Ah, yeah. About that . . ." he said, dark brows drawn down. He looked vaguely embarrassed by the ice rink on my finger. "If you still wanna change it for something smaller, that's okay with me. It is kinda big. I do get your point about that."

I couldn't shake the feeling I knew him from somewhere. Somewhere that wasn't last night or this morning or anything to do with the ridiculous beautiful ring on my finger.

"You bought me this?" I asked.

He nodded. "Last night at Cartier."

"Cartier?" My voice dropped to a whisper. "Huh."

For a long moment he just stared at me. "You don't remember?"

I really didn't want to answer that. "What is that, even? Two, three carats?"

"Five."

"Five? Wow."

"What do you remember?" he asked, voice hardening just a little.

"Well . . . it's hazy."

"No." His frown increased until it owned his handsome face. "You have got to be fucking kidding me. You seriously don't know?"

What to say? My mouth hung open, useless. There was a lot I didn't know. To my knowledge, however, Cartier didn't do costume jewelry. My head swam. Bad feelings unfurled within my stomach and bile burnt the back of my throat. Worse even than before.

I was not puking in front of this guy.

Not again.

He took a deep breath, nostrils flaring. "I didn't realize you'd had that much to drink. I mean, I knew you'd had a bit, but . . . shit. Seriously? You don't remember us going on the gondolas at the Venetian?"

"We went on gondolas?"

"Fuck. Ah, how about when you bought me a burger? Do you remember that?"

"Sorry."

"Wait a minute," he said, watching me through narrowed eyes. "You're just messing with me, aren't you?"

"I'm so sorry."

He physically recoiled from me. "Let me get this straight, you don't remember anything?"

"No," I said, swallowing hard. "What did we do last night?"

"We got fucking married," he growled.

This time, I didn't make it to the toilet.

———

I decided on divorce while I brushed my teeth, practiced what I would say to him as I washed my hair. But you couldn't rush these things. Unlike last night, when I'd apparently rushed into marriage. Rushing again would be wrong, foolish. That, or I was a coward taking the world's longest shower. Odds were on the latter.

Holy, holy hell. What a mess. I couldn't even begin to get my head wrapped around it. Married. Me. My lungs wouldn't work. Panic waited right around the corner.

No way could my desire for this disaster to go away come as a surprise to him. Puking on the floor had to have been a huge hint. I groaned and covered my face with my hands at the memory. His look of disgust would haunt me all my days.

My parents would kill me if they ever found out. I had plans, priorities. I was studying to be an architect like my father. Marriage to anyone at this stage didn't fit into those plans. In another ten, fifteen years, maybe. But marriage at twenty-one? Hell no. I hadn't even been on a second date in years and now I had a ring on my finger. No way did that make sense. I was doomed. This crazy wedding caper wasn't something I could hide from.

Or could I?

Unless my parents could not find out. Ever. Over the years I had made something of a habit of not involving them in things that might be seen as unsavory, unnecessary, or just plain stupid. This marriage quite possibly fell under all three categories.

Actually, maybe no one need know. If I didn't tell, how would they find out? They wouldn't. The answer was awe-inspiring in its simplicity.

"Yes!" I hissed and punched the air, clipping the shower head with the side of my fist. Water sprayed everywhere, including straight in my eyes, blinding me. Never mind, I had the answer.

Denial. I'd take the secret to my grave. No one would ever know of my extreme drunken idiocy.

I smiled with relief, my panic attack receding enough so that I could breathe. Oh, thank goodness. Everything would be okay. I had a new plan to get me back on track with the old one. Brilliant. I'd brave up, go and face him, and set things straight. Twenty-one-year-olds with grand life plans didn't marry complete strangers in Vegas, no matter how beautiful those strangers happened to be. It would be fine. He'd understand. In all likelihood, he sat out there right now, working out the most efficient method to dump and run.

The diamond still glittered on my hand. I couldn't bring myself to take it off just yet. It was like Christmas on my finger, so big, bright, and shiny. Though, upon reflection, my temporary husband didn't exactly appear to be rich. His jacket and jeans were both well-worn. The man was a mystery.

Wait. What if he was into something illegal? Maybe I'd married a criminal. Panic rushed back in with a vengeance. My stomach churned and my head throbbed. I knew nothing about the person waiting in the next room. Absolutely not a damn thing. I'd shoved him out the bathroom door without even getting his name.

A knock on the door sent my shoulders sky-high.

"Evelyn?" he called out, proving he at least knew my name.

"Just a second."

I turned off the taps and stepped out, wrapping a towel around myself. The width of it was barely sufficient to cover my curves, but my dress had puke on it. Putting it back on was out of the question.

"Hi," I said, opening the bathroom door a hand's length. He stood almost half a head taller than me, and I wasn't short by any means. Dressed in only a towel, I found him rather intimidating. However much he'd had to drink the previous night, he still looked gorgeous, as opposed to me—pale, pasty, and sopping wet. The aspirins hadn't done nearly as much as they should have.

Of course, I'd thrown them up.

"Hey." He didn't meet my eyes. "Look, I'm going to get this taken care of, okay?"

"Taken care of?"

"Yeah," he said, still avoiding all eye contact. Apparently the hideous green motel carpeting was beyond enticing. "My lawyers will deal with all this."

"You have lawyers?" Criminals had lawyers. Shit. I had to get myself divorced from this guy now.

"Yeah, I have lawyers. You don't need to worry about anything. They'll send you the paperwork or whatever. However this works." He gave me an irritated glance, lips a tight line, and pulled on his leather jacket over his bare chest. His T-shirt still hung drying over the edge of the tub. Sometime during the night I must have puked on it too. How gruesome. If I were him, I'd divorce me and never look back.

"This was a mistake," he said, echoing my thoughts.

"Oh."

"What?" His gaze jumped to my face. "You disagree?"

"No," I said quickly.

"Didn't think so. Pity it made sense last night, yeah?" He shoved a hand through his hair and made for the door. "Take care."

"Wait!" The stupid, amazing ring wouldn't come off my finger. I tugged and turned it, trying to wrestle it into submission. Finally it budged, grazing my knuckle raw in the process. Blood welled to the surface. One more stain in this whole sordid affair. "Here."

"For fuck's sake." He scowled at the rock sparkling in the palm of my hand as if it had personally offended him. "Keep it."

"I can't. It must have cost a fortune."

He shrugged.

"Please." I held it out, hand jiggling, impatient to be rid of the evidence of my drunken stupidity. "It belongs to you. You have to take it."

"No. I don't."

"But—"

Without another word, the man stormed out, slamming the door shut behind him. The thin walls vibrated with the force of it.

Whoa. My hand fell back to my side. He sure had a temper. Not that I hadn't given him provocation, but still. I wish I remembered what had gone on between us. Any inkling would be good.

Meanwhile my left butt cheek felt sore. I winced, carefully rubbing the area. My dignity wasn't the only casualty, it seemed. I must have scratched my behind at some stage, bumped into some furniture or taken a dive in my fancy new heels. The pricey ones Lauren had insisted went with the dress, the ones whose current whereabouts were a mystery. I hoped I hadn't lost them. Given my recent nuptials, nothing would surprise me.

I wandered back into the bathroom with a vague memory of a buzzing noise and laughter ringing in my ear, of him whispering to me. It made no sense.

I turned and raised the edge of my towel, going up on tippy-toes to inspect my ample ass in the mirror. Black ink and hot pink skin.

All the air left my body in a rush.
There was a word on my left butt cheek, a name:
David
I spun and dry-heaved into the sink.

CHAPTER TWO

Lauren sat beside me on the plane, fiddling with my iPhone. "I don't understand how your taste in music can be so bad. We've been friends for years. Have I taught you nothing?"

"To not drink tequila."

She rolled her eyes.

Above our heads the seat belt sign flashed on. A polite voice advised us to return our seats to the upright position as we'd be landing in a few minutes. I swallowed the dregs of my shitty plane coffee with a wince. Fact was, no amount of caffeine could help me today. Quality didn't even come into it.

"I am deadly serious," I said. "I'm also never setting foot in Nevada ever again so long as I live."

"Now, there's an overreaction."

"Not even a little, lady."

Lauren had stumbled back to the motel a bare two hours before our flight was due to leave. I'd spent the time repacking my small bag over and over in an attempt to get my life back into some semblance of order. It was good to see Lauren smiling, though getting to the airport in time had been a race. Apparently she and the cute waiter she'd met would be keeping in touch. Lauren had always been great with guys, while I was more closely related to your standard garden-variety wallflower. My plan to get laid in Vegas had been a deliberate attempt to get out of that rut. So much for that idea.

Lauren was studying economics, and she was gorgeous, inside and out. I was more kind of unwieldy. It was why I made a habit of walking everywhere I could in Portland and trying not to sample the contents of the cake display case at the café where I worked. It kept me manageable, waist-wise. Though my mom still saw fit to give me lectures on the subject because God forbid I dare put sugar in my coffee. My thighs would no doubt explode or something.

Lauren had three older brothers and knew what to say to guys. Nothing intimidated her. The girl oozed charm. I had one older brother, but we no longer interacted outside of major family holidays. Not since he moved out of our parents' home four years back leaving only a note. Nathan had a temper and a gift for getting into trouble. He'd been the bad boy in high school, always getting into fights and skipping classes. Though blaming my lack of success with guys on my nonexistent relationship with my brother was wrong. I could own my deficiencies with the opposite sex. Mostly.

"Listen to this." Lauren plugged my earphones into her phone, and the whine of electric guitars exploded inside my skull. The pain was exquisite. My headache roared back to sudden, horrific life. Nothing remained of my brain but bloody red mush. Of this I was certain.

I ripped out the earphones. "Don't. Please."

"But that's Stage Dive."

"And they're lovely. But, you know, another time maybe."

"I worry about you sometimes. I just want you to know that."

"There is nothing wrong with country music played softly."

Lauren snorted and fluffed up her dark hair. "There is nothing right with country music played at any volume. So what did you get up to last night? Apart from spending quality time heaving?"

"Actually, that about sums it up." The less said the better. How could I ever explain? Still, guilt slid through me and I squirmed in my seat. The tattoo throbbed in protest.

I hadn't told Lauren about my grand having-good-sex plan for the night. She'd have wanted to help. Honestly, sex didn't strike me as the sort of thing you should have help with. Apart from what was required from the sexual partner in question, of course. Lauren's assistance would have involved foisting me on every hottie in the room with promises of my immediate leg-open availability.

I loved Lauren, and her loyalty was above question, but she didn't have a subtle bone in her body. She'd punched a girl in the nose in fifth grade for teasing me about my weight, and we'd been friends ever since. With Lauren, you always knew exactly where you stood. Something I appreciated the bulk of the time, just not when discretion was called for.

Happily, my sore stomach survived the bumpy landing. As soon as those wheels hit the tarmac, I let out a sigh of relief. I was back in my hometown. Beautiful Oregon, lovely Portland, never again would I stray. With mountains in the distance and trees in the city, she was a singular delight. To limit myself to the one city for life might indeed be going overboard. But it was great to be home. I had an all-important internship starting next week that my father had pulled strings to get for me. There were also next semester's classes to start planning for.

Everything would be fine. I'd learned my lesson. Normally, I didn't go past three drinks. Three drinks were good. Three got me happy without tripping me face-first into disaster. Never again would I cross the line. I was back to being the good old organized, boring me. Adventures were not cool, and I was done with them.

We stood and grabbed our bags out of the overhead lockers. Everyone pushed forward in a rush to disembark. The hostesses gave us practiced smiles as we tramped up the aisle and out into the connecting tunnel. Next came security, and then we poured out into the baggage claim. Fortunately, we only had carry-on, so no delays there. I couldn't wait to get home.

I heard shouting up ahead. Lights were flashing. Someone famous must have been on the plane. People ahead of us turned and stared. I looked back too but saw no familiar faces.

"What's going on?" Lauren asked, scanning the crowd.

"I don't know," I said, standing on tippy-toes, getting excited by all the commotion.

Then I heard it, my name being called out over and over. Lauren's mouth pursed in surprise. Mine fell open.

"When's the baby due?"

"Evelyn, is David with you?"

"Will there be another wedding?"

"When will you be moving to LA?"

"Is David coming to meet your parents?"

"Evelyn, is this the end for Stage Dive?"

"Is it true that you got tattoos of each other's names?"

"How long have you and David been seeing each other?"

"What do you say to accusations that you've broken up the band?"

My name and his, over and over, mixed into a barrage of endless questions. All of which merged into chaos. A wall of noise I could barely comprehend. I stood gaping in disbelief as flashbulbs blinded me and people pressed in. My heart hammered. I'd never been great with crowds, and there was no escape that I could see.

Lauren snapped out of it first.

She shoved her sunglasses onto my face and then grabbed my hand. With liberal use of her elbows, she dragged me through the mob. The world became a blur, thanks to her prescription lenses. I was lucky not to fall on my ass. We ran through the busy airport and out a waiting taxi, jumping the queue. People started yelling. We ignored them.

The paparazzi were close behind.

The motherfucking paparazzi. It would have been surreal if it wasn't so frantic and in my face.

Lauren pushed me into the backseat of the cab. I scrambled across, then slumped down, doing my best to hide. Wishing I could disappear entirely.

"Go! Hurry!" she shouted at the driver.

The driver took her at her word. He shot out of the place, sending us sliding across the cracked vinyl seating. My forehead bounced off the back of the (luckily padded) passenger seat. Lauren pulled my seat belt over me and jammed it into the clasp. My hands didn't seem to be working. Everything jumped and jittered.

"Talk to me," she said.

"Ah . . ." No words came out. I pushed her sunglasses up on top of my head and stared into space. My ribs hurt, and my heart still pounded so hard.

"Ev?" With a small smile, Lauren patted my knee. "Did you somehow happen to get married while we were away?"

"I . . . yeah. I, uh, I did. I think."

"Wow."

And then it just all blurted out of me. "God, Lauren. I screwed up so badly and I barely even remember any of it. I just woke up and he was there and then he was so pissed at me and I don't even blame him. I didn't know how to tell you. I was just going to pretend it never happened."

"I don't think that's going to work now."

"No."

"Okay. No big deal. So you're married." Lauren nodded, her face freakily calm. No anger, no blame. Meanwhile, I felt terrible I hadn't confided in her. We shared everything.

"I'm sorry," I said. "I should have told you."

"Yes, you should have. But never mind." She straightened out her skirt like we were sitting down to tea. "So, who did you marry?"

"D-David. His name is David."

"David Ferris, by any chance?"

The name sounded familiar. "Maybe?"

"Where we going?" asked the cabdriver, never taking his eyes off the traffic. He wove in and out among the cars with supernatural speed. If I'd been up to feeling anything, I might have felt fear and more nausea. Blind terror, perhaps. But I had nothing.

"Ev?" Lauren turned in her seat, checking out the cars behind us. "We haven't lost them. Where do you want to go?"

"Home," I said, the first safe place to come to mind. "My parents' place, I mean."

"Good call. They've got a fence." Without pausing for breath, Lauren rattled off the address to the driver. She frowned and pushed the sunglasses back down over my face. "Keep them on."

I gave a rough laugh as the world outside turned back into a smudge. "You really think it'll help, now?"

"No," she said, flicking back her long hair. "But people in these situations always wear sunglasses. Trust me."

"You watch too much TV." I closed my eyes. The sunglasses weren't helping my hangover. Nor was the rest of it. All my own damn fault. "I'm sorry I didn't say something. I didn't mean to get married. I don't even remember what happened exactly. This is such a . . ."

"Clusterfuck?"

"That word works."

Lauren sighed and rested her head on my shoulder. "You're right. You really shouldn't drink tequila ever again."

"No," I agreed.

"Do me a favor?" she asked.

"Mm?"

"Don't break up my favorite band."

"Ohmygod." I shoved the sunglasses back up, frowning hard enough to make my head throb. "Guitarist. He's the guitarist. That's where I know him from."

"Yes. He's the guitarist for Stage Dive. Well spotted."

The David Ferris. He'd been on Lauren's bedroom wall for years. Granted, he had to be the last person I'd expect to wake up with, on a bathroom floor or otherwise. But how the hell could I not have recognized him? "That's how he could afford the ring."

"What ring?"

Shuffling farther down in the seat, I fished the monster out of my jeans pocket and brushed off the lint and fluff. The diamond glittered accusingly in the bright light of day.

Lauren started shaking beside me, muffled laughter escaping her lips. "Mother of God, it's huuuuge!"

"I know."

"No, seriously."

"I know."

"Fuck me. I think I'm about to pee myself," she squealed,

fanning her face and bouncing up and down on the car seat. "Look at it!"

"Lauren, stop. We can't both be freaking out. That won't work."

"Right. Sorry." She cleared her throat, visibly struggling to get herself back under control. "How much is that even worth?"

"I really don't want to guess."

"That. Is. Insane."

We both stared at my bling in awed silence.

Suddenly Lauren started bopping up and down in her seat again like a kid riding a sugar high. "I know! Let's sell it and go backpacking in Europe. Hell, we could probably circle the globe a couple of times on that sucker. Imagine it."

"We can't," I said, as tempting as it sounded. "I've got to get it back to him somehow. I can't keep this."

"Pity." She grinned. "So, congratulations. You're married to a rock star."

I tucked the ring back in my pocket. "Thanks. What the hell am I going to do?"

"I honestly don't know." She shook her head at me, her eyes full of wonder. "You've exceeded all of my expectations. I wanted you to let your hair down a little. Get a life and give mankind another chance. But this is a whole new level of crazy you've ascended to. Do you really have a tattoo?"

"Yes."

"Of his name?"

I sighed and nodded.

"Where, might I inquire?"

I shut my eyes tight. "My left butt cheek."

Lauren lost it, laughing so hard that tears started streaming down her face.

Perfect.

CHAPTER THREE

Dad's cell rang just before midnight. My own had long since been switched off. When the home phone wouldn't stop ringing, we'd unplugged it from the wall. Twice the police had been by to clear people out of the front yard. Mom had finally taken a sleeping pill and gone to bed. Having her neat, ordered world shot to hell hadn't gone down so well. Surprisingly, after an initial outburst, Dad had been dealing all right with the situation. I was suitably apologetic and wanted a divorce. He was willing to chalk this one up to hormones or the like. But that all changed when he looked at the screen of his cell.

"Leyton?" He answered the call, his eyes drilling into me from across the room. My stomach sank accordingly. Only a parent could train you so well. I had disappointed him. We both knew it. There was only one Leyton and only one reason why he'd be calling at this hour on this day.

"Yes," my father said. "It's an unfortunate situation." The lines around his mouth deepened, turning into crevices. "Understandably. Yes. Good night, then."

His fingers tightened around the cell and then he tossed it onto the dining room table. "Your internship has been canceled."

All of the air rushed out of me as my lungs constricted to the size of pennies.

"Leyton rightly feels that given your present situation . . ." My father's voice trailed away to nothing. He'd called in years-old favors to get me the internship with one of Portland's most prestigious architectural firms. It'd had taken only a thirty-second phone call, however, to make it disappear.

Someone banged on the door. Neither of us reacted. People had been hammering on it for hours.

Dad started pacing back and forth across the living room. I just watched in a daze.

Throughout my childhood, times such as this had always followed a certain pattern. Nathan got into a fight at school. The school called our mother. Our mother had a meltdown. Nate retreated to his room or, worse, disappeared for days. Dad got home and paced. And there I'd be among it all, trying to play mediator, the expert at not making waves. So what the hell was I doing standing in the middle of a fucking tsunami?

As kids went, I'd always been pretty low maintenance. I'd gotten good grades in high school and had gone on to the same local college as my father. I might have lacked his natural talent at design, but I put in the hours and effort to get the grades I needed to pass. I had been working part-time in the same coffee shop since I was fifteen. Moving in with Lauren had been my one grand rebellion. I was, all in all, fantastically boring. My parents had wanted me to stay home and save money. Anything else I'd achieved had been done through subterfuge so my parents could sleep soundly at night. Not that I'd gotten up to much. The odd party. The Tommy episode four years back. There'd been nothing to prepare me for this.

Apart from the press, there were people crying on the front lawn and holding signs proclaiming their love for David. One man was holding an old-style boom box high in the air, blasting out music. A song called "San Pedro" was their favorite. The yelling would reach a crescendo every time the singer made it to the chorus, "But the sun was low and we'd no place to go . . ."

Apparently, later they were planning on burning me in effigy.

Which was fine, I wanted to die.

My big brother Nathan had been over to collect Lauren and take her back to his place. We hadn't seen each other since Christmas, but desperate times and desperate measures. The apartment Lauren and I shared was likewise surrounded. Going there was out of the question, and Lauren didn't want to get her family or other friends involved. To say Nathan enjoyed my predicament would be unkind. Not untrue, but definitely unkind. He'd always been the one in trouble. This time, however, it was all on me. Nathan had never gotten accidentally married and inked in Vegas.

Because of course some asshat reporter had asked my mother how she felt about the tattoo, so that secret was out. Apparently now no decent boy from a good family would ever marry me. Previously, I'd been unlikely to land a man due to my various lumps and bumps. But now it was all on the tattoo. I'd decided to forgo pointing out to her that I was already married.

More banging on the front door. Dad just looked at me. I shrugged.

"Ms. Thomas?" a big voice boomed. "David sent me."

Yeah, right. "I'm calling the cops."

"Wait. Please," the big voice said. "I've got him on the phone. Just open the door enough so I can hand it in to you."

"No."

Muffled noises. "He said to ask you about his T-shirt."

The one he'd left behind in Vegas. It was in my bag, still damp. Huh. Maybe. But I still wasn't convinced. "What else?"

More talking. "He said he still didn't want the . . . excuse me, miss . . . 'fucking ring' back."

I opened the door but kept the chain on. A man who resembled a bulldog in a black suit handed me a cell phone.

"Hello?"

Loud music played in the background and there were lots of voices. Apparently this marriage incident hadn't slowed down David at all.

"Ev?"

"Yes."

He paused. "Listen, you probably want to lie low for a while until this all dies down, okay? Sam will get you out of there. He's part of my security team."

Sam gave me a polite smile. I'd seen mountains smaller than this guy.

"Where would I go?" I asked.

"He'll, ah . . . he'll bring you to me. We'll sort something out."

"To you?"

"Yeah, there'll be the divorce papers and shit to sign, so you may as well come here."

I wanted to say no. But taking this away from my parents' front doorstep was wildly tempting. Ditto with getting out of there before Mom woke up and heard about the internship. Still, with good reason or not, I couldn't forget the way David had slammed his way out of my life that morning. I had a vague backup plan taking shape. With the internship gone, I could return to work at the café. Ruby would be delighted to have me full-time for the summer and I loved being there. Turning up with this horde on my heels, however, would be a disaster.

My options were few and none of them appealed, but still I hedged. "I don't know . . ."

He gave a particularly pained-sounding sigh. "What else are you gonna do? Huh?"

Good question.

Out past Sam, the insanity continued. Lights flashed and people yelled. It didn't seem real. If this was what David's every-day life was like, I had no idea how he handled it.

"Look. You need to get the fuck out of there," he said, words brisk, brittle. "It'll calm down in a while."

My dad stood beside me, wringing his hands. David was right. Whatever happened, I had to get this away from the people I loved. I could do that much at least.

"Ev?"

"Sorry. Yes, I'd like to take you up on that offer," I said. "Thank you."

"Hand the phone back to Sam."

I did as asked, also opening the door fully so the big man could come inside. He wasn't overly tall, but he was built. The guy took up serious space. Sam nodded and said some "yes, sirs." Then he hung up. "Ms. Thomas, the car is waiting."

"No," said Dad.

"Dad—"

"You cannot trust that man. Look at everything that's hap-pened."

"It's hardly all his fault. I played my part in this." The whole situation embarrassed me. But running and hiding was not the answer. "I need to fix it."

"No," he repeated, laying down the law.

The problem was, I wasn't a little girl anymore. And this wasn't about me not believing that our backyard was too small for a pony. "I'm sorry, Dad. But I've made my decision."

His face pinked, eyes incredulous. Previously, on the rare occasions he'd taken a hard stance, I'd buckled (or quietly gone about my business behind his back). But this time . . . I was not convinced. For once my father seemed old to me, unsure. More than that, this problem was mine, all mine.

"Please, trust me," I said.

"Ev, honey, you don't have to do this," said Dad, trying a different tack. "We can figure something out on our own."

"I know we could. But he's got lawyers on the job already. This is for the best."

"Won't you need your own lawyer?" he asked. There were new lines on his face, as if just this one day had aged him. Guilt slunk through me.

"I'll ask around, find someone suitable for you. I don't want you being taken advantage of here," he continued. "Someone must know a decent divorce lawyer."

"Dad, it's not like I have any money to protect. We're going to make this as straightforward as possible," I said with a forced smile. "It's okay. We'll take care of it, and then I'll be back."

"We? Honey, you barely know this guy. You cannot trust him."

"The whole world is apparently watching. What's the worst that can happen?" I sent a silent prayer to the heavens that I'd never find out the answer to that.

"This is a mistake . . ." Dad sighed. "I know you're as disappointed over the internship as I am. But we need to stop and think here."

"I have thought about it. I need to get this circus away from you and Mom."

Dad's gaze went to the darkened hallway heading toward where Mom lay in her drug-induced slumber. The last thing I wanted was for my father to feel torn between the two of us.

"It'll be okay," I said, willing it to be true. "Really."

He hung his head at last. "I think you're doing the wrong

thing. But call me if you need anything. If you want to come home, I'll organize a flight for you right away."

I nodded.

"I'm serious. You call me if you need anything."

"Yes. I will." I wouldn't.

I picked up my backpack, still fresh from Vegas. No chance to refresh my wardrobe. All of my clothes were at the apartment. I smoothed back my hair, tucking it neatly behind my ears, trying to make myself look a little less like a train wreck.

"You were always my good girl," Dad said, sounding wistful.

I didn't know what to say.

He patted me on the arm. "Call me."

"Yeah," I said, my throat tight. "Say bye to Mom for me. I'll talk to you soon."

Sam stepped forward. "Your daughter is in safe hands, sir."

I didn't wait to hear Dad's reply. For the first time in hours I stepped outside. Pandemonium erupted. The instinct to turn tail, run, and hide was huge. But with Sam's big body beside me it wasn't quite so crazy frightening as before. He put an arm loosely around my shoulder and hustled me out of there, down the garden path, and toward the waiting crowd. Another man in a sharp black suit came toward us, making a way through the mob from the other side. The noise level skyrocketed. A woman yelled that she hated me and called me a cunt. Someone else wanted me to tell David that he loved him. Mostly, though, it was more questions. Cameras were shoved in my face, the flashbulbs glaring. Before I could stumble, Sam was there. My feet barely touched the ground as he and his friend hurried me into the waiting car. Not a limousine. Lauren would be disappointed. It was a fancy new sedan with an all-leather interior. The door slammed shut behind me and Sam and his friend climbed in. The driver nodded to me in the rearview mirror, then carefully accelerated. People banged on the windows and ran alongside. I huddled down in the middle of the seat. Soon we left them behind.

I was on my way back to David.

My husband.

CHAPTER FOUR

I slept on the short flight to LA, curled up in a super-comfortable chair in a corner of the private jet. It was a level of luxury above anything I'd ever imagined. If you had to turn your life upside down, you might as well enjoy the opulence while you were at it. Sam had offered me champagne and I'd politely declined. The idea of alcohol still turned me inside out. It was entirely possible I'd never drink again.

My career path had been temporarily shot to hell, but never mind, I had a new plan. Get divorced. It was breathtakingly simple. I loved it. I was back in control of my own destiny. One day, when I got married, if I got married, it would not be to a stranger in Vegas. It would not be a terrible mistake.

When I woke up, we were landing. Another sleek sedan stood waiting. I'd never been to LA. It looked every bit as wide-awake as Vegas, though less glam. Plenty of people were still out and about despite the hour of night.

I had to brave turning on my phone sometime. Lauren would be worried. I pushed the little black button and the screen flashed bright lights at me, coming to life. A hundred and fifty-eight text messages and ninety-seven missed calls. I blinked stupidly at the screen but the number didn't change. Holy hell.

Apparently everyone I knew had heard the news, along with quite a few people I did not.

My phone pinged.

Lauren: You okay? Where r u???

Me: LA. Going to him till things calm down. You all right?

Lauren: I'm fine. LA? Living the dream.

Me: Private jet was amazing. Though his fans are crazy.

Lauren: Your brother is crazy.

Me: Sorry about that.

Lauren: I can handle him. Whatever happens, do not break up the band!!!

Me: Got it.

Lauren: But break his heart. He wrote San Pedro after what's-her-face cheated on him. That album was BRIL-LIANT!

Me: Promise to leave him a broken quivering mess.

Lauren: That's the spirit.

Me: xx

It was after three in the morning by the time we reached the massive 1920s-era Spanish-style mansion in Laurel Canyon. It was lovely. Though Dad would not have been impressed—he preferred clean, contemporary lines with minimal fuss. Four-bedroom, two-bathroom houses for Portland's well-to-do. But I don't know, there was something beautiful and romantic about such extravagance. The decorative black wrought iron against the bare white walls.

A gaggle of girls and the obligatory pack of press milled about outside. News of our marriage had apparently stirred things up. Or maybe they always camped here. Ornate iron gates swung slowly open at our approach. Palm trees lined the long, winding driveway, large fronds waving in the wind as we drove by. The place looked like something out of a movie. Stage Dive were big business, I knew that much. Their last two albums had spawned numerous hit songs. Lauren had driven all over the countryside last summer, attending three of their shows in the space of a week. All of them had been in stadiums.

Still, that was a damn big house.

Nerves wound me tight. I wore the same jeans and blue top I'd had on all day. Dressing for the occasion wasn't an option. The best I could do was finger-brush my hair and spray on some perfume I had in my handbag. I might be lacking in glamour, but at least I'd smell all right.

Every light in the house blazed bright, and rock music boomed out into the warm night air. The big double doors stood open, and people spilled out of the house and onto the steps. It seemed the party to end all others was taking place.

Sam opened the car door for me and I hesitantly climbed out.

"I'll walk you in, Ms. Thomas."

"Thank you," I said.

I didn't move. After a moment Sam got the message. He forged ahead and I followed. A couple of girls were making out just inside the door, mouths all over each other. They were both slender and beyond gorgeous, dressed in tiny, sparkly dresses that barely hit their thighs. More people milled about drinking and dancing. A chandelier hung overhead and a grand staircase wound around an interior wall. The place was a Hollywood palace.

Thankfully, no one seemed to notice me. I could gawk to my heart's content.

Sam stopped to talk to a young man slouched against a wall, a bottle of beer to his lips. Long, blond hair stuck out every which way and his nose was pierced with a silver ring. Lots of tattoos. In ripped black jeans and a faded T-shirt, he had the same über-cool air as David. Maybe rock stars brought their clothes artfully aged. People with money were a pack apart.

The man gave me an obvious looking-over. I steadfastly resisted the urge to shrink back. Not happening. When he met my eyes, his gaze seemed curious but not unfriendly. The tension inside me eased.

"Hey," he said.

"Hi." I braved a smile.

"It's all good," he said to Sam. Then he tipped his chin at me. "Come on. He's out this way. I'm Mal."

"Hi," I said again, stupidly. "I'm Ev."

"Are you all right, Ms. Thomas?" asked Sam in a low voice.

"Yes, Sam. Thank you very much."

He gave me a polite nod and headed back the way we'd come. His broad shoulders and bald head soon disappeared among the crowd. Running after him and asking to be taken home wouldn't help, but my feet itched to do so. No, enough with the pity party. Time to pull up my big-girl panties and get on with things.

Hundreds of people had been packed into the place. The only thing in my experience that came close was my senior prom, and it paled significantly. None of the dresses here tonight compared. I could almost smell the money. Lauren was the dedicated celeb-watcher, but even I recognized a few of the faces. One of last year's Oscar winners and a lingerie model I'd seen on billboards back home. A teen pop queen who shouldn't have been swilling from a bottle of vodka, let alone sitting on the lap of a silver-haired member of . . . damn, what was that band's name?

Anyway.

I shut my mouth before someone noticed I had stars in my eyes. Lauren would have loved all this. It was amazing.

When a woman who most closely resembled a half-dressed Amazonian goddess sideswiped me, Mal stopped and frowned after her. "Some people, no manners. Come on."

The sluggish beat of the music moved through me, reawakening the dregs of my headache and putting a taint on the glitter. We weaved our way through a big room filled with plush velvet lounges and the people draped over them. Next came a space cluttered with guitars, amps, and other rock 'n' roll paraphernalia. Inside the house the air was smoky and humid, despite all the open windows and doors. My top clung beneath my arms. We moved outside onto the balcony, where a light breeze was blowing. I raised my face to it gratefully.

And there he was, leaning against a decorative iron railing. The strong lines of his face were in profile. Holy shit, how could I have forgotten? There was no explaining the full effect of David in real life. He fit in with the beautiful people just fine. He was one of them. I, on the other hand, belonged in the kitchen with the waitstaff.

My husband was busy talking to the leggy, enhanced-breasted brunette beside him. Perhaps he was a tit man and that's how we'd wound up wed. It was as good a guess as any. Dressed in only a teeny white bikini, the girl clung to him like she'd been surgically attached. Her hair was artfully messed in a way that suggested a minimum of two hours at a top-notch salon. She was beautiful and I hated her just a little. A trickle of sweat ran down my spine.

"Hey, Dave," Mal called out. "Company."

David turned, then saw me and frowned. In this light, his eyes looked dark and distinctly unhappy. "Ev."

"Hi."

Mal started to laugh. "That's about the only word I've been able to get out of her. Seriously, man, does your wife even speak?"

"She speaks." His tone of voice made it obvious he wished I wouldn't, ever again. Or at least not within his hearing.

I didn't know what to say. Generally, I wasn't after universal love and acceptance. Open hostility, however, was still kind of new to me.

The brunette tittered and rubbed her bountiful boobs against David's arm as if she was marking him. Sadly for her, he didn't seem to notice. She gave me a foul look, red mouth puckered. Charming. Though the fact that she saw me as competition was a huge boost to my ego. I stood taller and looked my husband in the eye.

Big mistake.

David's dark hair had been tied back in a little ponytail with strands falling around his face. What should have reeked of scummy drug dealer worked on him. Of course it did. He could probably make a dirty back alleyway seem like the honeymoon suite. A gray T-shirt molded to his thick shoulders and faded blue jeans covered his long legs. His black army-style boots were crossed at the ankles, easy as you please, because he belonged here. I didn't.

"You mind finding her a room?" David asked his friend.

Mal snorted. "Do I look like your fucking butler? You'll show your own wife to a room. Don't be an asshole."

"She's not my wife," David growled.

"Every news channel in the country would disagree with you there." Mal ruffled my hair with a big hand, making me feel all of eight years old. "Check you later, child bride. Nice to meet you."

"Child bride?" I asked, feeling clueless.

Mal stopped and grinned. "You haven't heard what they're saying?"

I shook my head.

"Probably for the best." With a last laugh, he wandered off.

David disentangled himself from the brunette. Her plump lips pursed in displeasure, but he wasn't looking. "Come on."

He put his hand out to usher me on, and there, spread across the length of his forearm, was his tattoo:

Evelyn

I froze. Holy shit. The man sure had chosen a conspicuous place to put my name. I didn't know how I felt about that.

"What?" His brows drew down and his forehead wrinkled. "Ah, yeah. Come on."

"Hurry back, David," cooed Bikini Girl, primping her hair. I had nothing against bikinis. I owned several despite my mom believing I was too big boned for such things. (I'd never actually worn them, but that was beside the point.) No, what I minded were the sneers and snarly looks Bikini Girl shot me when she thought David wasn't looking.

Little did she know he didn't care.

With a hand to the small of my back, he ushered me through the party toward the stairs. People called out and women preened, but he never slowed. I got the distinct feeling he was embarrassed to be seen with me. Being with David, I sure caught some scrutiny. Any money, I didn't fit the bill of a rock star's wife. People stopped and stared. Someone called out, asking if he could introduce us. No comment from my husband as he hurried me through the crowd.

Hallways spread out in both directions up on the second floor. We went left, down to the end. He threw open a door and there my bag sat, waiting on a big king-size bed. Everything in the sumptuous room had been done in white: the bed, walls, and carpets. An antique white love seat sat in the corner. It was beautiful, pristine. Nothing like my small, cramped room back at the apartment I shared with Lauren, where between the double bed and my desk, you had just enough room to get the cupboard door open, no more. This place went on and on, a sea of perfection.

"I'd better not touch anything," I mumbled, hands tucked into my back pockets.

"What?"

"It's lovely."

David looked around the room with nil interest. "Yeah."

I wandered over to the windows. A luxurious pool sat below, well lit and surrounded by palm trees and perfect gardens. Two people were in the water, making out. The woman's head fell back and her breasts bobbed on the surface. Oh, no, my mistake. They were having sex. I could feel the heat creep up my neck. I didn't think I was a prude, but still. I turned away.

"Listen, some people are going to come to talk to you about the divorce papers. They'll be here at ten," he said, hovering in the doorway. His fingers tapped out a beat on the doorframe. He kept casting longing looks down the hall, clearly impatient to be gone.

"Some people?"

"My lawyer and my manager," he told his feet. "They're rushing things, so . . . it'll all be, ah, dealt with as fast as it can."

"All right."

David sucked in his cheeks and nodded. He had killer cheekbones. I'd seen men in fashion magazines that couldn't have compared. But pretty or not, the frown never lifted. Not while I was around. It would have been nice to see him smile, just once.

"You need anything?" he asked.

"No. Thank you for all this. For flying me down here and letting me stay. It's very kind of you."

"No worries." He took a step back and started closing the door after him. "Night."

"David, shouldn't we talk or something? About last night?"

He paused, half hidden behind the door. "Seriously, Ev. Why fucking bother?"

And he was gone.

Again.

No door slam this time. I counted that as a step forward in our relationship. Being surprised was stupid. But disappointment held me still, staring around the room, seeing nothing. It wasn't that I suddenly wanted him to fall at my feet. But antipathy sucked.

Eventually I wandered back over to the window. The lovers were gone, the pool now empty. Another couple stumbled along the lit garden path, beneath the huge swaying palm trees. They headed toward what had to be the pool house. The man was David, and Bikini Girl hung off him, swishing her long hair and swaying her hips, working it to the nth degree. They looked good together. They fit. David reached out and tugged on the tie of her bikini top, undoing the neat bow and baring her from the waist up. Bikini Girl laughed soundlessly, not bothering to cover herself.

I swallowed hard, trying to dislodge the rock in my throat. Jealousy felt every bit as bad as antipathy. And I had no damn right to be jealous.

At the door to the pool house, David paused and looked back over his shoulder. His eyes met mine. Oh, shit. I ducked behind the curtain and idiotically held my breath. Caught spying—the shame of it. When I checked a moment later, they were gone. Light peeked out from the sides of the curtains in the pool house. I should have brazened it out. I wished I had. It wasn't like I was doing anything wrong.

The immaculate grandeur of the white room spread out before me. Inside and out, I felt a mess. The reality of my situation had apparently sunk in, and what a clusterfuck it was. Lauren had been right on with the word choice.

"David can do what he wants." My voice echoed through the room, startlingly loud even over the thumping of the music downstairs. I straightened my shoulders. Tomorrow I would meet with his people and the divorce would be sorted. "David can do what he wants and so can I."

But what did I want to do? I had no idea. So I unpacked my few items of clothing, settling in for the night. I hung David's T-shirt over a towel rail to finish drying. It was probably going to be needed for sleepwear. Organizing myself took five minutes, max. You could refold a couple of tank tops only so many ways before you just looked pathetic.

What now?

I hadn't been invited to the party downstairs. No way did I want to think about what might be happening in the pool house. Doubtless David was giving Bikini Girl everything I'd wanted in Vegas. No sex for me. Instead, he had sent me to my room like a naughty child.

What a room it was. The adjoining bathroom had a tub larger than my bedroom back home. Plenty of space to splash around. It was tempting. But I never had been much good at getting sent to my room. On the few occasions it happened at home, I used to climb out the window and sit outside with a book. As rebellions went, it lacked a lot, but I'd been satisfied. There was a lot to be said for being a quiet achiever.

Screw staying in the room of splendor. I couldn't do it.

No one noticed me as I crept back down the stairs. I slunk into the closest corner and settled in to watch the beautiful people at play. It was fascinating. Bodies writhed on an impromptu dance floor in the middle of the room. Someone lit up a cigar nearby, filling the air with a rich, spicy scent. Puffs of smoke billowed up toward the ceiling, a good twenty feet above. Diamonds glittered and teeth sparkled, and that was just some of the men. Open opulence fought grunge among the mixed crowd. You couldn't get better people-watching if you tried. No sign of Mal, sadly. At least he'd been friendly.

"You're new," a voice said from beside me, startling the crap out of me. I jumped a mile, or at least a few inches.

A man in a black suit lounged against the wall, sipping a glass of amber liquor. This slick black suit was something else. In all likelihood Sam's had come off the rack, but not this one. I'd never understood the appeal of a suit and tie before, but this man wore them incredibly well. He looked to be about David's age and he had short dark hair. Handsome, of course. Like David, he had the whole divine cheekbones thing going on.

"You know, if you move another foot over you'll disappear entirely behind that palm." He took another sip of his drink. "Then no one would see you."

"I'll give it some thought." I didn't bother denying I was in hiding. Apparently it was already obvious to all.

He smiled, flashing a dimple. Tommy Byrnes had dimples. He'd inured me to their power. The man leaned closer, so as to be heard more easily over the music, most likely. The fact that he backed it up by taking a decent-sized step toward me seemed unnecessary. Personal space was a wonderful thing. Something about this guy gave me the creeps, despite the swanky suit.

"I'm Jimmy."

"Ev."

He pursed his lips, staring at me. "Nope, I definitely don't know you. Why don't I know you?"

"You know everyone else?" I surveyed the room, highly dubious. "There are a lot of people here."

"There are," he agreed. "And I know them all. Everyone except you."

"David invited me." I didn't want to drop David's name, but I was being pushed into a corner, figuratively and literally as Jimmy closed in on me.

"Did he now?" His eyes looked wrong, the pupils pinpricks. Something was up with this guy. He stared down at the small amount of cleavage I had on display like he intended to plant his face there.

"Yeah. He did."

Jimmy didn't exactly seem pleased by the news. He threw back his drink, finishing it off in one large mouthful. "So, David invited you to the party."

"He invited me to stay for a few days," I said, which was not a lie. Happily, hopefully, he had somehow missed the news about David and me. Or maybe he was just too stoned to put two and two together. Either way, I wasn't filling him in.

"Really? That was nice of him."

"Yes, it was."

"What room did he put you in?" He stood in front of me and dropped his empty glass into the potted plant with a careless hand. His grin looked manic. My need to get away from him gained immediate urgency.

"The white one," I said, looking for a way around him. "Speaking of which, I'd better get back."

"The white room? My, my, aren't you special."

"Aren't I just? Excuse me." I pushed past him, giving up on social niceties.

He mustn't have expected it because he stumbled back a step. "Hey. Hold up."

"Jimmy." David appeared, earning my instant gratitude. "There a problem here?"

"Not at all," said Jimmy. "Just getting to know . . . Ev."

"Yeah, well, you don't need to know . . . Ev."

The guy's smile was expansive. "Come on. You know how I like pretty new things."

"Let's go," David said to me.

"It's not like you to cockblock, Davie," said Jimmy. "Didn't I see the lovely Kaetrin with you earlier out on the balcony? Why don't you go find her, get her to do what she's so damn good at? Me and Ev are busy here."

"Actually, no, we're not," I said. And why was David back so soon from his playtime with Bikini Girl? He couldn't possibly have been concerned about his little wife's well-being, surely.

Neither of them appeared to have heard me.

"So you invited her to stay in my house," said Jimmy.

"I was under the impression Adrian rented the place for all of us while we're working on the album. Something changed I don't know about?"

Jimmy laughed. "I like the place. Decided to buy it."

"Great. Let me know when the deal's going through and I'll be sure to get out. In the meantime, my guests are none of your business."

Jimmy looked at me, face alight with malicious glee. "It's her, isn't it? The one you married, you stupid son of a bitch."

"Come on." David grabbed my hand and dragged me toward the staircase. His jaw was clenched tight enough to make a muscle pop out on the side.

"I could have had her against a wall at a fucking party and you married her?"

Bullshit he could have.

David's fingers squeezed my hand tight.

Jimmy chortled like the cretin he was. "She is nothing, you sorry fuck. Look at her. Just look at her. Tell me this marriage didn't come courtesy of vodka and cocaine."

It wasn't anything I hadn't heard before. Well, apart from the marriage reference. But his words still bit. Before I could tell Jimmy what I thought of him, however, the iron-hard hold on my hand disappeared. David charged back to him, grabbing hold of his lapels. They were pretty evenly matched. Both were tall, well built. Neither looked ready to back down. The room hushed, all conversation stopping, though the music thumped on.

"Go for it, little brother," hissed Jimmy. "Show me who the star of this show really is."

David's shoulders went rigid beneath the thin cotton of his T-shirt. Then with a snarl he released Jimmy, shoving him back a step. "You're as bad as Mom. Look at you, you're a fucking mess."

I stared at the two of them, stunned. These two were the brothers in the band. Same dark hair and handsome faces. I clearly hadn't married into the happiest of families. Jimmy looked almost shamefaced.

My husband marched back past me, collecting my arm along the way. Every eye was on us. An elegant brunette took a step forward, hand outstretched. Distress lined her lovely face. "You know he doesn't mean it."

"Stay out of it, Martha," said my husband, not slowing down at all.

The woman shot me a look of distaste. Worse yet, of blame. With the way David was acting, I had a bad feeling that was going around.

Up the steps he dragged me, then down the hallway toward my room. We said nothing. Maybe this time he'd lock me in. Jam a chair under the door handle, perhaps. I could understand him being mad at Jimmy. That guy was a dick of epic proportions. But what had I done? Apart from escaping my plush prison, of course.

Halfway along the long hallway I liberated my limb from his tender care. I had to do something before he cut off the blood supply to my fingers.

"I know the way," I said.

"Still wanna get some, huh? You should have said something, I'd be more than happy to oblige," he said with a false smile. "And hey, you're not even shit-faced tonight. Chances are you'd remember."

"Ouch."

"Something I said untrue?"

"No. But I still think it's fair to say you're being an ass."

He stopped dead and looked at me, eyes wide, startled, if anything. "I'm being an ass? Fucking hell, you're my wife!"

"No, I'm not. You said so yourself. Right before you went off to play in the pool house with your friend," I said. Though he hadn't stayed long in the pool house, obviously. Five, six minutes maybe? I almost felt bad for Bikini Girl. That wasn't service with a smile.

Dark brows descended like thunderclouds. He was less than impressed. Bad luck. My feelings toward him were likewise at an all-time low.

"You're right. My bad. Should I take you back to my brother?"

he asked, cracking his knuckles like a Neanderthal and staring back down the hallway from where we'd come.

"No, thank you."

"That was real nice, making fuck-me eyes at him, by the way. Out of everyone down there, you had to be flirting with Jimmy," he sneered. "Classy, Ev."

"That's honestly what you think was happening?"

"What with you and him getting all fucking cozy in the corner?"

"Seriously?"

"I know Jimmy and I know girls around Jimmy. That's definitely what it looked like, baby." He held his arms out wide. "Prove me wrong."

I wasn't even certain I knew how to make fuck-me eyes. But I definitely hadn't been making them at that tool downstairs. No wonder so many marriages ended in divorce. Marriage sucked and husbands were the worst. My shoulders were caving in on me. I didn't think I'd ever felt so small.

"I think your brother issues might be even worse than your wife issues, and that's saying something." Slowly, I shook my head. "Thank you for offering me the opportunity to defend myself. I really appreciate it. But you know what, David? I'm just not convinced your good opinion is worth it."

He flinched.

I walked away before I said something worse. Forget anything amicable. The sooner we were divorced, the better.

CHAPTER FIVE

Sunlight poured in through the windows when I woke the next morning. Someone was hammering on the door, turning the handle, trying to get in. I'd locked it after the scene with David last night. Just in case he was tempted to return to trade some more insults with me. It had taken me hours to get to sleep with the music thrumming through the floor and my emotions running wild. But exhaustion won out in the end.

"Evelyn! Hello?" a female voice yelled from out in the hall-way. "Are you in there?" I crawled across the ginormous bed, tugging on the hem of David's T-shirt. Whatever he'd used to wash it in Vegas, it didn't smell of puke. The man had laundry skills. Fortunate for me, because apart from my dirty party dress and a couple of tops, I had nothing else to wear

"Who is it?" I asked, yawning loudly.

"Martha. I'm David's PA."

I cracked open the door and peered out. The elegant bru-nette from last night stared back at me, unimpressed. From be-ing made to wait or the sight of my bed hair, I didn't know. Did everyone in this house look like they'd just slunk off the cover of *Vogue*? Her eyes turned into slits at the sight of David's shirt.

"His representatives are here to meet with you. You might want to get your ass into gear." The woman spun on her heel and strode off down the hallway, heels clacking furiously against the terra-cotta tiled floor.

"Thanks."

She didn't acknowledge me, but, then, I didn't expect her to. This part of LA was clearly a colony for ill-mannered douches. I rushed through a shower, pulled on my jeans and a clean T-shirt. It was the best I could do.

The house stayed silent as I rushed down the hallway. There were no signs of life on the second level. I'd slapped on a little mascara, tied my wet hair back in a ponytail, but that was it. I could either hold people up or go without makeup. Politeness won. If coffee had been in the offering, however, I'd have left David's representatives hanging for at least two cups. Running on zero caffeine seemed suicidal given the stressful circumstances. I hurried down the stairs.

"Ms. Thomas," a man called, stepping out of a room to the left. He wore jeans and a white polo shirt. Around his neck hung a thick, gold chain. So who was this? Another of David's entourage?

"Sorry I'm late."

"It's fine." He smiled, but I didn't quite believe him despite the big white teeth. Nature had clearly played no part in his teeth or tan. "I'm Adrian."

"Ev. Hello."

He swept me into the room. Three men in suits sat waiting at an impressively long dining table. Overhead, another crystal chandelier sparkled in the morning light. On the walls were beautiful, colorful paintings. Originals, obviously.

"Gentlemen, this is Ms. Thomas," Adrian announced. "Scott Baker, Bill Preston, and Ted Vaughan are David's legal representatives. Why don't you sit here, Ev?"

Adrian spoke slowly, as if I were a feeble-minded child. He

pulled a chair out from the table for me directly opposite the team of legal eagles, then walked around to sit on their side. Wow, that sure told me. The lines had been drawn.

I rubbed my sweaty palms on the sides of my jeans and sat up straight, doing my best not to wilt beneath their hostile gazes. I could definitely do this. How hard could it be to get a divorce, after all?

"Ms. Thomas," the one Adrian had identified as Ted started. He pushed a black leather folder full of papers toward me. "Mr. Ferris asked us to draw up annulment papers. They'll cover all issues, including details of your settlement from Mr. Ferris."

The size of the stack of papers before me was daunting. These people worked fast. "My settlement?"

"Yes," Ted said. "Rest assured Mr. Ferris has been very generous."

I shook my head in confusion. "I'm sorry. Wha—"

"We'll deal with that last," Ted rushed on. "You'll notice here that the document covers all conditions to be met by yourself. The main issues include your not speaking to any member of the press with regard to this matter. This is nonnegotiable, I'm afraid. This condition remains in force until your death. Do you fully understand the requirement, Ms. Thomas? Under no circumstances may you talk to any member of the press regarding Mr. Ferris in any way while you're alive."

"So I can talk to them after I die?" I asked with a weak little laugh. Ted was getting on my nerves. I guess I hadn't gotten enough sleep after all.

Ted showed me his teeth. They weren't quite as impressive as Adrian's. "This is a very serious matter, Ms. Thomas."

"Ev," I said. "My name is Ev and I do realize the seriousness of this issue, Ted. I apologize for being flippant. But if we could get back to the part about the settlement? I'm a little confused."

"Very well." Ted looked down his nose at me and tapped a thick, gold pen on the paperwork in front of me. "As I said, Mr. Ferris has been very generous."

"No," I said, not looking at the papers, "you don't understand."

Ted cleared his throat and looked down at me over the top of his glasses. "It would be unwise of you to try and press for more given the circumstances, Ms. Thomas. A six-hour marriage in Las Vegas entered into while you were both heavily under the influence of alcohol? Textbook grounds for annulment."

Ted's cronies tittered and I felt my face fire up. My need to accidentally kick the prick under the table grew and grew.

"My client will not be making another offer."

"I don't want him to make another offer," I said, my voice rising.

"The annulment will go ahead, Ms. Thomas," said Ted. "There is no question of that. There will be no reconciliation."

"No, that's not what I meant."

Ted sighed. "We need to finalize this today, Ms. Thomas."

"I'm not trying to hold anything up, Ted."

The other two lawyers watched me with distaste, backing up Ted with sleazy, knowing smiles. Nothing pissed me off faster than a bunch of people trying to intimidate someone. Bullies had made my life hell back in high school. And really, that's all these people were.

Adrian gave me a big-toothed, faux-fatherly grin. "I'm sure Ev can see how kind David's being. There are not going to be any delays here, are there?"

These people, they blew my mind. Speaking of which, I had

to wonder where my darling husband was. Too busy banging bikini models to turn up to his own divorce, the poor guy. I pushed back my fringe, trying to figure out the right thing to say. Trying to get my anger managed. "Wait—"

"We all just want what's best for you given the unfortunate situation," Adrian continued, obviously lying through his big, bright teeth.

"Great," I said, fingers fidgeting beneath the table. "That's . . . that's really great of you."

"Please, Ms. Thomas." Ted tapped his pen imperiously alongside a figure on the paperwork and I dutifully looked, though I didn't want to. There were lots of zeros. I mean, really a lot. It was insane. In two lifetimes I couldn't earn that kind of money. David must have wanted me gone something fierce. My stomach rumbled nervously but my puking days were over. The whole scene felt horrific, like something out of a bad B movie or soap opera. Girl from the wrong side of the tracks hijacks hot, rich guy and tricks him into marriage. Now all that was left was for him to use his people to chase me off into the sunset.

Well, he won.

"This was all just a mistake," said Adrian. "I'm sure Ev is every bit as keen to put it behind her as David is. And with this generous financial settlement she can move forward to a bright future."

"You'll also never attempt to make contact with Mr. Ferris ever again, in any manner. Any attempt on your part to do so will see you in breach of contract." Ted withdrew his pen, sitting back in his seat with a false smile and his hands crossed over his belly. "Is that clear?"

"No," I said, scrubbing my face with my hands. They actually thought I'd fall over myself to get at that money. Money

I'd done nothing to earn, no matter how tempting accepting it was. Of course, they also thought I'd sell my story to the press and harass David every spare moment I got for the rest of my life. They thought I was cheap, trashy scum. "I think I can honestly say that nothing about this is clear."

"Ev, please." Adrian gave me a disappointed look. "Let's be reasonable."

"I'll tell you what . . ." I stood and retrieved the ring from my jeans pocket, throwing it onto the sea of paperwork. "You give this back to David and tell him I don't want any of it. None of this." I gestured at them, the table, the papers, and the entire damn house. The lawyers looked nervously among themselves as if they'd need more paperwork before they could allow me to go waving my arms about in such a disorderly fashion.

"Ev . . ."

"I don't want to sell his story, or stalk him, or whatever else you have buried in subclause 98.2. I don't want his money."

Adrian coughed out a laugh. Fuck him. The phony bastard could think what he liked.

Ted frowned at my big sparkly ring lying innocently among the mess. "Mr. Ferris didn't mention a ring."

"No? Well. Why don't you tell Mr. Ferris he can shove it wherever he feels it might best fit, Ted."

"Ms. Thomas!" Ted stood, his puffy face outraged. "That is unnecessary."

"Going to have to disagree with you there, Ted." I bolted out of the dining room of death and made straight for the front door as fast as my feet could carry me. Immediate escape was the only answer. If I could just get the hell away from them long enough to catch my breath, I could come up with a new plan to deal with this ridiculous situation. I'd be fine.

A brand new-black Jeep pulled up as I tore down the front steps.

The window lowered to show my guide from last night, Mal, sitting in the driver's seat. He smirked from behind black sunglasses. "Hey there, child bride."

I flipped him the finger and jogged down the long, winding driveway toward the front gates. Toward liberty and freedom and my old life, or whatever remained of it. If only I'd never gone to Vegas. If only I'd tried harder to convince Lauren that a party at home would be fine, none of this would have happened. God, I was such an idiot. Why had I drunk so much?

"Ev. Hold up." Mal pulled up alongside me in his Jeep. "What's wrong? Where're you going?"

I didn't answer. I was done with all of them. That and I had the worst feeling I was about to cry, damn it. My eyes felt hot, horrible.

"Stop." He pulled the brake and climbed out of the Jeep, running after me. "Hey, I'm sorry."

I said nothing. I had nothing to say to any of them.

His hand wrapped around my arm gently, but I didn't care. I swung at him. I'd never hit anyone in my life. Apparently, I wasn't about to start now. He dodged my flying fist with ease.

"Whoa! Okay." Mal danced back a step, giving me a wary look over the top of his shades. "You're mad. I get it."

Hands on hips, he looked back toward the house. Ted and Adrian stood on the front steps, staring after us. Even from this distance the dynamic duo did not appear happy. Evil bastards.

Mal hissed out a breath. "You're fucking joking. He sicced that ball sucker Ted onto you?"

I nodded, blinking, trying to get myself under control.

"Did you have anyone with you?" he asked.

"No."

He cocked his head. "Are you going to cry?"

"No!"

"Fuck. Come on." He held out his hand to me and I stared at in disbelief. "Ev, think. There're photographers and shit waiting out front. Even if you get past them, where are you going to go?"

He was right. I had to go back, get my bag. So stupid of me not to have thought of it. Just as soon as I had myself under control I'd go in and retrieve it, then get the hell out of here. I fanned my face with my hands, took a big breath. All good.

Meanwhile, his hand hovered, waiting. There were a couple of small blisters on it, situated in the join between thumb and finger. Curious.

"Are you the drummer?" I asked with a sniff.

For some reason he cracked up laughing, almost doubling over, clutching at his belly. Maybe he was on drugs or something. Or maybe he was just one more lunatic in this gigantic asylum. Batman would have had a hard time keeping this place in check.

"What is your problem?" I asked, taking a step away from him. Just in case.

His snazzy sunglasses fell off, clattering on the asphalt. He swiped them up and shoved them back on his face. "Nothing. Nothing at all. Let's get out of here. I've got a house at the beach. We'll hide out there. Come on, it'll be fun."

I hesitated, giving the jerks on the front steps a lethal look. "Why would you help me?"

"Because you're worth helping."

"Oh, really? Why would you think that?"

"You wouldn't like my answer."

"I haven't liked a single answer I've had all morning, why stop now?"

He smiled. "Fair enough. I'm David's oldest friend. We've gotten drunk and out of control more times than I can remember. He's had girls angling to snare him for years, even before we had money. He never was the slightest bit interested in marriage. It was never even on his radar before. So the fact that he married you, well, that suggests to me you're worth helping. Come on, Ev. Stop worrying."

Easy for him to say, his life hadn't been skewered by a rock star.

"I need to get my stuff."

"And get cornered by them? Worry about it later." He held his hand out, fingers beckoning for mine. "Let's get out of here."

I put my hand in his and we went.

CHAPTER SIX

"So, hang on, this song isn't about his dog dying or something?"

"You're not funny." I laughed.

"I so am." Mal sniggered at the opposite end of the couch as Tim McGraw let rip about his kind of rain on the flat-screen TV taking up the opposite wall. "Why do they all wear such big hats, do you think? I have a theory."

"Shush."

The way these people lived blew my tiny little mind. Mal, short for Malcolm, lived in a place at the beach that was mostly a three-story architectural feat of steel and glass. It was amazing. Not ridiculously huge like the place in the hills, but awe-inspiring just the same. My dad would have been in raptures over the minimalism of it, the cleanliness of the lines, or some such. I just appreciated having a friend in my time of need.

Mal's house was clearly a bachelor pad–slash–den of iniquity. I'd had a vague notion to make lunch to thank him for taking me in, but there wasn't a single speck of food in the house. Beer filled the fridge and vodka the freezer. Oh, no, there was a bag of oranges used as wedges to go with shots of vodka, apparently. He'd ruled out touching those. His super-slick coffee machine, however, made everything right. He even had decent beans. I wowed him by busting out a few of my barista moves. After drinking three cups in the space of an hour, I felt a lot more like my old well-planned, caffeinated self.

Mal dialed for pizza and we watched TV late into the night. Mostly he found his joy in mocking my taste in pretty much everything: movies, music, the lot. At least he did it good-naturedly. We couldn't go outside because a couple of photographers were waiting on the beach. I felt bad about it but he'd just shrugged it off.

"What about this song?" he asked. "You like this?"

Miranda Lambert strode on screen in a cool '50s frock and I grinned. "Miranda is mighty."

"I've met her."

I sat up straight. "Really?"

More sniggering from Mal. "You're impressed I've met Miranda Lambert but you didn't even know who I was. Honestly, woman, you are hard on the ego."

"I saw the gold and platinum records lining the hallway, buddy. I'm thinking you can take it."

He snorted.

"You know, you remind me a lot of my brother." I almost managed to duck the bottle cap he flicked at me. It bounced off my forehead. "What was that for?"

"Can't you at least pretend to worship me?"

"No. Sorry."

With total disregard for my Lambert love, Mal started surfing the channels. Home shopping, football, *Gone with the Wind*, and me. Me on TV.

"Wait," I said.

He groaned. "Not a good idea."

First my school pictures paraded past, followed by one of Lauren and me at our senior prom. They even had a reporter standing across the road from Ruby's, prattling on about my life before being elevated to the almighty status of David's wife. And then there was the man himself in some concert footage, guitar in his hands as he sang backup. The lyrics were your typical my-woman-is-mean, "She's my one and only, she's got me on my knees . . ." I wondered if he'd write songs about me. If so, odds were they'd be highly uncomplimentary. "Shit." I hugged a couch cushion tight to my chest.

Mal leaned over and fluffed my hair. "David's the favorite, darlin'. He's pretty, plays guitar, and writes the songs. Girlies faint when he walks by. Team that with your being a young 'un and you've got the news of the week."

"I'm twenty-one."

"And he's twenty-six. It's enough of a difference if they hype it just right." Mal sighed. "Face it, child bride. You got married in Vegas by an Elvis impersonator to one of rock 'n' roll's favorite sons. It was always bound to cause a shitstorm. Given there's also been some crap going on with the band lately . . . what with Jimmy partying like it's 1999 and Dave losing his music-writing mojo. Well, you get the picture. But next week, someone else will do something wacky and all the attention will move on."

"I guess so."

"I know so. People are constantly fucking up. It's a glorious thing." He sat back with his hands behind his head. "Go on, smile for Uncle Mal. You know you want to."

I smiled halfheartedly.

"That's a bullshit smile and I'm ashamed of you. You're not going to fool anyone with that. Try again."

I tried harder, smiling till my cheeks hurt.

"Damn. Now you just look like you're in pain."

Banging on the front door interrupted our merriment.

Mal raised his brows at me. "Wondered how long he'd take."

"What?" I trailed him to the front door, lurking behind a divider just in case it was more press.

He opened the door and David charged in, face tight and furious. "You piece of shit. You better not have touched her. Where is she?"

"The child bride is otherwise occupied." Mal cocked his head, taking David in with a cool glance. "Why the fuck do you even care?"

"Don't start with me. Where is she?"

Quietly, Mal shut the door, facing off against his friend. I hesitated, hanging back. All right, so I skulked in a cowardly fashion. Whatever.

Mal crossed his arms. "You left her to face Adrian and three lawyers on her own. You, my friend, are most definitely the piece of shit in this particular scenario."

"I didn't know Adrian would go at her with all that."

"You didn't want to know," said Mal. "Lie to everyone else out there, Dave. Not me. And sure as fuck not to yourself."

"Back off."

"You need some serious life advice, friend."

"Who are you, Oprah?"

Coughing out a laugh, Mal slumped against the wall. "Hell, yeah. Soon I'm gonna be giving out cars, so stick around."

"What did she say?"

"Who, Oprah?"

David just scowled at him. He didn't even notice me spying. Sad to say, even a scowling David was a thing of rare beauty. He did things to me. Complicated things. My heart tripped about in my chest. The anger and emotion in his voice couldn't be concern for me. That made no sense, not after last night and this morning. I had to be projecting, and it sucked that I even wanted him to care. My head made no sense. Getting away from this guy was the safest option all round.

"Dave, she was so upset she took a swing at me."

"Bullshit."

"I kid you not. She was nearly in tears when I found her," said Mal.

I banged my forehead in silent agony against the wall. Why the hell did Mal have to tell him that?

My husband hung his head. "I didn't mean for that to happen."

"Seems you didn't mean for a shitload to happen." Mal shook his head and tutted. "Did you even mean to marry her, dude? Seriously?"

David's face screwed up, his brow doing the wrinkly James Dean thing again. "I don't know anymore, okay? Fuck. I went to Vegas because I was so sick of all this shit, and I met her. She was different. She seemed different that night. I just . . . I wanted something outside of all this fucking idiocy for a change."

"Poor Davey. Did being a rock god get old?"

"Where is she?"

"I feel your manpain, bro. Really, I do. I mean, all you wanted was a girl who wouldn't kiss your ass for once and now you're pissed at her for the same damn reason. It's complicated, right?"

"Fuck you. Leave it alone, Mal. It's done." My husband huffed out a breath. "Anyway, she's the one who wanted the fucking divorce. Why aren't you giving her the third degree, huh?"

With a dramatic sigh, Mal flung out his arms. "Because she's really busy hiding around the corner, listening. I can't disturb her now."

David's body stilled and his blue eyes found me. "Evelyn."

Huh. Busted.

I stepped away from the wall and tried to put on a happy face. It didn't work. "Hi."

"She says that so well." Mal turned to me and winked. "So did you really ask the mighty David Ferris for a divorce?"

"She threw up on me when I told her we were married," my husband reported.

"What?" Mal dissolved into laughter, tears leaking from his eyes. "Are you serious? Fucking hell, that is fantastic. Oh, man, I wish I'd been there."

I gave David what I hoped to be the meanest look in all of time and space. He stared back, unimpressed.

"It was the floor," I clarified. "I didn't throw up on him."

"That time," said David.

"Please keep going," said Mal, laughing harder than ever. "This just gets better and better."

David didn't. Thank God.

"Seriously, I fucking love your wife, man. She's awesome. Can I have her?"

The look I got from David spoke of a much more reluctant affection. With the line between his brows, it was closer to outright irritation. I blew him a kiss. He looked away, hands fisted like he was barely holding himself back from throttling me. The feeling was entirely mutual.

Ah, marital bliss.

"You two are just the best." A chiming sound came from Mal's pocket and he pulled out a cell phone. Whatever he saw on the screen stopped his laughter dead. "You know, you should take her to your house, Dave."

"I don't think that's a good idea." David's mouth pulled wide in a truly pained expression.

I didn't think it was a good idea either. I'd happily go

through life without setting foot inside the house of horrors ever again. Maybe if I asked Mal nicely he'd fetch my stuff for me. Imposing on him further didn't appeal, but I was running low on options.

"Whoa." With a grim face, Mal shoved his cell at David.

"Fuck," David mumbled. He wrapped his hand around the back of his neck and squeezed. The worried glance he gave me from beneath his dark brows set every alarm ringing inside my head. Whatever was on that screen was bad.

Really bad.

"What is it?" I asked.

"Oh, you, ah . . . you don't need to worry about it." His gaze dropped to the phone again, then he passed it back to Mal. "My place would be cool, actually. We should do that. Fun. Yeah."

"No." For David to be so nice to me it had to be something truly bad. I held out my hand, fingers twitching from impatience or nerves or a bit of both. "Show me."

After a reluctant nod from David, Mal handed it over.

There could be no doubting what it was, even on the small screen. There was a lot of skin on account of my being bare from the waist down. My naked butt sat front and center in all its pale, dimpled glory. God, it looked huge. Had they used a wide-lens camera or something? The party dress had been pushed up and I stood, bent over a table while a tattoo artist worked hard inking my rear. My panties had been cinched down, barely covering the basics. Shit. Talk about a compromising position. Taking part in a porn shoot was definitely not part of the plan.

At the other end of the frame, our faces were close together and David was smiling. Huh. So that was what he looked like when he smiled.

I remembered it then, the buzz of the needle, and him talking to me, holding my hands. At first, that needle had stung. "You were pretending to bite my fingers. The tattoo artist got mad at us for messing around."

David tipped his chin. "Yeah. You were s'posed to be keeping still."

I nodded, trying to remember more but coming up empty.

People would see this picture. People had seen this. People I knew and strangers both. Anyone and everyone. My head spun woozily, the same as it had then. Only alcohol wasn't at fault this time.

"How did they get it?" I asked, my voice wavering and my heart at my toes. Or maybe that was just what remained of my tattered dignity.

David gave me sad eyes. "I don't know. We were in a private room. This should never have happened, but people get offered a lot of money for this sort of thing."

I nodded and handed Mal back his phone. My hand shook. "Right. Well . . ."

They both just looked at me, faces tense, waiting for me to burst into tears or something. Not happening.

"It's okay," I said, doing my best to believe it.

"Sure," said Mal.

David shoved his hands into his pockets. "It's not even that clear a picture."

"No, it's not," I agreed. The pity in his eyes was more than I could take. "Excuse me a minute."

Fortunately, the closest bathroom was only a short dash away. I locked the door and sat on the edge of the Jacuzzi, trying to slow my breathing, trying to be calm. There was nothing I could do. The picture was already out there. This was no death and dismemberment. It was a stupid picture of me in a compromising position showing more skin than I liked. But so what? Big deal. Accept it and move on. Despite the fact that everyone I knew would likely see it. Worse things had happened in the history of the world. I just needed to put it in context and stay calm.

"Ev?" David tapped lightly on the door. "Are you okay?"

"Yep." No. Not really.

"Let me in?"

I gave the door a pained look.

"Please."

Slowly, I stood and flicked the lock. David wandered in and shut the door behind him. No ponytail today. His dark hair hung down, framing his face. He had three small silver earrings in one ear playing peekaboo behind his hair. I stared at them because meeting his eyes was out of the question. I was not going to cry. Not about this. What the hell was even wrong with my eyes lately? Letting him in had been dumb.

With a heavy frown he stared down at me. "I'm sorry."

"It's not your fault."

"Yeah, it is. I should have looked after you better."

"No, David." I swallowed hard. "We were both drunk. God, this is all so horrifically, embarrassingly stupid."

He just stared at me.

"Sorry."

"Hey, you're allowed to be upset. That was a private moment. It shouldn't be out there."

"No," I agreed. "I . . . actually, I'd like to be alone for a minute."

He made a growly noise and suddenly his arms wrapped around me, pulling me in against him. He caught me off guard and I stumbled, my nose bumping into his chest. It hurt. But he smelled good. Clean, male, and good. Familiar. Some part of me remembered being this close to him and it was comforting. Something in my mind said "safe." But I couldn't remember how or why.

A hand moved restlessly over my back.

"I'm sorry," he said, "so fucking sorry."

The kindness was too much. Stupid tears flowed. "I'd hardly even shown anyone my ass and now it's all over the Internet."

"I know, baby."

He rested his head against the top of mine, holding on tight as I blubbered into his T-shirt. Having someone to hold on to helped. It would be okay. Deep down I knew it would be. But right then I couldn't see my way clear. Standing there with his arms around me felt right.

I don't know when we started swaying. David rocked me gently from side to side as if we were dancing to some slow song. The overwhelming temptation to stay like that with my face pressed into his shirt was what made me step back, pull myself together. His hands sat lightly on my hips, the connection not quite broken.

"Thanks," I said.

"S'okay." The front of his shirt had a damp patch, thanks to me.

"Your shirt's all wet."

He shrugged.

I ugly-cried. It was a gift of mine. The mirror confirmed it, demon-red eyes and flushed fluoro-pink cheeks. With an awkward smile I stepped away from him, and his hands fell back to his sides. I splashed my face with water and dried it on a towel while he stood idly by, frowning.

"Let's go for a drive," he said.

"Really?" I gave him a dubious look. David and me alone?

Given the marriage situation and our previous sober encounters, it didn't seem the wisest plan.

"Yeah." He rubbed his hands together, getting all enthused. "Just you and me. We'll get out of here for a while."

"David, like you said out there, I don't think that's a good idea."

"You want to stay in LA?" he scoffed.

"Look, you've been really sweet since you stepped through that door. Well, apart from telling Mal about me puking on you. That was unnecessary. But in the preceding twenty-four hours you dumped me alone in a room, went off with a groupie, accused me of trying to get it on with your brother, and sicced your posse of lawyers onto me."

He said nothing.

"Not that you going off with a groupie is any of my business. Of course."

He turned on his heel and paced to the other end of the bathroom, his movements tight, angry. Despite it being five times the size of the one back home, it still didn't leave enough room for a showdown like this. And he was between me and the door. Because suddenly exiting seemed a smart move.

"I just asked them to sort out the paperwork," he said.

"And they sure did." I put my hands on my hips, standing my ground. "I don't want any of your money."

"I heard." His face was carefully blank. My statement prompted in him none of the disbelief or mockery it had in the suited bullies. Lucky for him. I doubt he believed me, but at least he was willing to pretend. "They're drawing up new papers."

"Good." I stared him down. "You don't have to pay me off. Don't make assumptions like that. If you want to know something, ask. And I was never going to sell the story to the press. I wouldn't do that."

"Okay." He slumped against the wall, leaning his head back to stare up at nothing. "Sorry," he told the ceiling. I'm sure the plasterwork appreciated it immensely.

When I made no response, his gaze eventually found me. It had to be wrong, or at the very least immoral, to be so pretty. Normal people didn't stand a chance. My heart took a dive every time I looked at him. No, a dive didn't cover it. It plummeted.

Where was Lauren to tell me I was being melodramatic when I needed her most?

"I'm sorry, Ev," he repeated. "I know the last twenty-four hours have been shit. Offering to get out of here for a while was my way of trying to make things better."

"Thank you," I said. "And also for coming in here to check on me."

"No problem." He stared at me, eyes unguarded for once. And the honesty in his gaze changed things for me, the brief flash of something more. Sadness or loneliness, I don't know. A kind of weariness that was there and gone before I could understand. But it left its mark. There was a lot more to this man than a pretty face and a big name. I needed to remember that and not make my own assumptions.

"You really want to go?" I asked. "Really?"

His eyes were bright with amusement. "Why not?"

I gave him a cautious smile.

"We can talk over whatever we need to, just you and me. I need to make a couple of calls, then we'll head off, okay?"

"Thank you. I'd like that."

With a parting nod he opened the door and strode back out. He and Mal talked quietly about something in the lounge room. I took the opportunity to wash my face once more and finger-brush my hair for luck. The time had come to take control. Actually, it was well overdue. What was I doing, bouncing from one disaster to the next? That wasn't me. I liked being in control, having a plan. Time to stop worrying about what I couldn't change and take decisive action on what I could. I had money saved up. One of these days my poor old car would die and I'd been planning accordingly. Because once winter hit, and things turned cold, gray, and wet, walking wouldn't always appeal. The thought of using my savings didn't fill me with glee, but emergency measures and all that.

David's lawyers would draw up papers minus the money and I would sign them. No point worrying about that side of things. However, getting out of the public eye for a couple of weeks was well within my capabilities. I just needed to stop and think for a change instead of reacting. I was a big girl and I could take care of myself. The time had come to prove it. I'd go for the drive with him, sort out the basics, and get gone, first on a hideaway holiday, and then back to my very ordinary, well-ordered life devoid of any rock-star interventions.

Yes.

"Give me the keys to the Jeep," said David, squaring off against Mal in the lounge.

Mal winced. "I was joking about giving away cars."

"Come on. Quit bitching. I rode over on the bike and I don't have a helmet for her."

"Fine." With a sour face, Mal dropped his car keys into David's outstretched hand. "But only 'cause I like your wife. Not a scratch, you hear me?"

"Yeah, yeah." David turned and saw me. A hint of a smile curled his lips.

Except for that first day on the bathroom floor, I'd never

seen him smile, never even seen him come close. This bare trace of one made me light up inside. My knees wobbled. That couldn't be normal. I shouldn't be feeling all warm and happy just because he was. I couldn't afford to have any feelings for him at all. Not if I wanted to get out of this in one piece.

"Thanks for putting up with me today, Mal," I said.

"The pleasure was all mine," he drawled. "Sure you wanna go with him, child bride? Fucktard here made you cry. I make you laugh."

David's smile disappeared and he strode to my side. His hand sat lightly against the base of my spine, warm even through the layer of clothing. "We're out of here."

Mal grinned and winked at me.

"Where are we going?" I asked David.

"Does it matter? Let's just drive."

CHAPTER SEVEN

My neck had seized up. Pain shot through me as I slowly straightened and blinked the sleep from my eyes. I rubbed at the offending muscles, trying to get them to unlock. "Ow."

David took one hand off the steering wheel and reached out, rubbing the back of my neck with strong fingers. "You okay?"

"Yeah. I must have slept funny." I shuffled up in the seat, taking in our surroundings, trying not to enjoy the neck rub too much. Because of course he was crazy good with his hands. Mr. Magic Fingers cajoled my muscles back into some semblance of order with seemingly little effort. I couldn't be expected to resist. Impossible. So instead I moaned loudly and let him have his way with me.

Being barely awake was my only excuse.

The sun was just rising. Tall, shadowy trees rushed by outside. Trying to get out of LA, we'd gotten caught in a traffic jam the likes of which this Portland girl had never seen. For all my good intentions, we hadn't really talked. We'd stopped and gotten food and gas. The rest of the time, Johnny Cash had played on the stereo and I'd practiced speeches in my head. None of the words made it out of my mouth. For some reason, I was reluctant to call a halt to our adventure and go off on my own. It had nothing to do with pulling up my big-girl panties and everything to do with how comfortable I'd begun to feel with him. The silence wasn't awkward. It was peaceful. Refreshing, even, given the last day's worth of drama. Being with him on the open road . . . there was something freeing about it. At around two in the morning, I'd fallen asleep.

"David, where are we?"

He gave me a sidelong look, his hand still massaging my muscles. "Well . . ."

A sign flew past outside. "We're going to Monterey?"

"That's where my place is," he said. "Stop tensing up."

"Monterey?"

"Yeah. What've you got against Monterey, hmm? Have a bad time at a music festival?"

"No." I backpedaled fast, not wanting to appear ungrateful. "It's just a surprise. I didn't realize we were, umm . . . Monterey. Okay."

David sighed and pulled off the road. Dust flew and stones pinged off the Jeep. (Mal wouldn't be pleased.) He turned to face me, resting an elbow on the top of the passenger seat, boxing me in.

"Talk to me, friend," he said.

I opened my mouth and let it all tumble out. "I have a plan. I have some money put away. I was going to go someplace quiet for a couple of weeks until this blew over. You didn't have to put yourself out like this. I just need to get my stuff from back at the mansion and I can be out of your hair."

"All right." He nodded. "Well, we're here now and I'd like to go check out my place for a couple of days. So why don't you come with me? Just as friends. No big deal. It's Friday now, the lawyers said they'd have the new papers sent to us Monday. We'll sign them. I've got a show early next week back in LA.

If you want, you can lie low at the house for a few weeks till things calm down. Sound like a plan? We spend the weekend together, then go our separate ways. All sorted."

It did sound like a solid idea. But still, I deliberated for a second. Apparently, it was a second too long.

"You worried about spending the weekend with me or something? Am I that scary?" His gaze held mine, our faces a bare hand's breadth apart. Dark hair fell around his perfect face. For a moment I almost forgot to breathe. I didn't move. I couldn't. Outside a motorcycle roared past then all fell quiet again.

Was he scary? The man had no idea.

"No," I lied, throwing in some scoff for good measure.

I don't think he believed me. "Listen, I'm sorry about acting like a creep back in LA."

"It's okay, really, David. This situation would do anyone's head in."

"Tell me something," he said in a low voice. "You remembered about getting the tat. Anything else come back to you?"

Reliving my drunken rampage wasn't somewhere I wanted to go. Not with him. Not with anyone. I was paying the consequences by having my life upended and splashed about on the Internet. Ridiculous, given nothing in my past was even mildly sordid. Well, apart from the backseat of Tommy's parents' car. "Does this even matter? I mean, isn't it a bit late to be having this conversation?"

"Guess so." He shifted back in his seat and put a hand on the wheel. "You need to stretch your legs or anything?"

"A restroom would be great."

"No worries."

We pulled back out onto the road, and silence ensued for several minutes. He'd turned off the stereo sometime while I slept. The quiet was awkward now and it was all my doing. Guilt sucked first thing in the morning. It probably didn't improve later in the day, but first up, without even a drop of caffeine to fortify me, it was horrible. He'd been nice to me, trying to talk, and I'd shut him down.

"Most of that night is still a blur," I said.

He lifted a couple of fingers off the steering wheel in a little wave. Such was the sum total of his response.

I took a deep breath, fortifying myself to go further. "I remember doing shots at midnight. After that, it's hazy. I remember the sound of the needle at the tattoo parlor, us laughing, but that's about it. I've never blacked out in my life. It's scary."

"Yeah," he said quietly.

"How did we meet?"

He exhaled hard. "Ah, me and a group of people were leaving to go to another club. One of the girls wasn't looking where she was going, bumped into a cocktail waitress. Apparently the waitress was new or something and she crashed her tray. Luckily, it was only a couple of empty beer bottles."

"How did I get involved?"

He darted me a glance, taking his eyes off the road for a moment. "Some of them started giving the poor waitress shit, telling her they were going to get her fired. You just swooped in and handed them their asses."

"I did?"

"Oh, yeah." He licked his lips, the corner of his mouth curling. "Told them they were evil, pretentious, overpriced assholes who should watch where they were walking. You helped the girl pick up the beer bottles and then you insulted my friends some more. It was pretty fucking classic, actually. I can't remember everything you said. You got pretty creative with the insults by the end."

"Huh. And you liked me for that?"

He shut his mouth and said nothing. A whole wide world of nothing. Nothing could actually cover a lot of ground when you put that much effort into it.

"What happened next?" I asked.

"Security came over to throw you out. Not like they were gonna argue with the rich kids."

"No. I guess not."

"You looked panicky, so I got you out of there."

"You left your friends for me?" I watched him in amazement.

He did a one-shoulder shrug. As if it meant nil.

"What then?"

"We took off and had a drink in another bar."

"I'm surprised you stuck with me." Stunned was closer.

"Why wouldn't I?" he asked. "You treated me like a normal person. We just talked about everyday stuff. You weren't angling to get anything out of me. You didn't act like I was a different fucking species. When you looked at me it felt . . ."

"What?"

He cleared his throat. "I dunno. Doesn't matter."

"Yes, you do. And it does."

He groaned.

"Please?"

"Fuck's sake," he muttered, shifting around in the driver's seat all uncomfortable-like. "It felt real, okay? It felt right. I don't know how else to explain it."

I sat in stunned silence for a moment. "That's a good way to explain it."

Suddenly, he got decidedly smirky. "Plus, I'd never been propositioned quite like that."

"Yeeeah. Okay, stop now." I covered my face with my hands, and he laughed.

"Relax," he said. "You were very sweet."

"Sweet?"

"Sweet is not a bad thing."

He pulled the Jeep into a gas station, stopping in front of a pump. "Look at me."

I lowered my fingers.

David stared back at me, beautiful face grinning. "You said that you thought I was a really nice guy. And that it would be great if we could go up to your room and have sex and just hang out for a while, if maybe that was something I'd be interested in doing."

"Ha. I have all the moves." I laughed. There might have been more embarrassing conversations in my life. Doubtful, though. Oh, good God, the thought of me trying out my smooth seduction routine on David. He who had groupies and glamour models throwing themselves at him on a daily basis. If there'd been enough room under the car seat, I'd have hid down there. "What did you say?"

"What do you think I said?" Without taking his gaze off me, he popped the glove box and pulled out a baseball cap. "Looks like the restrooms are around the side."

"This is so mortifying. Why couldn't you have forgotten too?"

He just looked at me. The smirk was long gone. For a long moment he held my gaze captive, unsmiling. The air in the car seemed to drop by about fifty degrees.

"I'll be right back," I said, fingers fumbling with the seat belt.

"Sure."

I finally managed to unbuckle the stupid thing, heart galloping inside my chest. The conversation had gotten crazy heavy toward the end. It had caught me unawares. Knowing he'd stood up for me in Las Vegas, that he'd chosen me over his friends . . . it changed things. And it made me wonder what else I needed to know about that night.

"Wait." He rifled among the collection of sunglasses, pulled out a pair of designer aviator shades, and handed them to me. "You're famous now too, remember?"

"My butt is."

He almost smiled. He fit the baseball cap to his head and rested an arm on the steering wheel. The tattoo of my name was right there, in all its glory. It was pink around the edges and some of the letters had small scabs on them. I wasn't the only one permanently marked by this.

"See you in a bit," he said.

"Right." I opened the door and slowly climbed out of the car. Tripping and landing on my ass in front of him must be avoided at all costs.

I saw to the necessities, then washed my hands. The girl in the restroom mirror looked wild-eyed and then some. I splashed water on my face and did a little damage control on my hair. What a joke. This adventure I was on was undoing any and all attempts at keeping control. Me, my life, all of it seemed to be in a state of flux. That shouldn't have felt as strangely good as it did.

When I got back he was standing by the Jeep, signing an autograph for a couple of guys, one of whom was busy doing an enthusiastic air guitar performance. David laughed and clapped him on the back and they talked for a couple of minutes more. He was kind, gracious. He stood smiling, chatting with them, until he noticed me hovering nearby. "Thanks, guys. If you could keep this quiet for a couple of days I'd appreciate it, hey? We could do with a break from the fuss."

"No worries." One of the guys turned and grinned at me. "Congratulations. You're way prettier in person than in your pictures."

"Thanks." I waved a hand at them, not quite knowing what else to do.

David winked at me and opened the passenger door for me to hop in.

The other man pulled out a cell phone and started snapping pictures. David ignored him and jogged around to the other side of the vehicle. He didn't speak till we were back out on the road.

"It's not far now," he said. "We still going to Monterey?"

"Absolutely."

"Cool."

Hearing David talk about our first meeting had put a new spin on things. That conversation had aroused my curiosity. That he'd chosen me to some degree that night . . . I don't think the possibility had occurred to me before. I'd figured we'd both let tequila do the thinking and somehow fallen into this mess together. I was wrong. There was more to the story. Much more. David's reluctance to answer certain questions made me wonder.

I wanted answers. But I needed to tread carefully.

"Is it always like that for you?" I asked. "Being recognized? Having people approach you all the time?"

"They were fine. The crazies are a worry, but you handle it. It's part of my job. People like the music, so . . ."

A bad feeling crept through me. "You did tell me who you were that night, didn't you?"

"Yeah, of course I did." He gave me a snarky look, his brows bunched up.

My bad feeling crept away, only to be replaced by shame. "Sorry."

"Ev, I wanted you to know what the fuck you were getting into. You said you really liked me, but you weren't that keen on my band." He fiddled with the stereo, another half smile on his face. Soon some rock song I didn't know played quietly over the speakers. "You felt pretty bad about it, actually. You kept apologizing over and over. Insisted on buying me a burger and shake to make up for it."

"I just prefer country."

"Believe me, I know. And stop apologizing. You're allowed to like whatever the hell you want."

"Was it a good burger and shake?"

He gave me a one-shoulder shrug. "It was fine."

"I wish I remembered."

He snorted. "There's a first."

I don't know what exactly came over me. Maybe I just wanted to see if I could make him smile. With a knee beneath me I pulled out a length of seat belt, raised myself up, and kissed him quick on the cheek. A surprise attack. His skin was warm and smooth against my lips. The man smelled so much better than he had any right to.

"What was that for?" he asked, shooting me a look out of the corners of his eyes.

"For getting me out of Portland and then LA. For talking to me about that night." I shrugged, trying to play it off. "For lots of things."

A little line appeared above the bridge of his nose. When he spoke, his voice was gruff. "Right. No problem."

His mouth stayed shut and his hand went to his cheek, touching where I'd been. The frown-faced side-on looks continued for quite some time. Each one made me wonder a bit more if David Ferris was just as scared of me as I was of him. This reaction was even better than a smile.

———

The log-and-stone house rose out of the trees, perched on the edge of a cliff. The place was awe-inspiring on a whole different level from the mansion back in LA. Below, the ocean went about its business of being spectacular.

David climbed out of the car and walked up to the house, fiddling with a set of keys from his pocket. He opened the front door, then stopped to punch numbers into a security system.

"You coming?" he yelled.

I lingered beside the car, looking up at the magnificent house. Him and me alone. Inside there. Hmm. Waves crashed on the rocks nearby. I swore I could hear the swell of an orchestral accompaniment not too far off in the distance. The place was decidedly atmospheric. And that atmosphere was pure romance.

"What's the problem?" David came back down the stone path toward me.

"Nothing . . . I was just—"

"Good." He didn't stop. I didn't know what was going on until I found myself hanging upside down over his shoulder in a fireman's hold.

"Shit. David!"

"Relax."

"You're going to drop me!"

"I'm not going to drop you. Stop squirming," he said, his arm pressing against the back of my legs. "Show some trust."

"What are you doing?" I battered my hands against the ass of his jeans.

"It's traditional to carry the bride across the threshold."

"Not like this."

He patted my butt cheek, the one with his name on it. "Why would we wanna start being conventional now, huh?"

"I thought we were just being friends."

"This is friendly. You should probably stop feeling my ass, though, or I'm gonna get the wrong idea about us. Especially after that kiss in the car."

"I'm not feeling your ass," I grumbled, and stopped using his butt cheeks for a handhold. Like it was my fault the position left me no alternative but to hold on to his firm butt.

"Please, you're all over me. It's disgusting."

I laughed despite myself. "You put me over your shoulder, you idiot. Of course I'm all over you."

Up the steps we went, then onto the wide wooden patio and into the house. Hardwood floors in a rich brown and moving boxes, lots and lots of moving boxes. I couldn't see much else.

"This could be a problem," he said.

"What could be?" I asked, still upside down, my hair obscuring my view.

"Hang on." Carefully, he righted me, setting my feet on the floor. All the blood rushed from my head and I staggered. He grabbed my elbows, holding me upright.

"Okay?" he asked.

"Yeah. What's the problem?"

"I thought there'd be more furniture," he said.

"You've never been here before?"

"I've been busy."

Apart from boxes there were more boxes. They were everywhere. We stood in a large central room with a huge stone fireplace set in the far wall. You could roast a whole cow in the thing if you were so inclined. Stairs led to a second floor above and another level below this one. A dining room and open-plan kitchen came next. The place was a combination of floor-to-ceiling glass, neat lines of logs, and gray stonework. The perfect mix of old and new design techniques. It was stunning. But then all the places he lived in seemed to be.

I wondered what he'd make of my and Lauren's tiny bedraggled apartment. A silly thought. As if he'd ever see it.

"At least they got a fridge." He pulled one of the large stainless steel doors open. Every inch of space inside had been packed with food and beverages. "Excellent."

"Who are 'they'?"

"Ah, the people that look after the place for me. Friends of mine. They used to look after it for the previous owner too. I rang them, asked them to sort some stuff out for us." He pulled out a Corona and popped the lid. "Cheers."

I smiled, amused. "For breakfast?"

"I've been awake for two days. I want a beer, then I want a bed. Man, I hope they thought to get a bed." Beer in hand, he ambled back through the lounge and up the stairs. I followed, curious.

He pushed open one bedroom door after another. There were four all up and each had its own bathroom because cool, rich people clearly couldn't share. At the final door at the end of the hall he stopped and sagged with relief. "Thank fuck for that."

A kingdom of a bed made up with clean, white sheets waited within. And a couple more boxes.

"What's with all the boxes?" I asked. "Did they only get one bed?"

"Sometimes I buy stuff on my travels. Sometimes people give me stuff. I've just been sending it all here for the last few years. Take a look if you want. And yes, there's only one bed." He took another swig of beer. "You think I'm made of money?"

I huffed out a laugh. "Says the guy who got Cartier to open so I could pick out a ring."

"You remember that?" He smiled around the bottle of beer.

"No, I just assumed given what time of night it must have

been." I wandered over to the wall of windows. Such an amazing view.

"You tried to pick some shitty little thing. I couldn't believe it." He stared at me, but his gaze was distant.

"I threw the ring at the lawyers."

He flinched and studied his shoes. "Yeah, I know."

"I'm sorry. They just made me so mad."

"Lawyers do that." He took another swig of the beer. "Mal said you took a swing at him."

"I missed."

"Probably for the best. He's an idiot but he means well."

"Yeah, he was really kind to me." Crossing my arms, I checked out the rest of his big bedroom, wandering into the bathroom. The Jacuzzi would have made Mal's curl up in shame. The place was sumptuous. Yet again the feeling of not belonging, of not fitting in with the décor, hit me hard.

"That's some heavy frown, friend," he said.

I attempted a smile. "I'm just still trying to figure things out. I mean, is that why you took the plunge in Vegas? Because you're unhappy? And apart from Mal you're surrounded by jerks?"

"Fuck." His let his head fall back. "Do we have to keep talking about that night?"

"I'm just trying to understand."

"No," he said. "It wasn't that, okay?"

"Then what?"

"We were in Vegas, Ev. Shit happens."

I shut my mouth.

"I don't mean . . ." He wiped a hand across his face. "Fuck. Look, don't think it was just all drinking and partying and that's the only reason anything happened. Why we happened. I wouldn't want you to think that."

I flailed. It seemed the only proper response. "But that's what I do think. That's exactly what I think. That's the only way this fits together in my head. When a girl like me wakes up married to a guy like you, what else can she possibly think? God, David, look at you. You're beautiful, rich, and successful. Your brother was right, this makes no sense."

He turned on me, face tight. "Don't do that. Don't run yourself down like that."

I just sighed.

"I'm serious. Don't you ever give what that asshole said another thought, understood? You are not nothing."

"Then give me something. Tell me what it was like between us that night."

He opened his mouth, then snapped it closed. "Nah. I don't want to dredge it all up, you know, water under the bridge or whatever. I just don't want you thinking that the whole night was some alcohol-fueled frenzy or something, that's all. Honestly, you didn't even seem that drunk most of it."

"David, you're hedging. Come on. It's not fair that you remember and I don't."

"No," he said, his voice hard, cold, in a way I hadn't heard it. He loomed over me, jaw set. "It's not fair that I remember and you don't, Evelyn."

I didn't know what to say.

"I'm going out." True to his word, he stormed out the door. Heavy footsteps thumped along the hallway and back down the stairs. I stood staring after him.

I gave him awhile to cool off, then followed him out onto the beach. The morning light was blinding, clear blue skies all the way. It was beautiful. Salty sea air cleared my head a little.

David's words raised more questions than they answered. Puzzling that night out consumed my thoughts. I'd reached two conclusions. Both worried me. The first was that the night in Vegas was special to him. My prying or trivializing the experience upset him. The second was, I suspected, he hadn't been all that drunk. It sounded like he knew exactly what he was doing. In which case, how the hell must he have felt the next morning? I'd rejected him and our marriage out of hand. He must have been heartsore, humiliated.

There'd been good reasons for my behavior. I'd still, however, been incredibly thoughtless. I didn't know David then. But I was beginning to now. And the more we talked, the more I liked him.

David sat on the rocks with a beer in hand, staring out to sea. A cool ocean wind tossed his long hair about. The fabric of his T-shirt was drawn tight across his broad back. He had his knees drawn up with an arm wrapped around them. It made him seem younger than he was, more vulnerable.

"Hi," I said, squatting beside him.

"Hey." Eyes squinted against the sun, he looked up at me, face guarded.

"I'm sorry for pushing."

He nodded, stared back out at the water. "S'okay."

"I didn't mean to upset you."

"Don't worry about it."

"Are we still friends?"

He huffed out a laugh. "Sure."

I sat down next to him, trying to figure out what to say next, what would set things right between us. Nothing I could think of saying was going to make up for Vegas. I needed more time with him. The ticking clock of the annulment papers grew louder by the minute. It unnerved me, thinking our time would be cut short. That it would soon all be over and I wouldn't see or talk to him again. That I wouldn't get to figure out the puzzle that was us. My skin grew goose pimples from more than the wind.

"Shit. You're cold," he said, wrapping an arm around my shoulders, pulling me in closer against him.

And I got closer, happily. "Thanks."

He put down the beer bottle, wrapping both arms around me. "Should probably get you inside."

"In a bit." My thumbs rubbed over my fingers, fidgeting. "Thank you for bringing me here. It's a lovely place."

"Mm."

"David, really, I'm so sorry."

"Hey." He put a finger beneath my chin, raising it. The anger and hurt were gone, replaced by kindness. He gave me one of his little shrugs. "Let's just let it go."

The idea actually sent me into a panic. I didn't want to let go of him. The knowledge was startling. I stared up at him, letting it sink in. "I don't want to."

He blinked. "All right. You want to make it up to me?"

I doubted we were talking about the same thing, but I nodded anyway.

"I've got an idea."

"Shoot."

"Different things can jog your memory, right?"

"I guess so," I said.

"So if I kiss you, you might remember what we were like together."

I stopped breathing. "You want to kiss me?"

"You don't want me to kiss you?"

"No," I said quickly. "I'm okay with you kissing me."

He bit back a smile. "That's very kind of you."

"And this kiss is for the purposes of scientific research?"

"Yep. You want to know what happened that night and I don't really want to talk about it. So, I figure, easier all around if you can maybe remember some of it yourself."

"That makes sense."

"Excellent."

"How far did we go that night?"

His gaze dropped to the neck of my tank top and the curves of my breasts. "Second base."

"Shirt on?"

"Off. We were both topless. Topless cuddles are best." He watched as I absorbed the information, his face close to mine.

"Bra?"

"Absolutely not."

"Oh." I licked my lips, breathing hard. "So, you really think we should do this?"

"You're overthinking it."

"Sorry."

"And stop apologizing."

My mouth opened to repeat the sentiment but I snapped it shut.

"S'okay. You'll get the hang of it."

My brain stuttered and I stared at his mouth. He had the most beautiful mouth, with full lips that pulled up slightly at the edges. Stunning.

"Tell me what you're thinking," he said.

"You said not to think. And honestly, I'm not."

"Good," he said, leaning even closer. "That's good."

His lips brushed against mine, easing me into it. Soft but firm, with no hesitation. His teeth toyed with my bottom lip. Then he sucked on it. He didn't kiss like the boys I knew, though I couldn't exactly define the difference. It was just better and . . . more.

Infinitely more. His mouth pressed against mine and his tongue slipped into my mouth, rubbing against mine. God, he tasted good. My fingers slid into his hair as if they'd always wanted to. He kissed me until I couldn't remember anything that had come before. None of it mattered.

His hand slid around the nape of my neck, holding me in place. The kiss went on and on. He lit me up from top to toe. I never wanted it to end.

He kissed me till my head spun, and I hung on for dear life. Then he pulled back, panting, and set his forehead against mine once again.

"Why did you stop?" I asked when I could form a coherent sentence. My hands pulled at him, trying to bring him back to my mouth.

"Shh. Relax." He took a deep breath. "Did you remember something? Anything about that familiar to you?"

My kiss-addled mind came up blank. Damn it. "No. I don't think so."

"That's a pity." A ridge appeared between his brows. The dark smudges beneath his beautiful blue eyes seemed to have darkened. I'd disappointed him again. My heart sank.

"You look tired," I said.

"Yeah. Might be time to get some shut-eye." He planted a quick kiss on my forehead. Was it a friend's kiss, or more? I couldn't tell. Maybe it too was just for scientific purposes.

"We tried, huh?" he said.

"Yeah. We did."

He rose to his feet, collecting his beer bottle. Without him to warm me, the breeze blew straight through me, shaking my bones. It was the kiss, though, that had really shaken me. It had blown my ever-lovin' mind. To think I'd had a night of kisses like that and forgotten it. I needed a brain transplant at the earliest convenience.

"Do you mind if I come with you?" I asked.

"Not at all." He held out a hand to help me to my feet.

Together, we wandered back up to the house, up the stairs into the master bedroom. I tugged off my shoes as David dealt with his own footwear. We lay down on the mattress, not touching. Both of us staring at the ceiling like there might be answers there.

I kept quiet. For all of about a minute. My mind was wide awake and babbling at me. "I think I understand a little better now how we ended up married."

"Do you?" He turned his head to face me.

"Yes." I'd never been kissed like that before. "I do."

"C'mere." A strong arm encircled my waist, dragging me into the center of the bed.

"David." I reached for him with a nervous smile. More than ready for more kisses. More of him.

"Lie on your side," he said, his hands maneuvering me until he lay behind me. One arm slipped beneath my neck and the other was slung over my waist, pulling me in closer against him. His hips fit against my butt perfectly.

"What are we doing?" I asked, bewildered.

"Spooning. We did it that night for a while. Until you felt sick."

"We spooned?"

"Yep," he said. "Stage two in the memory rehab process, spooning. Now go to sleep."

"I only woke up an hour ago."

He pressed his face into my hair and even threw a leg over mine for good measure, pinning me down. "Bad luck. I'm tired and I wanna spoon. With you. And the way I figure it, you owe me. So we're spooning."

"Got it."

His breath warmed the side of my neck, sending shivers down my spine.

"Relax. You're all tense." His arms tightened around me.

After a moment, I picked up his left hand, running the pads of my fingers over his calluses. Using him for my fidget toy. The tips of his fingers were hard. There was also a ridge down his thumb and another slight one along the bottom of his fingers where they joined the palm of his hand. He obviously spent a lot of time holding guitars. On the back of his fingers the word *Free* had been tattooed. On his right hand was the word *Live*. I couldn't help but wonder if marriage would impinge on that freedom. Japanese-style waves and a serpentine dragon covered his arm, the colors and detail impressive.

"Tell me about your major," he said. "You're doin' architecture, right?"

"Yes," I said, a little surprised he knew. I'd obviously told him in Vegas. "My dad's one."

He meshed his fingers with mine, putting the kibosh on my fidgeting.

"Did you always want to play guitar?" I asked, trying not to get too distracted by the way he was wrapped around me.

"Yeah. Music's the only thing that ever really made sense to me. Can't imagine doing anything else."

"Huh." It must be nice, having something to be so passionate about. I liked the idea of being an architect. Many of my childhood games had involved building blocks or drawing. But I didn't feel driven to do it, exactly. "I'm pretty much tone deaf."

"That explains a lot." He chuckled.

"Be nice. I was never particularly good at sports either. I

like drawing and reading and watching movies. And I like to travel, not that I've done much of it."

"Yeah?"

"Mm."

He shifted behind me, getting comfortable. "When I travel, it's always about the shows. Doesn't leave much time for looking around."

"That's a pity."

"And being recognized can be a pain in the ass sometimes. Now and then, it gets ugly. There's a fair bit of pressure on us, and I can't always do what I want. Truth is, I'm kind of ready to slow things down, hang out at home more."

I said nothing, turning his words over inside my head.

"The parties get old after a while. Having people around all the damn time."

"I bet." And yet, back in LA he'd still had a groupie hanging off him, cooing at his every word. Obviously parts of the lifestyle still appealed. Parts that I wasn't certain I could compete with even if I wanted to. "Won't you miss some of it?"

"Honestly, it's all I've done for so long, I don't know."

"Well, you have a gorgeous home to hang out in."

"Hmm." He was quiet for a moment. "Ev?"

"Yeah?"

"Was being an architect your idea or your dad's?"

"I don't remember," I admitted. "We've always talked about it. My brother was never interested in taking up the mantle. He was always getting into fights and skipping class."

"You said you had a tough time at high school too."

"Doesn't everyone?" I wriggled around, turned over so I could see his face. "I don't usually talk about that with other people."

"We talked about it. You said you got picked on because of

your size. I figured that's what set you off with my friends. The fact that they were bullying that girl like a pack of fucking schoolkids."

"I guess that would do it." The teasing wasn't a subject I liked to raise. Too easily, it bought back all of the crappy feelings associated with it. David's arms didn't allow for any of that to slip through, however. "Most of the teachers just ignored it. Like it was an extra hassle they didn't need. But there was this one teacher, Miss Hall. Anytime they started in on me or one of the other kids, she'd intercede. She was great."

"She sounds great. But you didn't really answer my question. Do you want to be an architect?"

"Well, it's what I've always planned to do. And I, ah, I like the idea of designing someone's home. I don't know that being an architect is my divine calling, like music is for you, but I think I could be good at it."

"I'm not doubting that, baby," he said, his voice soft but definite.

I tried not to let the endearment reduce me to a soggy mess on the mattress. Subtlety was the key. I'd hurt him in Vegas. If I was serious about this, about wanting him to give us another go, I needed to be careful. Give him good memories to replace the bad. Memories we could both share this time.

"Ev, is it what you want to do with your life?"

I stopped. Having already trotted out the standard responses, extra thought was required. The plan had been around for so long I didn't tend to question it. There was safety and comfort to be had there. But David wanted more and I wanted to give it to him. Maybe this was why I'd spilled my secrets to him in Vegas. Something about this man drew me in, and I didn't want to fight it. "Honestly, I'm not sure."

"That's okay, you know." His gaze never shifted from mine. "You're only twenty-one."

"But I'm supposed to be an adult now, taking responsibility for myself. I'm supposed to know these things."

"You've been living with your friend for a few years, yeah? Paying your own bills and doing your classes and all that?"

"Yes."

"Then how are you not taking responsibility for yourself?" He tucked his long dark hair behind an ear, getting it out of his face. "So you start out in architecture and see how you go."

"You make it sound so simple."

"It is. You either stick with that or try something else, see how it works for you. It's your life. Your call."

"Do you only play guitar?" I asked, wanting to know more about him. Wanting the topic of conversation to be off me. The knot of tension building inside me was not pleasant.

"No." A smile tugged at the corner of his mouth—he knew exactly what I was about. "Bass and drums too. Of course."

"Of course?"

"Anyone passable at guitar can play bass if they put their mind to it. And anyone who can pick up two sticks at the same time can play drums. Be sure to tell Mal I said that next time you see him, yeah? He'll get a kick out of that."

"You got it."

"And I sing."

"You do?" I asked, getting excited. "Will you sing something for me? Please?"

He made a noncommittal noise.

"Did you sing to me that night?"

He gave me a small pained smile. "Yeah, I did."

"So it might bring back a memory."

"You're going to use that now, aren't you? Anytime you want something you're going to throw it at me."

"Hey, you started it. You wanted to kiss me for scientific purposes."

"It was for scientific purposes. A kiss between friends for reasons of pure logic."

"It was a very friendly kiss, David."

A lazy smile lit his face. "Yes, it was."

"Please sing me something?"

"Okay," he huffed. "Turn back around, then. We were in spoon position for this."

I snuggled back down against him and he shuffled closer. Being David's cuddle toy was a wonderful thing. I couldn't imagine anything better. Pity he was sticking with the scientific rationale. Not that I could blame him. If I were him, I'd be wary of me.

His voice washed over me, deep, rough in the best way possible as he sang the ballad.

I've got this feeling that comes and goes
Ten broken fingers and one broken nose
Dark waters very cold
I know I'll make it home
This sorry sun has burned the sky
She's out of touch and she's very high
Her bed was made of stone
I know I'll break her throne
These aching bones won't hold me up
My swollen shoes they have had enough
These smokestacks burn them down
This ocean let it drown

When he finished I was quiet. He gave me a squeeze, probably checking I was still alive. I squeezed his arms right back, not turning over so he couldn't see the tears in my eyes. The combination of his voice and the moody ballad had undone me. I was always making a mess of myself around him, crying or puking. Why he wanted anything to do with me, I had no idea.

"Thank you," I said.

"Anytime."

I lay there, trying to decipher the lyrics. What it might mean that he'd chosen that song to sing to me. "What's it called?"

"'Homesick.' I wrote it for the last album." He rose up on one elbow, leaning over to check out my face. "Shit, I made you sad. I'm sorry."

"No. It was beautiful. Your voice is amazing."

He frowned but lay back down, pressed his chest against my spine. "I'll sing you something happy next time."

"If you like." I pressed my lips to the back of his hand, to the veins tracing across, and the dusting of dark hair. "David?"

"Hmm?"

"Why don't you sing in the band? You have such a great voice."

"I do backup. Jimmy loves the limelight. It was always more his thing." His fingers twined with mine. "He wasn't always the asshole he is now. I'm sorry he hassled you in LA. I could have killed him for saying that shit."

"It's okay."

"No, it's not. He was off his face. He didn't have a fucking clue what he was talking about." His thumb moved restlessly over my hand. "You're gorgeous. You don't need to change a thing."

I didn't know what to say at first. Jimmy had said some

horrible things and it had stayed with me. Funny how the bad stuff always did.

"I've both puked and cried on you. Are you entirely sure about that?" I joked, finally.

"Yes," he said simply. "I like you the way you are, blurting out whatever shit crosses your mind. Not trying to play me, or use me. You're just . . . being with me. I like you."

I lay there speechless for a moment, taken aback. "Thank you."

"You're welcome. Anytime, Evelyn. Anytime at all."

"I like you too."

His lips brushed against the back of my neck. Shivers raced across my skin. "Do you?"

"Yes. Very much."

"Thanks, baby."

It took a long time for his breathing to even out. His limbs got heavier and he stilled, asleep against my back. My foot went fuzzy with pins and needles, but never mind. I hadn't slept with anyone before, apart from the occasional platonic bed-sharing episode with Lauren. Apparently, sleeping was all I'd be doing today.

In all honesty, it felt good, lying next to him.

It felt right.

CHAPTER EIGHT

"Hey." David padded down the stairs seven hours later, wearing a towel wrapped around his waist. He'd slicked his wet hair back and his tattoos were displayed to perfection, defining his lean torso and muscular arms. There was a lot of skin on show. The man was a visual feast. I made a conscious effort to keep my tongue inside my head. Keeping the welcoming grin off my face was beyond my abilities. I'd planned to play it cool so as not to spook him. That plan had failed.

"Whatcha doin'?" he asked.

"Nothing much. There was a delivery for you." I pointed to the bags and boxes waiting by the door. All day I'd pondered the problem of us. The only thing I'd come up with was that I didn't want our time to end. I didn't want to sign those annulment papers. Not yet. The idea made me want to start puking all over again. I wanted David. I wanted to be with him. I needed a new plan.

The pad of my thumb rubbed over my bottom lip, back and forth, back and forth. I'd gone for a long walk up the beach earlier, watching the waves crash on the shore and reliving that kiss. Over and over again, I'd played it inside my mind. The same went for our conversations. In fact, I'd picked apart every moment of our time together, explored every nuance. Every moment I could remember, anyway, and I'd tried damn hard to remember all of it.

"A delivery?" He crouched down beside the closest package and started tearing at the wrapping. I averted my eyes before I caught a glimpse up his towel, despite being wildly curious.

"Would you mind if I used your phone?" I asked.

"Ev, you don't need to ask. Help yourself to whatever."

"Thanks." Lauren and my folks were probably freaking out, wondering what was going on. It was time to brave up to the butt-picture repercussions. I groaned on the inside.

"This one's for you." He handed me a thick brown-paper parcel done up with string, followed by a shopping bag with some brand I'd never heard of printed on the side. "Ah, this one too, by the look."

"It is?"

"Yeah. I asked Martha to order some stuff for us."

"Oh."

"Oh? No." David shook his head. Then he kneeled down in front of me and tore into the brown package in my hands. "No 'oh.' We need clothes. It's really simple."

"That's very kind of you, David, but I'm fine."

He wasn't listening. Instead he held up a red dress the same thigh-baring length as those girls at the mansion had worn. "What the fuck? You're not wearing this." The designer dress went flying, and he ripped into the shopping bag at my feet.

"David, you can't just throw it on the ground."

"Sure I can. Here, this is a little better."

A black tank top fell into my lap. At least this one looked the right size. The thigh-high red dress had been a size-four joke. Quite possibly a mean one, given Martha's dislike of me back in LA. No matter.

A tag dangled from the tank. The price. Shit. They couldn't be serious.

"Whoa. I could pay my rent for weeks with this top."

In lieu of a response he threw a pair of skinny black jeans at me. "Here, they're okay too."

I put the jeans aside. "It's a plain cotton tank top. How can this possibly cost two hundred dollars?"

"What do you think of this?" A length of silky blue fabric dangled from his hand. "Nice, huh?"

"Do they sew the seams with gold thread? Is that it?"

"What are you talking about?" He held up the blue dress, turning it this way and that. "Hell no, it's backless. The top of your ass will probably show in that." It joined the red dress on the floor. My hands itched to rescue them, fold them away nicely. But David just ripped into the next box. "What were you saying?"

"I'm talking about the price of this top."

"Shit, no. We're not talking about the price of that top because we're not talking about money. It's an issue for you, and I'm not going there." A micromini denim skirt came next. "What the fuck was Martha thinking ordering you this sort of stuff?"

"Well, to be fair, you do normally have girls in bikinis hanging off you. In comparison, the backless dress is quite sedate."

"You're different. You're my friend, aren't you?"

"Yes." I didn't entirely believe the tone of my own voice.

His forehead wrinkled up with disdain. "Damn it. Look at the length of this. I can't even tell if it's meant to be a skirt or a fucking belt."

Laughter burst out of me and he gave me a hurt look, big blue puppy-dog eyes of extreme sadness and displeasure. Clearly, I had hurt his heart.

"I'm sorry," I said. "But you sound like my father."

He shoved the micromini back into its bag. At least it wasn't on the floor. "Yeah? Your dad and I should meet. I think we'd get along great."

"You want to meet my father?"

"Depends. Would he shoot me on sight?"

"No." Probably not.

He just gave me a curious look and burrowed into the next box. "That's better. Here."

He passed me a couple of sedate T-shirts, one black and one blue.

"I don't think you should be selecting nun's clothing for me, friend," I said, amused at his behavior. "It's vaguely hypo-critical."

"They're not nun's clothes. They just cover the essentials. Is that too much to ask?" The next bulging bag was passed to me in its entirety. "Here."

"You do admit it's just a tiny bit hypocritical, though, right?"

"Admit nothing. Adrian taught me that a long time ago. Look in the bag."

I did so and he burst out laughing, whatever expression I wore being apparently hilarious.

"What is this?" I asked, feeling all wide-eyed with wonder. It might have been a thong if the makers had seen fit to invest just a little more material into it.

"I'm dressing you like a nun."

"La Perla." I read the tag, then turned it over to check out the price.

"Shit. Will you not look at the price, please, Ev?" David dived at me and I lay back, trying to make out the figures on the crazily swaying tag that was bigger than the scrap of lace.

His larger hand closed over mine, engulfing the thong. "Don't. For fuck's sake."

The back of my head hit the edge of a step and I winced, my eyes filling with tears. "Ow."

"You all right?" His body stretched out above mine. A hand rubbed carefully at the back of my skull.

"Um, yeah." The scent of his soap and shampoo was pure heaven, Lord help me. But there was something more than that. His cologne. It wasn't heavy. Just a light scent of spice. There was something really familiar about it.

The tag hanging down in front of my face momentarily distracted me however. "Three hundred dollars?"

"It's worth it."

"Holy shit. No, it's not."

He hung the thong from the tip of a finger, a crazy cool smile on his face. "Trust me. I'd have paid ten times that amount for this. No questions asked."

"David, I could get the exact same thing for less than a tenth of that price in a normal store. That's insane."

"No, you couldn't." He balanced his weight on an elbow set on the step beside my head and started reading from the tag. "See, this exquisite lace is handmade by local artists in a small region of northern Italy famous for just such craftsmanship. It's made from only the finest of silks. You can't get that at Walmart, baby."

"No, I guess not."

He made a pleased humming sound and looked at me with eyes soft and hazy. Then his smile faded. He pulled back and scrunched the thong up in his hand. "Anyway."

"Wait." My fingers curled around his biceps, keeping him in place.

"What's up?" he asked, his voice tightening.

"Just, let me . . ." I lifted my face to his neck. The scent was strongest there. I breathed him deep, letting myself get high off the scent of him. I shut my eyes and remembered.

"Evelyn?" The muscles in his arms flexed and hardened. "I'm not sure this is a good idea."

"We were in the gondolas at the Venetian. You said you couldn't swim, that I'd have to save you if we capsized."

His Adam's apple jumped. "Yeah."

"I was terrified for you."

"I know. You hung on to me so tight I could barely breathe." I drew back so I could see his face.

"Why do you think we stayed on them for so long?" he asked. "You were practically sitting in my lap."

"Can you swim?"

He laughed quietly. "Of course I can swim. I don't even think the water was that deep."

"It was all a ruse. You're tricky, David Ferris."

"And you're funny, Evelyn Thomas." His face relaxed, his eyes softening again. "You remembered something."

"Yes."

"That's great. Anything else?"

I gave him a sad smile. "No, sorry."

He looked away, disappointed, I think, but trying not to let it show.

"David?"

"Mm?"

I leaned forward to press my lips to his, wanting to kiss him, needing to. He pulled back again. My hopes dived. "Sorry. I'm sorry."

"Ev. What are you doing?"

"Kissing you?"

He said nothing. Jaw rigid, he looked away.

"You're allowed to kiss me and cuddle me and buy me insanely priced lingerie and I can't kiss you back?" My hands slid down to his and he held them. At least he wasn't rejecting me totally.

"Why do you wanna kiss me?" he asked, his voice stern.

I studied our entwined fingers for a moment, getting my thoughts in order. "David, I'm probably not ever going to remember everything about that night in Vegas. But I thought we could maybe make some new good memories this weekend. Something we can both share."

"Just this weekend?"

My heart filled my throat. "No. I don't know. It just . . . it feels like there's meant to be more between us."

"More than friends?" He watched me, eyes intent.

"Yes. I like you. You're kind and sweet and beautiful and you're easy to talk to. When we're not always arguing about Vegas. I feel like . . ."

"What?"

"Like this weekend is a second chance. I don't want to just let it slip by. I think I'd regret that for a long time."

He nodded, cocked his head. "So what was your plan? Just kiss me and see what happened?"

"My plan?"

"I know about you and your plans. You told me all about how anal you are."

"I told you that?" I was an idiot.

"Yeah. You did. You especially told me about the big plan." He stared down at me, eyes intense. "You know . . . finish school then spend three to five years establishing yourself at midrange firm before moving up the ranks somewhere more prestigious and starting your own small consultancy business by thirty-five. Then there'd maybe time to get a relationship and those pesky 2.4 kids out of the way."

My throat was suddenly a dry, barren place. "I was really chatty that night."

"Mm. But what was interesting was the way you didn't talk about that plan like it was a good thing. You talked about it like it was a cage and you were rattling the bars."

I had nothing.

"So, come on," he said softly, taunting me. "What's the plan here, Ev? How were you going to convince me?"

"Oh. Well, I was um . . . I was going to seduce you, I guess. And see what happened. Yeah . . ."

"How? By complaining about me buying you stuff?"

"No. That was just an added bonus. You're welcome."

He licked his lips, but I saw the smile. "Right. Come on, then, show me your moves."

"My moves?"

"Your seduction techniques. Come on, time's a-wasting." I hesitated and he clicked his tongue, impatient. "I'm only wearing a towel, baby. How hard can this be?"

"Fine, fine." I held his fingers tight, refusing to let go. "So, David?"

"Yes, Evelyn?"

"I was thinking . . ."

"Hmm?"

I was so hopelessly outclassed with him. I gave him the only thing I could think of. The only thing that I knew had a track record of working. "I think you're a really nice guy and I was wondering if you'd maybe like to come up to my room and have sex with me and maybe hang out for a while. If that's maybe something you'd be interested in doing . . ."

His eyes darkened, accusing and unhappy. He started to pull back again. "Now you're just being funny."

"No." I slipped my hand around the back of his neck, beneath his damp hair, trying to bring him back to me. "No, I'm very, very serious."

Jaw tensed, he stared at me.

"You asked me this morning in the car if I thought you were scary. The answer is yes. You scare me shitless. I don't know what I'm doing here. But I hate the thought of leaving you."

His gaze searched my face, but still he said nothing. He was going to turn me down. I knew it. I'd asked for too much, pushed him too far. He'd walk away from me, and who could blame him after everything?

"It's okay," I said, gathering what remained of my pride up off the floor.

"Ah, man." He sighed. "You're kinda terrifying too."

"I am?"

"Yeah, you are. And wipe that smile off your face."

"Sorry."

He angled his head and kissed me, his lips firm and so good. My eyes closed and my mouth opened. The taste of him took me over. The mint of his toothpaste and the slide of his tongue against mine. All of it was beyond perfect. He lay me back against the stairs. The new bruise at the back of my head throbbed in protest when I bumped it yet again. I flinched but didn't stop. David cupped the back of my skull, guarding against further injury.

The weight of his body held me in place, not that I was trying to escape. The edge of the steps pressed into my back and I couldn't care less. I'd have happily lain there for hours with him above me, the warm scent of his skin making me high. His hips held my legs wide open. If not for my jeans and his towel, things would get interesting fast. God, I hated cotton just then.

We didn't once break the kiss. My legs wrapped around his waist and my hands curved around his shoulders. Nothing had ever felt this good. My ache for him increased and caught fire, spreading right through me. My legs tightened around him, muscles burning. I couldn't get close enough. Talk about frustrating. His mouth moved over my jaw and down my neck, lighting me up from inside. He bit and licked, finding sensitive spots below my ear and in the crook of my neck. Places I hadn't known I had. The man had magic. He knew things I didn't. Where he'd learned his tricks didn't matter. Not right then.

"Up," he said in a rough voice. Slowly he stood, one hand beneath my ass and the other still protecting my skull.

"David." I scrambled to tighten my hold on his back.

"Hey." He drew back just enough to look into my eyes. His pupils were huge, almost swallowing the blue iris whole. "I am not going to drop you. That's never going to happen."

I took a deep breath. "Okay."

"You trust me?"

"Yes."

"Good." His hand slid down my back. "Now put your arms around my neck."

I did, and my balance immediately felt better. Both of David's hands gripped my butt and I locked my feet behind his back, holding on tight. His face showed no sign of pain or imminent back breakage. Maybe he was strong enough to carry me around after all.

"That's it." He smiled and kissed my chin. "All good?"

I nodded, not trusting myself to speak.

"Bed?"

"Yes."

He chuckled in a way that did bad things to me. "Kiss me," he said.

Without hesitation, I did so, fitting my mouth to his. Sliding my tongue between his lips and getting lost in him all over again. He groaned, his hands holding me hard against him.

Which was when the doorbell rang, making a low, mournful sound that echoed in my heart and groin. "Nooo."

"You're fucking joking." David's face screwed up and he gave the tall double doors the foulest of looks. At least I wasn't alone. I groaned and gave him a tight full-body hug. It would have been funny if it didn't hurt so much.

A hand rubbed at my back, sliding beneath the hem of my tank to stroke the skin beneath. "It's like the universe doesn't want me inside you or something, I swear," he grumbled.

"Make them go away. Please."

He chuckled, clutching me tighter.

"It hurts."

He groaned and kissed my neck. "Let me answer the door and get rid of them, then I'll take care of you, okay?"

"Your towel is on the floor."

"That's a problem. Down you hop."

I reluctantly loosened my hold and put my feet back on firm ground. Again the gonglike sound filled the house. David grabbed a pair of black jeans out of a bag and quickly pulled them on. All I caught was a flash of toned ass. Keeping my eyes mostly averted might have been the hardest thing I'd ever done.

"Hang back just in case it's press." He looked into a small screen embedded beside the door. "Ah, man."

"Trouble?"

"No. Worse. Old friends with food." He gave me a brief glance. "If it makes you feel any better, I'll be hurting too."

"But—"

"Anticipation makes it sweeter. I promise," he said, then

threw open the door. A hand tugged down the front of his T-shirt, trying to cover the obvious bulge beneath his jeans. "Tyler. Pam. Hey, good to see you."

I was going to kill him. Slowly. Strangle him with the overpriced thong. A fitting death for a rock star.

A couple about my parents' age came in, laden down with pots and bottles of wine. The man, Tyler, was tall, thin, and covered in tats. Pam looked to have Native American in her heritage. Beautiful long black hair hung down her back in a braid, thick as my wrist. They both wore wide grins and gave me curious glances. I could feel my face heat when they took in the lingerie and clothing strewn about on the floor. It probably looked like we'd been about to embark on a two-person orgy. Which was the truth, but still.

"How the hell are ya?" Tyler roared in an Australian accent, giving David a one-armed hug on account of the Crock-Pot he held in the other. "And this must be Ev. I have to read about it in the damn paper, Dave? Are you serious?" He gave my husband a stern look, one brow arched high. "Pam was pissed."

"Sorry. It was—ah, it was sudden." David kissed Pam on the cheek and took a casserole dish and a laden bag from her. She patted him on the head in a motherly fashion.

"Introduce me," she said.

"Ev, this is Pam and Tyler, old friends of mine. They've also been taking care of the house for me." He looked relaxed standing between these people. His smile was easy and his eyes were bright. I hadn't seen him looking so happy before. Jealousy reared its ugly head, sinking its teeth in.

"Hello." I put out my hand for shaking, but Tyler engulfed me in a hug.

"She's so pretty. Isn't she pretty, hon?" Tyler stepped aside and Pam came closer, a warm smile on her face.

I was being a jerk. These were nice people. I should be profoundly grateful not every female David knew rubbed her boobs on him. Damn my screaming hormones for making me surly.

"She sure is. Hello, Ev. I'm Pam." The woman's coffee-brown eyes went liquid. She seemed ready to burst into tears. In a rush, she took my hands and squeezed my fingers tight. "I'm just so happy he found a nice girl, finally."

"Oh, thank you." My face felt flammable.

David gave me a wry grin.

"Okay, enough of that," Tyler said. "Let's let these lovebirds have their privacy. We can visit another time."

David stood aside, still holding the casserole dish and bag. When he saw me watching, he winked.

"I'll have to show you the setup downstairs sometime," Tyler said. "You here for long?"

"We're not sure," he said, giving me a glance.

Pam clung to my hands, reluctant to leave. "I made chicken enchiladas and rice. Do you like Mexican? It's David's favorite." Pam's brows wrinkled. "But I didn't think to check if that was all right with you. You might be vegetarian."

"No, I'm not. And I love Mexican," I said, squeezing her fingers back, though not as hard. "Thank you so much."

"Phew." She grinned.

"Hon," called Tyler.

"I'm coming." Pam gave my fingers a parting pat. "If you need anything at all while you're here, you give me a call. Okay?"

David said nothing. It was clearly my decision if they stayed or went. My body was still abuzz with need. That, and we seemed to do better alone. I didn't want to share him because I was shallow and wanted hot sex. I wanted him all to myself.

But it was the right thing to do. And if anticipation made it sweeter, well, maybe this once the right thing to do was also the best thing to do.

"Stay," I said, stammering out the words. "Have dinner with us. You've made so much. We could never possibly finish it all."

David's gaze jumped to me, a smile of approval on his face. He looked almost boyish, trying to contain his excitement. Like I'd just told him his birthday had been brought forward. Whoever these people were, they were important to him. I felt as though I'd just passed some test.

Pam sighed. "Tyler is right, you're newlyweds."

"Stay. Please," I said.

Pam looked to Tyler.

Tyler shrugged but smiled, obviously delighted.

Pam clapped her hands with glee. "Let's eat!"

CHAPTER NINE

Warm hands pushed up my tank top as the sun rose. Next came hot kisses down my back, sending a shiver up my spine. My skin came to immediate goose-pimpled attention, despite the truly horrible time of day.

"Ev, baby, roll over." David whispered in my ear.

"What time is it?"

We'd all gone downstairs to the recording studio after dinner for a "quick look." At midnight Pam had bailed, saying Tyler could call her when they were done. No one anticipated that being anytime soon, since they'd opened a bottle of bourbon. I'd stretched out on the big couch down there while David and Tyler messed around, moving between the control room and the studio. I'd wanted to be close to David, to listen to him play guitar and sing snippets of songs. He had a beautiful voice. What he could do with a six-string in his hands blew my mind. His eyes would take on this faraway look and he was gone. It was like nothing else existed. Sometimes, I actually felt a little lonely, lying there watching him. Then the song would end and he'd shake his head, stretch his fingers, returning to earth. His gaze would find me and he'd smile. He was back.

At some stage I'd dozed off. How I'd gotten up to bed I had

no idea. David must have carried me. One thing was certain: I could smell booze.

"It's almost five in the morning," he said. "Roll over."

"Tired," I mumbled, staying right where I was.

The mattress shifted as he straddled my hips and put an arm either side of my head, bending down over me, covering me.

"Guess what?" he asked.

"What?"

Gently he pushed my hair back off my face. Then he licked my ear. I squirmed, ticklish.

"I wrote two songs," he said, his voice a little slurred, soft around the edges.

"Mm." I smiled without opening my eyes. Hopefully he'd take that as being supportive. I couldn't manage much more on fewer than four hours' sleep. I simply wasn't wired that way. "That's nice."

"No, you don't understand. I haven't written anything in over two years. This is fucking amazing." He nuzzled my neck. "And they're about you."

"Your songs?" I asked, stunned. And still dazed. "Really?"

"Yeah, I just . . ." He breathed deep and nipped my shoulder, making my eyes pop open.

"Hey!"

He leaned over so I could see his face, his dark hair hanging down. "There you are. So, I think of you and suddenly I have something to say. I haven't had anything I wanted to say in a long time. I didn't give a fuck. It was all just more of the same. But you changed things. You fixed me."

"David, I'm glad you got your mojo back, but you're incredibly talented. You were never broken. Maybe you just needed some time off."

"No." From upside down, he frowned at me. "Roll over. I

can't talk to you like this." I hesitated and he slapped my butt. The nontattooed cheek, lucky for him. "Come on, baby."

"Watch it with the biting and spanking, buddy."

"So move already," he growled.

"Okay. Okay."

He climbed off me onto the other side of the mammoth mattress and I sat, drawing my knees up to my chest. The man was shirtless, staring back at me with only a pair of jeans on. How the hell did he keep losing his shirt? The sight of his bare chest brought me to the dribble point. The jeans pushed me right over. No one wore jeans like David. And having caught a glimpse of him without them only made it worse. My imagination went into some sort of sexual berserker rage. The pictures that filled my head . . . I have no idea where they all came from. The images were surprisingly raw and detailed. I was quite certain I wasn't flexible enough to achieve some of them.

All of the air left the room. Truth was, I wanted him. All of him. The good and the bad and the bits in between. I wanted him more than I'd ever wanted anything before in my life.

But not when he'd been drinking. We'd already been there, made that mistake. I didn't know quite what was going on between us, but I didn't want to mess it up.

So, right. No sex. Bad.

I had to stop looking at him. So I took a deep breath and studied my knees. My bare knees. I'd gone to sleep wearing jeans. Now I had only panties and my tank top on. My bra had also mysteriously disappeared. "What happened to the rest of my clothes?"

"They left," he said, face serious.

"You took them?"

He shrugged. "You wouldn't have been comfortable sleeping in them."

"How on earth did you manage to get my bra off without waking me?"

He gave me a sly smile. "I didn't do anything else. I swear. I just . . . removed it for safety reasons. Underwire is dangerous."

"Riiiight."

"I didn't even look."

I narrowed my eyes on him.

"That's a lie," he admitted, rolling his shoulders. "I had to look. But we are still married, so looking is okay."

"It is, huh?" It was pretty much impossible to be mad at him when he looked at me like that. My foolish girl parts got giddy.

No. Sex.

"What are you doing up that end of the bed? That's not going to work," he said, totally unaware of my wakening hormones and distress at same.

Faster than I'd have thought possible given the amount of booze on his breath, he grabbed my feet and dragged me down the bed. My back hit the mattress and my head bounced off the pillow. David sprawled out on top of me before I could attempt any more evasive maneuvers. His weight pressed me into the mattress in the best possible way. Saying no under these conditions was a big ask.

"I don't think we should have sex now," I blurted out.

The side of his mouth kicked up. "Relax. There's no way we're fucking right now."

"No?" Damn it, I actually whined. My patheticness knew no end.

"No. When we do it the first time we'll both be stone-cold sober. Trust me on that. I'm not waking up in the morning again to find you're freaking out because you don't remember or you've changed your mind or something. I'm done being the asshole here."

"I never thought you were an asshole, David." Or at least, not exactly. A jerk maybe, and definitely a bra thief, but not an asshole.

"No?"

"No."

"Not even in Vegas when I started swearing at you and slamming doors?" His fingers slid into my hair, rubbing at my scalp. Impossible not to push into his touch like a happy kitty. He had magic hands. He even made mornings bearable. Though five o'clock was pushing it.

"That wasn't a good morning for either of us," I said.

"How about in LA with that girl hanging off me?"

"You planned that?"

He shut one eye and looked down at me. "Maybe I needed some armor against you."

I didn't know what to say. At first. "It's none of my business who you have hanging off you."

His smile was one of immense self-satisfaction. "You were jealous."

"Do we have to do this right now?" I pushed against his hard body, getting nowhere. "David?"

"Can't own up to it, can you?"

I didn't reply.

"Hey, I couldn't bring myself to touch her. Not with you there."

"You didn't?" I calmed down a lot at that statement. My heart palpitations eased. "I wondered what happened. You came back so fast."

He grunted, got closer. "Seeing you with Jimmy . . ."

"Nothing was going on. I swear."

"No, I know. I'm sorry about that. I was out of line."

My pushing hands turned to petting. Funny that. They slid over his shoulders, around his neck to fiddle with his hair. I just wanted to feel the heat of his skin and keep him near. He made for an emotional landslide, turning me from sleep deprived and cranky to adoring in under eight seconds. "It's great that you wrote some songs."

"Mm. How about when I left you with Adrian and the lawyers? Were you mad at me then?"

I huffed out a breath. "Fine. I might admit to being a bit upset about that."

He nodded slowly, his eyes never leaving mine. "When I got back and they told me what had happened, that you'd taken off with Mal, I lost it. Trashed my favorite guitar, used it to take apart Mal's kit. Still can't believe I did that. I was just so fucking angry and jealous and mad at myself."

I could feel my face scrunch up in disbelief. "You did?"

"Yeah." His eyes were stark, wide. "I did."

"Why are you telling me this now, David?"

"I don't want you hearing it from someone else." He swallowed, making the line of his throat move. "Listen, I'm not like that, Ev. It won't happen again, I promise. I'm just not used to this. You get to me. This whole situation does. I dunno, I'm fucking rambling. Do you understand?"

Later, he mightn't even remember any of this. But right now, he looked so sincere. My heart hurt for him. I looked into his bloodshot eyes and smiled. "I think so. It definitely won't happen again?"

"No. I swear." The relief in his voice was palpable. "We're okay?"

"Yes. Are you going to play the songs for me later?" I asked. "I'd love to hear them."

"They're not done yet. When they're done, I will. I want them perfect for you."

"Okay," I said. He'd written songs about me. How incredible, unless they were the uncomplimentary kind, in which case we needed to talk. "They're not about how much I annoy you sometimes, are they?"

He seesawed his hand in the air. "A little. In a good way, though."

"What?" I cried.

"Trust me."

"Do you actually state what a pain in the ass I am in these songs?"

"Not those words exactly. No." He chuckled, his good humor returned. "You don't want me to lie and say everything's always fucking unicorns and rainbows, do you?"

"Maybe. Yes. People are going to know these are about me. I have a reputation as a constant delight to protect."

He groaned. "Evelyn, look at me."

I did so.

"You are a constant fucking delight. I don't think anyone could ever doubt that."

"You're awful pretty when you lie."

"Am I, now? They're love songs, baby. Love isn't always smooth or straightforward. It can be messy and painful," he said. "Doesn't mean it isn't still the most incredible thing that can ever happen to you. Doesn't mean I'm not crazy about you."

"You are?" I asked, my voice tight with emotion.

"Of course I am."

"I'm crazy about you too. You're beautiful, inside and out, David Ferris."

He lay his forehead against mine, closing his eyes for a moment. "You're so fucking sweet. But, you know, I like that you can bite too. Like you did in Vegas with those assholes. I like that you cared, standing up for that girl. I even kind of like it when you piss me off. Not all the time, though. Shit. I'm rambling again . . ."

"It's okay," I whispered. "I like you rambling."

"So you're not angry at me for losing my temper?"

"No, David. I'm not angry at you."

Without another word, he crawled off me and lay at my side. He pulled me into his arms, arranging an arm beneath me and another over my hip. "Ev?"

"Hmm?"

"Take your shirt off. I wanna be skin to skin," he said. "Please? Nothing more, I promise."

"Okay." I sat up and pulled the tank top off over my head, then snuggled back down against him. Topless had a lot going for it. He tucked me in beneath his chin, and the feel of his warm chest was perfect, thrilling and calming all at once. Every inch of my skin seemed alive with sensation. But being like this with him soothed the savage storm within or something. It never occurred to me to worry about my belly or hips or any of that crap.

Never mind the lingering scent of booze on his skin, I just wanted to be close to him.

"I like sleeping with you," he said, his hand stroking over my back. "Didn't think I'd be able to sleep with someone else in the bed, but with you it's okay."

"You've never slept with anyone before?"

"Not in a long time. I need my space." His fingers toyed with the band on my boy-leg shorts, making me squirm.

"Huh."

"This with you is torture, but it's good torture."

Everything fell quiet for a few minutes and I thought he might have fallen asleep. But he hadn't. "Talk to me, I like hearing your voice."

"All right. I had a nice time with Pam, she's lovely."

"Yeah, she is." His fingers trailed up and down along my spine. "They're good people."

"It was really kind of them to bring us dinner." I didn't know what to say. I wasn't ready to confess I'd been thinking about what he'd said about my becoming an architect. That I'd started questioning the almighty plan. Saying I was scared I'd mess up and somehow ruin things between us didn't seem smart either. Maybe the fates would be listening and screw me over first chance they got. God, I hoped not. So instead I chose to talk trivial. "I love how you can hear the ocean here."

"Mm," he hummed his agreement. "Baby, I don't want to sign those papers on Monday."

I held perfectly still, my heart pounding. "You don't?"

"No." His hand crept up, fingers stroking below my breast, tracing the line of my rib cage. I had to remind myself to breathe. But he didn't even seem to be aware he did it, like he was just doodling on my skin the same way you would on paper. His arms tightened around me. "There's no reason it can't wait. We could spend some time together, see how things went."

Hope rushed through me, hot and thrilling. "David, are you serious about this?"

"Yeah, I am." He sighed. "I know I've been drinking. But I've been thinking it over. I don't . . . shit, I didn't even like having you out of my sight the last few hours, but you looked like you needed to sleep. I don't want us to sign those papers."

I squeezed my eyes tight and sent up a silent prayer. "Then we won't."

"You sure?"

"Yes."

He pulled me in tight against him. "Okay. Okay, that's good."

"We're going to be fine." I sighed happily. The relief made me weak. If I hadn't been lying down I'd have landed on the floor.

Suddenly he sniffed at his shoulder and underarms. "Shit, I stink of bourbon. I'm going to have a shower." He gave me a quick kiss and rolled out of the bed. "Kick me out of bed next time I try to come in smelling like this. Don't let me cuddle up to you."

I loved that he was talking about our being together like it would be an everyday thing. I loved it so much, I didn't even care how bad he smelled.

True love.

CHAPTER TEN

The gong of the doorbell echoed through the house just after ten. David slept on against my back. He didn't stir at all. With a couple more hours' sleep I felt happily half human. I crawled out from beneath his arm, trying not to disturb him. I pulled my top and jeans back on and dashed down the stairs, doing my best not to break my neck in the process. In all likelihood it would be more deliveries.

"Child bride! Let me in!" Mal hollered from the other side of the door. He followed it up with an impressive percussive performance, banging his hands against the solid wood. Definitely the drummer. "Evvie!"

No one called me Evvie. I'd stamped out that nickname years ago. However, it might be better than child bride.

I opened the door and Mal barreled in, Tyler dragging himself along after. Considering Tyler had sat up drinking and playing music with David until the wee small hours, I wasn't really surprised at his condition. The poor man clearly suffered with the hangover from hell. He looked like he'd been punched in both eyes, the bruises from lack of sleep were so bad. An energy drink was attached to his lips.

"Mal. What are you doing here?" I stopped, rubbed the

sleep from my eyes. Wake-up call, it wasn't even my house. "Sorry, that was rude. It's just a surprise to see you. Hi, Tyler."

I'd been hoping to have my husband to myself today, but apparently it wasn't to be.

Mal dropped my backpack at my feet. He was so busy looking around the place he didn't even seem to have heard my question, rude or not.

"David is still asleep," I said, and rifled through the contents of my bag. Oh, my stuff. My wonderful stuff. My purse and phone in particular were a delight to lay eyes on. Many text messages from Lauren, plus a few from my dad. I hadn't even known he could text. "Thank you for bringing this."

"Dave called me at four in the morning and told me he'd written some new stuff. Figured I'd come up and see what was going on. Thought you'd like your gear." Hands on hips, Mal stood before the wall of windows pondering the magnificence of nature. "Man, check out that view."

"Nice, huh?" said Tyler from behind his drink. "Wait till you see the studio."

Mal cupped his hands around his mouth. "Hipster King. Get down here!"

"Hi, sweetie." Pam wandered in, twirling a set of keys on her finger. "I tried to make them leave it a few more hours, but as you can see, I lost. Sorry."

"Never mind," I said. I'm not much of a hugger normally. We didn't do a lot of it in my family. My parents preferred a more hands-free method. But Pam was so nice that I hugged her back when she threw her arms around me.

We'd talked for hours the night before down in the recording studio. It had been illuminating. Married to a popular session player and producer, she'd lived the lifestyle for over twenty years. Touring, recording, groupies . . . she'd experienced the whole rock 'n' roll shebang. She and Tyler had attended a music festival and fallen in love with Monterey with its jagged coastline and sweeping ocean views.

"The lounge and another couple of beds are on their way, should be here soon. Mal, Tyler, help move the boxes. We'll stack them against the fireplace." Suddenly Pam stopped, giving me a cautious smile. "Hang on. You're the woman of the house. You give the orders here."

"Oh, against the fireplace sounds great, thanks," I said.

"You heard her, boys. Get moving."

Tyler grumbled but put down his can and lumbered toward a box, dragging his feet like the walking dead.

"Hold up." Mal smacked his lips at Pam and me. "I haven't gotten my hello kisses yet." He caught Pam up in a bear hug, lifting her off her feet and twirling her around until she laughed. Arms wide, he stepped toward me next. "Come to daddy, bed-head girl."

I put a hand out to halt him, laughing. "That's actually really disturbing, Mal."

"Leave her be," said David from the top of the stairs, yawning and rubbing the sleep from his eyes. Still wearing just the jeans. He was my kryptonite. All the strength of my convictions to be careful disappeared. My legs actually wobbled. I hated that.

Were we married or not today? He'd had a hell of a lot to drink last night. Drunk people and promises did not go well together—we'd both learned that the hard way. I could only hope he remembered our conversation and still felt the same way.

"What the fuck are you doing here?" growled my husband.

"I want to hear the new stuff, asswipe. Deal with it." Mal stared up at him, his jaw set in a hard line. "I should beat the living crap out of you. Fuck, man. That was my favorite kit!"

Body rigid, David started down the stairs. "I said I'm sorry. I meant it."

"Maybe. But it's still time to pay, you dickwad."

For a moment David didn't reply. Tension lined his face but there was a look of inevitability in his weary eyes. "All right. What?"

"It's gotta hurt. Bad."

"Worse than you turning up when Ev and me are having time alone?"

Mal actually looked a little shamefaced.

David stopped at the foot of the steps, waiting. "You wanna take this outside?"

Pam and Tyler said nothing, just watched the byplay. I got the feeling this wasn't the first time these two had faced off. Boys will be boys and all that. But I stood beside Mal, every muscle tensed. If he took one step toward David, I'd jump him. Pull his hair or something. I didn't know how, but I'd stop him.

Mal gave him a measuring look. "I'm not hitting you. I don't want to mess up my hands when we've got work to do."

"What, then?"

"You already trashed your favorite guitar. So it's going to have to be something else." Mal rubbed his hands together. "Something money can't buy."

"What?" asked David, his eyes suddenly wary.

"Hi, Evvie." Mal grinned, and slung an arm around my shoulder, pulling me in against him.

"Hey," I protested.

In the next moment his mouth covered mine, entirely un-welcome. David shouted a protest. An arm wrapped around my back and Mal dipped me, kissing me hard, bruising my lips. I grabbed at his shoulders, afraid I'd hit the floor. When he tried to put his tongue in my mouth, however, I didn't hesitate to bite him.

The idiot howled.

Take that.

Just as fast as he'd dipped me, he set me to rights. My head spun. I put a hand to the wall to stop from stumbling. I rubbed at my mouth, trying to get rid of the taste of him, while Mal gave me a wounded look.

"Damn it. That hurt." He carefully touched his tongue, searching for damage. "I'm bleeding!"

"Good."

Pam and Tyler chuckled, highly amused.

Arms wrapped around me from behind and David whispered in my ear, "Nice work."

"Did you know he was going to do that?" I asked, sounding distinctly pissy.

"Fuck no." He rubbed his face against the side of my head, mussing my bed hair. "I don't want anyone else touching you."

It was the right answer. My anger melted away. I put my hands on top of his, and the grip on me tightened.

"You want me to beat the shit out of him?" asked David. "Just say the word."

I pretended to consider it for a moment while Mal watched us with interest. We obviously looked a lot friendlier than we had in LA. But it was nobody's business. Not his friend's, not the press's, nobody's.

"No," I whispered back, my belly doing backflips. I was falling so fast for him it scared me. "I guess you'd better not."

David turned me in his arms and I fit myself against him, wrapping my arms around his waist. It felt natural and right. The scent of his skin made me high. I could have stood there breathing him in for hours. It felt like maybe we were together, but I no longer trusted my own judgment, if I ever had to begin with.

"Malcolm is joining you on your honeymoon?" Pam's voice was heavy with disbelief.

David chuckled. "No, this isn't our honeymoon. If we have a honeymoon it'll be somewhere far away from everyone. Sure as hell, he won't be there."

"If?" she asked.

I really did love Pam.

"When," he corrected, holding me tight.

"This is all real cute, but I came to make music," Mal announced.

"Then you're just going to have to fucking wait," said David. "Ev and I have plans this morning."

"We've been waiting two years to come up with something new."

"Tough shit. You can wait a few more hours." David took my hand and led me back toward the stairs. Excitement ran rife through me. He'd chosen me and it felt wonderful.

"Evvie, sorry about the mouth mauling," Mal said, sitting himself down on the nearest box.

"You're forgiven," I said with a queenly wave, feeling magnanimous as we headed up the stairs.

"You going to apologize for biting me?" Mal asked.

"Nope."

"Well, that's not very nice," he called out after us.

David sniggered.

"Okay, people, we need to move boxes." I heard Pam say.

David rushed us down the hallway, then closed and locked the bedroom door behind us.

"You put your clothes back on," he said. "Get them off."

He didn't wait for me to do it, grabbing the hem of my shirt and lifting it up over my head and raised arms.

"I didn't think answering the door mostly naked was a good idea."

"Fair enough," he murmured, pulling me in against him and backing me up against the door. "You looked worried about something downstairs. What was it?"

"It was nothing."

"Evelyn." There was something about the way he said my name. It made me a quivering mess. Also the way he cornered me, pressing his body against mine. I put my hands flat on his hard chest. Not pushing him away, just needing to touch him.

"I was wondering," I said. "After our talk this morning, when we, um, discussed signing the papers on Monday."

"What about it?" he asked, staring straight at me. I couldn't have looked away if I'd tried.

"Well, I wasn't sure if you still felt the same way. About not signing them, I mean. You'd had a lot to drink."

"I haven't changed my mind." His pelvis aligned with mine and his hands swept up my sides. "You changed yours?"

"No."

"Good." His warm hands cupped my breasts, and I lost all ability to think straight.

"You okay with this?" He gave his hands a pointed a look.

I nodded. Talking had gone with thinking, apparently.

"Then here's the plan. Because I know how you like your plans. We're going to stay in this room until we're both satisfied we're on the same page when it comes to us. Agreed?"

I nodded again. Without a doubt, the plan had my full support.

"Good." He placed the palm of one hand between my breasts, flat against my chest. "Your heart's beating real fast."

"David."

"Hmm?"

Nope, I still had no words. So instead, I covered his hand with my own, holding it against my heart. He smiled.

"This is a dramatic reenactment of the night we got married," he announced, looking at me from beneath dark brows. "Hang on. We were sitting on the bed in your motel room. You were straddling me."

"I was?"

"Yeah." He led me to the bed and sat at the edge. "Come on."

I climbed onto his lap, my legs wrapped around him. "Like this?"

"That's it." His hands gripped my waist. "You refused to go back to my suite at the Bellagio. Said I was out of touch with real life and needed to see how the little people lived."

I groaned with embarrassment. "That doesn't sound the least bit arrogant of me."

His mouth curved into a small smile. "It was fun. But also, you were right."

"Better not tell me that too often or it'll go to my head."

His chin rose. "Stop making jokes, baby. I'm being serious. I needed a dose of reality. Someone who'd actually say no to me occasionally and call bullshit on that scene. That's what we do. We push each other out of our comfort zones."

It made sense. "I think you're right . . . Is it enough?"

He held his hand to my heart again and bumped the tip of his nose against mine. "Can you feel what we're doing here? We're building something."

"Yes." I could feel it, the connection between us, the overwhelming need to be with him. Nothing else mattered. There was the physical, the way he went to my head faster than anything I'd ever experienced. How wonderful he smelled all sleep warm first thing in the morning. But I wanted more from him than just that. I wanted to hear his voice, hear him talk about everything and anything.

I felt all lit up inside. Like a potent mix of hormones was racing through me at light speed. His other hand curled around the back of my neck, bringing my mouth to his. Kissing David threw kerosene on the mix within me. He slid his tongue into my mouth to stroke against my own, before teasing over my teeth and lips. I'd never felt anything so fine. Fingers caressed my breast, doing wonderful things and making me gasp. God, the heat of his bare skin. I shuffled forward, seeking more, needing it. His hand left my breast to splay across my back, pressing me against him. He was hard. I could feel him through both layers of denim. The pressure that provided between my legs was heavenly. Amazing.

"That's it," he murmured as I rocked against him, seeking more.

Our kisses were fierce, hungry. His hot mouth moved over my jaw and chin, my neck. Where my neck met my chest, he stopped and sucked. Everything in me drew tight.

"David—"

He pulled back and looked at me, his eyes dilated. Every bit as affected as I was. Thank God I wasn't alone with the panting. A finger traced a slow path between my breasts down to the waistband of my jeans.

"You know what happened next," he said. His hand slipped beneath. "Say it, Ev." When I hesitated, he leaned forward and nipped at my neck. "Go on. Tell me."

Biting had never appealed to me before, neither in thought

nor in action. Not that there'd been much action. But the sensation of David's teeth pressing into my skin turned me inside out. I shut my eyes tight. A bit from the bite and a lot from having to say the words he wanted.

"I've only done this once before."

"You're nervous. Don't be nervous." He kissed me where he'd just bitten. "So, anyway, let's get married."

My eyelids opened and a startled laugh flew out of me. "I bet that's not what you said that night."

"I might have been a little concerned by your inexperience. And we might have had words about it." He gave me a faint smile and kissed the side of my mouth. "But everything worked out fine."

"What words? Tell me what happened."

"We decided to get married. Lie back on the bed for me."

He grasped my hips, helping me climb off him and onto the mattress. My hands slid over the smooth, cool cotton sheet. I lay on my back and he swiftly undid my jeans and disposed of them. The bed shifted beneath me as he knelt above me. I felt ready to implode, my heart hammering, but he seemed perfectly calm and in control. Nice that one of us was. Of course, he'd done this dozens of times.

Probably more, what with groupies and all that. Hundreds? Thousands, even?

I really didn't want to think about it.

His gaze rose to meet mine as he hooked fingers into my panties. In no rush at all, he dragged the last of my clothing down my legs. The urge to cover myself was overwhelming. But I fisted the sheet instead, rubbing the fabric between my fingers.

He undid his jeans. The rustles of his clothing were the only sounds. We didn't break eye contact. Not until he turned to the bedside table and retrieved a condom, discreetly tucking it underneath the pillow next to me.

David naked defied description. Beautiful didn't begin to cover it, all the hard lines of his body and the tattoos covering his skin, but he didn't give me much time to look.

He climbed back onto the bed, lying at my side, raised up on one elbow. His hand curled over my hip. Dark hair fell forward, blocking his face from view. I wanted to see him. He leaned down, kissing me gently this time on my lips, my face. His hair brushed against my skin.

"Where were we?" he asked, his voice a low rumble in my ear.

"We decided to get married."

"Mm, because I'd just had the best night of my life. First time I hadn't felt alone in so fucking long. The thought of not having you with me every other night . . . I couldn't do it." His mouth traveled up my neck. "I couldn't let you go. Especially once I knew you'd only been with one other guy."

"I thought that bothered you?"

"It bothered me, all right," he said, and kissed my chin. "You were obviously ready to give sex another try. If I was stupid enough to let you go, you might have met someone else. I couldn't stand the thought of you fucking anyone but me."

"Oh."

"Oh," he agreed. "Speaking of which, any second thoughts about what we're doing here?"

"No." Lots of nerves but no second thoughts.

The hand on my hip traced over my stomach. It circled my belly button before dipping lower, making me shiver.

"You are so damn pretty," he breathed. "Every piece of you. And when I dared you to put aside your plan and run away with me, you said yes."

"I did?"

"You did."

"Thank God for that."

Fingers stroked over the top of my sex before moving on to my thigh muscles clenched tight together. If I wanted this to go any further I was going to need to open my legs. I knew this. Of course I did. Memories of the pain from last time made me hesitate. My toes were curled and a cramp was threatening to start up in my calf muscle from all of the tensing. Ridiculous. Tommy Byrnes had been a thoughtless prick. David wasn't like that.

"We can go as slow as you want," he said, reading me just fine. "Trust me, Ev."

His warm hand smoothed over my thigh as his tongue traveled the length of my neck. It felt wonderful, but it wasn't enough.

"I need . . ." I turned my face to him, searching for his mouth. He fit his lips to mine, making everything right. Kissing David healed every ill. The knot of tension inside me turned into something sweet at the taste of him, the feel of his body against mine. One arm was trapped underneath me, but the other I made full use of, touching all of him within reach. Kneading his shoulder and feeling the hard, smooth planes of his back.

When I sucked on his tongue, he moaned in the back of his throat and my confidence soared. His hand slipped between my legs. Just the pressure of his palm had me seeing stars. I broke off the kiss, unable to breathe. He touched me gently at first, letting me get used to him. The things his fingers could do.

"Elvis couldn't be with us today," he said.

"What?" I asked, mystified.

He stopped and put two fingers into his mouth, wetting them or tasting me I didn't know. Didn't matter. What was important was him putting his hand back on me, fast.

"I didn't want to share this with anyone." The tip of his finger pushed into me, easing inside just a little. Pulling back before pressing in again. It didn't have the same thrill attached to it that came with him stroking me, but it didn't hurt. Not yet.

"So, no Elvis. I'll have to ask the questions," he said.

I frowned at him, finding it hard to focus on what he was saying. It couldn't be as important as him touching me. The pursuit of pleasure ruled my mind. Maybe he babbled during foreplay. I didn't know. If he wanted, I was more than willing to listen to him later.

His gaze lingered on my breasts until finally he dipped his head, taking one into his mouth. My back bowed, pushing his finger further inside. The way his mouth drew on me erased any discomfort. He stroked me between my legs and the pleasure grew. I tingled in the best way possible. When I did this, it was nice. When David did it, it reached the heights of spectacular, stellar. I knew he was crazy good at guitar, but this had to be where his true talent lay. Honestly.

"God, David." I arched against him when he moved to my other breast. Two fingers worked inside me, a little uncomfortable but nothing I couldn't handle. Not so long as he kept his mouth on me, lavishing my breasts with attention. His thumb rubbed around a sweet spot and my eyes rolled back into my head. So close. The strength of what was building was staggering. Mind-blowing. My body was going to be blown to dust, atoms, when this hit.

If he stopped, I'd cry. Cry, and beg. And maybe kill.

Happily, he didn't stop.

I came, groaning, every muscle drawn taut. It was almost too much. Almost. I floated, my body limp, satiated for all time. Or at least until the next time.

When I opened my eyes again, he was there waiting. He ripped open the condom with his teeth and then put it on. I'd barely caught my breath when he rose over me, moved between my legs.

"Good?" he asked, with a smile of satisfaction.

A nod was the best I could do.

He took the bulk of his weight onto his elbows, his body pressing me into the bed. I'd noticed he enjoyed using his size to the advantage of both of us. It worked. Certainly, there was nothing boring or claustrophobic about the position. I don't know why I'd thought there would be. In the back of Tommy Byrnes's parents' car I'd been cramped and uncomfortable, but this was nothing like that. Lying underneath him, feeling the heat of his skin against mine was perfect. And there could be no doubting how much he wanted this. I lay there, waiting for him to push into me.

Still waiting.

He brushed his lips against mine. "Do you, Evelyn Jennifer Thomas, agree to stay married to me, David Vincent Ferris?"

Oh, that was the Elvis he'd been talking about. The one who'd married us. Huh. I held back his hair, needing to see his eyes. I should have asked him to tie it back. It made it hard to try and gauge his seriousness.

"You really want to do this now?" I asked, a little thrown. I'd been so busy worrying about the sex I hadn't seen this coming.

"Absolutely. We're doing our vows again right now."

"Yes?" I said.

He cocked his head, narrowing his eyes at me. The look on his face was distinctly pained. "Yes? You're not sure?"

"No. I mean, yes," I repeated, more definitely. "Yes. I'm sure. I am."

"Thank fuck for that." His hand rifled under the pillow next to me, returning with the ring of stupendousness sparkling between his fingers. "Hand."

I held my hand between us and he slid the ring on. My cheeks hurt, I was smiling so hard. "Did you say yes too?"

"Yes." He took my mouth in a hard kiss. His hand slid down my side, over my stomach to cup me between my legs. Everything there was still sensitive and no doubt wet. The hunger in his kisses and the way he touched me assured me he certainly didn't mind.

He fit himself to me and pushed in. This was it. And suddenly, shit, I couldn't relax. The memory of pain from the last time I'd attempted this messed with my mind. Wet didn't matter when my muscles wouldn't give. I gasped, my thighs squeezing his hips. David was hard and thick and it hurt.

"Look at me," he said. The blue of his eyes had darkened and his jaw was set. His damp skin gleamed in the low lighting. "Hey."

"Hey." My voice sounded shaky even to my own ears.

"Kiss me." He lowered his face and I did so, pressing my tongue into his mouth, needing him. Carefully, he rocked against me, moving deeper inside me. The pad of his thumb played around my clit, counteracting the hurt. The pain eased, coming closer to being plain old discomfort with an edge of pleasure. No problem. This I could handle.

Fingers wrapped around my leg before sliding down to cup a butt cheek. He pulled me in against him and moved deeper inside me. Rocking against me until I'd taken him all. Which was a problem, because there wasn't enough damn room in me for him.

"It's okay," he groaned.

Easy for him to say.

Shit.

Bodies flush against each another, we lay there, unmoving. My arms were around his head so tight, clinging to him, that I'm not certain how he breathed. Somehow he managed to turn his face enough to kiss my neck, lick the sweat from my skin. Up, over my jaw to my mouth. The death grip I had on him eased when he kissed me.

"That's it," he said. "Try and relax for me."

I nodded jerkily, willing my body to unwind.

"You are so damn beautiful and, God, you feel fucking amazing." His big hand petted my breast, calloused fingers stroking down my side, easing me. My muscles began to relax incrementally, adjusting to his presence. The hurt faded more every time he touched me, whispering words of praise.

"This is good," I said at last, my hands resting on his biceps. "I'm okay."

"No, you're better than okay. You're amazing."

I gave him a giddy smile. He said the best things.

"You mean I can move?" he asked.

"Yes."

He started rocking against me again, moving a little more each time. Gradually gaining momentum as our bodies moved slickly together. We fit, mostly. And we were actually doing it, the deed. Talk about feeling close to someone. You couldn't get physically closer. I was so profoundly glad it was him. It meant everything.

Tommy had lasted two seconds. Long enough to break my hymen and hurt me. David touched me and kissed me and took his time. Slowly, the sweet heat, that sensation of pressure building, came again. He tended to it with care, feeding me long, wet kisses. Stroking himself into me in a way that brought only pleasure. He was incredible, watching me so closely, gauging my reactions to everything he did.

Eventually, I clung onto him and came hard. It felt like the New Year's fireworks display inside me, hot and bright and perfect. So much more with inside and over me, his skin plastered to mine. I stuttered out his name and he pressed hard against me. When he groaned, his whole body shuddered. He buried his face in my neck, his breath heating my skin.

We'd done it.

Huh.

Wow.

Things did ache a little. People were right about that. But nothing like last time.

Carefully, he moved off me, collapsing on the bed at my side.

"We did it," I whispered.

His eyes opened. His chest was still heaving, working to get more air into him. After a moment, he rolled onto his side to face me. There'd never been a better man. Of this I was certain.

"Yeah. You okay?" he asked.

"Yes." I shuffled closer, seeking out the heat of his body. He slid an arm over my waist, drawing me in. Letting me know I was wanted. Our faces were a bare hand's width apart. "It was so much better than last time. I think I like sex after all."

"You have no idea how relieved I am to hear that."

"Were you nervous?"

He chuckled, shuffling closer. "Not as nervous as you were. I'm glad you liked it."

"I loved it. You're a man of many talents."

His smile took on a certain glow.

"You're not going to get all cocky on me now, are you? All puns intended."

"I wouldn't dare. I trust you to keep me grounded, Mrs. Ferris."

"Mrs. Ferris," I said, with no small amount of wonder. "How about that?"

"Hmm." His fingers stroked my face.

I caught his bare hand, inspecting it. "You don't have a ring."

"No, I don't. We'll have to fix that."

"Yes, we will."

He smiled. "Hey, Mrs. Ferris."

"Hey, Mr. Ferris."

There wasn't enough room in me for all the feelings he inspired.

Not even close.

CHAPTER ELEVEN

We spent the afternoon back down in the recording studio with Tyler and Mal. When David wasn't playing, he pulled me onto his lap. When he was busy on guitar, I listened, in awe of his talent. He didn't sing, so I remained in the dark about the lyrics. But the music was beautiful in a raw, rock 'n' roll sort of way. Mal seemed pleased with the new material, bopping his head along in time.

Tyler beamed behind the splendid board of buttons and dials. "Play that lick again, Dave." My husband nodded and his fingers moved over the fretboard, making magic.

Pam had been busy while we'd been upstairs, starting on unpacking the collection of boxes. When she made a move to return to the job in the early evening, I went with her. Asked or not, it wasn't fair that she got lumped with the task on her own. Plus, it pleased my inner need to organize. I snuck back downstairs now and then as the hours passed, stealing kisses, before heading back up to help Pam again. David and company remained immersed in the music. They'd come up seeking food or drink but returned immediately to the studio.

"This is what it's like when they're recording. They lose track of time, get caught up in the music. The number of dinners Tyler has missed because he simply forgot!" said Pam, hands busy unpacking the latest box.

"It's their job, but it's also their first love," she continued, dusting off an Asian-style bowl. "You know that one old girl-friend that's always hanging around the fringes, drunk-dialing them at all hours and asking them to come over?"

I laughed. "How do you deal with never getting to come first?"

"You have to strike a balance. Music's a part of them that you have to accept, hon. Fighting it won't work. Have you ever been really passionate about something?"

"No," I answered in all honesty, eyeing up another stringed instrument I'd never seen the likes of. It had intricate carving encircling the sound hole. "I enjoy college. I love being a barista, it's a great job. I really like the people. But I can't sling coffee for the rest of my life." I stopped, grimaced. "God, those are my father's words. Forget I ever said that."

"You can totally sling coffee for the rest of your life, if you so choose," she said. "But sometimes it takes time to find your thing. There's no rush. I was a born and bred photographer."

"That's great."

Pam smiled, her gaze going distant. "That's how Tyler and I met. I went on tour for a couple of days with the band he was in at the time. I ended up going right around Europe with them. We got married in Venice at the end of the tour and we've been together ever since."

"That's a wonderful story."

"Yeah." Pam sighed. "It was a wonderful time."

"Did you study photography?"

"No, my father taught me. He worked for National Geo-graphic. He put a camera in my hand at age six and I refused to give it back. The next day he brought me an old secondhand one. I carried it everywhere I went. Everything I saw was through its lens. Well, you know what I mean . . . the world made sense when I looked at it that way. Better than that, it made everything beautiful, special." She pulled a couple of books out of a box, adding them to the shelves built into one wall. We'd already managed to half fill them with various books and mementoes.

"You know, David's dated a lot of women over the years. But he's different with you. I don't know . . . the way he watches you, I think it's adorable. It's the first time he's brought anyone here in six years."

"Why was the place empty so long?"

Pam's smile faded and she avoided my eyes. "He wanted it to be his place to come home to, but then things changed. The band was just hitting it big. I guess things got complicated. He could explain it to you best."

"Right," I said, intrigued.

Pam sat back on her haunches, looking around the room. "Listen to me rabbiting on. We've been at this all day. I think we deserve a break."

"I second that."

Nearly half the boxes were open. The contents we couldn't think of an immediate home for were lined up along one wall. A big plush black couch had been delivered. It fit the house and its owner perfectly. With various rugs, pictures, and instruments strewn about, the place had almost begun to look like a home. I wondered if David would approve. Easily, I could picture us spending time here when I wasn't in classes. Or maybe holidays would be spent touring. Our future was a beautiful, dazzling thing, filled with promise.

In the here and now, however, I still hadn't caught up with Lauren. A fact that caused me great guilt. Explaining this situation didn't appeal, nor did confessing my fast-growing feelings for David.

"Come on, let's go grab some food from down the road. The bar does the best ribs you've ever tasted. Tyler goes crazy for them," said Pam.

"That's a brilliant idea. I'll just let him know we're going. Do I need to change?" I had on the black jeans and tank top, a pair of Converses. The only shoes I'd been able to find among Martha's buys that didn't feature four-inch-plus heels. For once, I looked almost rock 'n' roll–associated. Pam wore jeans and a white shirt, a heavy turquoise necklace around her throat. It was casual in theory, but Pam was a striking woman.

"You're dressed fine," she said. "Don't worry. It's very relaxed."

"All right."

The sound of music still drifted up from downstairs. When I went down there, the door was shut and the red light shining. I could see Tyler with headphones on, busy at the console. I'd forgotten to charge my phone with all the recent excitement. But I didn't have David's phone number so I couldn't have texted him anyway. I didn't want to interrupt. In the end, I left a note on the kitchen bench. We wouldn't be gone long. David probably wouldn't even notice.

The bar was a traditional wooden wonderland with a big jukebox and three pool tables. Staff called out "hellos" to Pam as we walked in. No one even blinked at me, which was a relief. The place was packed. It felt good to be back out among people, just part of the crowd. Pam had phoned ahead, but the order wasn't ready yet. Apparently the kitchen was every bit as busy as the bar. We grabbed a couple of drinks and settled in to wait. It was a nice place, very relaxed. There was lots of laughter, and country music blared from the jukebox. My fingers tapped along in time.

"Let's dance," said Pam, grabbing my hand and tugging me out of my chair. She bopped and swayed as I followed her onto the crowded dance floor.

It felt good to let loose. Sugarland turned into Miranda Lambert and I raised my arms, moving to the music. A guy came up behind me and grabbed my hips, but he backed up a step when I shook my head with a smile. He grinned back at me and kept dancing, not moving away. A man spun Pam and she whooped, letting him draw her into a loose hold. They seemed to know each other.

When the guy beside me moved a little closer, I didn't object. He kept his hands to himself and it was all friendly enough. I didn't know the next song, but it had a good beat and we kept right on moving. My skin grew damp with sweat, my hair clinging to my face. Then Dierks Bentley came on. I'd had a terrible crush on him since age twelve, but it was all about his pretty blond hair and nothing to do with his music. My love for him was a shameful thing.

Dude One moved away and another took his place, slipping an arm around my waist and trying to pull me in against him. I planted my hands on his chest and pushed back, giving him the same smile and headshake that had worked on the last. He might have been only about my height, despite the huge hat, but he was built solid. He had a big barrel of a chest and he stank of cigarette smoke.

"No," I said, still trying to push him off me. "Sorry."

"Don't be sorry, darlin'," he yelled in my ear, knocking me in the forehead with the brim of his hat. "Dance with me."

"Let go."

He grinned and his hands slapped down hard on both my butt cheeks. The jerkoff started grinding himself against me.

"Hey!" I pushed against him, getting nowhere. "Get off me."

"Darlin'." The letch leaned in to kiss me, smacking me in the nose with the brim of his hat again. It hurt. Also, I hated him. If I could just wiggle my leg between his and knee the asswipe in the groin, I'd be able to even the playing field. Or leave him writhing on the floor crying for his mommy. An outcome I was fine with.

I shoved my foot between the two of his, getting closer to my objective. Closer . . .

"Let her go." David miraculously appeared out of the crowd beside us, a muscle jumping in his jaw. Oh, shit. He looked ready to kill.

"Wait your turn," the cowboy yelled back, pushing his pelvis into me. God, it was disgusting. Puking could happen. It would be no less than he deserved.

David snarled. Then he grabbed the man's hat and sent it flying off into the crowd. The man's eyes went round as plates and his hands dropped away from me.

I skipped back a step, free at last. "David—"

He looked to me, and in that moment, the cowboy swung. His fist clipped David's jaw. David's head snapped back and he stumbled. The cowboy dove at him. They landed hard, sprawled across the dance floor. Fists flew. Feet kicked. I could barely see who did what. People formed a circle around them, watching. No one doing anything to stop it. Blood spurted, spraying the floor. The pair rolled and pushed, and David came out on top. Then just as fast he fell aside. My pulse pounded behind my ears. The violence was startling. Nathan used to get into fights regularly after school. I'd hated it. The blood and the dirt, the mindless rage.

But I couldn't just stand by, caught in a cold stupor. I wouldn't.

A strong hand grabbed my arm, halting my forward momentum.

"No," said Mal.

Then he and another couple of guys stepped in. Relief poured through me. Mal and Tyler wrestled David off the cowboy. Another pair restrained the bloody-faced fool who bellowed on and on about his hat. Goddamn idiot.

They hustled David out of the bar, dragging him backward. Through the front doors and down the steps they went while his feet kicked out, trying to get back into it. And he kept right on fighting until they threw him up against Mal's big black Jeep.

"Knock it off!" Mal yelled in his face. "It's over."

David slumped against the vehicle. Blood seeped from one nostril. His dark hair hung in his face. Even in the shadows he looked swollen, misshapen. Not half as bad as the other guy, but still.

"Are you okay?" I stepped closer to check the extent of his wounds.

"I'm fine," he said, shoulders still heaving as he stared at the ground. "Let's go."

Moving in slow motion, he turned and opened the passenger-side door, climbing in. With a mumbled good-bye, Pam and Tyler headed for their own car. A couple of people stood on the steps leading into the bar, watching. One guy held a baseball bat as if he expected further trouble.

"Ev. Get in the car." Mal opened the door to the backseat and ushered me in. "Come on. Cops could be coming. Or worse."

Worse was the press. I knew that now. They'd be all over this in no time.

I got in the car.

CHAPTER TWELVE

Mal disappeared as soon as we got home. David stomped up the stairs to our bedroom. Was it really ours? I didn't have a clue. But I followed. He turned and faced me as soon as I entered the room. His expression was fierce, dark brows down and his mouth a hard line. "You call that giving us a chance?"

Whoa. I licked my lips, giving myself a moment. "I call it going out to pick up some food. The kitchen was running late so we got a beer. We liked the music so we decided to get up to dance for a couple of songs. Nothing more."

"He was all over you."

"I was about to knee him in the balls."

"You left without a fucking word!" he shouted.

"Don't yell at me," I said, searching for a calm I didn't have in me just then. "I left you a note in the kitchen."

He shoved his hands through his hair, visibly fighting for calm. "I didn't see it. Why didn't you come talk to me?"

"The red light was on. You were recording and I didn't want to disturb you. We weren't supposed to be gone for long."

Bruised face furious, he walked a few steps away, then turned and marched back. No calmer from what I could tell despite the pacing. But at least he seemed to be trying. His temper was the third person in the room, and it took up all the damn space. "I was worried. You didn't even have your phone on you, I found it on the fucking table. Pam's phone kept ringing out."

"I'm sorry you were worried." I held out my hands, out of excuses for both of us. "I forgot to charge my phone. It happens sometimes. I'll try to be more careful in future. But David, nothing was going on. I'm allowed to leave the house."

"Fuck. I know that. I just . . ."

"You're doing your thing, and that's great."

"This was some sort of fucking punishment?" He forced the hard words out through gritted teeth. "Is that it?"

"No. Of course not." I sighed. Quietly.

"So you weren't trying to get picked up?"

"I'm going to pretend you didn't say that." Slapping him upside the head wasn't out of the question. I kept my clenched fists safely at my sides, resisting the urge.

"Why'd you let him touch you?"

"I didn't. I asked him to move back and he refused. That's when you arrived." I rubbed at my mouth with my fingers, fast running out of patience. "We're just going around in circles here. Maybe we should talk about this later when you've had a chance to calm down."

Hands shaking, I turned toward the door.

"You're leaving? Fucking perfect." He threw himself back onto the bed. Laughter wholly lacking in humor came out of his mouth. "So much for us sticking together."

"What? No. I don't want to fight with you, David. I'm going downstairs before we start saying things we don't mean. That's all."

"Go," he said, his voice harsh. "I fucking knew you would."

"God," I growled, turning back to face him. The desire to scream and shout at him, to try to make some sense of this, boiled over inside of me. "Are you even listening to me? Are you hearing me at all? I'm not leaving you. Where is this coming from?"

He didn't answer, just stared at me, eyes accusing. It made no sense.

I almost tripped getting back to him, my feet fumbling. Landing on my face would be perfect. It was exactly where this was heading. I didn't even understand what we were fighting about anymore, if I ever had.

"Who are you comparing me to here?" I asked, every bit as angry as him now. "Because I am not her."

He kept right on glaring at me.

"Well?"

His lips stayed shut and my frustration and fury skyrocketed. I wanted to grab him and shake him apart. Make him admit to something, anything. Make him tell me what the hell was really going on.

I crawled onto the bed, getting in his face. "David, talk to me!"

Nothing.

Fine.

I pushed back with trembling legs and tried to clamber off the mattress. He grabbed at my arms, trying to hold on. And like fuck he was. I pushed back hard. All brawling limbs, we tumbled off the bed and rolled onto the floor. His back hit the hardwood floor. Immediately, he rolled us again, putting me on the bottom. My blood pounded behind my ears. I kicked and pushed and wrestled him with all the hurt he'd inspired. Before he could get his bearings I rolled us again, regaining the uppermost position. He couldn't stop me, the bastard. Escape was imminent.

But it didn't happen.

David grabbed my face in both hands and mashed his lips to mine, kissing the stuffing out of me. I opened my mouth and his tongue slipped in. The kiss was rough and wet. Breathing was an issue. We both had anger management problems and neither of us entirely refrained from biting. With his bruised mouth, he definitely had the most to lose. It wasn't long before the metallic taste of blood hit my tongue.

He pulled back with a hiss, fresh blood on his swollen top lip. "Fuck."

He grabbed my hands. I didn't make it easy on him, struggling for all I was worth. But he was stronger. He pinned them to the floor above my head with relative ease. The press of his hard-on between my legs felt exquisite, insane. And the more I bucked against him, the better it got. Adrenaline had already been pouring through me, amping me up. The need to have him sat just below the surface, prickling my skin, making me hyperaware of everything.

So this was angry sex. I couldn't bring myself to hurt him, not really. But there were other ways to assert myself in this situation. He came back to my mouth and I nipped him again in warning.

A mad smile appeared on his face. It probably matched my own. We were both panting, fighting for air. Both as stubborn as hell. Without another word, he released my wrists and drew back. Quickly, he grabbed my waist and turned me over, pulling me up onto my elbows and knees. Arranging me how he wanted me. Rough hands tore at the button and zip on my jeans. He yanked down my denim and my crazily overpriced thong, body poised over mine.

His hands smoothed over my ass. Teeth dragged over the sensitive skin of one cheek, just above the tattoo of his name. A hand slipped beneath to cup my sex. The press of his fingers against me had me seeing stars. When they started stroking me, working me higher, I couldn't hold back my moan. He nipped me on the rump, a sharp sting of sensation. Then he pressed kisses up my spine. Stubble from his chin scratched my shoulder.

The lack of words, the absolute silence apart from our heavy breathing made it more. It made it different.

One finger slid inside me. Not nearly enough, damn it. He slid in a second finger, stretching me a little. Once, twice he slowly pumped them into me. I pushed back against his hand, needing more. Next came the sound of the bedside drawer sliding open as he searched for a condom. His fingers slid out of me and the loss was excruciating. I heard his zipper being lowered, the rustle of clothes, and the crinkle of a condom wrapper. Then his cock pressed against me, rubbing over my opening. He pushed in slow and steady, filling me up until there was nothing left that wasn't me and him. For a moment he stopped, letting me adjust.

But not for long.

Hands gripped my hips and he began to move. Each thrust was a little faster and harder than the last. Labored breathing and the slap of skin against skin swallowed the silence. The scent of sex hung heavy in the air. I pushed back against him, meeting him thrust for thrust, spurring him on. It was nothing like the sweet and slow of this morning. Neither of us was tender. My jeans shackled me at the knees, making me slip forward a little with each thrust. His fingers dug into my hips, holding me in place. He stroked over something inside me and I gave a startled gasp. Again and again he concentrated on that spot, making me mindless. I felt superheated. Like fire burned through me. Sweat dripped off my skin. I hung my head, closed my eyes, and held onto the floor with all my might. My voice called out without my consent, saying his name. Damn it. My body wasn't my own. I came hard, awash with sensation. My back bowed, every muscle drawn tight.

David pounded into me, hands slipping over my slick skin. He came a moment later in silence, holding himself deep. His face rested against my back, arms wrapped around my body, which was lucky. I'd lost all traction. Slowly I slid to the floor. If he hadn't been holding me I'd have face-planted. I doubt I'd have even cared.

In silence, he picked me up and carried me into the bathroom, sat me on the sink. Without fuss he dealt with the condom, started running a bath, holding a hand beneath the faucet to check the temperature. He undressed me like I was a child, pulling off my sneakers and socks, my jeans and panties. He tugged off my shirt and unclipped my bra. His own clothes were ripped off with far less care. I felt curiously naked with him now, the way he was treating me. Being so careful with me despite my biting and big-boned unwieldiness. He treated me like I was precious. Like I was a china doll. One he could apparently have rough sex with upon occasion. Once more, he checked the water, then he picked me up again and into the bath we went.

I huddled against him, my skin cooling off fast. My teeth chattered. He held me tighter, resting his cheek against the top of my head.

"I'm sorry if I was too rough," he said finally. "I didn't mean it, accusing you of shit like that. I just . . . fuck. I'm sorry."

"Rough wasn't a problem, but the trust issue . . . we're going to need to talk about it sometime." I rested my head against his shoulder, stared up into his troubled eyes.

His chin jerked as he gave me a tight nod.

"But right now, I'd like to talk about Vegas."

The arms around me tensed. "What about Vegas?"

I stared back at him, still trying to think everything through. Not wanting to get this wrong, whatever this was.

Marriage, that's what it was.

Shit.

"We've covered a lot of ground in the last twenty-four hours," I said.

"Yeah, I guess we have."

I held up my hand, my sparkly ring. The size of the diamond didn't matter. That David had put it on me was what made it important. "We talked about lots of things. We slept together, and we made promises to each other, important ones."

"You regretting any of it?"

My hand slid around the back of his neck. "No. Absolutely not. But if you woke up tomorrow, and you'd somehow forgotten all of this. If it was all gone for you, like it had never happened, I would be furious at you."

His forehead wrinkled.

"I'd hate you for forgetting all this when it's meant everything to me."

He licked his lips and turned off the tap with a foot. Without the water gushing out, the room quieted instantly.

"Yeah," he said. "I was angry."

"I'm not going to let you down like that again."

Beneath me his chest rose and fell heavily. "Okay."

"I know it takes time to learn to trust someone. But in the meantime, I need you to at least give me the benefit of the doubt."

"I know." Wary blue eyes watched me.

I sat up and reached for the washcloth on the edge of the bath. "Let me clean you up a little."

A dark lump sat on his jaw. Blood lingered beneath his nose and near his mouth. He was a mess. A big red mark was on his ribs.

"You should see a doctor," I said.

"Nothing's broken."

Carefully, I wiped the blood from the side of his mouth and beneath his nose. Seeing him in pain was horrible. Knowing I was the cause made my stomach twist and turn. "Tell me if I press too hard."

"You're fine."

"I'm sorry you got hurt. In the bar tonight, and in Vegas. I didn't mean for that to happen."

His eyes softened and his hands slid over me. "I want you to come back to LA with me. I want you with me. I know school will start back eventually and we're gonna have to work something out. But whatever happens, I don't want us apart."

"We're not going to be."

"Promise?"

"Promise."

CHAPTER THIRTEEN

Morning light woke me. I rolled over and stretched, working out the kinks. David lay on his back beside me, fast asleep. He had an arm flung over his face, covering his eyes. With him there, everything was right with my world. But also, everything was on show. He'd kicked off the sheet sometime during the night. So the morning wood thing was true. There you go. Lauren had been right on that count.

Waking up beside him with my wedding ring back on my finger had me grinning like a loon. Of course waking up beside a bare-naked David would have made just about anybody smile. Between my legs felt a little sore from last night's efforts, but nothing too bad. Nothing sufficient to distract me from the view that was my husband.

I shuffled down the bed a bit, checking him out at my leisure for once. He didn't have much of a belly button. It was basically a small indent followed by a fine trail of dark hair leading down across his flat stomach directly to it. And it was hard, thick, and long.

"It" being his penis, of course.

Gah. No, that didn't sound right.

His cock. Yeah, much better.

We'd sat in the warm bath for a while last night at his insistence, soaking. We'd just talked. It had been lovely. There'd been no mention of the woman who'd obviously cheated on him and/or left him at sometime in his past. But I'd felt her presence lurking. Time would kick her out the back door, I was sure of it.

He smelled faintly of soap, a little musky, perhaps. Warm wasn't something I'd ever registered as having a smell before, but that's what David smelled of. Warmth, like he was liquid sunshine or something. Heat and comfort and home.

I quickly checked his face. His eyes were still closed beneath the length of his arm, thank goodness. His chest rose and fell in a steady rhythm. I really didn't need him catching me sniffing at his crotch, no matter how poetic my thoughts. That would be embarrassment on a scale I'd prefer not to experience.

The skin looked super smooth despite the veins, and the head stood out distinctly. He was uncircumcised. Curiosity got the better of me, or maybe it already had. With all of his front half at my disposal, look where I'd wound up. I gently laid the palm of my hand atop him. The skin was soft and warm. Carefully, I wrapped my fingers around him. His cock twitched and I jerked back, startled.

David burst out laughing, loud and long.

Bastard.

Embarrassment was a dam that had burst wide open inside of me. Heat flashed up my neck.

"I'm sorry," he said, reaching for me with his hand. "But you should have seen your face."

"It's not funny."

"Baby, you wouldn't believe how fucking funny it was." He wrapped his fingers around my wrist, dragging me up and onto him. "Come here. Aw, the tips of your ears are all pink."

"No, they're not," I mumbled, lying across his chest.

He stroked my back, still sniggering. "Don't let this scar you for life, though, hey? I like you touching me."

I huffed noncommittally.

"You know, if you play with my dick, things will always happen. I guarantee it."

"I know that." The crook of his neck was handy for burying my hot face in, so I took full advantage. "I just got a surprise."

"You sure did." He squeezed me tight, then slid a hand down to cup my bottom. "How are you feeling?"

"Okay."

"Yeah?"

"A little sore," I admitted. "A lot happy. Though that was before you callously mocked me."

"Poor baby. Let me see," he said, rolling me over onto the mattress until he was on top.

"What?"

He sat up between my legs with a hand holding my knees open. With a practiced eye he checked me over. "You don't look too swollen. Probably just a bit sore inside, yeah?"

"Probably." I tried to pull my legs up, to close them. Because I heartily doubted having him look at me there in that way helped the color of my ear tips.

"I have to be more careful with you."

"I'm fine. Not that breakable, honestly."

"Mm."

"Takes more than a round of rough sex on the hardwood floor to worry me."

"That so? Stay still for me," he said, shuffling back to lie down at the end of the mattress.

This situated him distinctly between my legs, face-to-face with my girl bits, guaranteeing I wouldn't be going anywhere.

I'd heard good things about this, things that made my embarrassment levels redundant. Plus, I was curious.

He brushed his lips against my sex, the warmth of his breath making me shiver. My stomach muscles spasmed in anticipation.

His gaze met mine over the top of my torso. "Okay?"

I gave him a jerky nod, impatient.

"Put the other pillow behind your head too," he instructed. "I want you to be able to watch."

My husband had the best ideas. I did as asked, settling in to watch though my legs were aquiver. He kissed the inside of my thighs, first one, then the other. Everything in me focused on the sensations emanating from there. My world was a small perfect place. Nothing existed outside our bed.

His eyes closed but mine stayed open. He kissed his way over the lips of my sex and then traced the divide with the tip of his tongue. That worked. Warmth suffused me inside. Hands wrapped around the underneath of my thighs, fingers rubbing small circles into my skin. His lips never left my sex. It was exactly as if he was kissing me there. Mouth open wide and tongue stroking, making me writhe. The grip on my thighs tightened, holding me to him. Even the brush of his hair and the prickle of his stubble against me were thrilling things. I don't know when I stopped watching. My eyes shut of their own accord as the pleasure took over. It was amazing. I didn't want it to end. But the pressure inside me built until I couldn't contain it any longer. I came with a shout, my body drawn tight from top to toe. Every part of me tingled. He didn't pull back until I lay perfectly still, concentrating on just breathing.

"Am I forgiven for laughing at you?" he asked, crawling up the bed to plant a kiss on my shoulder.

"Sure."

"How about the rough sex on the hardwood floor? Am I forgiven for that too?"

"Mmhmm."

The mattress shifted beneath me as he hovered above. His wet mouth lingered over the curve of my breast, the line of my collarbone.

"I really liked that," I said, my voice low and lazy. Gradually I opened my eyes.

"Fuck drunk suits you, Evelyn." A hand smoothed over my hip, and he smiled down at me. "I'll eat you out whenever you like. You only have to ask."

I smiled back at him. And the smile may have twitched a little at the edges. Talking about this kind of thing was still new to me.

"Tell me you liked me licking your gorgeous pussy."

"I said I liked it."

"You're embarrassed." David's brows drew together. There was mischief in his eyes. "You can talk rough sex on hardwood floors but not cunnilingus, hey? Say 'pussy.'"

I rolled my eyes. "Pussy."

"Again. Not as in 'cat.'"

"I'm not saying it as in 'cat.' Pussy. Pussy, pussy, pussy. Pussy not as in 'cat.' Happy?" I laughed, moving a hand to slide down his chest, heading for his groin. "Can I do something for you now?"

He stopped my hand, brought it to his mouth and kissed it. "I'm going to wait till tonight when we can make love again, if you're feeling okay."

"We're making love tonight, Mr. Smooth?"

"Sure." He smirked, climbing off the bed. "We'll make love again and then we'll fuck again. I think we should put some serious time into exploring the differences. It'll be fun."

"Okay," I quickly agreed. I wasn't stupid.

"That's my girl." He held a hand out for me, eyes intent. "You are so damn pretty. You know, I'm never going to be able to wait until tonight."

"No?"

"Nope. Look at you lying all naked on my bed. I've never seen anything I've liked more." He shook his head, mouth rueful as his eyes traveled over my body. My husband was incredibly good for my ego. But he made me feel humble at the same time, grateful. "I was a fucking idiot to suggest waiting," he said, taking a step back and crooking his finger at me. "And you know how I hate being away from you. Come help me in the shower? It'll give you some good hands-on experience."

I crawled off the bed after him. "That so?"

"Oh, yeah. And you know how seriously I take you and your education."

"You suck," said Lauren, her voice echoing down the line. Pam had warned me some parts of the coast could be iffy with cell coverage.

"I'm not saying I don't still love you," she said. "But, you know . . ."

"I know. I'm sorry," I said, settling into the corner of the lounge. The menfolk were busy downstairs making music. Pam had gone running errands in town. I had calls to make. Boxes to unpack. Dreams of blissful wedlock to work up to insane, impossible proportions inside my head.

"Never mind. Update me," she demanded.

"Well, we're still married. In a good way this time."

Lauren screamed in my ear. It took her a good couple of

minutes to calm down. "Oh, my God, I was hoping something would work out. He's so fucking hot."

"Yes, indeed he is. But he's more than that. He's wonderful."

"Keep going."

"I mean, really wonderful."

She huffed out a laugh. "You already used 'wonderful.' Try a new word, Cinderella. Give my inner fangirl something to work with here."

"Don't crush on my husband. That's not cool."

"You're six years too late with that warning. I was crushing on David Ferris long before you put a ring on him in Vegas."

"Actually, he doesn't have a ring."

"No? You should fix that."

"Hmm." I stared out the window at the ocean. Out in the distance a bird drifted in lazy circles high up in the sky. "We're at his place in Monterey. It's beautiful here."

"You left LA?"

"LA was not so great. What with the groupies and lawyers and business managers and everything, it was pretty shitty."

"Details, babe. Gimme."

I drew my knees up to my chest and fidgeted with the seam of my jeans, feeling conflicted. Discussing our personal details behind David's back didn't sit well with me. Not even with Lauren. Things had changed. Most noticeably, our marriage had changed. But there were still some things I could share. "The people there were like something from another planet. I did not fit in. Though you would have liked seeing the parties they threw. All the glamorous people packed into this mansion. It was impressive."

"You're making me insanely jealous. Who was there?"

I gave her a couple of names as she oohed and aahed.

"But I don't miss LA. Things are so good now, out here, Lauren. We've put the annulment on hold. We're going to see how things go."

"That's so romantic. Tell me you've jumped that fine-looking man's bones, please. Don't make me cry."

"Lauren." I sighed.

"Yes or no?"

I hesitated, and she got screamy at me, rather predictably. "YES OR NO?"

"Yes. All right? Yes."

This time, her shriek definitely did my eardrums permanent damage. All I could hear was ringing. When it ended, someone was mumbling in the background. Someone male.

"Who was that?" I asked.

"No one. Just a friend."

"A friend-friend or a friend?"

"Just a friend. Hang on, changing rooms. And we were talking about you, partner of David Ferris, world-famous lead guitarist for Stage Dive."

"A friend that I know?" I asked, curiosity now fully aroused.

"You are aware of the picture of your ass making the rounds, aren't you?"

Cue the squirming. "Uh, yeah. I am."

"Bummer. Haha! But seriously, you look good. Mine wouldn't have looked half as nice. Bet you're glad you walked to campus last semester instead of driving all the time like lazy ol' me. That sure was some night you had in Vegas, missy."

"Let's talk about your friend instead of my butt. Or Vegas."

"Or we could talk about your sex life. Because we've been talking about mine for a couple of years now, but we haven't much been able to talk about yours, girlfriend," she said in a glee-filled singsong voice.

"Evvie! Want a soda?" Mal shouted as he sailed past on his way to the kitchen, having emerged from below.

"Yes, please."

"Who is that?" asked Lauren.

"The drummer. They're doing some work in the studio downstairs."

Lauren gasped. "The whole band is there?"

"No, just Mal and another friend of David's."

"Malcolm is there? He's really hot, but a total man slut," she supplied helpfully. "You should see the number of women he gets photographed with."

"Here you go, child bride." Mal passed me an icy-cold bottle, the top already removed.

"Thanks, Mal," I said.

He winked and wandered off again.

"None of my business," I told Lauren.

She clucked her tongue. "You haven't been on the Internet to find anything out about them, have you? You're flying totally blind in this situation."

"It feels wrong checking up on them behind their backs."

"Naïveté is only sexy up to a point, chica."

"It's not naïveté, chica. It's respecting their personal lives."

"Which you're now a part of."

"Privacy matters. Why should they trust me if I'm stalking them online?"

"You and your excuses." Lauren sighed. "So you don't know that the band started touring when David was only sixteen? They got a gig supporting a band through Asia and have pretty much stayed on the road or in the recording studio from then onward. Hell of a life, huh?"

"Yeah. He said he's ready to slow down."

"I'm not surprised. Rumors about the band breaking up are

everywhere. Do try and stop that from happening if you can, please. And get your husbo to get his shit into gear and hurry up and write a new album. I'm counting on you."

"No problem," I said, not sharing that David was writing me songs. That was private. For now, at least. The list of things I didn't feel I could share with Lauren was growing exponentially.

"I wanted you to crush that boy's heart so we could have another album like *San Pedro*. But I can tell you're going to be difficult about that."

"Your powers of perception are uncanny."

She chuckled. "You know there's a song about the Monterey house on that album?"

"There is?"

"Oh, yeah. That's the famous 'House of Sand.' Epic love song. David's high school sweetheart cheated on him while he was touring in Europe at age twenty-one. He'd bought that house for them to live in."

"Stop, Lauren. This is . . . shit, this is personal." My heart and mind raced. "This house?"

"Yeah. They'd been together for years. David was gutted. Then some bitch he slept with sold her story to the tabloids. Also, his mother left when he was twelve. Expect there to be some issues all around where women are concerned."

"No, Lauren, stop. I'm serious," I said, nearly strangling the phone. "He'll tell me things like that when he's ready. This doesn't feel right."

"It's just being prepared. I don't see what the problem is."

"Lauren."

"Okay. No more. You did need to know those tidbits, though, seriously. Events like that leave a permanent scar."

She had a point. The information did explain his accusations regarding my leaving and the strength of his reactions to that. Two of the most important women in his world had deserted him.. Though finding out this way about his history still felt wrong. When he trusted me enough to tell me, he would. But I hadn't had enough of a chance yet to earn that sort of trust from him. Personal information didn't just roll off the tongue at the first meeting. How horrible to have it all set out there on the Internet just waiting for people to look it up and mull it over for their entertainment. So much for privacy. Little wonder he'd been worried about my talking to the press.

I took a sip of the soda, then rested the cold bottle against my cheek. "I really want this to work."

"I know you do. I can hear it in your voice when you talk about him—you're in love with him."

My spine snapped to attention. "What? No. That's crazy talk. Not yet, at least. It's only been a couple of days. Do I sound in love? Really?"

"Time is irrelevant where the heart is concerned."

"Maybe," I said, concerned.

"Listen, Jimmy has been dating Liv Andrews. If you meet her, I definitely want an autograph. Loved her last film."

"Jimmy is not the greatest. That could get uncomfortable."

She huffed. "Fine. But you are in love."

"Hush now."

"What? I think it's nice."

Mutterings from Lauren's mysterious friend interrupted my rising fear.

"I've got to go," she said. "Keep in touch, okay? Call me."

"I will."

"Bye."

I said "bye," but she was already gone.

CHAPTER FOURTEEN

"You're frowning." David walked up behind me slowly. His head cocked to the side, making his dark hair fall over the side of his face. He tucked it behind an ear and moved closer. "Why are you doing that, hmm?"

I'd been putting together dinner. I'd found pizza crusts in the freezer, so I took them out to defrost and started cutting up toppings and grating cheese, while worrying about what Lauren had told me, of course. The house didn't seem so welcoming anymore. Armed with the knowledge that it had been bought with another woman in mind, my feelings toward the place had shifted. I was back to feeling like an interloper. Horrible but true. Insecurities sucked.

"Gimme." From behind me he snagged my wrist and brought my hand to his mouth, sucking a smear of tomato paste from my finger. "Mm. Yum."

My stomach squeezed tight in response. God, his mouth on me this morning. His plans for us tonight. It all felt like a dream, a crazy beautiful dream that I didn't want to wake from. Nor did I need to. All would be well. We'd work things out. We were married again now, committed. He snaked an arm around me and pressed himself against my back, leaving no room between us for doubt.

"How are things going downstairs?" I asked.

"Real good. We've got four songs shaping up nicely. Sorry we ran a bit over," he said, planting a kiss on the side of my neck, chasing the last of the bad thoughts far away. "But now it's our time."

"Good."

"Making pizza?"

"Yeah."

"Can I help?" he asked, still nuzzling the side of my neck. The stubble on his jaw scratched lightly at my skin, feeling strange and wonderful all at once. He made me shivery. Right up until he stopped. "You're putting broccoli on it?"

"I like vegetables on pizza."

"Zucchini too. Huh." His voice sounded slightly incredulous and he perched his chin on my shoulder. "How about that?"

"And bacon, sausage, mushrooms, peppers, tomatoes, and three different types of cheeses." I pointed the chopping knife at my excellent collection of ingredients. "Wait till you taste them. They're going to be the best pizzas ever."

"Course they are. Here, I'll put them together." He turned me to face him, rearing back when my chopping knife accidentally waved at him. His hands fastened onto my hips and he lifted me up onto the kitchen island. "Keep me company."

"Sure thing."

From the fridge he took a beer for him and a soda for me, since I was still avoiding alcohol. Tyler's and Mal's voices drifted through from the lounge room.

"We working again tomorrow?" Tyler called out.

"Sorry, man. We gotta head back to LA," said David, washing his hands at the sink. He had great hands, long, strong fingers. "Give me a couple of days to sort shit out down there then we'll be up again."

Tyler stuck his head around the corner, giving me a wave. "Sounds good. The new stuff is coming together well. Bringing Ben and Jimmy back with you next time?"

David's brow wrinkled, his eyes not so happy. "Yeah, I'll see what they're up to."

"Cool. Pammy's outside, so I gotta run. It's date night."

"Have fun." I waved back.

Tyler grinned. "Always do."

Chuckling quietly, Mal ambled in. "Date night, seriously . . . what the fuck is that about? Old people are the weirdest. Dude, you can't put broccoli on pizza."

"Yeah, you can." David kept busy, scattering peppers around the little trees of broccoli.

"No," said Mal. "That's just not right."

"Shut up. Ev wants broccoli on the pizza, then that's what she gets."

Ice-cold lovely sweet soda slid down my throat, feeling all sorts of good. "Don't stress, Mal. Vegetables are your friend."

"You lie, child bride." His mouth stretched wide in disgust and he retrieved a bottle of juice from the fridge. "Never mind. I'll just pick it off."

"No, you're going out," said David. "Me and Ev are having date night too."

"What? You're fucking kidding me. Where am I supposed to go?"

David just shrugged and scattered pepperoni atop his steadily growing creations.

"Oh, come on. Evvie, you'll stand up for me, won't you?" Mal gave me the most pitiful face in all of existence. It was sadness blended with misery with a touch of forlorn on top. He even bent over and laid his head on my knee. "If I stay in town they'll know we're here."

"You've got your car," said David.

"We're in the middle of nowhere," Mal complained. "Don't let him throw me out into the wild. I'll get eaten by fucking bears or something."

"I'm not sure they have bears around here," I said.

"Cut the shit, Mal," said David. "And get your head off my wife's leg."

With a growl, Mal straightened. "Your wife is my friend. She's not going to let you do this to me!"

"That so?" David looked at me and his face fell. "Fuck, baby. No. You cannot be falling for this shit. It's only one night."

I winced. "Maybe we could go up to our room. Or he could just stay downstairs or something."

David shoved his hands through his hair. The bruise on his poor cheek, I needed to kiss it better. His forehead did that James Dean wrinkling thing as he studied his friend. "Jesus. Stop making that pathetic face at her. Have some dignity."

He cuffed the back of Mal's head, making his long blond hair fly in his face. Skipping back, Mal retreated beyond the line of fire. "All right, I'll stay downstairs. I'll even eat your shitty broccoli pizza."

"David." I grabbed his T-shirt and tugged him toward me. And he came, abandoning his pursuit of Mal.

"This is supposed to be our time," he said.

"I know. It will be."

"Yes!" hissed Mal, getting gone while he was ahead. "I'll be downstairs. Yell when dinner's ready."

"He's got a girl in every city," said David, scowling after him. "No way was he sleeping in his car. You've been played."

"Maybe. But I would have worried about him." I tucked his dark hair behind his ears, then trailed my hands down to the back of his neck, drawing him closer. The studs in his ears were all small, silver. A skull, an X, and a super-tiny winking diamond. He pressed his earlobe between his thumb and a finger, blocking my view.

"Something wrong?" he asked.

"I was just looking at your earrings. Do they mean anything special?"

"Nope." He gave me a quick peck on the cheek. "Why were you frowning earlier?" He picked up a handful of mushrooms and started adding them to the pizzas. "You're doing it again now."

Crap. I kicked my heels, turned all the excuses over inside my head. I had no idea how he'd react to my knowing the things Lauren had told me. What would he think if I asked about them? Starting a fight did not appeal. But lying didn't either. Withholding was lying, deep down where it mattered. I knew that.

"I talked to my friend Lauren today."

"Mmhmm."

I pushed my hands down between my legs and squeezed them tight, delaying. "She's a really big fan."

"Yeah, you said." He gave me a smile. "Am I allowed to meet her, or is she off-limits like your dad?"

"You can meet my dad if you want."

"I want. We'll take a trip to Miami sometime soon and I'll introduce you to mine, okay?"

"I'd like that." I took a deep breath, let it out. "David, Lauren told me some things. And I don't want to keep secrets from you. But I don't know how happy you're going to be about these things that she told me."

He turned his head, narrowed his eyes. "Things?"

"About you."

"Ah. I see." He picked up two handfuls of grated cheese and sprinkled them across the pizzas. "So you hadn't looked me up on Wikipedia or some shit?"

"No," I said, horrified at the thought.

He grunted. "It's no big deal. What do you want to know, Ev?"

I didn't know what to say. So I picked up my soda and downed about half of it in one go. Bad idea—it didn't help. Instead, it gave me a mild case of brain freeze, stinging above the bridge of my nose.

"Go on. Ask me whatever you want," he said. He wasn't happy. The angry monobrow from drawing his eyebrows together clued me in to that. I didn't think I'd ever met anyone with such an expressive face as David. Or maybe he just fascinated me full stop.

"All right. What's your favorite color?"

He scoffed. "That's not one of the things your friend told you about."

"You said I could ask whatever I wanted, and I want to know what your favorite color is."

"Black. And I know it's not really a color. I did miss a lot of school, but I was there that day." His tongue played behind his cheek. "What's yours?"

"Blue." I watched as he opened the gargantuan oven door. The pizza trays clattered against the racks. "What's your favorite song?"

"We're covering all the basics, huh?"

"We are married. I thought it would be nice. We sort of skipped a lot of the getting-to-know-you stuff."

"All right." The side of his mouth kicked up and he gave me a look that said he was onto my game of avoidance. The faint smile set the world to rights.

"I got a lot of favorite music," he said. " 'Four Sticks' by Led Zeppelin, that's up there. Yours is 'Need You Now' by Lady Antebellum, as sung by an Elvis impersonator. Sadly."

"Come on, I was under the influence. That's not fair."

"But it is true."

"Maybe." I still wished I could remember it. "Favorite book?"

"I like graphic novels. Stuff like *Hellblazer*, *Preacher*."

I took another mouthful of soda, trying to think up a genius question. Only all the blatantly obvious ones appeared inside my head. I sucked at dating. It was probably just as well that we'd skipped that part.

"Wait," he said. "What's yours?"

"*Jane Eyre*. How about your favorite movie?"

"*Evil Dead 2*. Yours?"

"*Walk the Line*."

"The one about the Man in Black? Nice. Okay." He clapped his hands together and rubbed them. "My turn. Tell me something terrible. Something you did that you've never confessed to another living soul."

"Ooh, good one." Scary, but good. Why couldn't I have thought of a question like that?

He grinned around the top of his bottle of beer, well pleased with himself.

"Let me think . . ."

"There's a time limit."

I screwed up my face at him. "There is not a time limit."

"There is," he said. "Because you can't try and think up something half-assed to tell me. You've gotta give me the first worst thing that comes into your head that you don't want anyone else ever knowing about. This is about honesty."

"Fine." I sniffed. "I kissed a girl named Amanda Harper when I was fifteen."

His chin rose. "You did?"

"Yes."

He sidled closer, eyes curious. "Did you like it?"

"No. Not really. I mean, it was okay." I gripped the edge of the bench, hunching forward. "She was the school lesbian and I wanted to see if I was one too."

"There was just the one lesbian at your school?"

"Oh, I suspected quite a few people, but only she was open about it. She gave herself the title."

"Good for her." His hands settled on my knees and pushed them apart, making room for him. "Why did you think you were a lesbian?"

"To be accurate, I was hoping I was bi," I said. "More options. Because, honestly, the guys at school were . . ."

"They were what?" He gripped my butt and pulled me across the bench, bringing me closer. No way did I resist.

"They didn't really interest me, I guess."

"But kissing your lesbian friend Amanda didn't do it for you either?" he asked.

"No."

He clicked his tongue. "Damn. That's a sad story. You're cheating, by the way."

"What? How?"

"You were meant to tell me something terrible." His smile left a mile way behind. "Telling me you tongue-kissed a girl isn't even remotely terrible."

"I never said there was tongue."

"Was there?"

"A little. The briefest of touches, maybe. But then I got weirded out and stopped it."

He took another swig of beer. "Your ear tips are doing the pink thing again."

"I bet they are." I laughed and ducked my head. "I didn't cheat. I never told anyone about that kiss. I was going to take it to my grave. You should feel honored by my trust in you."

"Yeah, but telling me something I'm likely to find a huge turn-on is cheating. You were meant to tell me something terrible. The rules were clear. Go again and give me something bad this time."

"It's a huge turn-on, huh?"

"Next time I hit the shower I'm definitely using that story."

I bit my tongue and looked away. Memories from this morning of David soaping up my hands and then putting them on him assailed my mind. The thought of him masturbating to my brief bout of teen sexual experimentation . . . "honored" wasn't quite the right word. But I couldn't say I wasn't pleased by the notion. "Well, remember to make me older. Fifteen is a bit skeevy."

"You only kissed her."

"You'll leave it at that in your head? You'll respect accuracy and legalities, and not take it any further between Amanda and me?"

"Fine, I'll make you older. And wildly fucking curious." He pulled me closer, using the hands-on-my-butt method again, and I put my arms around him.

"Now, go again, and do it right this time."

"Yeah, yeah."

He gave the side of my neck a lingering kiss. "You weren't lying about Amanda, were you?"

"No."

"Good. I like that story. You should tell it to me often. Now go again."

I ummed and ahhed, procrastinating my little heart out. David rested his forehead against mine with a heavy sigh. "Just fucking tell me something."

"I can't think of anything."

"Bullshit."

"I can't," I whined. Not anything I wanted to share, anyway.

"Tell me."

I groaned and bumped my forehead against his ever so lightly. "David, come on, you're the last person I want to make myself look bad in front of."

He drew back, inspecting me down the length of his nose. "You're worried about what I think of you?"

"Of course I am."

"You're honest and good, baby. Nothing you might have done is gonna be that bad."

"But honest isn't always good," I said, trying to explain. "I've opened my mouth plenty of times when I shouldn't have. Given people my opinion when I should have kept quiet. I react first and think later. Look at what happened in Vegas, between us. I didn't ask any of the right questions that morning. I'm always going to regret that."

"Vegas was a pretty extreme situation." His hand rubbed my back, reassuring me. "You got nothing to worry about."

"You asked me how I felt when you had that groupie hanging off you in LA. I dealt with it then. But the fact is, if that happened now and some woman tried to come on to you, I'd probably get stabby. I'm not always going to react well to the rock star hoopla that surrounds you. What happens then?"

He made a noise in his throat. "I dunno, I finally have to realize that you're human? That you fuck up sometimes just like everybody else?"

I didn't answer.

"We'll both screw up, Ev. That's a given. We just gotta be patient with each other." He put a finger beneath my chin, raising it up so he could kiss me. "Now tell me about what Lauren told you today."

I stared at him, caught and cornered. The contents of my stomach curdled for real. I had to tell him. There would be no getting around it. How he reacted was beyond my control. "She told me that your first girlfriend cheated on you."

He blinked. "Yeah. That happened. We'd been together a long time, but . . . I was always either recording or on the road," he said. "We'd been touring Europe for eight, nine months when it happened. Touring fucks up a lot of couples. The groupies and the whole lifestyle can really screw with you. Being left behind all the time is probably no picnic either."

I bet it wasn't. "When do you tour next?"

He shook his head. "There're none booked. Won't be until we get this new record down, and that hasn't been going so well until now."

"Okay. How does this work? I mean, do you believe what happens on the road, stays on the road?" I asked. The boundaries of our relationship had never really been established. Exactly what did our marriage mean? He wanted us to stick together, but I had school to consider, my job, my life. Maybe the good wives just dumped it all and went with the band. Or maybe wives weren't even invited. I didn't have a clue.

"You asking me if I'm planning on cheating on you?"

"I'm asking how we fit into each other's lives."

"Right." He pinched his lips between his thumb and finger. "Well, I think not fucking around on each other would be a good start. Let's just make that a rule for us, okay? As for the band and stuff, I guess we take it as it comes."

"Agreed."

Without a word he stepped back from me, crossing over to the staircase. "Mal?"

"What?"

"Close the door down there and lock it," David yelled. "Don't you come up here under any circumstances. Not till I tell you it's okay. Understood?"

There was a pause, then Mal yelled back, "What if there's a fire?"

"Burn."

"Fuck you." The door downstairs slammed shut.

"Lock it!"

Mal's reply was muffled, but the pissy tone carried just fine. These two were more akin to actual brothers than David and his biological sibling. Jimmy was a jerk and just one of the very good reasons we should never return to LA. Sadly, hiding out in Monterey wasn't a viable long-term solution.

School, band, family, friends, blah blah blah.

David reached for the back of his T-shirt and dragged it off over his head. "Rule number two, if I take my shirt off you have to take off yours. The shirt-off rule now applies to these sorts of conversations. I know we need to talk about stuff. But there's no reason we can't make it easier."

"This'll make it easier?" Highly doubtful. All that smooth, hot skin just waiting for my touch, and my fingers itching to do so. Keeping my tongue inside my mouth while his flat stomach and six-pack were revealed tested my moral fortitude no end. All that beautiful inked skin on display, driving any attempt at a coherent thought straight out of my mind. Good God, the man had some power over me. But wait up, we were married. Morally, I was obliged to ogle my husband. It would be unnatural and wrong to do otherwise.

"Get it off," he said, tipping his chin at my offending items of clothing.

The staircase sat calm and quiet. No signs of life.

"He ain't coming up here. I promise." David's hands gripped the bottom of my T-shirt and carefully pulled it off over my head, rescuing my ponytail when it got caught.

When he reached for my bra, I pressed my forearms to my chest, holding it in place. "Why don't I keep the bra, just in case . . ."

"It's against the rules. You really wanna go breaking rules already? That's not like you."

"David."

"Evelyn." The bra's band relaxed as he undid the clasp. "I need to see your bare breasts, baby. You have no idea how much I fucking love them. Let it go."

"Why do you get to make all the rules?"

"I only made that one. Oh, no—two. We have the no-cheating rule as well." He tugged at my bra and I eased my grip, letting him take it. No way was I moving my arms, though.

"Go on, you make some rules," he said, running his fingers over my arms, making every little hair stand on end.

"Are you just trying to distract me from the conversation with the no-clothes thing?"

"Absolutely not. Now make a rule."

My hands stayed tucked beneath my chin, arms covering all the essentials, just in case. "No lies. Not about anything."

"Done."

I nodded, relieved. We could do this marriage thing. I knew it in my head, my heart. We were going to be okay. "I trust you."

He stopped, stared. "Thanks. That's big."

I waited, but he said no more.

"Do you trust me?" I asked, filling the silence. The minute the words left my lips I wanted them back. If I had to demand his faith and affection, it didn't mean a damn thing. Worse than that, it did damage. I could feel it, a sudden jagged wound between us. One that I'd made. Of all the stupid times for me to get impatient! I wished it was the middle of winter so I could go stick my head in a snowdrift.

His gaze wandered away, over my shoulder. There was my answer right there. Honesty had already shown me who was boss. How about that? I suddenly felt cold, and though it had nothing to do with losing my shirt, I really wanted to put it back on.

"I'm getting there, Ev. Just . . . give me time." Frustration lined his face. He pressed his lips together till they whitened. Then he looked me in the eye. Whatever he saw didn't help matters. "Shit."

"It's okay, really," I said, willing it to be true.

"You lying to me?"

"No. No. We'll be fine."

In lieu of an answer, he kissed me.

You couldn't beat a well-timed distraction. Heat rushed back into me. His regret and my hurt both took a backseat when I placed my hands on top of his. With fingers meshed, I moved our combined hands to cover my breasts. We both groaned. The heat of his palms felt sublime. The chill of disappointment couldn't combat it. Our chemistry won out every time. I had to believe more feelings would follow. My shoulders pushed forward, pressing me harder into his hands as if gravity had shifted toward him. But also, I wanted his mouth. Hell, I wanted to crawl around inside him and read his mind. I wanted everything. Each dark corner of him. Every stray thought.

Our lips met again and he groaned, hands kneading my breasts. His tongue slipped into my mouth, and that fast and easy I ached for him. Needed him. My insides squeezed tight and my legs wrapped around him, holding on. Let him try and get away now. I'd fight tooth and nail to keep him. Thumbs stroked over my nipples, teasing me. My hands slid up his arms, curved over his shoulders, holding steady. Hot kisses trailed over my face, my jaw, the side of my neck. Half naked or not, I don't think I'd have cared if my high school marching band paraded through the room. They could bring baton twirlers and all. Only this mattered.

No wonder people took sex so seriously, or not seriously enough at all. Sex addled your wits and stole your body. It was like being lost and found all at once. Frankly, it was a little frightening.

"We will be fine," he said, teasing my earlobe with his teeth. Rubbing his hardness against me. God bless whoever had thought to put a seam right there in jeans. Lights danced before my eyes. Did it feel as good for him? I wanted it to be the best and I wanted him to be right about us being fine.

"Sweet baby, just need time," he said, his warm breath skating over my skin.

"Because of her," I said, needing it to be out there in the open. No secrets.

"Yeah," he said, his voice faint. "Because of her."

The truth bit.

"Evelyn, there's just you and me in this. I swear." He returned to my mouth and kissed me as if I was delicate, giving me only the briefest taste of him. An awareness of warmth, the firmness of his lips.

"Wait," I said, making my legs give up their grip on him.

He blinked dark, hazy eyes at me.

"Move back. I want to hop down."

"You do?" His lovely mouth turned down at the edges. The front of his jeans was in a state of obvious distress. I'd done that to him. A victory lap around the kitchen counter would probably be taking it too far, but still, it felt good. That knowledge sat well within me. She didn't do that to him these days. I did.

I shuffled off the edge of the counter and he grabbed my hips, easing my descent to the floor. Just as well. My legs were liquid. He stared down at me, his brow wrinkled.

"There's something I want to do," I explained, fingers shaking from nerves and excitement. First I wrangled with the button of his jeans before moving on to the straining zipper.

His hands gripped my wrists. "Hey. Wait."

I hesitated, wanting to hear what he had to say. Surely he wouldn't try to tell me he didn't want this. Every guy liked this, or so I'd been told. He looked perplexed, as if I was a piece that refused to fit the puzzle. I honestly didn't know if he meant to stop me or hurry me onward.

"Is there a problem?" I asked, when he didn't speak.

Slowly he removed his hands from my wrists, setting me free. He held them up like I'd pointed a gun at him. "This is what you want?"

"Yes. David, why is this a big deal? Don't you want my mouth on you?"

A soft smile curved his lips. "You have no idea how much I want that. But this is another first for you, isn't it?"

I nodded, fingers fiddling with the waistband of his jeans, but going no further.

"That's why it's a big deal. I want all your firsts to be perfect. Even this. And I'm pretty fucking worked up here just at the thought of you sucking me."

"Oh."

"I've been thinking about you all damn day. I kept fucking things up, couldn't concentrate for shit. Amazing we got anything done." He pushed his fingers through his long hair, pulling it back from his face. His hands stayed on top of his head, stretching out his lean, muscular torso. The bruise on his ribs from the bar fight last night was a dark gray smudge, marring perfection. I leaned in, kissing it. His gaze never left me because my bare breasts were still most definitely a part of me. My eyes, my mouth, my breasts: he couldn't seem to decide what fascinated him the most.

Carefully, I lowered the zipper over his erection. No underwear. At least I didn't jump this time when his hard-on made its sudden appearance. With two hands I pushed down his jeans, freeing his cock. It stood tall and proud. Just like this morning, I pressed my hand against the underside, feeling the heat of the silken skin. Funny, the idea of the male appendage had never particularly moved me before. But now I felt moved, as my clenched thighs attested.

Moved and more than a little proprietary.

"You're mine," I whispered, my thumb rubbing around the edge of the head, feeling out the ridge and the dip in the middle. Learning him.

"Yeah."

The sweet spot sat below that little tuck. Over the years, I'd read enough magazines and listened to enough of Lauren's tales of sexcapades to know as much. She did love her details. I made a mental note to thank her, take her out to dinner somewhere nice.

I moved my hand around so that I gripped him and massaged the area with the pad of my thumb, waiting to see what happened. Much easier to see what was going on without the soap bubbles in the way. It didn't take long. Especially not once I tightened my hold on him a little and pumped slightly. His stomach muscles flinched and danced, the same as they had this morning in the shower. My fingers moved the soft, smooth skin, massaging the hard flesh beneath, pumping once, twice. A bead of milky fluid leaked from the small slit in the top.

"That means you're fucking killing me," my husband supplied helpfully, his voice guttural. "Just in case you were wondering."

I grinned.

He swore.

"I swear it gets bigger every time I see it."

His smile was lopsided. "You inspire me."

I stroked him again and his chest heaved. "Evelyn. Please."

Time to put him out of his misery. I knelt, the floor uncomfortably hard beneath me. If you were going to kneel in front of someone, some minor discomfort seemed an obvious part of the territory. It all added to the atmosphere, the experience. The musky scent of him was stronger later in the day. I took his cock in hand and nuzzled his hip bone, breathing him in deep.

He still watched. I checked to be sure. Hell, his eyes were huge and dark and focused solely on me. Beside him, his hands gripped the counter as if he expected a tremor to hit at any time, knuckles white.

When I took him into my mouth, he moaned. My inexperience and his size prevented me from taking him too deep. He didn't seem to mind. The salty taste of his skin and the bitterness of that liquid, the warm scent of him and the feel of his hardness merged into one unique experience. Pleasing David was a brilliant thing.

He groaned and his hips jerked, pushing him farther into my mouth. My throat tightened in surprise and I gagged slightly. His hand flew to my hair, patting, soothing. "Fuck, baby. Sorry."

I resumed my ministrations, rubbing my tongue against him, drawing on him. Figuring out the best way to fit him into my mouth. Doing everything I could to make him tremble and cuss. What a glorious thing giving head was. His hand tightened in my hair, pulling some, and I loved it. All of it. Anything with the ability to reduce my world-weary husband to a stammering mess while giving him such pleasure deserved a serious time investment. His hips shifted restlessly and his cock jerked against my tongue, filling my mouth with that salty, bitter taste faster than I could swallow.

So it was messy. Never mind. My jaw hurt a little. Big deal. And I could have done with a glass of water. But his reaction . . .

David dropped to his knees and gathered me up in his arms, all the better to squish me against him. My ribs creaked, and his dug into me over and over as he fought for breath. I pressed my face against his shoulder and waited till he'd calmed down some to seek my acclaim.

"Was it okay?" I asked, reasonably certain of a favorable response. Which is always the best time to ask, in my opinion.

He grunted.

That was it? I sat there feeling rather proud of myself and he gave me a grunt. No, I needed more validation than that. I both wanted and deserved it. "Are you sure?"

He sat back on his heels and stared at me. Then he looked around, searching for something. The T-shirt he'd left forgotten on the floor. And then he wiped beneath my chin, cleaning me up. Nice.

"There's some on your shoulder too." I pointed at the unfortunate spillage I'd obviously transferred onto him. He wiped it up as well.

"Sex can get messy," he said.

"Yes, it can."

"You on the pill?"

"You can't get pregnant that way, David."

The side of his mouth twitched. "Cute. Are you on the pill?"

"No, but I have the birth control thing implanted in my arm because my periods are erratic so—" His mouth slammed over the top of mine, kissing me hard and deep. Shutting me up really effectively. A hand cradled the back of my head as he took me down to the floor, stretching out on top of me. The cold, hard flooring beneath my bare back barely registered. It didn't matter so long as he kissed me. My hands clung to his shoulders, fingers sliding over slick skin.

"I care about your periods, Ev. Honest to fuck I do." He kissed my cheeks, my forehead.

"Thanks."

"But right now I wanna know how you feel about us going bare?"

"You mean more than losing the shirts, I take it?"

"I mean fucking without a condom." His hands framed my face as he stared down at me, eyes that intense shade of blue. "I'm clean. I've been tested. I don't do drugs and I always used protection, ever since I broke up with her. But it's your call."

The mention of "her" cooled me a bit, but not much or for long. Impossible with David sprawled all over me and the scent of sex so heavy in the air. Plus pizza. But mostly David. He made my mouth water, forget about the food. Thinking wasn't easy given the situation. I'd said I trusted him and I did.

"Baby, just think about it," he said. "There's no rush. Okay?"

"No, I think we should."

"Are you certain?"

I nodded.

He exhaled a deep breath and kissed me again.

"I fucking love your mouth." With the top of a finger he traced my lips, still swollen from what we'd been up to.

"You did like it? It was okay?"

"It was perfect. Nothing you do could be wrong. I almost lose it just knowing it's you. You could accidentally bite me and I'd probably think it was fucking hot." He gave a rough laugh, then hastened to add, "But don't do that."

"No." I arched my neck and pressed my lips to his, kissing him sweet and slow. Showing him what he meant to me. We were still rolling around on the kitchen floor when the buzzer on the oven screeched, startling us apart. Then the phone rang.

"Shit."

"I'll get the pizza," I said, wriggling out from beneath him.

"I'll grab the phone. No one should even have this damn number."

An oven mitt sat waiting on the counter and I slipped it over my hand. Hot air and the rich scent of melted cheese wafted out when I opened the oven door. My stomach rumbled. So maybe I was hungry after all. The pizzas were a touch burnt around the edges. Nothing too bad, though. The tips of my broccoli were toasted golden brown. We could concentrate on the middle. I transferred the pizzas onto the cool stovetop and turned off the heat.

David talked quietly in the background. He stood in front of the bank of windows, legs spread wide and shoulders set like he was bracing himself for an attack. Relaxed, happy people didn't strike that pose. Outside the sun was setting. The violet and gray of evening cast shadows on his skin.

"Yeah, yeah, Adrian. I know," he said.

Trepidation tightened me one muscle at a time. God, please, not now. We were doing so well. Couldn't they stay away just a little longer?

"What time's the flight?" he asked.

"Fuck," came next.

"No, we'll be there. Relax. Yeah, bye."

He turned to face me, phone dangling from his hand. "There's some stuff going on in LA that Mal and I need to be there for. Adrian's sending a chopper for us. We all need to get ready."

My smile strained my face, I could feel it. "Okay."

"Sorry we're getting cut short here. We'll come back soon, yeah?"

"Absolutely. It's fine."

That was a lie, because we were going back to LA.

CHAPTER FIFTEEN

David's knee jiggled all the way back to LA. When I put my hand on his leg, he took to toying with my wedding ring instead, turning it around on my finger. Seemed we were both fidgeters, given the right circumstances.

I'd never been in a helicopter before. The view was spectacular, but it was loud and uncomfortable—I could see why people preferred planes. A chain of lights, from streetlights to houses to the blazing high-rise towers in LA, lit the way. Everything about the situation had changed, but I was the same bundle of nervous energy in need of sleep that I had been leaving Portland not so many days back. Mal had thrown himself into the corner, closed his eyes, and gone to sleep. Nothing fazed him. Of course, there was no reason this should. He was part of the band, welded into David's life.

We landed a little before four in the morning, having left sometime after midnight. Bodyguard Sam stood waiting at the helicopter pad with a business face on.

"Mrs. Ferris. Gentlemen." He ushered us into a big black SUV waiting nearby.

"Straight back home, thanks, Sam," David said. His home, not mine. LA had no happy memories for me.

Then we were ensconced in luxury, locked away behind

dark windows. I sank back against the soft seating, closing my eyes. It kind of amazed me I could be so damn tired and worried all at once.

Back at the mansion, Martha waited, leaning against the front door, wrapped up in some expensive-looking red shawl. His PA gave me all the bad feelings. But I was determined to fit in this time. David and I were together. Screw her, she'd have to adapt. Her dark hair shone, flowing over her shoulders, not a strand out of place. No doubt I looked like someone who'd been awake for over twenty hours.

Sam opened the SUV door and offered me a hand. I could feel Martha's eyes zero in on the way David slung an arm around me, keeping me close. Her face hardened to stone. The look she gave me was poison. Whatever her issues, I was too damn tired to deal with them.

"Martie," Mal crowed, running up the steps to slip an arm around her waist. "Help me find breakfast, O gorgeous one."

"You know where the kitchen is, Mal."

The curt dismissal didn't stop Mal from sweeping her off with him. Martha's first few steps faltered, but then she strutted once more, ever on show. Mal had cleared the way. I could have kissed his feet.

David said nothing as we made our way up the stairs to the second floor, our footsteps echoing in the quiet. When I went to turn toward the white room, the one I'd stayed in last time, he steered me right instead. At a set of double doors we stopped and he fished a key out of his pocket. I gave him a curious look.

"So I have trust issues." He unlocked the door.

Inside, the room was simple, lacking the antiques and flashy décor of the rest of the house. A huge bed made up with dark gray linens. A comfortable sofa to match. Lots of guitars. An open wardrobe, full of clothes. Mostly, there was empty space.

Room for him to breathe, I think. This room felt different from the rest of the house, less showy, calmer.

"It's okay, you can look around." His hand slid down to the base of my spine, resting just above the curve of my ass. "It's our room now," he said.

God, I hoped he didn't want to live here permanently. I mean, I did have school to go back to eventually. We hadn't yet gotten around to discussing where we'd live. But the thought of Martha, Jimmy, and Adrian being around all the time sent me into a panic. Shit. I couldn't afford to think like that. Negativity would swallow me whole. What was important was being with David. Sticking together and making it work.

How horrible, being forced to live in the lap of luxury with my wonderful husband. Poor me. I needed a good slap and a cup of coffee. Or twelve hours' sleep. Either would work wonders.

He drew the curtains, blocking out the dawn's early light. "You look beat. Come lie down with me?"

"That's, umm . . . yeah, good idea. I'll just use the bathroom."

"Okay." David started stripping, dumping his leather jacket on the lounge chair, pulling off his T-shirt. The normal hoorah of my hormones was sorely missing in action. Drowned out by the nerves. I fled into the bathroom, needing a minute to pull myself together. I closed the door and switched on the lights. The room blazed to life, blinding me. Spots flickered before my eyes. I stabbed switches at random until finally it dimmed to a soft glow. Much better.

A giant white tub that looked like a bowl, gray stone walls, and clear glass partitions. Simply put, it was opulent. One day I'd probably become inured to all this, but I hoped not. Taking it for granted would be terrible.

A shower would soothe me. Sitting in the giant soup bowl

would have been nice. But I didn't totally trust myself to get into it without falling on my butt and breaking something. Not in the overtired, wound-up state I was in.

No, a long, hot shower would be perfect.

I stepped out of my flats and undid the zip on my jeans, getting undressed in record time. The shower could have fit me and ten close friends. Steaming hot water poured out from overhead and I stepped into it, grateful. It pounded down in the best way possible, making my muscles more pliable in minutes, relaxing me. I loved this shower. This shower and I needed to spend quality time together, often. Apart from David, and occasionally Mal, this shower was the best damn thing in the whole house.

David's arms slipped around me from behind, drawing me back against him. I hadn't even heard him come in.

"Hi." I leaned back against him, lifting my arms to thread them around his neck. "I think I'm in love with your shower."

"You're cheating on me with the shower? Damn, Evelyn. That's harsh." He picked up a bar of soap and started washing me, rubbing it over my belly, my breasts, softly between my legs. Once the soapsuds had reached critical mass, he helped the warm water chase the bubbles away. His big hands slid over my skin, bringing it to life and returning my hormones to me tenfold. One strong arm wrapped around my waist. The fingers of his other hand, however, lingered atop my sex, stroking lightly.

"I know you're worried about being here. But you don't need to be. Everything'll be fine." His lips brushed against my ear as the magic he was working on me grew. I could feel myself turning liquid hot like the water. My thighs trembled. I widened my stance, giving him more room.

"I—I know."

"It's you and me against the world."

I couldn't have kept the smile off my face if I tried.

"My lovely wife. Let's go this way." With careful steps he turned us, so that his back was to the water. I braced my hands on the glass wall. The tip of his finger teased between the lips of my sex, coaxing me open. God, he was good at this. "Your pussy is the sweetest fucking thing I've ever seen."

My insides fluttered with delight. "Whatever I did to deserve you, I need to do it much more often."

He chuckled, his mouth fixing to the side of my neck and sucking, making me groan. I swear the room spun. Or that might have been my blood rushing about. For certain, my hips bucked of their own volition. But he didn't let me go far. The hard length of him pressed against my butt and my lower back. My sex clenched unhappily, aching for more.

"David."

"Hmm?"

I tried to turn, but his splayed hand against my middle stopped me. "Let me."

"Let you what? What do you want, baby? Tell me and it's yours."

"I just want you."

"You've got me. I'm all over you. Feel." He pressed himself hard against me, holding me tight.

"But—"

"Now, let's see what happens when I strum your clit."

Feather-light strokes worked me higher and higher, all centered around that one magic spot. No great surprise he could play me to perfection. He'd already proved it several times over. And the way he rubbed himself against me drove me out of my mind. My body knew exactly what it wanted and it wasn't his damn clever fingers. I wanted to feel that connection with him again.

"Wait," I said, my voice high and needy.

"What, baby?"

"I want you inside of me."

He eased a finger into me, massaging an area behind my clit that made me see stars. Still, it was wrong, wildly insufficient. Not a bit funny. It would be a tragedy to have to kill him, but he was really pushing it.

"David. Please."

"No good?"

"I want you."

"And I want you. I'm crazy about you."

"But—"

"How about I get you off with a showerhead? Wouldn't that be nice?"

I actually stamped my foot, despite my wobbling knees. "No."

At which point my husband cracked up laughing and I hated him.

"I thought you were in love with the shower." He tittered away, highly amused with himself and all but begging for death.

Tears of frustration actually welled in my eyes. "No."

"You sure? I'm pretty certain I remember hearing you say it."

"David, for fuck's sake, I'm in love with you."

He stilled completely. Even the finger embedded within me stopped moving. There was only the sound of the water falling. You'd think those words would have lost their power. Weren't we already married? Hadn't we decided to stay married? Invoking the *l*-word should have lost its mystical punch, given our crazy situation. But it hadn't.

Everything changed.

Strong hands turned me and lifted me, leaving my feet dangling precariously in the air. It took me a second to figure out where I was and what had happened. I wrapped my legs and arms around him for safekeeping, holding on tight. His face . . . I'd never seen such a fierce, determined expression. It went well beyond lust and closer toward being what I needed from him.

His hands gripped my rear, taking my weight and holding me to him. Slowly, steadily, he lowered me onto him. There was none of the pain this time to rob me of pleasure. Nothing to distract me from the feel of him filling me. It was such a strange, wonderful sensation, having him inside of me. I squirmed, trying to get more comfortable. Instantly, his fingers dug into my butt cheeks.

"Fuck," he groaned.

"What?"

"Just . . . just stay still for a minute."

I scrunched up my nose, concentrated on catching my breath. This sex stuff was tricky. Also, I wanted to memorize every moment of this perfect experience. I didn't want to forget a thing.

He balanced my back against the shower wall and pushed more fully into me. A startled sound burst out of my mouth. Most closely it resembled "argh."

"Easy," he murmured. "You okay?"

I felt really full. Stretched. And it might have felt good. It was hard to tell. I needed him to do something so I could figure out where this new sensation was taking me. "Are you going to move now?"

"If you're okay now."

"I'm okay."

He did move then, watching my face all the while. The slide

out lit me up inside in a lovely rush, but the thrust back in got my immediate attention. Whoa. Good or bad, I still couldn't quite tell. I needed more. He gave it to me, his pelvis shifting against me, keeping the warmth and tension building. My blood felt fever hot, surging through me, burning beneath my skin. I fit my mouth to his, wanting more. Wanting it all. The wet of his mouth and the skill of his tongue. All of him. No one kissed like David. As though kissing me beat breathing, eating, sleeping, or anything else he might have otherwise planned to do with the rest of his life.

My back bumped hard against the glass wall and our teeth clinked together. He broke the kiss with a wary look, but he never stopped moving. Harder, faster, he rocked into me. It just got better and better. We needed to do this all the time. Constantly. Nothing else mattered when it was like this between us. Every worry disappeared.

It was so damn good. He was all that I needed.

Then he hit upon some spot inside of me and my whole body seized up, nerves tingling and running riot. My muscles squeezed him tight, and he thrust in deep several times in rapid succession. The world blacked out, or I closed my eyes. The pressure inside me shattered into a million amazing pieces. It went on and on. My mind left the stratosphere, I was sure of it. Everything sparkled. If it felt anything like that for David, I don't know how he stayed on his feet. But he did. He stood strong and whole with me clutched tight against him like he'd never let me go.

Eventually, about a decade later, he did set me down. His hands hovered by my waist, just in case. Once my limbs proved trustworthy, he turned me to face the water. With a gentle hand, he cleaned me between my legs. I didn't get what he was up to at first and tried to back away. Touching anything there right then didn't seem a smart idea.

"It's okay," he said, drawing me back into the spray of water. "Trust me."

I stood still, flinching out of instinct. He took nothing but care. The whole world seemed weird, everything too close and yet buffered at the same time. Weariness and the best orgasm of my life had undone me.

Next he reached over and turned off the water, stepped out, and grabbed two towels. One he tied around his waist, the other he patted me dry with.

"That was good, right?" I asked as he dried off my hair, tending to me. My body still shook and quivered. It seemed like a good sign. My world had been torn apart and remade into some sparkly surreal love-fest thing. If he said it was only okay, I might hit him.

"That was fucking incredible," he corrected, throwing my towel onto the bathroom counter.

Even my grin quivered. I saw it in the mirror. "Yes. It was."

"Us together, always is."

Hand in hand we walked back into the bedroom. Being naked in front of him didn't feel weird for once. There was no hesitation. He discarded his towel and we climbed onto his giant-size bed, gravitating naturally toward the middle and each other. We both lay on our sides, face-to-face. I could slip into a coma, I was so worn out. Such a pity to have to close my eyes when he lay right there in front of me. My husband.

"You swore at me," he said, eyes amused.

"Did I?"

His hand sat atop of my thigh, his thumb sliding back and

forth over my hip bone. "Gonna pretend you don't remember what you said? Really?"

"No. I remember." Though I hadn't meant to say it, neither the cuss word nor the declaration of love. But I had. Big-girl-panties time. "I said I was in love with you."

"Mm. People say stuff during sex. It happens."

He was giving me an out, but I couldn't take it. I wouldn't take it, no matter how tempting. I wasn't about to diminish the moment like that.

"I am in love with you," I said, feeling awkward. The same as when I'd said I trusted him, he was going to leave me hanging here too. I knew it.

His gaze lingered on my face, patient and kind. It hurt. Something inside me felt brittle and he brought it straight to the fore. Love made spelunking look sensible. BASE jumping and wrestling bears couldn't be far behind. But it was much, much too late to worry. The words were already out there. If love was for fools, then so be it. At least I'd be an honest one.

He stroked my face with the back of his fingers. "That was a beautiful thing to say."

"David, it's okay—"

"You're so fucking important to me," he said, stopping me short. "I want you to know that."

"Thank you." Ouch, not exactly the words I wanted to hear after I admitted I loved him.

Rising up on one elbow, he brought his lips to mine, kissing me silly. Stroking my tongue with his and taking me over. It left no room for worry.

"I need you again," he whispered, kneeling between my legs.

This time we did make love. There was no other word for it. He rocked into me at his own pace, pressing his cheek against mine, scratching me with his stubble. His voice went on and on, whispering secrets in my ear. How no one had ever been this right for him. How he wanted to stay just like this as long as could. Sweat dripped off his body, running over my skin before soaking into the bedsheet. He made himself a permanent part of me. It was bliss. Sweet, tender, and slow. Maddeningly slow near the end.

It felt like it went on for forever. I wish it had.

CHAPTER SIXTEEN

Adrian went ballistic over the bruises on David's face. He didn't seem too pleased to see me again, either. There was a brief flash of shark's teeth before I was hustled into a corner of the big dressing room out of harm's way. Security stood outside, letting only those invited into the inner sanctum.

The show was in a ballroom at one of the big, fancy hotels in town. Lots of twinkling chandeliers and red satin, big round tables crammed full of stars and the pretty-people posses that accompanied them. Luckily, I'd worn a blue dress, the only one that remotely covered everything, and a pair of the mile-high shoes Martha had ordered. Kaetrin, Bikini Girl, David's old friend, had been on the other side of the room, wearing a red frock and a scowl. She was going to get wrinkles if she kept that up. Happily, she got bored with pouting at me after a while and wandered away. I didn't blame her for being mad. If I'd lost David, I'd be pissed too. Women hovered near David, hoping for his attention. I could have high-fived someone over the way he ignored them.

There was no sign of Jimmy. Mal sat with a stunning Asian girl on one knee and a busty blond on the other, much too busy to talk to me. I still hadn't met the fourth member of the band, Ben.

"Hey," David said, exchanging my untouched glass of Cristal for a bottle of water. "Thought you might prefer this. Everything okay?"

"Thank you. Yes. Everything's great."

Wonderful man, he knew I still hadn't recovered enough from Vegas to risk the taste of alcohol. He nodded and passed the glass of champagne off to a waiter. Then he started slipping out of his leather jacket. Other people might put on tuxedos, but David stuck to his jeans and boots. His one concession to the occasion was a black button-down shirt. "Do me a favor and put this on."

"You don't like my dress?"

"Sure I do. But the air-conditioning's a bit cold in here," he said, wrapping the jacket around my shoulders.

"No, it's not."

He gave me a lopsided grin that would have melted the hardest of hearts. Mine didn't stand a chance. With an arm either side of my head, he leaned in, blocking out the rest of the room and everyone in it.

"Trust me, you're finding it a bit cool." His gaze fell to my chest and understanding dawned on me. The dress was made from some light, gauzy fabric. Gorgeous, but not so subtle in certain ways. And obviously my bra wasn't helping at all.

"Oh," I said.

"Mm. And I'm over there, trying to talk business with Adrian, but I can't. I'm totally fucking distracted because I love your rack."

"Excellent." I put an arm over my chest as subtly as possible.

"They're so pretty and they fill my hands just right. It's like we were made for one another, you know?"

"David." I grinned like the horny, lovesick fool I was.

"Sometimes there's this almost-smile on your face. And I wonder what you're thinking, standing over here watching everything."

"Nothing in particular, just taking it all in. Looking forward to seeing you play."

"Are you, now?"

"Of course I am. I can't wait."

He kissed me lightly on the lips. "After I'm finished we'll get out of here, yeah? Head off somewhere, just you and me. We can do whatever you feel like. Go for a drive or get something to eat, maybe."

"Just us?"

"Absolutely. Whatever you want."

"It all sounds good."

His graze dipped back to my chest. "You're still a little cold. I could warm you up. Where do you stand on me copping a feel in public?"

"That's a no." I turned my face to take a sip of the water. Arctic air or no, I needed cooling down.

"Yeah, that's what I thought. Come on. With great breasts come great responsibility." He took my hand and led me through the crowd of party people as I laughed. He didn't stop for anyone.

There was a small room attached to the back with a rack of garment bags and some makeup scattered around. Mirrors on the walls, a big bouquet of flowers, and a sofa that was very much occupied. Jimmy sat there in another dapper suit, legs spread with a woman kneeling between them. Her face was in his lap, head bobbing. No prizes for guessing what they were up to. The red of her dress clued me in to her identity, though I could have lived a long and happy life never knowing. Kaetrin's dark hair was wrapped tight around Jimmy's fist. In his other hand he held a bottle of whiskey. Two neat white lines of powder sat on the coffee table along with a small silver straw.

Holy crap. So this was the rock 'n' roll lifestyle. Suddenly my palms felt sweaty. But this wasn't what David was into. This wasn't him. I knew that.

"Ev," Jimmy said in a husky voice, a sleazy, slow smile spreading across his face. "Looking good, darlin'."

I snapped my mouth shut.

"Come on." David's hands clutched my shoulders, turning me away from the scene. He was livid, his mouth a bitter line.

"What, not going to say hi to Kaetrin, Dave? That's a bit harsh. Thought you two were good friends."

"Fuck off, Jimmy."

Behind us Jimmy groaned long and loud as the show on the couch reached its obvious conclusion. David slammed the door shut. The party continued on, music pumping out of the sound system, glasses clinking, and lots of loud conversation. We were out of there, but David stared off into the middle distance, oblivious of everything, it seemed. His face was lined with tension.

"David?"

"Five minutes," yelled Adrian, clapping his hands high in the air. "Showtime. Let's go."

David's eyelids blinked rapidly, as if he was waking up in the middle of a bad dream.

The atmosphere in the room was suddenly charged with excitement. The crowd cheered and Jimmy staggered on out with Kaetrin in tow. More cheering and shouts of encouragement for the band to take to the stage, along with some knowing laughter over Jimmy and the girl's reappearance.

"Let's do this!" shouted Jimmy, shaking hands and clapping people on the back as he moved through the room. "Come on, Davie."

My husband's shoulders hiked up. "Martha."

The woman sauntered over, her face a careful mask. "What can I do for you?"

"Look after Ev while I'm onstage."

"Sure."

"Look, I've got to go but I'll be right back," he said to me.

"Of course. Go."

With a final kiss to my forehead, he went, shoulders hunched in protectively. I had the maddest impulse to go after him. To stop him. To do something. Mal joined him at the door and slung an arm around his neck. David didn't look back. The bulk of the people followed them. I stood alone, watching the exodus. He'd been right, the room was cold. I clutched his jacket around me tighter, letting the scent of him soothe me. Everything was fine. If I kept telling myself that, sooner or later it would become true. Even the bits I didn't understand would work out. I had to have faith. And damn it, I did have faith. But my smile was long gone.

Martha watched me, her immaculate expression never altering.

After a moment, her red lips parted. "I've known David a very long time."

"That's nice," I said, refusing to be cowed by her cool gaze.

"Yes. He's enormously talented and driven. It makes him intense about things, passionate."

I said nothing.

"Sometimes he gets carried away. It doesn't mean anything." Martha stared at my ring. With an elegant motion she tucked her dark hair back behind her ear. Above a beautifully set cluster of dark red stones sat a single, small, winking diamond. Little more than a chip, it didn't really seem to fit Martha's expensive veneer. "When you're ready, I'll show you where you can watch the show from."

The sensation of spiraling that had started when David walked away from me became stronger. Beside me, Martha waited patiently, not saying a word, for which I was grateful. She'd said more than enough already. Only the clutter of red stones hung from her other ear. Paranoia wasn't pretty. Could this be the mate to the diamond earring David wore? No. That made no sense.

Lots of people wore tiny diamond solitaire earrings. Even millionaires.

I pushed my water aside, forcing a smile. "Shall we go?"

Watching the show was amazing. Martha took me to a spot to the side of the stage, behind the curtains, but it still felt like I was right in the thick of things. And things were loud and thrilling. Music thrummed through my chest, making my heart race. The music was a great distraction from my worries about the earring. David and I needed to talk. I'd been all for waiting until he felt comfortable enough to tell me things, but my questions were getting out of hand. I didn't want to be second-guessing him in this way. We needed honesty.

With a guitar in his hands, David was a god. Little wonder people worshiped him. His hands moved over the strings of his electric guitar with absolute precision, his concentration total. The muscles flexing in his forearms made his tattoos come to life. I stood in awe of him, mouth agape. There were other people onstage too, but David held me spellbound. I'd only seen the private side of him, who he was when he was with me. This seemed to be almost another entity. A stranger. My husband had taken a backseat to the performer. The rock star. It was actually a little daunting. But in that moment, his passion made perfect sense to me. His talent was such a gift.

They played five songs, then it was announced another big-name artist would take to the stage. All four of the band members exited by the other side. Martha had disappeared. Hard to be upset about that, despite backstage being a maze of hallways and dressing rooms. The woman was a monster. I was better off alone.

I made my way back on my own, taking tiny, delicate steps because my stupid shoes were killing me. Blisters lined my toes where the strap cut across, rubbing away at my skin. Didn't matter, my joy would not be dimmed. The memory of the music stayed with me. The way David had looked all caught up in the performance, both exciting and unknown. Talk about a rush.

I smiled and swore, quietly, ignoring my poor feet and wending my way through the mix of roadies, sound technicians, makeup artists, and general hangers-on.

"Child bride." Mal smacked a noisy kiss on my cheek. "I'm heading to a club. You guys coming or taking off back to your love nest?"

"I don't know. Just let me find David. That was amazing, by the way. You guys were brilliant."

"Glad you liked it. Don't tell David I carried the show, though. He's so precious about that sort of thing."

"My lips are sealed."

He laughed. "He's better with you, you know? Artistic types have a bad habit of disappearing up their own asses. He's smiled more in the last few days with you than I've seen him do in the last five years put together. You're good for him."

"Really?"

Mal grinned. "Really. You tell him I'm going to Charlotte's. See you there later, maybe."

"Okay."

Mal took off and I made my way toward the band's dressing room through the even bigger and better crush of people assembled. Inside the dressing room, however, things were quiet. Jimmy and Adrian had stood huddled out in the hallway, deep in conversation as I passed on by. Definitely not stopping. Sam and a second security person nodded to me as I passed.

The door to the back room where Jimmy had been busy earlier stood partly open. David's voice carried to me, clear as day, despite the noise outside. It was like I was becoming tuned in to him on some cosmic level. Scary but exhilarating at the same time. I couldn't wait to get out of here with him and do whatever. Go meet Mal or take off on our own. I didn't mind, so long as we were together.

I just wanted to be with him.

The sound of Martha's raised voice from within the same room decreased my happy.

"Don't," someone said from behind me, halting me at the door.

I turned to face the fourth member of the band: Ben. I remembered him now from some show Lauren had made me sit through years ago. He played bass, and he made Sam the bodyguard look like a cute, fluffy kitten. Short dark hair and the neck of a bull. Attractive in a strange, serial-killer kind of way. Though it might have just been the way he looked at me, eyes dead serious and jaw rigid. Another one on drugs, perhaps. To me, he felt nothing but bad.

"Let them sort it out," he said, voice low. His gaze darted to the partially open doorway. "You don't know what they were like when they were together."

"What?" I edged back a bit and he noticed, taking a step to the side to get closer to the door. Trying to maneuver me to the outer.

Ben just looked at me, his thick arm barring the way. "Mal said you're nice and I'm sure you are. But she's my sister. David and her have always been crazy about each other, ever since we were kids."

"I don't understand." I flinched, my head shaking.

"I know."

"Move, Ben."

"I'm sorry. Can't do that."

Fact was, he didn't need to. I held his gaze, making sure I had his full attention. Then I balanced my weight on one of my hooker heels, using the other to kick the door open. Since it had never been fully closed, it swung inward with ease.

David stood with his back partially turned toward us. Martha's hands were in his hair, holding him to her. Their mouths were mushed together. It was a hard, ugly kiss. Or maybe that was just the way it looked from the outside.

I didn't feel anything. Seeing that should have been big, but it wasn't. It made me small and it shut me down inside. If anything, it felt almost oddly inevitable. The pieces had all been there. I'd been so stupid, trying not to see this. Thinking everything would be fine.

A noise escaped my throat and David broke away from her. He looked over his shoulder at me.

"Ev," he said, face drawn and eyes bright.

My heart must have given up. Blood wasn't flowing. How bizarre. My hands and feet were ice-cold. I shook my head. I had nothing. I took a step back, and he flung out a hand to me.

"Don't," he said.

"David." Martha gave him a hazardous smile. No other

word for it. Her hand stroked over his arm as if she could sink her nails into him at any time. I guessed she could.

David came toward me. I took several hasty steps back, stumbling in my heels. He stopped and stared at me like I was a stranger.

"Baby, this is nothing," he said. He reached for me again. I held my arms tight to my chest, guarding myself from harm. Too late.

"It was her? She's the high school sweetheart?"

The familiar old muscle in his jaw went pop. "That was a long time ago. It doesn't matter."

"Jesus, David."

"It has nothing to do with us."

The more he spoke, the colder I felt. I did my best to ignore Ben and Martha hovering in the background.

David swore. "Come on, we're getting out of here."

I shook my head slowly. He grabbed my arms, stopping me from retreating any farther. "What the fuck are you doing, Evelyn?"

"What are *you* doing, David? What have you done?"

"Nothing," he said, teeth gritted. "I haven't done a damn thing. You said you trusted me."

"Why do you both still wear the earrings if it's nothing?"

His hand flew to his ear, covering the offending items. "It's not like that."

"Why does she still work for you?"

"You said you trusted me," he repeated.

"Why keep the house in Monterey all these years?"

"No," he said and then stopped.

I stared at him, incredulous. "No? That's it? That's not enough. Was I supposed to just not see all this? Ignore it?"

"You don't understand."

"Then explain it to me," I pleaded. His eyes looked right through me. I might as well not have spoken. My questions went unanswered, same as they ever had. "You can't do it, can you?"

I took another step back and his face hardened to fury. His hands fisted at his sides. "Don't you dare fucking leave me. You promised!"

I didn't know him at all. I stared at him, transfixed, letting his anger wash over me. It couldn't hope to pierce the hurt. Not a chance.

"You walk out of here and it's over. Don't you fucking think of coming back."

"Okay."

"I mean it. You'll be nothing to me."

Behind David, Ben's mouth opened but nothing came out. Just as well. Even numb had its limits.

"Evelyn!" David snarled.

I slipped off the stupid shoes and went barefoot for my grand exit. Might as well be comfortable. Normally I'd never wear heels like that. There was nothing wrong with normal. I was long overdue for a huge heaping dose of it. I'd wrap myself in normal like it was cotton wool, protecting me from everything. I had the café to get back to, school to start thinking about. I had a life waiting.

A door slammed shut behind me. Something thumped against it on the other side. The sound of shouting was muted.

Outside the dressing room door, Jimmy and Adrian were still deep in conversation. By which I mean Adrian spoke and Jimmy stared at the ceiling, grinning like a lunatic. I doubted a rocket ship could have reached Jimmy just then, he looked that high.

"Excuse me," I said, butting in.

Adrian turned and frowned, the flash of bright teeth coming a moment too late. "Evelyn. Honey, I'm just in the middle of something here—"

"I'd like to go back to Portland now."

"You would? Okay." He rubbed his hands together. Ah, I'd pleased him. His smile was huge, genuine for once and glaringly bright. Headlights had nothing on him. He'd apparently been holding back previously.

"Sam!" he yelled.

The bodyguard appeared, weaving through the crowd with ease. "Mrs. Ferris."

"Miss Thomas," Adrian corrected. "Would you mind seeing her safely returned to her home, thanks, Sam?"

The polite professional expression didn't falter for a second. "Yes, sir. Of course."

"Excellent."

Jimmy started laughing, big belly laughs that shook his whole body. Then he started cackling, the noise vaguely reminiscent of the Wicked Witch of the West in *The Wizard of Oz*. If she'd been on crack or cocaine or whatever Jimmy had been digging into, of course.

These people, they made no sense.

I didn't belong here. I'd never belonged here.

"This way." Sam pressed a hand lightly to the small of my back, which was sufficient to get me moving. Time to go home, wake up from the too-good-to-be-true dream that had twisted into this warped nightmare.

The laughter got louder and louder, ringing in my ears, until suddenly it cut off. I turned in time to watch Jimmy slump to the ground, his slick suit a mess. One woman gasped. Another chuckled and rolled her eyes.

"Fuck's sake," growled Adrian, kneeling beside the unconscious man. He slapped at his face. "Jimmy. Jimmy!"

More burly bodyguards appeared, crowding around the fallen singer, blocking him from view.

"Not again," Adrian ranted. "Get the doctor in here. God-damn it, Jimmy."

"Mrs. Ferris?" asked Sam.

"Is he all right?"

Sam scowled at the scene. "He's probably just passed out. It's been happening a lot lately. Shall we go?"

"Get me out of here, Sam. Please."

I was back in Portland before the sun rose. I didn't cry on the trip. It was as if my brain had diagnosed the emergency and cau-terized my emotions. I felt numb, as if Sam could swerve the car into the oncoming traffic and I wouldn't utter a peep. I was done, frozen solid. We went via the mansion so Sam could collect my bag before heading to the airport. He put me on the jet and we flew to Portland. He got me off the jet and drove me home.

Sam insisted on carrying my bag, just like he'd insisted on calling me by my married name. The man did the best subtle, concerned sidelong glance I'd ever seen. Never said much, though, which I appreciated immensely.

I sleepwalked my sorry self up the stairs to the apartment Lauren and I shared. Home was a garlic-scented hallway cour-tesy of Mrs. Lucia downstairs, constantly cooking. Peeling green wallpaper and worn wooden floorboards, scuffed and stained. Lucky I'd put the Converses on, or my feet would have been full of splinters. This floor was nothing like the gloss and gleam of David's house. You could see yourself in that sucker.

Shit. I didn't want to think of him. All of those memories belonged in a box buried in the back of my mind. Never again would they see the light of day.

My key still fit the lock. It comforted me. I might as well have been missing for years instead of days. It hadn't even been a week. I'd left early Thursday morning and now it was Tuesday. Less than six short days. That was insane. Everything felt different. I pushed open the door, being quiet because of the early hour. Lauren would be asleep. Or she might not be. I heard laughing.

She might, in fact, be spread out over our small breakfast table, giggling as some guy stuffed his head beneath one of the old oversized T-shirts she slept in. He buried his face in her cleavage and tickled her. Lauren squirmed, making all sorts of happy noises. Thankfully the guy's pants were still on, whoever he was. They were really into it, didn't notice our entry at all.

Sam stared at the far wall, avoiding the scene. Poor guy, the things he must have witnessed over the years.

"Hi," I said. "Um, Lauren?"

Lauren screeched and rolled, twisting the guy up in her shirt as he fought to get free. If she accidentally strangled him, at least he'd go happy, given the view.

"Ev," she panted. "You're back."

The guy finally liberated his face.

"Nathan?" I asked, stupefied. I cocked my head just to be sure, narrowed my eyes.

"Hi." My brother raised one hand while pulling down Lauren's shirt with the other. "How are you?"

"Fine, yeah," I said. "Sam, this is my friend Lauren and my brother, Nate. Guys, this is Sam."

Sam did his polite nod and set down my bag. "Can I do anything else for you, Mrs. Ferris?"

"No, Sam. Thank you for seeing me home."

"You're very welcome." He looked to the door then back at

me, a small wrinkle between his brows. I couldn't be certain, but I think it was as close as Sam got to an actual frown. His facial expressions seemed limited. Restrained was probably a better word. He reached out and gave me a stiff pat on the back. Then he left, closing the door behind him.

My eyes heated, threatening tears. I blinked like crazy, holding it in. His kindness nearly cracked the numb, damn it. I couldn't afford that yet.

"So, you two?" I asked.

"We're together. Yes," said Lauren, reaching behind her. Nate took her hand and held on tight. They actually looked good together. Though, seriously, how much stranger could things get? My world had changed. It felt different, though the small apartment looked the same. Things were pretty much where I'd left them. Lauren's collection of demented porcelain cats still sat on a shelf collecting dust. Our cheap or second-hand furniture and turquoise blue walls hadn't altered. Though I might never use the table again, considering what I'd seen. Lord knew what else they'd been up to on there.

I flexed my fingers, willing some life back into my limbs. "I thought you two hated each other?"

"We did," confirmed Lauren. "But, you know . . . now we don't. It's a surprisingly uncomplicated story, actually. It just kind of happened while you were away."

"Wow."

"Nice dress," said Lauren, looking me over.

"Thanks."

"Valentino?"

I smoothed the blue fabric over my stomach. "I don't know."

"That's a statement, matching it with the sneakers," Lauren said. Then she gave Nate a look. They apparently already had the silent communication thing down because he tippy-toed off toward her bedroom. Interesting . . .

My best friend and my brother. And she'd never said a word. But then, there were plenty of things I hadn't told her either. Maybe we were past the age of sharing every last little detail of our lives. How sad.

Loneliness and a healthy dose of self-pity cooled me right off and I wrapped my arms around myself.

Lauren came over and pried one of my hands loose. "Hon, what happened?"

I shook my head, warding off questions. "I can't. Not yet."

She joined me leaning against the wall. "I have ice cream."

"What kind?"

"Triple choc. I was thinking of torturing your brother with it later in a sexually explicit manner."

There went my vague interest in ice cream. I scrubbed my face with my hands. "Lauren, if you love me, you'll never say anything like that to me ever again."

"Sorry."

I almost smiled. My mouth definitely came close to it but faltered at the last. "Nate makes you happy, doesn't he?"

"Yeah, he really does. It just feels like . . . I don't know, it's like we're in tune or something. Ever since the night he picked me up from your folks' place we've pretty much been together. It feels right. He's not angry like he used to be in high school. He's given up his man-slut ways. He's calmed down and grown up. Shit, out of the two of us, he's the sensible one." She mock pouted. "But our days of sharing every last detail about our lives really are over, aren't they?"

"I guess they are."

"Ah, well. We'll always have middle school."

"Yeah." I managed a smile.

"Hon, I'm sorry things went bad. I mean, that's obviously why you're back looking like shit in that absolutely exquisite dress." She eyed up my gown with great lust.

"You can have it." Hell, she could have all of the other stuff as well. I never wanted to touch any of it ever again. His jacket I'd left with Sam, the ring stuffed into a pocket. Sam would take care of it. See that it got back to him. My hand seemed bare without it, lighter. Lighter and freer should have gone together, but they didn't. Inside me sat a great weight. I'd been dragging my sorry ass around for hours now. Onto the plane. Off the plane. Into the car. Up the stairs. Neither time nor distance had helped so far.

"I want to hug you but you're giving off that don't-touch-me vibe," she said, propping her hands on her slim hips. "Tell me what to do."

"Sorry." The smile I gave her was twisted and awful. I could feel it. "Later?"

"How much later? Because frankly, you look like you need it bad."

I couldn't stop the tears this time. They just started flowing, and once they started, they wouldn't stop. I wiped at them uselessly, then just gave up and covered my face with my hands. "Fuck."

Lauren threw her arms around me, held me tight. "Let it go."

I did.

CHAPTER SEVENTEEN

Twenty-eight days later . . .

The woman was taking forever to order. Her eyes kept shifting between me and the menu as she leaned across the counter. I knew that look. I dreaded that look. I loved being in the café, with the aroma of coffee beans and the soothing blend of music and chatter. I loved the camaraderie we had going on behind the counter and the fact that the work kept my hands and brain busy. Weirdly enough, being a barista relaxed me. I was good at it. With my studies a constant struggle, I reveled in that fact. If everything ever hit the wall, I'd always have coffee to fall back on. It was the modern-day Portland equivalent of typing. The city ran on coffee beans and cafés. Coffee and beer were in our blood.

Lately, however, some customers had been a pain in the ass to deal with.

"You seem really familiar," she started, much as they all did. "Weren't you all over the Internet a while back? Something to do with David Ferris?"

At least I didn't flinch at his name anymore. And it had been days since I'd felt the urge to actually vomit. Definitely not pregnant, just getting annulled.

After the first few days of hiding in bed, crying my eyes

out, I took every shift the café would give me to keep busy. I couldn't mourn him forever. Pity my heart remained unconvinced. He was in my dreams every night when I closed my eyes. I had to chase him out of my mind a thousand times a day.

By the time I surfaced, the few lingering paparazzi had cleared off back to LA. Apparently Jimmy had gone into rehab. Lauren switched channels every time I walked in, but I couldn't help but catch enough news to know what was going on. It seemed Stage Dive were being talked about everywhere. Someone had even asked me to sign a picture of David striding into the treatment facility, head hanging down and hands stuffed in his pockets. He'd looked so alone. Several times, I'd almost called him. Just to ask if he was okay. Just to hear his voice. How stupid was that? And what if I rang and Martha answered?

At any rate, Jimmy's meltdown was much more interesting than me. I barely rated a mention on the news these days.

But people, customers, they drove me nuts. Outside of work, I'd become a complete shut-in. That had its own issues on account of my brother basically living with us now. People in love were sickening. It was a proven medical fact. Customers with speculation shining bright in their beady little eyes weren't much better.

"You're mistaken," I told the nosy woman.

She gave me a coy look. "I don't think so."

Ten bucks said she was working her way up to asking me for his autograph. This would make the eighth attempt to obtain one today. Some of them wanted to take me home for intimate relations because, you know, rock star's ex. My vagina clearly had to be something special. I sometimes wondered if they thought there was a little plaque on my inner thigh saying David Ferris had been there.

This chick, however, wasn't checking me out. No, she wanted an autograph.

"Look," she said, speculation turning to wheedling. "I wouldn't ask, it's just that I'm such a huge fan of his."

"I can't help you, sorry. We're actually about to close. So would you like to order something before that happens?" I asked, pleasant smile firmly in place. Sam would have been proud of that smile, as fake as it was. But with my eyes I told the woman the truth. That I was all used up and I honestly had no fucks left to give. Especially when it came to David Ferris.

"Can you at least tell me if the band is really breaking up? Come on. Everyone's saying an announcement's going to be made any day now."

"I don't know anything about it. Would you liked to order something, or not?"

Further denial generally led to either anger or tears. She chose anger. A good choice, because tears annoyed the living hell out of me. I was sick of them, both on myself and others. Despite it being common knowledge that I'd been dumped, they still figured I had connections. Or so they hoped.

She did a fake little laugh. "There's no need to be a bitch about it. Would letting me know what's happening really have killed you?"

"Leave," said my lovely manager, Ruby. "Right now. Get out."

The woman switched to incredulous, mouth open wide. "What?"

"Amanda, call the cops." Ruby stood tall beside me.

"On it, boss." Amanda snapped open her cell and punched in the numbers, leveling the woman with her evil eye. Amanda, having moved on from being my high school's sole lesbian, was studying drama. These confrontations were her favorite part of the day. They might have sapped my strength, but Amanda sucked all of her power from them. A dark, malevolent force, to be sure, but it was all hers and she reveled in it. "Yes, we've got a fake blonde with a bad tan giving us trouble, Officer. I'm pretty certain I saw her at a frat party doing some serious underage drinking last week. I don't want to say what happened after that but the footage is available on YouTube for your viewing pleasure if you're over eighteen."

"No wonder he dropped you. I saw the picture, your ass is wide as fucking Texas," the woman sneered, and then sped out of the café.

"Do you really have to stir them up?" I asked.

Amanda clucked her tongue. "Please. She started it."

I'd heard worse than what she'd said. Way worse. Several times now I'd had to change my e-mail address to stop the hate mail from flooding in. I had closed my Facebook account early on.

Still, I checked my butt to be sure. It was a close call, but I was pretty sure Texas was, in fact, wider.

"As far as I can tell you're living on a diet of breath mints and lattes. Your ass is not a concern." Amanda had long since forgiven me for the bad kiss back in high school, bless her. I was beyond lucky to have the friends I did. I really don't know how I'd have made it through the last month without them.

"I eat."

"Really? Whose jeans are those?"

I started cleaning the coffee machine because it really was getting on closing time. That, and for reasons of subject avoidance. Fact was, getting cheated on and lied to by rock 'n' roll's favorite son did make for quite the diet. Definitely not one I'd recommend. My sleep was shot to shit and I was tired all the time. I was depression's bitch. Inside and out, I didn't feel like me. The time I'd spent with David, the way it had changed things, was a constant agitation, an itch I couldn't scratch. Partly because I lacked the power but also because I lacked the will. You could sing "I Will Survive" only so many times before the urge to throttle yourself took over.

"Lauren doesn't wear these. Said they were the wrong shade of dark wash and that the placement of the back pockets made her look hippy. Apparently pocket placement matters."

"And you started wearing that skinny cow's clothes when?"

"Don't call her that."

Amanda rolled her eyes. "Please, she takes it as a compliment."

True. "Well, I think the jeans are nice. Are you wiping down the tables, or would you like me to?"

Amanda just sighed. "Jo and I want to thank you for helping us move last weekend. So we're taking you out tonight. Drinking and dancing ahoy!"

"Oh." Alcohol and I already had a bad reputation. "I don't know."

"I do."

"I had plans to—"

"No you don't. This is why I left it to the last minute to tell you. I knew you'd try to make excuses." Amanda's dark eyes brooked no nonsense. "Ruby, I'm taking our girl out for a night on the town."

"Good idea," Ruby called out from the kitchen. "Get her out of here. I'll clean up."

My practiced pleasant smile fell off my face. "But—"

"It's the sad eyes," said Ruby, confiscating my cleaning cloth. "I can't bear them any longer. Please go out and have some fun."

"Am I that much of a killjoy?" I asked, suddenly worried. I honestly thought I'd been putting on a good front. Their faces told me otherwise.

"No. You're a normal twenty-one-year-old going through a breakup. You need to get back out there and reclaim your life." Ruby was in her early thirties and soon to be wed. "Trust me. I know best. Go."

"Or," said Amanda, waggling a finger at me, "you could sit at home watching *Walk the Line* for the eight hundredth time while listening to your brother and best friend going hard at it in the room next door."

When she put it like that . . . "Let's go."

"I want to be bi," I announced, because it was important. A girl had to have goals. I pushed back my chair and rose to my feet. "Let's dance. I love this song."

"You love any song that's not by the band who shall not be named." Amanda laughed, following me through the crowd. Her girlfriend, Jo, just shook her head, clinging to her hand. Vodka was doubtless as bad an idea as tequila, but I did feel somewhat unwound, looser. It was good to get out, and on an empty stomach three drinks went a long way, clearly. I did suspect Amanda had made at least one of them a double. It felt great to dance and laugh and let loose. Out of all of the getting-over-a-breakup tactics I'd attempted, keeping busy worked best. But going out dancing and drinking all dressed up shouldn't be mocked.

I tucked my hair behind my ears because my ponytail had started falling apart again. Perfect metaphor for my life. Nothing worked right since I'd gotten back from LA. Nothing lasted. Love was a lie, and rock 'n' roll sucked. Blah blah blah. Time for another drink.

And I'd been in the middle of making an important point.

"I'm serious," I said. "I'm going bi. It's my new plan."

"I think that's a great plan," yelled Jo, moving next to me. Jo also worked at the café, which was how the two had met. She had long blue hair that was the envy of all.

Amanda rolled her eyes at me. "You're not bi. Babe, don't encourage her."

Jo grinned, totally unrepentant. "Last week she wanted to be gay. Before that she talked monasteries. I think this is a constructive step toward her forgiving every penis-possessing human and moving on with her life."

"I am moving on with my life," I said.

"Which is why you two have been talking about him for the past four hours?" Amanda grinned, throwing her arms around Jo's shoulders.

"We weren't talking about him. We were insulting him. How do you say 'useless stinking sheep fornicator' in German again?" I asked, leaning in to be heard over the music. "That was my favorite."

Jo and Amanda got busy close dancing and I let them go, unperturbed. Because I wasn't afraid of being alone. I was action-packed, full of single-girl power. Fuck David Ferris. Fuck him good and hard.

The music all blended into one long time-bending beat, and so long as I kept moving it was all perfect. Sweat slicked my neck and I popped another button on my dress, widening the neckline. I ignored the other people dancing around me. I shut my eyes, staying safe in my own little world. The alcohol had given me a nice buzz.

For some reason, the hands sliding over my hips didn't bother me, even though they were uninvited. They went no farther, made no demands on me. Their owner danced behind me, keeping a small safe distance between us. It was nice. Maybe the music had hypnotized me. Or maybe I had been lonely, because I didn't fight it. Instead I relaxed against him. For all of the next song we stayed like that, melded together, moving. The beat slowed down and I raised my arms, linking my hands behind his neck. After a month of avoiding almost all human contact, my body woke. The short, soft hair at the back of his neck brushed over my fingers. Smooth, warm skin beneath.

God, it was so nice. I hadn't realized how touch starved I was.

I leaned my head back against him and he whispered something softly. Too soft for me to hear. The bristles on his cheek and jaw lightly prickled the side of my face. Hands slid over my ribs, up my arms. Calloused fingers lightly stroked the sensitive underside of my arms. His body was solid behind me, strong, but he kept his touch light, restrained. I wasn't in the market for a rebound. My heart was too bruised for that, my mind too wary. I couldn't bring myself to move away from him, however. It felt too good there.

"Evelyn," he said, his lips teasing my ear.

My breath caught, my eyelids shot open. I turned to find David staring back at me. The long hair was gone. It was still longish on top but cut short at the sides. He could probably do a neat Elvis pompadour if the fancy took him. A short, dark beard covered his lower face.

"Y-you're here," I stuttered out. My tongue felt thick and useless inside my dry mouth. Christ, it was really him. Here in Portland. In the flesh.

"Yeah." His blue eyes burned. He didn't say anything else. Music kept playing, people kept moving. The world only stopped turning for me.

"Why?"

"Ev?" Amanda put a hand to my arm and I jumped, the spell broken. She gave David a quick glance, and then her face screwed up in distaste. "What the fuck is he doing here?"

"It's okay," I said.

Her gaze moved between David and me. She didn't really seem convinced. Fair enough.

"Amanda. Please." I squeezed her fingers, nodded. After a moment she turned back to Jo, who stared at David with open disbelief. And a healthy dose of star-struck. His new look made for a brilliant disguise. Unless you knew who you were looking for, of course.

I pushed through the crowd, getting the hell out of there. I knew he'd follow. Of course he would. It was no accident he was there, though I had no damn idea how he'd found me. I needed to get away from the heat and the noise so I could think straight. Down the back hallway past the men's and women's toilets. There, that was what I wanted. A big black door opened onto a back alleyway. Open night air. A few brave stars twinkled high overhead. Otherwise it was dark back here, damp from earlier summer rain. It was horrible and dirty and hateful. An ideal setting.

I might have been feeling a bit dramatic.

The door slammed shut behind David. He faced me, hands on hips. He opened his mouth to start talking and no, not happening. I snapped.

"Why are you here, David?"

"We need to talk."

"No, we don't."

He rubbed at his mouth. "Please. There're things I have to tell you."

"Too late."

Looking at him revived the pain. As if I had wounds lingering just beneath the skin, waiting to resurface. I couldn't help staring at him, however. Parts of me were desperate for the sight of him, the sound of him. My head and heart were a wreck. David didn't appear so great himself. He looked tired. There were shadows beneath his eyes and he seemed a little pale, even in this crappy lighting. The earrings were missing, all of them gone. Not that I cared.

He rocked back on his heels, eyes watching me desperately. "Jimmy went into rehab and there were other things going on I had to deal with. We had to do therapy together as part of his treatment. That's why I couldn't come right away."

"I'm sorry to hear about Jimmy."

He nodded. "Thanks. He's doing a lot better."

"Good. That's good."

Another nod. "Ev, about Martha—"

"Whoa." I held up a hand, backing up. "Don't."

His mouth turned down at the edges. "We have to talk."

"Do we?"

"Yes."

"Because now you've decided you're ready? Fuck you, David. It's been a month. Twenty-eight days without a word. I'm sorry about your brother, but no."

"I wanted to make sure I was coming after you for the right reasons."

"I don't even know what that means."

"Ev—"

"No." I shook my head, hurt and fury pushing me hard. So I pushed at him even harder, sending him back a step. He hit the wall and I had nowhere else to go with him. But that didn't stop me.

I went to push at him again and he grabbed my hands. "Calm down."

"No!"

His hands encircled my wrists. He gritted his teeth, grinding his molars together. I heard it. Impressive that he didn't crack anything. "No what? No to talking now? What? What do you mean?"

"I mean no to everything and anything to do with you." My words echoed through the narrow alleyway, up the sides of the buildings until they emptied out into the uncaring night sky. "We're finished, remember? You're fucking done with me. I'm nothing to you. You said so yourself."

"I was wrong. Goddamn it, Ev. Calm down. Listen to me."

"Let me go."

"I'm sorry. But it's not what you think."

Out of options, I got in his face. "You don't get to come here now. You lied to me. You cheated on me."

"Baby—"

"Don't you dare call me that," I yelled.

"I'm sorry." His gaze roamed my face, searching for sense, maybe. He was shit out of luck. "I'm sorry."

"Stop."

"I'm sorry. I'm sorry." Over and over he said, chanting the most worthless words in all of time and space. I had to stop it. Shut him up before he drove me insane. I smashed my mouth to his, halting the useless litany. He groaned and kissed me back hard, bruising my lips, hurting me. But then I hurt him too. The pain helped. I pushed my tongue into his mouth, taking what was supposed to be mine. In that moment I hated him and I loved him. There didn't seem to be any difference.

My hands were freed and I wound them around his neck.

He turned us, setting my back to the rough brick wall. His touch burned through my skin and bones. It all happened so fast, there wasn't time to wonder about the wisdom of it. He pushed up my dress and tore at my panties. They didn't stand a chance. The cool of the night air and the heat of his palms smoothed over my thighs.

"I missed you so fucking much," he groaned.

"David."

He lowered his zipper and pushed down the front of his jeans. Then he lifted my leg, bringing it up to his hip. My hands dragged at his neck. I think I was trying to climb him. There wasn't much thought going into it. Just the drive to get as close to him as physically possible. He nipped at my lips, taking my mouth in another hard kiss. His cock pushed against me, easing into me. The feel of him filling me made my head spin. The slight ache as he stretched me. His other hand slid around beneath my butt, then he lifted me up, pushing in all the way, making me moan. I wrapped my legs around him and held on tight. He pounded himself into me with nil finesse. Rough suited both our moods. My fingernails clawed at his neck, my heels drumming his ass. His teeth pressed hard into the side of my neck. The pain was perfect.

"Harder," I panted.

"Fuck yes."

The rough brickwork abraded my back, pulling at the fabric of my dress. The hard drive of his cock took my breath away. I clung on tight, trying to savor the feel of him, the tension building inside me. It was all too much and still not enough. The thought that this could be our last time, a brutally angry joining like this . . . I wanted to cry but I didn't have the tears. His fingers dug into my ass cheeks, marking my flesh. The pressure inside me grew higher and higher. He changed his angle slightly, hitting my clit, and I came hard, my arms wrapped around his head, my cheek pressed against his. His beard brushed against up my face. My whole body shuddered and shook.

"Evelyn," he snarled, grinding himself into me, emptying himself inside me.

Every muscle in my body went liquid. It was all I could do to hang on to him.

"It's fine, baby." His mouth pressed against my damp face. "It'll be okay, I promise. I'll fix it."

"P-put me down."

His shoulders rose and fell on a harsh breath, and carefully he did so. Quickly I pulled down the skirt of my dress, set myself to rights. Like that was even possible. This situation was out of control. Without fuss he pulled up his jeans, made himself presentable. I looked everywhere but at him. An alleyway. Holy hell.

"Are you all right?" His fingers brushed over my face, tucked back my hair. Until I put a hand to his chest, forcing him back a step. Well, not forcing him. He chose to give me my space.

"I . . . um." I licked my lips and tried again. "I need to go home."

"Come on, I'll get us a cab."

"No. I'm sorry. I know I started this. But . . ." I shook my head.

David hung his.

"That was good-bye."

"Like fuck it was. Don't you even try to tell me that." His finger slid beneath my chin, making me look at him. "We are not finished, you hear me? Not even fucking remotely. New plan. I'm not leaving Portland until we've talked this out. I promise you that."

"Not tonight."

"No. Not tonight. Tomorrow, then?"

I opened my mouth but nothing came out. I had no idea what I wanted to say. My fingernails dug into my sides through my dress. What I wanted these days was a mystery even to me. To stop hurting would be nice. To remove all memory of him from my head and heart. To get my breathing back under control.

"Tomorrow," he repeated.

"I don't know." Now I felt tired, facing him. I could have slept for a year. My shoulders slumped and my brain stalled.

He just stared at me, eyes intense. "Okay."

Where that left us, I had no idea. But I nodded as if something had been decided.

"Good," he said, taking a deep breath.

My muscles still trembled. Semen slid down the inside of my leg. Shit. We'd had the talk, but things had been different back then.

"David, you practiced safe sex, right, the last month?"

"You have nothing to worry about."

"Good."

He took a step toward me. "As far as I'm concerned we're still married. So no, Evelyn, I haven't been fucking around on you."

I had nothing. My knees wavered. Probably due to the recent action they'd seen. Relief over him not taking to the groupies with a vengeance after our split couldn't be part of it, surely. I didn't even want to think about Martha, that tentacle-wielding sea monster from the deep.

Sex was so messy. Love was far and away worse.

One of us had to go. He made no move, so I left, hightailing it back toward the club to find Amanda and Jo. I needed new panties and a heart transplant. I needed to go home. He followed me, opening the door. The heavy bass of the music boomed out into the night.

I rushed into the ladies' room and locked myself into a stall to clean up. When I came out to wash my hands, looking in the mirror was hard. The harsh fluorescent lighting did me no favors. My long blond hair hung around my face a knotted mess thanks to David's hands. My eyes were wide and wounded. I looked terrified, but of what I didn't want to say. Also, there was the mother of all hickeys forming on my neck. Hell.

A couple of girls came in, giggling and casting longing looks back over their shoulders. Before the door swung shut, I caught a glance of David leaning against the wall opposite, waiting, staring at his boots. The girls' excited chatter was jarringly loud. But they made no mention of his name. David's disguise was holding up. Arms wrapped around myself, I went out to meet him.

"Ready to go?" he asked, pushing off from the wall.

"Yeah."

We made our way back through the club, dodging dancers and drunks, searching for Amanda and Jo. They were on the edge of the dance floor, talking. Amanda had her cranky face on.

She took me in and a brow arched. "Are you fucking kidding me?"

"Thanks for asking me out, guys. But I'm going to head home," I said, ignoring the pointed look.

"With him?" She jerked her chin at David, who lurked at my shoulder.

Jo stepped forward, wrapping me up in her arms. "Ignore her. You do what's right for you."

"Thanks."

Amanda rolled her eyes and followed suit, pulling me in for a hug. "He hurt you so bad."

"I know." My eyes welled with tears. Highly unhelpful. "Thanks for asking me out."

I'd bet all the money I had Amanda was roasting David over my shoulder with her eyes. I almost felt bad for him. Almost.

We left the club as one of his songs came over the speakers. There were numerous cries of "Divers!" Jimmy's voice purred out the lyrics, "Damn I hate these last days of love, cherry lips and long good-byes . . ."

David ducked his head and we rushed out. Outside in the open air, the song was no more than the faraway thumping of bass and drums. I kept sneaking sidelong glances, checking he was really there and not some figment of my imagination. So many times I'd dreamed he'd come to me. And every time I'd woken up alone, my face wet with tears. Now he was here and I couldn't risk it. If he broke me again, I wasn't convinced I'd manage to get back up a second time. My heart might not make it. So I did my best to keep my mouth and my mind shut.

It was still relatively early and there weren't many people milling about outside. I held out my hand to the passing traffic and a cab cruised to a stop soon after. David held the door open for me. I climbed in without a word.

"I'm seeing you home." He slid in after me and I scurried across the seat in surprise.

"You don't need—"

"I do. Okay. I do need to do that much, so just . . ."

"All right."

"Where to?" The cabdriver asked, giving us an uninterested look in the rearview mirror. Another feuding couple in his backseat. I'm sure he saw at least a dozen a night.

David rattled off my address without blinking. The taxi pulled out into the flow of traffic. He could have gotten my address from Sam, and as for the rest . . .

"Lauren," I sighed, sinking back against the seat. "Of course, that's how you knew where to find me."

He winced. "I talked to Lauren earlier. Listen, don't be mad at her. She took a lot of convincing."

"Right."

"I'm serious. She ripped me a new one for messing things up with you, yelled at me for half an hour. Please don't be mad at her."

I gritted my teeth and stared out the window. Until his fingers slid over mine. I snatched back my hand.

"You'll let me inside you but you won't let me hold your hand?" he whispered, his face sad in the dim glow of the passing cars and streetlights.

It was on the tip of my mouth to say that it had been an accident. That what had happened between us was wrong. But I couldn't do it. I knew how much it would hurt him. We stared at each other as my mouth hung open, my brain useless.

"I missed you so fucking much," he said. "You have no idea."

"Don't."

His lips shut but he didn't look away. I sat there caught by his gaze. He looked so different with his long hair gone, with the short beard. Familiar but unknown. It wasn't a long trip home, though it seemed to take forever. The cab stopped outside the old block of flats, and the driver gave us an impatient look over his shoulder.

I pushed open the car door, ready to be gone but hesitating just the same. My foot hovered in thin air above the curb. "I honestly didn't think I'd ever see you again."

"Hey," he said, his arm stretching out across the back of the seat. His fingers reached toward me but fell short of making contact. "You're going to see me again. Tomorrow."

I didn't know what to say.

"Tomorrow," he repeated, voice determined.

"I don't know if it'll make any difference."

He lifted his chin, inhaling sharply. "I know I fucked us up, but I'm going to fix it. Just don't make up your mind yet, all right? Give me that much."

I gave him a brief nod and hurried inside on unsteady legs. Once I'd locked myself inside, the cab pulled away, its tail-lights fading to black through the frosted glass of the downstairs door.

What the hell was I supposed to do now?

CHAPTER EIGHTEEN

I was running late for work. Rushing about like a mad thing trying to get ready. I ran into the bathroom, jumped in the shower. Gave my face a good scrub to get rid of the remnants of last night's makeup. Gruesome, crusty stuff. It would serve me right if I got the pimple from hell. Last night had all been some bizarre dream. But this was real life. Work and school and friends. My plans for the future. Those were the things that were important. And if I just kept telling myself that, everything would be fine and dandy. Someday.

Ruby didn't much mind what we wore at work beyond the official café T-shirt. Her roots were strongly alternative. She'd planned to be a poet but wound up inheriting her aunt's coffee shop in the Pearl District. Urban development had upped property prices and Ruby became quite the well-to-do businesswoman. Now she wrote her poetry on the walls in the café. I don't think you could find a better boss. But late was still late. Not good.

I'd stayed up worrying about what had happened with David in that alleyway. Reliving the moment where he told me he considered us still married. Sleep would have been far more beneficial. Pity my brain wouldn't switch off.

I pulled on a black pencil skirt, the official café T-shirt, and a pair of flats. Done. Nothing was going to help the bruises beneath my eyes. People had pretty much gotten used to them on me lately. It took about half a stick of concealer to cover the bruise on my neck.

I roared out of the bathroom in a cloud of steam, just in time to see Lauren waltz out of the kitchen, broad smile on her face. "You're late for work."

"That I am."

I looped my handbag over my shoulder, grabbed my keys off the table, and got going. There wasn't time for this. Not now. Quite possibly not ever. I couldn't imagine her ever having a good enough reason for siding with David. Over the last month she'd spent many nights by my side, letting me talk myself hoarse about him when I needed to. Because eventually, it all had to come out. Daily I told her that I didn't deserve her, and she'd smack a kiss on my cheek. Why betray me now? I thumped down the stairs with extra oomph.

"Ev, wait." Lauren ran after me as I stormed down the front steps.

I turned on her, house keys held before me like a weapon. "You told him where I was."

"What was I supposed to do?"

"Oh, I don't know. Not tell him? You knew I didn't want to see him." I looked her over, noticing all sorts of things I didn't want to. "Full hair and makeup at this hour? Really, Lauren? Were you expecting him to be here, perhaps?"

Her chin dipped as she had the good grace to look embarrassed at last. "I'm sorry. You're right, I got carried away. But he's here to make amends. I thought you might at least want to hear what he has to say."

I shook my head, fury bubbling away inside me. "Not your call."

"You've been miserable. What was I supposed to do?" She threw her arms sky-high. "He said that he'd come to make things right with you. I believe him."

"Of course you do. He's David Ferris, your very own teen idol."

"No. If he wasn't here to kiss your feet I'd have killed him. No matter who he is, he hurt you." She seemed sincere, her mouth pinched and eyes huge. "I'm sorry about dressing up this morning. It won't happen again."

"You look great. But you're wasting your time. He's not going to be here. That isn't going to happen."

"No? So who gave you that monster on your neck?"

I didn't even need to answer that. Damn it. The sun beat down overhead, warming up the day.

"If there's a chance you think he might be the one," she said, making my stomach twist. "If you think you two can sort this out somehow . . . He's the only one that ever got to you. The way you talk about him . . ."

"We were only together a few days."

"You really think that matters?"

"Yes. No. I don't know," I flailed. It wasn't pretty. "We never made sense, Lauren. Not from day one."

"Gah," she said, making a strangled noise to accompany it. "This is about your fucking plan, isn't it? Let me clue you in on something. You don't have to make sense. You just have to want to be together and be willing to do whatever it takes to make that happen. It's amazingly simple. That's love, Ev, putting each other first. Not worrying about if you fit into some fucktard plan that your dad brainwashed you into believing was what you wanted out of life."

"It's not about the plan." I scrubbed at my face with my hands, holding back tears of frustration and fear. "He broke me. It feels like he broke me. Why would anyone willingly take that chance again?"

Lauren looked at me, her own eyes bright. "I know he hurt you. So punish the bastard, keep him waiting. The fucker, he deserves it. But if you love him, then think about hearing what he has to say."

Maybe I was coming down with a cold, tight chest and itchy eyes. Having your heart broken should come with some positives, some perspective to balance out the bad. I should have been wiser, tougher, but I didn't feel it just then. I jangled my house keys. Ruby was going to kill me. I'd have to forgo my usual walk and catch a streetcar to have even a hope in hell of not getting my Texas-size ass fired. "I have to go."

Lauren nodded, face set. "You know, I love you so much more than I ever loved him. Without question."

I snorted. "Thanks."

"But has it occurred to you that you wouldn't be this upset if you didn't still love him at least a little bit?"

"I don't like you making sense at this hour of the morning. Stop it."

She took a step back, giving me a smile. "You were always there talking sense at me when I needed it. So I'm not going to stop nagging you just because you don't like what you're hearing. Deal with it."

"I love you, Lauren."

"I know, you Thomas kids are crazy for me. Why, just last night, your brother did this thing . . ."

I fled from the sound of her evil laughter.

Work was fine. Two guys came in to ask me to a frat party that was coming up. I'd never received such invites pre-David. I therefore declined them post-David. If I was indeed post-David. Who knew? Various people tried for autographs or information, and I sold them coffee and cake instead. We closed up at dusk.

All day I'd been on edge, wondering if he'd put in an appearance. Tomorrow was today, but I hadn't seen any sign of him. Maybe he'd changed his mind. Mine changed from one minute to the next. My promise to him not to decide yet was safe and sound.

We were just locking up when Ruby jabbed me in the ribs with her elbow. Probably a bit harder than she meant to because I'm pretty sure I sustained a kidney injury.

"He's really here," she hissed, nodding at David who did indeed lurk nearby, waiting. He was here, just like he'd said he'd be. Nervous excitement bubbled up inside of me. With a ball cap on and the beard, he blended well. Especially with the haircut. My heart sobbed a little at the loss of his long dark hair. But I'd never admit to it. Amanda had told Ruby about his reappearance last night. Given the lack of paparazzi and screaming fans in the vicinity, it must still be a secret from the rest of the city.

I stared at him, unsure how to feel. Last night at the club had been surreal. Here and now, this was me living my normal life. Seeing him in it, I didn't know how I felt. Discombobulated was a good word.

"Do you want to meet him?" I asked.

"No, I'm reserving judgment. I think actually meeting him might render me partial. He's very attractive, isn't he?" Ruby gave him a slow look-over, lingering on his jeans-clad legs longer than necessary. She had a thing for men's thighs. Soccer players sent her into a frenzy. Odd for a poet, but then I'd found no one ever really fit a certain type. Everyone had their quirks.

Ruby continued looking him over like he was meat at market. "Maybe don't divorce him."

"You sound very impartial. See you later."

Her hand hooked my arm. "Wait. If you stay with him will you still work for me?"

"Yes. I'll even try to be on time more often. Night, Ruby."

He stood on the sidewalk, hands stuffed into the pockets of his jeans. Seeing him felt similar to standing at a cliff's edge. The little voice in the back of my head whispered damn the consequences, you know you can probably fly. If you can't, imagine the thrill of the fall. Reason, on the other hand, screamed bloody murder at me.

At what point exactly could you decide you were going insane?

"Evelyn."

Everything stopped. If he ever figured out what it did to me when he said my name like that, I was done for. God, I'd missed him. It'd been like having a piece of me missing. But now that he was back, I didn't know how we fit together anymore. I didn't even know if we could.

"Hi," I said.

"You look tired," he said, mouth turning downward. "I mean, you look good, of course. But . . ."

"It's fine." I studied the sidewalk, took a deep breath. "It was a busy day."

"So this is where you work?"

"Yeah."

Ruby's café sat quiet and empty. Fairy lights twinkled in the windows alongside a host of flyers taped to the glass advertising this and that. Streetlights flickered on around us.

"Looks nice. Listen, we don't have to talk right now," he said. "I just wanna walk you home."

I crossed my arms over my chest. "You don't have to do that."

"It's not like it's a chore. Let me walk you home, Ev. Please."

I nodded and after a moment started a hesitant stride down

the city street. David fell into step beside me. What to talk about? Every topic seemed loaded. An open pit full of sharp stakes lay waiting around every corner. He kept shooting me wary sidelong glances. Opening his mouth and then shutting it. Apparently the situation sucked for both of us. I couldn't bring myself to talk about LA. Last night seemed safer territory. Wait. No, it wasn't. Bringing up alley sex was never going to pass for smart.

"How was your day?" he asked. "Apart from busy."

Why couldn't I have thought of something innocuous like that?

"Ah, fine. A couple of girls came in with stuff for you to sign. Some guys wanted me to give you a demo tape of their garage-reggae-blues band. One of the big-name jocks from school came in just to give me his number. He thinks we could have fun sometime," I babbled, trying to lighten the mood.

His face became thunderous, dark brows drawn tight together. "Shit. That been happening often?"

And I was an idiot to have opened my mouth. "It's no big deal, David. I told him I was busy and he went away."

"So he fucking should." He tipped his chin, giving me a long look. "You trying to make me jealous?"

"No, my mouth just ran away without my head. Sorry. Things are complicated enough."

"I am jealous."

I stared at him in surprise. I don't know why. He'd made it clear last night he was here for me. But the knowledge that maybe I wasn't alone out on the lovelorn precipice, thinking of throwing myself off . . . there was a lot of comfort in that.

"Come on," he said, resuming the walking. At the corner we stopped, waiting for the traffic to clear.

"I might get Sam up here to keep an eye on you," he said. "I don't want people bothering you at work."

"As much as I like Sam, he can stay where he is. Normal people don't take bodyguards to work."

His forehead scrunched up, but he said nothing. We crossed the road, continuing on. A streetcar rumbled past, all lit up. I preferred walking, getting in some outside time after being shut inside all day. Plus, Portland's beautiful: cafés and breweries and a weird heart. Take that, LA.

"So what did you do today?" I asked, proving myself a total winner in the creative conversation stakes.

"Just had a look around town, checking things out. I don't get to play the tourist too often. We're going left here," he said, turning me off the normal path toward home.

"Where are we going?"

"Just bear with me. I need to pick something up." He escorted me into a pizza place I went to occasionally with Lauren. "Pizza's the only thing I know you definitely eat. They were willing to stick on every fucking vegetable I could think of, so I hope you'll like it."

The place was only about a quarter full due to the early hour. Bare brick walls and black tables. A jukebox blared out something by the Beatles. I stood in the doorway, hesitant to go farther with him. The man nodded to David and fetched an order from the warmer behind him. David thanked him and headed back toward me.

"You didn't have to do that." I stepped back out onto the street, giving the pizza box suspicious glances.

"It's just pizza, Ev," he said. "Relax. You don't even have to ask me to share it with you if you don't want. Which way is it to your place from here?"

"Left."

We walked another block in silence with David carrying the pizza box up high on one hand.

"Stop frowning," he said. "When I picked you up last night you were lighter than in Monterey. You've lost weight."

I shrugged. Not going there. Definitely not remembering him lifting me and my legs going around him and how badly I'd missed him and the sound of his voice as he—

"Yeah, well, I liked you the way you were," he said. "I love your curves. So I came up with another plan. You're getting pizza with fifteen cheeses on it until you've got them back."

"My first instinct here is to say something snarky about how my body is no longer any of your business."

"Lucky you thought twice about saying that, huh? Especially since you let me back into your body last night." He met my scowl with one of his own. "Look, I just don't want you losing weight and getting sick, especially not on my account. It's that simple. Forget the rest and stop giving the pizza dirty looks or you'll hurt its feelings."

"You're not the boss of me," I muttered.

He barked out a laugh. "You feel better for saying that?"

"Yes."

I gave him a wary smile. Having him beside me again felt too easy. I shouldn't get comfortable, who knew when it would once again blow up in my face? But the truth was, I wanted him there so bad it hurt.

"Ba—" He cleared his throat and tried again, without the sentiment that would have earned him an automatic smackdown. "Friend. Are we friends again?"

"I don't know."

He shook his head. "We're friends. Ev, you're sad, you're tired, and you've lost weight, and I fucking hate that I'm the cause of it. I'm going to make this right with you one step at a time. Just . . . give me a little room to maneuver here. I promise I won't step on your toes too badly."

"I don't trust you anymore, David."

His teasing smile fell. "I know you don't. And when you're ready we're gonna talk about that."

I swallowed hard against the lump in my throat.

"When you're ready," he reiterated. "Come on. Let's get you home so you can eat this while it's still hot."

We walked the rest of the way home in silence. I think it was companionable. David gave me occasional small smiles. They seemed genuine.

He tramped up the stairs behind me, not really bothering to look around. I'd forgotten he'd been here last night when he got my whereabouts from Lauren. I unlocked the door and took a peek inside, still scarred from catching Lauren and my brother on the couch last week. Living with them wasn't going to work long term. I think everyone was getting to the point of needing their own space.

The last month, though, had been beneficial for Nate and me. It had given us a chance to talk. We were closer than we'd ever been. He loved his job at the mechanic shop. He was happy and settled. Lauren was right, he'd changed. My brother had figured out what he wanted and where he belonged. Now if I could just get my shit together and do the same.

Rock music played softly and Nate and Lauren danced in the middle of the room. An impromptu thing, obviously, given my brother's still-greasy work clothes. Lauren didn't seem to care, holding on to him tight, staring into his eyes.

I cleared my throat to announce our arrival and stepped into the room.

Nate looked over and gave me a welcoming smile. But then he saw David. Blood suffused his face and his eyes changed. The temperature in the room seemed to rocket.

"Nate," I said, making a grab for him as he charged David.

"Shit." Lauren ran after him. "No!"

Nate's fist connected with David's face. The pizza went flying. David stumbled back, blood gushing from his nose.

"You fucking asshole," my brother yelled.

I jumped on Nate's back, trying to wrestle him back. Lauren grabbed at his arm. David did nothing. He covered his bloody face but made no move to protect himself from further damage.

"I'm going to fucking kill you for hurting her," Nate roared.

David just looked at him, eyes accepting.

"Stop, Nate!" My feet dragged at the floor, my arms wrapped around my brother's windpipe.

"You want him here?" Nate asked me, incredulous. "Are you fucking serious?" Then he looked at Lauren tugging at his arm. "What are you doing?"

"This is between them, Nate."

"What? No! You saw what he did to her. What she's been like for the last month."

"You need to calm down. She doesn't want this." Lauren's hands patted over his face. "Please, babe. This isn't you."

Slowly, Nate pulled back. His shoulders dropped back to normal levels, his muscles relaxing. I gave up my choke hold on him, not that it had done much good. My brother did the raging bull thing scarily well. Blood leaked out from between David's fingers, dripped onto the floor. "Crap. Come on." I grabbed his arm and led him into our bathroom.

He leaned over the sink, swearing quietly but profusely. I bundled up some toilet paper and handed it to him. He stuffed it beneath his bloody nostrils.

"Is it broken?"

"I dunno." His voice was muffled, thick.

"I'm so sorry."

"S'okay." From his back jeans pocket came a ringing noise.

"I'll get it." Carefully, I extracted his phone. The name flashing on screen stopped me cold. The universe had to be playing a prank. Surely. Except it wasn't. It was just the same old heartbreak playing out all over again inside of me. I could already feel the ice-cold numbness spreading through my veins.

"It's her." I held the phone out to him.

Above the ball of bloody toilet paper his nose looked wounded but intact. Violence wasn't going to help. No matter the anger working through me, winding me up just then.

His gaze jumped from the screen to me. "Ev."

"You should go. I want you to go."

"I haven't talked to Martha since that night. I've had nothing to do with her."

I shook my head, out of words. The phone rang shrilly, the noise piercing my eardrums. It echoed on and on inside the small bathroom. It vibrated in my hand and my whole body trembled. "Take it before I break it."

Bloodstained fingers took it from my hand.

"You gotta let me explain," he said. "I promise, she's gone."

"Then why is she calling you?"

"I don't know and I'm not answering. I haven't spoken to her once since I fired her. You gotta believe me."

"But I don't. I mean, how can I?"

He blinked pained eyes at me. We just stared at one another as realization dawned. This wasn't going to work. This had never been going to work. He was always secrets and lies, and I was always on the outside looking in. Nothing had changed. My heart was breaking all over again. Surprising, really, that there was enough of it left to worry over.

"Just go," I said, my stupid eyes welling up.

Without another word, he walked out.

CHAPTER NINETEEN

David and I didn't speak after that. But every afternoon after work he was there, waiting across the street. He'd be watching me from beneath the brim of his baseball cap. All ready to stalk me home safely. It pissed me off, but in no way did I feel threatened. I'd ignored him for three days as he trailed me. Today was day number four. He'd traded his usual black jeans for blue, boots for sneakers. Even from a distance, his upper lip and nose looked bruised. The paparazzi were still missing in action, though today someone had asked me if he was in town. His days of moving around Portland unknown were probably coming to an end. I wondered if he knew.

When I didn't just ignore him as per my usual modus operandi, he took a step forward. Then stopped. A truck passed between us among a steady stream of city traffic. This was crazy. Why was he still here? Why hadn't he just gone back to Martha? Moving on was impossible with him here.

Decision half made, I rushed across during the next break in traffic, meeting him on the opposite sidewalk.

"Hi," I said, not fussing with the strap on my bag at all. "What are you doing here, David?"

He stuffed his hands in his pockets, looked around. "I'm walking you home. Same as I do every day."

"This is your life now?"

"Guess so."

"Huh," I said, summing up the situation perfectly. "Why don't you go back to LA?"

Blue eyes watched me warily and he didn't answer at first. "My wife lives in Portland."

My heart stuttered. The simplicity of the statement and the sincerity in his eyes caught me off guard. I wasn't nearly as immune to him as I should have been. "We can't keep doing this."

He studied the street, not me, his shoulders hunched over. "Will you walk with me, Ev?"

I nodded. We walked. Neither of us rushed, instead strolling past shop fronts and restaurants, peering into bars just getting going for the evening. I had a bad feeling that once we stopped walking we'd have to start talking, so dawdling suited me fine. Summer nights meant there were a fair number of people around.

An Irish bar sat on a street corner about halfway home. Music blared out, some old song by the White Stripes. Hands still stuffed into his pockets, David gestured toward the bar with an elbow. "Wanna get a drink?"

It took me a moment to find my voice. "Sure."

He led me straight to a table at the back, away from the growing crowd of after-work drinkers. He ordered two pints of Guinness. Once they arrived, we sat in silence, sipping. After a moment, David took off his cap and set it on the table. Shit, his poor face. I could see it more clearly now, and he looked like he had two black eyes.

We sat there staring at one another in some bizarre sort of standoff. Neither of us spoke. The way he looked at me, like he'd been hurt too, like he was hurting . . . I couldn't take it. Waiting to drag this whole sorry mess of a relationship out into the light wasn't helping either of us. Time for a new plan. We'd clear the air, then get on with our respective lives. No more hurt and heartache. "You wanted to tell me about her?" I prompted, sitting up straighter, preparing myself for the worst.

"Yeah. Martha and I were together a long time. You probably already know, she was the one who cheated on me. The one we talked about."

I nodded.

"We started the band when I was fourteen, Mal and Jimmy and me. Ben joined a year later and she'd hang around too. They were like family," he said, brow puckered. "They are family. Even when things went bad I couldn't just turn my back on her . . ."

"You kissed her."

He sighed. "No, she kissed me. Martha and I are finished."

"I'm guessing she doesn't know that, since she's still calling you and all."

"She's moved to New York, no longer working for the band. I don't know what the phone call was about. I didn't return it."

I nodded, only slightly appeased. Our problems weren't that clear-cut. "Does your heart understand you're finished with her? I guess I mean your head, don't I? The heart's just another muscle, really. Silly to say it decides anything."

"Martha and I are finished. We have been for a long time. I promise."

"Even if that's true, doesn't that just make me the consolation prize? Your attempt at a normal life?"

"Ev, no. That's not the way it is."

"Are you sure about that?" I asked, disbelief thick in my voice. I picked up my beer, gulping down the bitter dark ale and creamy foam. Something to calm the nerves. "I was getting over you," I said, my voice a pitiful, small thing. My shoulders were right back where they belonged, way down. "A month. I didn't really give up on you until day seven, though. Then I knew you weren't coming. I knew it was over then. Because if I'd been so important to you, you'd have said something by then, right? I mean, you knew I was in love with you. So you'd have put me out of my misery by then, wouldn't you?"

He said nothing.

"You're all secrets and lies, David. I asked you about the earring, remember?"

He nodded.

"You lied."

"Yeah. I'm sorry."

"Did you do that before or after our honesty rule? I can't remember. It was definitely after the cheating rule, though, right?" Talking was a mistake. All of the jagged thoughts and emotions he inspired caught up with me too fast.

He didn't deign to reply.

"What's the story behind the earrings, anyway?"

"I brought them with my first paycheck after the record company signed us."

"Wow. And you both wore them all this time. Even after she cheated on you and everything."

"It was Jimmy," he said. "She cheated on me with Jimmy."

Holy shit, his own brother. So many things fell into place with that piece of information. "That's why you got so upset about finding him and that groupie together. And when you saw Jimmy talking to me at that party."

"Yeah. It was all a long time ago, but . . . Jimmy flew back for an appearance on a TV show. We were in the middle of a big tour, playing Spain at the time. The second album had just hit the top ten. We were finally really pulling in the crowds."

"So you forgave them to keep the band together?"

"No. Not exactly. I just got on with things. Even back then Jimmy was drinking too much. He'd changed." He licked his lips, studied the table. "I'm sorry about that night. More fucking sorry than I can say. What you walked in on . . . I know how it must have looked. And I hated myself for lying to you about the earring, for still wearing it in Monterey."

He flicked at his ear in annoyance. There was a visible wound there with shiny, pink, nearly healed skin around it. It didn't look like a fading earring hole at all.

"What did you do there?" I asked.

"Cut across it with a knife." He shrugged. "An earring hole takes years to grow over. Made a new cut when you left so it could heal properly."

"Oh."

"I waited to come talk to you because I needed some time. You walking out on me after you'd promised you wouldn't . . . that was hard to take."

"I didn't have any choice."

He leaned toward me, his eyes hard. "You had a choice."

"I'd just seen my husband kissing another woman. And then you refused to even discuss it with me. You just started yelling at me about leaving. Again." My hands gripped the edge of the table so tight I could feel my fingernails pressing into the wood. "What the fuck should I have done, David? Tell me. Because I've played that scene over in my head so many times and it always works out the same way, with you slamming the door shut behind me."

"Shit." He slumped back in his seat. "You knew you leaving was a problem for me. You should have stuck with me, given me a chance to calm down. We worked it out in Monterey after that bar fight. We could have done it again."

"Rough sex doesn't fix everything. Sometimes you actually have to talk."

"I tried to talk to you the other night at that club. Wasn't what was on your mind."

I could feel my face heat up. It just pissed me off even more.

"Fuck. Look," he said, rubbing at the back of his neck. "The thing is, I needed to get us straight in my head, okay? I needed to figure out if us being together was the right thing. Honestly, Ev, I didn't want to hurt you again."

A month he'd left me to stew in my misery. It was on the tip of my tongue to give him a flippant thank-you. Or even to flip him off. But this was too serious.

"You got us straight in your head? That's great. I wish I could get us straight in my head." I stopped babbling long enough to drink more beer. My throat was giving sandpaper serious competition.

He held himself perfectly still, watching me crash and burn with an eerie calm.

"So, I'm kind of beat." I looked everywhere but at him. "Does that cover everything you wanted to talk about?"

"No."

"No? There's more?" Please, God, don't let there be more.

"Yeah."

"Have at it." Time to drink.

"I love you."

I spat beer across the table, all over our combined hands. "Shit."

"I'll get some napkins," he said, releasing my hand and rising out of his chair. A moment later he was back. I sat there like a useless doll while he cleaned my arm and then the table, trembling was all I was good for. Carefully, he pulled back my seat, helped me to my feet, and ushered me out of the bar. The hum of traffic and rush of city air cleared my senses. I had room to think out on the street.

Immediately my feet got moving. They knew what was up. My boots stomped across the pavement, putting serious distance between me and there. Getting the hell away from him and what he'd said. David stayed right on my heels, however.

We stopped at a street corner and I punched the button, waiting for the Walk light. "Don't say that again."

"Is it such a surprise, really? Why the fuck else would I be doing this, huh? Of course I love you."

"Don't." I turned on him, face furious.

His lips formed a tight line. "All right. I won't say that again. For now. But we should talk some more."

I growled, gnashed my teeth.

"Ev."

Crap. Negotiation wasn't my strong suit. Not with him. I wanted him gone. Or at least I was pretty certain I wanted him gone. Gone so I could resume my mourning for him and us and everything we might have been. Gone so I didn't have to think about the fact that he now thought he loved me. What utter emotional bullshit. My tear ducts went crazy right on cue. I took huge deep breaths trying to get myself back under control.

"Later, not today," he said, in an affable, reasonable voice. I didn't trust it or him at all.

"Fine."

I strode another block with him hanging at my side until again a red light stopped us cold, leaving room for conversation. He had better not speak. At least not until I got my shit together and figured all this out. I straightened my pencil skirt, tucked back my hair, fidgeted. The light took forever. Since when did Portland turn against me? This wasn't fair.

"We're not finished," he said. It sounded like both a threat and a promise.

The first text arrived at midnight while I was lying on my bed, reading. Or trying to read. Because trying to sleep had been a bust. School started back soon, but I was finding it hard to raise my usual enthusiasm for my studies. I had the worst feeling that the seed of doubt David had planted regarding my career choices had taken root inside my brain. I liked architecture, but I didn't love it. Did that matter? Sadly, I had no answers. Lots of excuses—some bullshit and some valid—but no answers.

David would probably say I could do whatever the fuck I wanted to. I knew all too well what my father would say. It wouldn't be pretty.

I'd been avoiding seeing my parents since I got back. Easy enough to do considering I'd hung up on the lecture my father had attempted to give me the second day after my return. Relations had been frosty since then. The real surprise was that I wasn't surprised. They had never encouraged anything that didn't directly support the plan. There was a reason I'd never returned their calls when I was in Monterey. Because I couldn't tell them the things they wanted to hear anymore, it had seemed safer to stay mute.

Nathan had been running interference with the folks, which I appreciated, but my time was up. We'd all been summoned to dinner tomorrow night. I figured the text was my mother ensuring I wasn't going to try and weasel out of it. Sometimes she sat up late watching old black-and-white movies when her sleeping pills didn't kick in.

I was wrong.

David: She surprised me when she kissed me. That's why I didn't stop her right away. But I didn't want it.

I stared at my cell, frowning.

David: You there?
Me: Yeah.
David: I need to know if you believe me about Martha.

Did I? I took a breath, searched deep. There was frustration, plenty of confusion, but my anger had apparently burned itself out at long last. Because I didn't doubt he'd told me the truth.

Me: I believe you.
David: Thank you. I keep thinking of more. Will you listen?
Me: Yes.
David: My folks got married because of Jimmy. Mom left when I was 12. She drank. Jimmy's been paying her to keep quiet. She's been hustling him for years.
Me: Holy hell!
David: Yeah. I got lawyers onto it now.
Me: Glad to hear it.
David: We retired Dad to Florida. I told him about you. He wants to meet.
Me: Really? I don't know what to say . . .
David: Can I come up?
Me: You're here??

I didn't wait for a reply. Forget my pajama shorts and ragged old T-shirt, washed so many times its original color was a faded memory. He'd just have to take me as he found me. I unlocked the front door of our apartment and padded down the stairs on bare feet, my cell still in my hand. Sure enough, a tall shadow loomed through the frosted glass of the building's front door. I pushed it open to find him sitting on the step. Outside, the night was still, peaceful. A fancy silver SUV was pulled up at the curb.

"Hey," he said, a finger busy on the screen of his cell. Mine beeped again.

David: Wanted to say good night.

"Okay," I said, looking up from the screen. "Come in."

The side of his mouth lifted and he looked up at me. I met his gaze, refusing to feel self-conscious. He didn't seem put off by my slacker bedtime style. If anything, his smile increased, his eyes warming. "You about to go to bed?"

"I was just reading. Couldn't sleep."

"Is your brother here?" He stood and followed me back up the stairs, his sneakers loud on the old wooden floors. I half expected Mrs. Lucia from downstairs to come out and yell. It was a hobby of hers.

"No," I said, closing the door behind us. "He and Lauren went out."

He looked around the apartment with interest. As usual he took up all the space. I don't know how he did that. It was like a magician's trick. He was somehow so much bigger than he actually seemed. And the man didn't seem small to begin with. In no rush at all, his gaze wandered around the room, taking in bright turquoise walls (Lauren's doing) and the shelves of neatly stacked books (my doing).

"Is this yours?" he asked, poking his head into my bedroom.

"Ah, yes. It's a bit of a mess right now, though." I squeezed past him and started speed-cleaning, picking up the books and other assorted debris scattered across the floor. I should have asked him to give me five minutes before coming up. My mother would be horrified. Since returning from LA I'd let my world descend into chaos. It suited my frazzled state of mind. Didn't mean David needed to see it. I needed to make a plan to clean up my act and actually stick to it this time.

"I used to be organized," I said, flailing, my fallback position for everything lately.

"It doesn't matter."

"This won't take a minute."

"Ev," he said, catching hold of my wrist in much the same manner that his gaze caught me. "I don't care. I just need to talk to you."

A sudden horrible thought entered my mind. "Are you leaving?" I asked, today's dirty work shirt clutched in my suddenly shaking hand.

His grip tightened around my wrist. "You want me to leave?"

"No. I mean, are you leaving Portland? Is that why you're here, to say good-bye?"

"No."

"Oh." The pincer grip my ribs had gotten on my heart and lungs eased back a little. "Okay."

"Where did that come from?" When I didn't answer, he tugged me gently toward him. "Hey."

I took a reluctant step in his direction, dropping the dirty laundry. He pressed for more, sitting on my bed and pulling me down alongside him. I sort of stumbled my butt onto the double mattress as opposed to doing it with any grace. Story of my life. Object achieved, he gave up his grip on me. My hands clenched the edge of the bed.

"So, you got a weird look on your face and then you asked me if I was leaving," he said, blue eyes concerned. "Care to explain?"

"You haven't turned up at midnight before. I guess I wondered if there was more to it than just dropping by."

"I drove by your apartment and I saw your light was on. Figured I'd send you a text, see what mood you were in after our talk today." He rubbed at his bearded chin with the palm of his hand. "Plus, like I said, I keep thinking of stuff I need to tell you."

"You drive by my apartment often?"

He gave me a wry smile. "Only a couple of times. It's my way of saying good night to you."

"How did you know which window was mine?"

"Ah, well, that time I talked to Lauren when I was first came to town? She had the light on in the other room. Figured this one must be yours." He didn't look at me, choosing instead to check out the photos of me and my friends on the walls. "You mad that I've been around?"

"No," I answered honestly. "I think I might be running out of mad."

"You are?"

"Yeah."

He let out a slow breath and stared back at me, saying nothing. Dark bruises lingered beneath his eyes, though his swollen nose had gone back to normal size.

"I really am sorry Nate hit you."

"If I was your brother, I'd have done the exact same fucking thing." He braced his elbows on his knees but kept his face turned toward me.

"Would you?"

"Without question."

Males and their penchant for beating on things, it knew no end.

The silence dragged out. It wasn't uncomfortable, exactly. At least we weren't fighting or rehashing our breakup one more time. Being broken and angry got old.

"Can we just hang out?" I asked.

"Absolutely. Lemme see this." He picked up my iPhone and started flicking through the music files. "Where are the ear-buds?"

I hopped up and retrieved them from among the crap on my desk. David plugged them in, then handed me an earbud. I sat at his side, curious what he'd choose out of my music. When the rocking, jumpy beat of "Jackson" by Johnny Cash and June Carter started, I looked at him in amusement. He smirked and mouthed the lyrics. We had indeed gotten married in a fever.

"You making fun of me?" I asked.

Light danced in his eyes. "I'm making fun of us."

"Fair enough."

"What else have you got here?"

Cash and Carter finished and he continued his search for songs. I watched his face, waiting for a reaction to my musical tastes. All I got was a smothered yawn.

"They're not that bad," I protested.

"Sorry. Big day."

"David, if you're tired, we don't have to—"

"No. I'm fine. But do you mind if I lie down?"

David on my bed. Well, he was already on my bed but . . . "Sure."

He gave me a cagey look but started tugging off his sneak-ers. "You just being polite?"

"No, it's fine. And, I mean, legally the bed is still half yours,"

I joked, pulling out the earbud before his movements did it for me. "So, what did you do today?"

"Been working on the new album and sorting out some stuff." Hands behind his head, he stretched out across my bed. "You lying down too? We can't share the music if you don't."

I crawled on and lay down next to him, wriggling around a bit, making myself comfortable. It was, after all, my bed. And he would be the only male who'd ever lain on it. The slight scent of his soap came to me, clean and warm and David. All too well, I remembered. For once, hurt didn't seem to come attached to the memory. I poked around inside my head, double-checking. When I'd said I was out of mad, it had apparently been nothing more than the truth. We had our issues, but him cheating on me wasn't one of them. I knew that now and it meant a lot.

"Here." He handed me back the earbud and started playing with my cell again.

"How's Jimmy?" I rolled onto my side, needing to see him. The strong line of his nose and jaw was in profile, the curve of his lips. How many times had I kissed him? Not nearly enough to last me if it never happened again.

"He's doing a lot better. Seems to have really gotten himself right. I think he's going to be okay."

"That's great news."

"At least he comes by his problems honestly," he said, his tone turning bitter. "Our mother is a fucking disaster from what I hear. But then, she always was. She used to take us to the park because she needed to score. She'd turn up to school plays and parent-teacher nights high as a kite."

I kept my mouth shut, letting him get it out. The best thing I could do for him was to be there and listen. The pain and anger in his voice were heartbreaking. My parents had their overbearing issues, certainly, but nothing like this. David's childhood had been terrible. If I could have bitch-slapped his mother right then for putting that pain in his voice, I would have. Twice over.

"Dad ignored her using for years. He could. He was a long-haul truck driver, away most of the time. Jimmy and me were the ones that had to put up with her shit. The number of times we'd come home to find her babbling all sorts of stuff or passed out on the couch. There'd be no food in the house 'cause she'd spent the grocery money on pills. Then one day we came home from school and she and the TV were gone. That was it." He stared up at nothing, his face drawn. "She didn't even leave a note. Now she's back and she's been hurting Jimmy. It drives me nuts."

"That must have been hard for you," I said. "Hearing about her from Jimmy."

One of his shoulders did a little lift. "He shouldn't have had to deal with her on his own. Said he wanted to protect me. Seems my big brother isn't a completely selfish prick."

"Thank you for texting me."

"S'okay. What do you feel like listening to?" The sudden change in topic told me he didn't want to talk about his family anymore. He yawned again, his jaw cracking. "Sorry."

"The Saint Johns."

He nodded, flicking through to find the only song I had of theirs. The strum of the guitar started softly, filling my head. He put the cell on his chest and his eyelids drifted down. A man and a woman took turns singing about their head and their heart. Throughout it, his face remained calm, relaxed. I started to wonder if he'd fallen asleep. But when the song finished, he turned to look at me.

"Nice. A bit sad," he said.

"You don't think they'll be together in the end?"

He rolled onto his side too. There was no more than a hand's width between us. With a curious look, he handed me the cell. "Play me another song you like."

I scrolled through the screens, trying to decide what to play for him. "I forgot to tell you, someone was in saying she'd seen you today. Your anonymity might be about to run out."

He sighed. "Bound to happen sooner or later. They'll just have to get used to me being around."

"You're really not leaving?" I tried to keep my voice light, but it didn't work.

"No. I'm really not." He looked at me and I just knew he saw everything. All of my fears and dreams and the hopes I did my best to keep hidden, even from myself. But I couldn't hide from him if I tried. "Okay?"

"Okay," I said.

"You asked me if you were my attempt at normal. I need you to understand, that's not it at all. Being with you, the way I feel about you, it does ground me. But that's because it makes me question fucking everything. It makes me want to make things better. Makes me want to be better. I can't hide from shit or make excuses when it comes to you, because that won't work. Neither of us is happy when things are that way, and I want you to be happy . . ." His forehead furrowed and his dark brows drew tight. "Do you understand?"

"I think so," I whispered, feeling so much for him right then I didn't know which way was up.

He yawned again, his jaw cracking. "Sorry. Fuck, I'm beat. You mind if I close my eyes for five minutes?"

"No."

He did so. "Play me another song?"

"On it."

I played him "Revelator" by Gillian Welch, the longest, most soothing song I could find. I'd guess he fell asleep about half-way through. His features relaxed and his breathing deepened. Carefully, I pulled out the earbuds and put the cell away. I switched on the bedside lamp and turned off the main one, shut the door so Lauren and Nate's eventual return didn't wake him. Then I lay back down and just stared at him. I don't know for how long. The compulsion to stroke his face or trace his tattoos made my fingers itch, but I didn't want to wake him. He obviously needed the sleep.

When I woke up in the morning, he was gone. Disappointment was a bitter taste. I'd just had the best night's sleep I'd had in weeks, devoid of the usual tense and angsty dreams I seemed to specialize in of late. When had he left? I rolled onto my back and something crinkled, complaining loudly. With a hand, I fished out a piece of paper. It had obviously been torn from one of my notepads. The message was brief but beautiful:

I'm still not leaving Portland.

CHAPTER TWENTY

I think I'd have preferred to find Genghis Khan staring back at me from across the café counter than Martha. I don't know—a Mongol horde versus Martha, tough call. Both were horrible in their own unique ways.

The lunchtime crowd had eased to a few determined patrons, settling in for the afternoon with their lattes and friands. It had been a busy day and Ruby had been distracted, messing up orders. Not like her usual self at all. I'd sat her at a corner table with a pot of tea for a while. Then we'd gotten busy again. When I'd asked what was wrong, she'd just waved me away. Eventually, I'd corner her.

And now here was Martha.

"We need to talk," she said. Her dark hair was tied back and her makeup minimal. There was none of the LA flashiness to her now. If anything, she seemed somber, subdued. Still just a touch smarmy, but hey, this was Martha, after all. And what the hell was she doing here?

"Ruby, is it okay if I take my break?" Jo was out back stocking shelves. She'd just come back from her break, making me due for mine. Ruby nodded, giving Martha a covert evil eye. No matter what was going on with her, Ruby was good people. She recognized a man-stealing sea monster when she saw one.

Martha headed back outside with her nose in the air, and I followed. The usual flow of city traffic cruised by. Overhead, the sky was clear blue, a perfect summer's day. I'd have felt more comfortable if nature had been about to dump a bucketload of rain on top of her perfect head, but it was not to be.

After a brief inspection of the surface, Martha perched on the edge of a bench. "Jimmy called me."

I sat down a little way away from her.

"Apparently he has to apologize to people as part of his rehab process." Perfectly manicured nails tapped at the wooden seat. "It wasn't much of an apology, actually. He told me I needed to come to Portland and clean up the shit I'd caused between you and David."

She stared determinedly ahead. "Things aren't great between Ben and him. I love my brother. I don't want him on the outs with Dave because of me."

"What do you expect me to do here, Martha?"

"I don't expect you to do anything for me. I just want you to listen." She ducked her chin, shut her eyes for a second. "I always figured I could get him back whenever I wanted. After he'd had a few years to calm down, of course. He never got to screw around, we were each other's first. So I just bided my time, let him sow all the wild oats. I was his one true love, right, no matter what I'd done? He was still out there playing those songs about me night after night, wearing our earring even after all those years . . ."

Traffic roared past, people chatted, but Martha and I were apart from it. I wasn't sure I wanted to hear this, but I soaked up every word anyway, desperate to understand.

"Turns out artists can be very sentimental." Her laughter sounded self-mocking. "It doesn't necessarily mean anything." She turned to me, eyes hard, hateful. "I think I was just a habit for him back then. He never gave up a damn thing for me. He sure as hell never moved cities to fit in with what I wanted."

"What do you mean?"

"He's got the album written, Ev. Apparently the new songs are brilliant. The best he's ever done. There's no reason he couldn't be in whatever studio he wanted putting it together, doing what he loves. Instead he's here, recording in some setup a few streets over. Because being close to you means more to him." She rocked forward, her smile harsh. "He's sold the Monterey house, bought a place here. I waited years for him to come back, to have time for me. For you he reorganizes every-thing in the blink of a fucking eye."

"I didn't know," I said, stunned.

"The band is all here. They're recording at a place called the Bent Basement."

"I've heard of it."

"If you're stupid enough to let him go, then you deserve to be miserable for a very long time." The woman looked at me like she had firsthand experience with that situation. She stood, brushed off her hands. "That's me done."

Martha walked away. She disappeared among the crowds of midafternoon shoppers like she'd never been.

David was recording in Portland. He'd said he was working on the new album. I hadn't imagined that meant actually re-cording here. Let alone buying a place.

Holy shit.

I stood and moved in the opposite direction from the one Martha had taken. First I walked, trying to figure out what I was doing, giving my brain a chance to catch up with me. Then I gave it up as a lost cause and ran, dodging pedestrians and café tables, parked cars and whatever. Faster and faster my Doc Martens boots carried me. I found the Bent Basement two blocks over, situated down a flight of stairs, between a micro-brewery and an upmarket dress shop. I slapped my hands against the wood, pushed it open. The unassuming green door was unlocked. Speakers carried the strains of an almighty electric guitar solo through the dark-painted rooms. Sam sat on a sofa, reading a magazine. For once his standard black suit was missing, and he wore slacks and a short-sleeved Hawaiian shirt.

"Mrs. Ferris." He smiled.

"Hi, Sam," I panted, trying to catch my breath. "You look very cool."

He winked at me. "Mr. Ferris is in one of the sound booths at the moment, but if you go through that door there you'll be able to observe."

"Thanks, Sam. Good to see you again."

The thick door led to the soundboard setup. A man I didn't know sat behind it with headphones on. This setup left the small studio at Monterey in the dust. Through the window I could see David playing, his eyes closed, enmeshed with the music. He too wore headphones.

"Hey," Jimmy said quietly. I hadn't realized the rest of them were behind me, lounging, waiting to take their turn.

"Hi, Jimmy."

He gave me a strained smile. His suit was gone. So were the pinprick eyes. "It's good to see you here."

"Thanks." I didn't know what the etiquette was regarding rehab. Should I ask after his health, or sweep the situation under the rug? "And thank you for calling Martha."

"She came to talk to you, huh? Good. I'm glad." He slid his hands into the pockets of his black jeans. "Least I could do. I'm sorry about our previous meetings, Ev. I was . . . not where I should have been. I hope we can move on from that."

Off the drugs, the similarities between him and David were

more pronounced. But his blue eyes and his smile didn't do to me the things David's did. No one else's ever could. Not in five years, not in fifty. For the first time in a long time, I could accept that. I was good with it, even. The epiphanies seemed to be coming thick and fast today.

Jimmy waited patiently for me to come back from wherever I was and say something. When I didn't, he continued on. "I've never had a sister-in-law before."

"I've never had a brother-in-law."

"No? We're useful for all sorts of shit. Just you wait and see."

I smiled and he smiled back at me, far more relaxed this time.

Ben sat on the corner of a black leather lounge, talking with Mal. Mal tipped his chin at me, and I did the same back. All Ben gave me was a worried look. He was still every bit as big and imposing, but he seemed more afraid of me than I was of him today. I nodded hello to him and he returned it, with a tight smile. After talking to Martha, I could understand a little better where he'd been coming from that night. We'd never be besties, but there would be peace for David's sake.

The guitar solo cut off. I turned back to see David watching me, pulling off his headphones. Then he lifted his guitar strap off over his head and headed for the connecting door.

"Hey," he said, coming toward me. "Everything okay?"

"Yes. Can we talk?"

"Sure." He ushered me back into the booth. "Won't be long, Jack."

The man at the board nodded and fiddled with some buttons, turning off the microphones, I assume. He didn't seem overly irritated with the interruption. Instruments and microphones were everywhere. The place was organized chaos. We stood in the corner, out of view of the rest.

"Martha came to see me," I said once he'd closed the door. He stood tall in front of me, blocking out everything else. I rested my back against the wall and looked up at him, still trying to catch my breath. My heart had been calming down after the sprint. Had been. But now he was here and he was so damn close. I put my hands behind my back before they started grabbing at him.

David did the wrinkly brow thing. "Martha?"

"It's okay," I rushed on. "Well, you know, she was her usual self. But we talked."

"About what?"

"You two, mostly. She gave me some things to think about. Are you busy tonight?"

His eyes widened slightly. "No. Would you like to do something?"

"Yeah." I nodded. "I missed you this morning when I woke up, when I realized you'd gone. I've missed you a lot, the last month. I don't think I ever told you that."

He exhaled hard. "No . . . no, you haven't. I missed you too. I'm sorry I couldn't stay this morning."

"Another time."

"Definitely." He took a step closer till the toes of his boots touched mine. No one had ever been more welcome in my personal space. "I'd promised we'd start here early or I would have been there when you woke."

"You didn't tell me about the band recording here."

"We've had other things to deal with. I thought it could wait."

"Right. That makes sense." I stared at the wall beside me, trying to get my thoughts in order. After a whole lot of slow and painful, everything seemed to be happening at once.

". . . About tonight, Ev?"

"Oh, I'm going to dinner at my parents'."

"Am I invited?"

"Yes," I said. "Yes, you are."

"Okay. Great."

"Did you actually buy a house here?"

"A three-bedroom condo a couple of blocks up. I figured it was close to your work and not too far from your school . . . you know, just in case." He studied my face. "Would you like to see it?"

"Wow." I changed the subject to buy some time. "Uh, Jimmy's looking well."

He smiled and put his hands either side of my head, closing the distance between us. "Yeah. He's doing good. Relocating up here is working out well for pretty much everyone. Seems I wasn't the only one ready for a break from all the fuckwittery in LA. Our playing's sharper than it's been in years. We're focusing on the important stuff again."

"That's great."

"Now, what did Martha say to you, baby?"

The endearment came accompanied by the warm old familiar feeling. I almost swayed, I was so grateful. "Well, we talked about you."

"I get that."

"I guess I'm still making sense of everything."

He nodded slowly, leaning in until our noses almost brushed. The perfect intimacy of it, the faint feel of his breath against my face. My need to get close to him had never disappeared. No matter how I'd tried to shut it down. Love and heartbreak made you breathtakingly stupid, desperate, even. The things you'd try to tell yourself to make it through, hoping one day you'd believe it.

"All right," he said. "Anything I can help you with?"

"No. I just wanted to check you were really here, I think."

"I'm here."

"Yes."

"That's not changing, Evelyn."

"No. I think I get that now. I guess I can be a little slow sometimes picking up on these things. I just wasn't sure, you know, with everything that's happened. But I still love you." Apparently I was back to blurting crap out whenever it occurred to me. With David, though, it was okay. I was safe. "I do."

"I know, baby. The question is, when are you going to come back to me?"

"It's really big, you know? It hurt so much when it fell apart last time."

He nodded sadly. "You left me. I think that's about the worst fucking thing I've ever experienced."

"I had to go, but also . . . part of it was me wanting to hurt you like you'd hurt me, I think." I needed to hold his hand again, but I didn't feel like I could. "I don't want to be vindictive like that, not with you, not ever again."

"I said some horrible shit to you that night. Both of us were hurting. We're just going to have to forgive each other and let it go."

"You didn't write a song about it, did you?"

He looked away.

"No! David," I said, aghast. "You can't. That was such a terrible night."

"On a scale of one to ten, how pissed would you be exactly?"

"Where one is divorce?"

He moved his lower body closer, placing his feet between mine. There was no more than a hair's breadth between us. I'd never catch my breath at this rate. Never.

"No," he said, his voice soft. "You don't even remember us getting married, so divorce or annulment or what-the-fuck-ever is not on. It never was. I just told the lawyers to keep looking busy for the last month while I figured things out. Did I forget to mention that?"

"Yeah, you did." I couldn't help but smile at that. "So what's one?"

"One is now. It's this, us living apart and being fucking miserable without each other."

"That is pretty horrible."

"It is," he agreed.

"Is the song a headliner, or are you just going to shove it in somewhere and hope no one notices? It's just a B-side or something, right? Unlisted and hidden at the end?"

"Let's pretend we'd been talking about making one of the songs the name of the album."

"One of them? How much of this brilliant album I've been hearing about is going to be about us?"

"I love you."

"David." I tried to maintain the mock angry, but it didn't work. I didn't have the strength for it.

"Can you trust me?" He asked, his face suddenly serious. "I need you to trust me again. About more than just the songs. Seeing that worry in your eyes all the time is fucking killing me."

"I know." I frowned, knitting my fingers together behind my back. "I'm getting there. And I'll learn to deal with the songs. Really. Music is a big part of who you are, and it's a huge compliment that you feel that strongly for me. I was mostly just teasing."

"I know. And they're not all about us splitting up."

"No?"

"No."

"That's good. I'm glad."

"Mm."

I licked my lips and his eyes tracked the movement. I waited for him to close the distance between us and kiss me. But he didn't and I didn't either. For some reason, it wasn't right to rush this. It should be perfect. Everything between us settled. No people waiting in the next room. Us being this close together, however, hearing the low rumble of his voice, I could have stayed there all day. But Ruby would be wondering what the hell had happened to me. I also had a small errand to run before I returned.

"I'd better get back to work," I said.

"Right." He drew back, slowly. "What time would you like me to pick you up tonight?"

"Ah, seven?"

"Sounds good." A shadow passed over his face. "Do you think your parents will like me?"

I took a deep breath and let it go. "I don't know. It doesn't matter. I like you."

"You do?"

I nodded.

The light in his eyes was like the sun rising. My knees trembled and my heart quaked. It was powerful and beautiful and perfect.

"That's all that matters, then," he said.

CHAPTER TWENTY-ONE

My parents hadn't liked him. For the better part of the meal they'd ignored David's presence. Every time they blatantly passed him over, I'd opened my mouth to object and David's foot would nudge mine beneath the table. He'd given me a small shake of the head. I'd sat and steamed, my anger growing by the moment. Things had long since moved beyond awkward, though Lauren had done her best to cover the silences.

David, for his part, had gone all out, wearing a gray button-down shirt with the sleeves secured to his wrists. It covered the bulk of his tattoos. Black jeans and plain black boots completed his meet-the-parents wardrobe. Considering he'd refused to dress up for a ballroom full of Hollywood royalty, I was impressed. He'd even poofed up his hair into a vaguely James Dean do. On most men I would not have liked it. David was not most men. Frankly, he looked gosh-almighty awesome, even with the fading bruises beneath his eyes. And the gracious manner with which he dealt with my parents' abysmal behavior only reinforced my belief in him. My pride that he'd chosen to be with me. But back to the dinner conversation.

Lauren was giving a detailed synopsis of her plans for classes for the upcoming semester. My dad nodded and listened intently, asking all the appropriate questions. Nate's falling for her was beyond my parents' wildest dreams. She'd been a de facto part of the family for a long time now. They couldn't have been more delighted. But more than that, she seemed to make them take a look at their son anew, noticing the changes in him. When Lauren talked about Nate's work and his responsibilities, they listened.

Meanwhile, David was only on the other side of the table, but I missed him. There was so much to talk about that I didn't know where to start. And hadn't we already talked over the bulk of it? So what was the problem? I had the strangest sensation that something was wrong, something was slipping away from me. David had moved to Portland. All would be well. But it wasn't. Classes started back soon. The threat of the plan still hung over my head because I allowed it to.

"Ev? Is something wrong?" Dad sat at one end of the table, his face drawn with concern.

"No, Dad," I said, my smile full of gritted teeth. There'd been no mention of my hanging up on him. I suspected it had been chalked up to brokenhearted girl rage or something similar.

Dad frowned, first at me and then at David. "My daughter goes back to school next week."

"Ah, yes," said David. "She did mention that, Mr. Thomas."

My father studied David from over the top of his glasses. "Her studies are very important."

A cold kind of panic gripped me as the horror unrolled right before my eyes. "Dad. Stop."

"Yes, Mr. Thomas," said David. "I have no intention of interrupting them."

"Good." Dad steepled his hands in front of him, settling in to give a lecture. "But the fact is, young women imagining themselves in love have a terrible tendency to not think."

"Dad—"

My dad held up a hand to stop me. "Ever since she was a little girl, she's planned to become an architect."

"Okay. No."

"What if you go on tour, David?" my father asked, continuing despite my commotion. "As you inevitably will. Do you expect her to drop everything and just follow you?"

"That would be up to your daughter, sir. But I don't plan on doing anything to make her have to choose between me and school. Whatever she wants to do, she's got my support."

"She wants to be an architect," Dad said, his tone absolute. "This relationship has already cost her dearly. She had an important internship canceled when all of this nonsense happened. It's set her back considerably."

I pushed back, rising from my chair. "That's enough."

Dad gave me the same glare he'd first dealt David, hostile and unwelcome. He looked at me like he no longer recognized me.

"I won't have you throwing away your future for him," he thundered.

"Him?" I asked, horrified at his tone. Anger had been pooling inside of me all night, filling me up. No wonder I'd barely touched my dinner. "The person you've both been unconscionably rude to for the past hour? David is the last person who would expect me to throw away anything that mattered to me."

"If he cared for you, he would walk away. Look at the damage he's done." A vein bulged on the side of my father's forehead as he stood too. Everyone else watched in stunned silence. It could be said I'd gone the bulk of my life backing down. But those had all been about things that didn't matter, not really. This was different.

"You're wrong."

"You're out of control," my father snarled, pointing his finger at me.

"No," I said to my father. Then I turned and said what I should have said a long time ago to my husband. "No, I'm not. What I am is the luckiest fucking girl in the entire world."

A smile lit David's eyes. He sucked in his bottom lip, trying to keep the happy contained in the face of my parents' fury.

"I am," I said, tearing up and not even minding for once.

He pushed back his chair and rose to his feet, facing me across the table. The promise of unconditional love and support in his eyes was all the answer I needed. And in that one perfect moment, I knew everything was fine. We were fine. We always would be if we stuck together. There wasn't a single doubt inside of me. In silence, he walked around the table and stood at my side.

The look on my parents' faces . . . whoa. They always said it was best to rip the Band-Aid off all at once, though, get it over and done with. So I did.

"I don't want to be an architect." The relief in finally saying it was staggering. I'm almost certain my knees knocked. There'd be no backing down, however. David took my hand in his, gave it a squeeze.

My father just blinked at me. "You don't mean that."

"I'm afraid I do. It was your dream, Dad. Not mine. I should never have gone along with this. That was my mistake and I'm sorry."

"What will you do?" asked my mother, her voice rising. "Make coffee?"

"Yes."

"That's ridiculous. All that money we spent—" Mom's eyes flashed in anger.

"I'll pay it back."

"This is insane," Dad said, his face going pale. "This is about him."

"No. This is about me, actually. David just made me start questioning what I really wanted. He made me want to be a better person. Lying about this, trying to fit in with your plan for so long . . . I was wrong to do that."

My father glared at me. "I think you should leave now, Evelyn. Think this over carefully. We'll talk about it later."

I guessed we would, but it wouldn't change anything. My good-girl status had well and truly taken a dive.

"You forgot to tell her that whatever she decides, you still love her." Nathan got to his feet, pulling out Lauren's chair for her. He faced my father with his jaw set. "We'd better go too."

"She knows that." Face screwed up in confusion, Dad stood at the head of the table.

Nate grunted. "No, she doesn't. Why do you think she fell into line for so many years?"

Mom knotted her hands.

"That's ridiculous," sputtered Dad.

"No, he's right," I said. "But I guess everyone has to grow up sometime."

Dad's eyes turned even colder. "Being an adult is not about turning your back on your responsibilities."

"Following in your footsteps is not my responsibility," I said, refusing to back down. The days of my doing that were gone. "I can't be you. I'm sorry I wasted so many years and so much of your money figuring that out."

"We only want what's best for you," said Mom, voice thick with emotion.

"I know you do. But that's for me to decide now." I turned

back to my husband, keeping a firm hold on his hand. "And my husband isn't going anywhere. You need to accept that."

Nate walked around the table, gave Mom a kiss. "Thanks for dinner."

"One day," she said, looking between the both of us, "when you have your own children, then you'll understand how hard it is."

Her words pretty much wrapped things up. My dad just kept shaking his head and huffing out breaths. I felt guilty for disappointing them. But not bad enough to return to my former ways. I'd finally reached an age where I understood that my parents were people too. They weren't perfect or omnipotent. They were every bit as fallible as me. It was my job to judge what was right.

I picked up my handbag. It was time to go.

David nodded to both my parents and escorted me out. A sleek new silver Lexus Hybrid sat waiting by the curb. It wasn't a big SUV like the ones Sam and the other bodyguards used. This one came in a more user-friendly size. Behind us, Nate and Lauren climbed into his car. Nothing much was said. Mom and Dad stood in the house's open doorway, dark silhouettes from the light behind them. David opened the door for me and I climbed into the passenger seat.

"I'm sorry about my father. Are you upset?" I asked.

"No." He shut my door and walked around to the driver's side.

"No? That's it?"

He shrugged. "He's your dad. Of course he's going to be concerned."

"I thought you might have been running for the hills by now with all the drama."

He flicked on the indicator and pulled out onto the road. "Did you really?"

"No. Sorry, that was a stupid thing to say." I watched my old neighborhood passing by, the park I'd played in and the path I'd taken to school. "So I'm a college dropout."

He gave me curious glance. "How does that feel?"

"God, I don't know." I shook my hands, rubbed them together. "Tingly. My toes and hands feel tingly. I don't know what I'm doing."

"Do you know what you want to do?"

"No. Not really."

"But you know what you don't want to do?"

"Yes," I answered definitely.

"Then there's your starting point."

A full moon hung heavy in the sky. The stars twinkled on. And I'd just upended my entire existence. Again. "You're now officially married to a college dropout who makes coffee for a living. Does that bother you?"

With a sigh, David flicked on the indicator and pulled over in front of a neat row of suburban houses. He picked up one of my hands, pressing it gently between both of his. "If I wanted to quit the band, would that bother you?"

"Of course not. That's your decision."

"If I wanted to give all the money away, what would you say?"

I shrugged. "You made the money, it's your choice. I guess you'd have to come live with me then. And I'm telling you now, the apartment we'd have on my salary alone would be small. Minuscule. Just so you know."

"But you'd still take me in?"

"Without question." I covered one of his hands with my

own, needing to borrow a bit of his strength just then. "Thank you for being there tonight."

Little creases lined his perfect dark blue eyes. "I didn't even say anything."

"You didn't have to."

"You called me your husband."

I nodded, my heart stuck in my throat.

"I didn't kiss you at the studio today because it felt like there was still too much up in the air between us. It didn't feel right. But I want to kiss you now."

"Please," I said.

He leaned into me and I met him halfway. His mouth covered mine, lips warm and firm and familiar. The only ones I wanted or needed. His hands cupped my face, holding me to him. The kiss was so sweet and perfect. It was a promise, one that wouldn't be broken this time. We'd both learned from our mistakes and we'd keep learning all our lives. That was marriage.

His fingers eased into my hair and I stroked my tongue against his. The taste of him was as necessary to me as air. The feel of his hands on me was the promise of everything to come. What started out as an affirmation turned into more at light speed. The groan that came out of him. Holy hell. I wanted to hear that noise for the rest of my life. My hands dragged at his shirt, trying to pull him closer. We had some serious time to make up for.

"We have to stop," he whispered.

"We do?" I asked, in between panting breaths.

"Sadly." He chuckled, nudged the tip of my nose with his. "Soon, my luckiest fucking girl in the world. Soon. Did you really have to throw the 'fucking' in there?"

"I really did."

"Your parents looked about ready to have kittens."

"I'm so sorry about the way they treated you." I ran my fingers over the spiky short dark hair on the side of his head, feeling the bristles.

"I can deal."

"You shouldn't have to. You won't have to. I'm not sitting by and—"

He shut down my rant by kissing me. Of course, it worked. His tongue played over my teeth, teasing me. I undid my seat belt and crawled into his lap, needing to get closer. Nobody kissed like David. His hands slipped beneath my top, molding to the curves of my breasts. Thumbs stroked my nipples. The poor things were so damn hard it hurt. Talking of which, I could feel David's erection pressing into my hip. We kept our lips locked until a car full of kids went by, horn blaring. Apparently our makeout session was somewhat visible from the street despite the fogged-up windows. Classy.

"Soon," he promised, his breathing harsh against my neck. "Fuck, it's good to get you alone. That was intense. But I'm proud of you for standing up for yourself. You did good."

"Thank you. You think we'll understand when we have kids, like my mom said?"

He looked up at me, his beautiful face and serious eyes so wonderfully familiar I could cry.

"We've never talked about kids," he said. "Do you want them?"

"One day. Do you?"

"One day, yeah. After we've had a few years' worth of alone time."

"Sounds good," I said. "You going to show me this condo of yours?"

"Of ours. Absolutely."

"I think you're going to need to take your hands out of my top if you're planning on driving us there."

"Mm. Pity." He gave my breasts a final squeeze before slipping his hands free of my clothing. "And you're going to have to hop back into your seat."

"Okeydokey."

His hands wrapped around my hips, helping me climb back over to my side of the vehicle. I refastened my seat belt while he took a deep breath. With a wince he adjusted himself, obviously trying to get more comfortable. "You're a terror."

"Me? What did I do?"

"You know what you did," he grouched, pulling back out onto the road.

"I don't know what you're talking about."

"Don't you give me that," he said, giving me a narrow-eyed look. "You did it in Vegas and then you did it in Monterey and LA too. Now you're doing it in Portland. I can't take you anywhere."

"Are you talking about the state of your fly? Because I'm not the one in control of your reactions to me, buddy. You are."

He barked out a laugh. "I've never been in control of my reactions to you. Not once."

"Is that why you married me? Because you were helpless against me?"

"You make me tremble in fear, rest assured." The smile he gave me made me tremble, and fear had nothing to do with it. "But I married you, Evelyn, because you made sense to me. We make sense. We're a whole lot better together than apart. You notice that?"

"Yeah, I really did."

"Good." His fingers stroked over my cheekbone. "We need to get home. Now."

I'm pretty sure he broke several speed limits on the drive. The condo was only a couple of blocks back from Ruby's café. It was located in a big old brown-brick building with Art Deco stonework surrounding the glass double doors. David punched in a code and led me into a white marble lobby. A statue of what looked like driftwood stood tall in the corner. Security cameras hid in the ceiling corners. He didn't give me time to look, rushing me through. I practically had to run to keep up with him.

"Come on," he said, tugging on my hand, drawing me into the elevator.

"This is all very impressive."

He pushed the button for the top floor. "Wait till you see our place. You're moving in with me now, right?"

"Right."

"Ah, we've got some visitors at the moment, by the way. Just while we record the album and all that. A few more weeks, probably." The elevator doors slid open and we stepped into the hall. At which point David took my handbag from me. Then he bent and set his shoulder to my stomach, lifting me high. "Here we are."

"Hey," I squeaked.

"I got you. Time to get carried over the threshold again."

"David, I'm wearing a skirt." It nearly went to my knees, but still. I'd rather not flash his guests and band members if I could avoid it.

"I know you are. Have I thanked you for that yet? I really appreciate having that easy access." His black boots thumped along the marble flooring. I took the opportunity to grope his ass because I was allowed to. My life was fucking fantastic like that.

"You're not wearing any underwear," I informed him.

"That so?"

A hand felt up my rear. Over my clothing, thankfully.

"You are," he said, voice low and growly in the best way possible. "Which ones you wearing, baby? Boy shorts by the feel."

"I don't think you've seen these."

"Yeah, well we're gonna change that real soon. Trust me."

"I do."

I heard the sound of a door opening, and the marble beneath me turned to a glossy, black-painted wooden floor. The walls were a pristine white. And I could hear male voices, laughing and trash-talking nearby. Music played in the background, Nine Inch Nails, I think. Nate had been playing his music at the apartment and they were a favorite of his. Of course the condo looked amazing. There were dark wooden dining room chairs and green couches. Plenty of space. Guitar cases were strewn about the place. From what I could see, it looked beautiful and lived in. It looked like a home.

Our home.

"You kidnapped a girl. That's awesome but illegal, Davie. You're probably going to have to give her back." My hair was lifted and Mal appeared, crouched beside me. "Hey there, child bride. Where's my hello kiss?"

"Leave my wife alone, you dickwad." David lifted one booted foot and negligently pushed him aside. "Go get your own."

"Why the fuck would I want to get married? That's for crazy folk like you two fine people. And while I applaud your insanity, no goddamn way am I following in your footsteps."

"Who the fuck would have him?" Jimmy's smoother voice moved up alongside me. "Hey, Ev."

"Hi, Jimmy." I took a hand off the seat of my husband's jeans and waved at him. "David, do I have to stay upside down?"

"Ah, right. It's date night," my husband announced.

"Got it," Mal said. "Come on, Jimmy. We'll go find Benny-boy. He was going to that Japanese place for a bite."

"Right." Jimmy's sneakers headed for the door. "Later, guys."

"Bye!" I gave him another wave.

"Night, Evvie." Mal left too, and the door slammed shut behind them.

"Alone at last." David sighed and started moving again, down a long hallway. With me still over his shoulder. "You like the place?"

"What I can see of it is lovely."

"That's good. I'll show you the rest later. First things first, I really need to get into those panties of yours."

"I don't think they'd fit you." I giggled. He slapped me on the ass. White-hot lightning, though it was more of a shock than anything. "Christ, David."

"Just warming you up, funny girl." He turned into the last room at the end of the hallway, kicked the door shut. My handbag was thrown into a chair. Without a word of warning, he upended me onto a king-size bed. My body bounced on the mattress. The blood was rushing around in my head, making it spin. I pushed my hair out of my face and rose up onto my elbows.

"Don't move," he said, voice guttural.

He stood at the end of the bed, undressing. The most amazing sight in existence. I could watch him do this always. He reached back and pulled off his shirt and I knew bone deep I wasn't the luckiest fucking girl in the world. I was the luckiest fucking girl in the entire universe. That was the truth. Not just because he was beyond beautiful and I was the only one that got to see him do this, but the way he watched me through hooded eyes the entire time. Lust was there, but also a whole lot of love.

"You have no idea how often I've imagined you lying on that bed in the last week." He pulled off his boots and socks, tossing them aside. "How many times I nearly called you in the last month."

"Why didn't you?"

"Why didn't you?" he asked, undoing the top button on his jeans.

"Let's not do that again."

"No. Never." He crawled onto the bed, smoothing his hands down my calf muscles. My shoes went flying and his fingers slipped beneath my skirt, easing it up, higher and higher. Without breaking eye contact, he dragged down my boy shorts. He obviously wasn't interested in checking out my panties after all. The man had priorities. "Tell me you love me."

"I love you."

"Again."

"I love you."

"I missed the taste of you so fucking much." Big hands parted my legs, exposing me to his gaze. "I might just spend a few days with my head between your legs, all right?"

Oh, God. He rubbed his beard against my inner thigh, making my skin prickle with awareness. I couldn't speak if I tried.

"Say it again."

I swallowed hard, trying to get myself back under control.

"I'm waiting."

"I l-love you," I stuttered, my voice sounded barely there, breathy. My pelvis almost shot off the bed at the first touch of his mouth. Every bit of me was wound tight and trembling.

"Keep going." His tongue parted the lips of my sex, sliding between before delving within. The sweet, firm feel of his mouth and the ticklish sensation of his beard.

"I love you."

Strong hands slid beneath my ass, holding me to his mouth. "More."

I groaned out something. It must have been enough. He didn't stop or speak again. David attacked me. There was nothing easy about it. His mouth worked me hard, driving me sky-high in a matter of moments. The knot inside me tightened and grew as his tongue laved me. Electricity streaked up my spine. I don't know when I started shaking. But the strength went out of me and my back hit the mattress once again. I fisted my hands in his hair, fingers gripping at the short, gelled strands.

It was almost too much. I didn't know if I needed to get closer or get away. Either way, his hands held me to him. Every muscle in me tensed and my mouth opened on a soundless cry. Fireworks filled my mind. I came and came.

When my heart eased up on the hammering, I opened my eyes. David knelt between my legs. His jeans had been pushed down and his erection grazed his flat stomach. Dark blue eyes stared down at me.

"I can't wait."

"No. Don't." I tightened my legs around his hips. One of his hands remained beneath my ass, holding me high. With the other, he guided himself into me. He didn't rush. We were both still at least half dressed, him on the bottom and me on the top. There was no time to waste. We were too needy to wait and do this skin to skin. Next time.

He entered me so slowly I couldn't breathe. The only thing that mattered was feeling. And God, the feel of him thick and hard pushing inside of me. The perspiration on his bare chest gleamed in the low lighting. The muscles in his shoulders stood out in stark relief as he began to move.

"Mine," he said.

I could only nod.

He looked down on me, watching my breasts jiggle beneath my top with each thrust. Fingers gripped my hips hard. Mine clutched at the bedding, trying to find purchase so I could push back against him. His expression was wild, mouth swollen and wet. Only this was real, me and him together. Everything else could come and go. I'd found what was worth fighting for.

"I love you."

"C'mere." He picked me up off the mattress, holding me tight again him. My legs were braced around his waist, muscles burning from how hard I'd been holding on. I wound my arms around his neck as he sat me on his cock.

"I love you too." His hands slid beneath the back of my top. We moved harshly together. Our furious breaths mingled into one. Sweat slicked both our skins, the fabric of my shirt sticking to me. The heat gathered low inside me again. It didn't take long in this position. Not with the way he ground himself against me. His mouth sucked at the section of skin where my neck met my body, and I shuddered in his arms, coming again. The noises he made and the way he said my name . . . I never wanted to forget. Not a moment of it.

Eventually, he laid us both back on the bed. I wasn't willing to let him go, so he covered my body with his. The weight of him pressing me down into the bed, the feel of his mouth on the side of my face. We should never move. In the best-case scenario, we'd just stay like this forever.

But actually, I did have something I had to do.

"I need my bag," I said, squirming beneath him.

"What for?" He rose up on his elbows.

"I have to do something."

"What could be more important than this?"

"Roll over," I said, already urging him in that direction.

"All right. But this had better be good." He relaxed and let me roll him. I scampered across the mattress, trying to tug my skirt back down at the same time. David must have liked what he saw, because he came after me with snapping teeth.

"Get back here, wife," he ordered.

"Give me a second."

"My name looks good on your ass," he said. "The tattoo has healed very nicely."

"Well, thank you." I finally got off the mattress and set my pencil skirt to rights. In the month we'd been apart, I'd ignored my ink. But now, I was glad it was there.

"That skirt's coming off."

"Just wait."

"And that top. We have a lot more making up to do."

"Yes, in a minute. I've missed my topless cuddles."

He'd dumped my bag on a blue velvet wing-back chair by the door. Whoever had decorated the condo had done a hell of a job. It was beautiful. But I'd check it out later. Right now I had something important to do.

"I bought you a present today, after we talked at the studio."

"Did you, now?"

I nodded, searching my bag for the treasure. Bingo. The fancy little box was right where I'd left it. With it hidden in my hand, I walked back to him, a wide smile on my face. "Yes, I did."

"What have you got in your hand?" He climbed off the bed. Unlike me, he stripped off his jeans. My husband stood before me naked and perfectly disheveled. He looked at me like I was everything. As long as I lived, I knew I wouldn't want anyone else.

"Evelyn?"

For some reason I felt suddenly shy, awkward. Any money, the tips of my ears glowed bright pink.

"Give me your left hand." I reached for his hand and he

gave it to me. Carefully I slid on the thick platinum band I'd blown my savings on that afternoon, working it past his big knuckle. Perfect. I'd walk all winter and freeze my ass off, happily. David meant more to me than replacing my crappy old car. Given the money I now owed my parents, the timing wasn't brilliant. But this was more important.

Except the ring covered half of the second-to-last *E* on his *Live Free* tattoo. Shit, I hadn't thought of that. He probably wasn't going to want to wear it.

"Thank you."

My gaze darted to his face, trying to judge his sincerity. "You like it?"

"I fucking love it."

"Really? Because I forgot about your ink, but—"

He shut me up by kissing me. I kind of liked his new habit of doing that. His tongue stroked into my mouth and my eyes slid shut, every worry forgotten. He kissed me until not a single doubt remained as to how taken with his ring he was. Fingers fussed with the buttons on my top, slipping it off my shoulders. Next the band on my bra loosened.

"I love my ring," he said, his lips traveling over my jaw and down my neck. My bra straps slid down my arms and my breasts were free. Next he started in on my skirt, wrestling with the zip and pushing it down over my hips. He didn't stop until I was every bit as bare as him. "I'm never taking it off."

"I'm glad you like it."

"I do. And I need to get you naked right now and show you how much I like it. But then I'll give you back your ring. I promise."

"No rush," I murmured, arching my neck to give him better access. "We've got forever."

CHAPTER TWENTY-TWO

We'd planned to meet Amanda, Jo, and a few other friends at one of the local bars the next night. My insides were in a permanent state of upheaval. Excited and nervous and a hundred other emotions I couldn't begin to process. But not doubtful. Never that. I'd talked to Ruby about continuing on with the extra shifts at the café and she'd been delighted. It turned out her distraction the previous day had been on account of her finding out she was pregnant. My dropping out of college couldn't come at a better time as far as she was concerned. Eventually I'd go back to school. I liked the idea of teaching, maybe. I don't know. There was time.

The bar was one of the smaller ones, not far from our new home. A four-piece rock band on the small corner stage played grunge classics interspersed with a few new songs. Jo waved us over to a table out of the way. Meeting David was obviously big for her. Puppies jumped less.

"David. It's so great," she said over and over. That was about it. If she started to hump his leg, I was stepping in.

Amanda, on the other hand, needed to turn that frown upside down. At least, unlike my parents', her protest was silent. I appreciated her concern, but she'd just have to get used to David being around.

David ordered drinks for us and settled into a seat pulled up beside me. The music was really too loud for conversation. Soon afterward, Nate and Lauren arrived. A fragile peace had emerged between my brother and my husband, for which I was profoundly grateful.

David shuffled closer. "I wanna ask you something."

"What?"

He slipped a hand around my waist, drawing me closer. I did the job better by simply planting myself in his lap. With a warm smile, his arms wound around me, holding me tight. "Hey."

"Hey," I said. "What did you want to ask me?"

"I was wondering . . . would you like to hear one of the songs I wrote for you?"

"Really? I'd love to."

"Excellent," he said, his hand smoothing over the back of my simple black dress. Worn because it was his favorite color, of course. Also, I'd strongly suspected the V-neck would appeal to him. Tonight, I was all about pleasing my husband. There'd no doubt be times in the future when we needed to kick each other's asses, but not tonight. We were here to celebrate.

Lauren led Nate out onto the dance floor and Amanda and Jo followed, abandoning us to our private talk. I honest to God had the best brother and friends in the whole wide world. All of them had taken the news of the plan going boom with calm faces. They had hugged me, and not one word of doubt over my sudden change in direction had been voiced. When Lauren recounted her version of how David stood beside me at dinner, I'd caught Amanda giving him a nod of approval. It gave me great hope.

I'd even called my mother earlier. The conversation had been brief, but I was glad I had. We were still family.

David had eventually given me my ring back the night before. Turned out his list of things to do to me was long. He fed me ice cream in bed for breakfast while the sun rose. Best night ever.

It felt right having the ring back on my hand. The weight and fit of it were perfect. As promised, his own had stayed put. He'd been proudly showing it to his brother when I'd stumbled out in search of coffee at midday. Once I'd been caffeinated, David and Jimmy had moved me into the condo. Mal and Ben had been busy at the studio. Nate and Lauren had helped move me too, once David and Jimmy finished signing everything Divers-related she could find. Despite her protestations that she'd miss me, I think she was also looking forward to having the apartment for her and Nate alone. They were good together.

"I've got something else I want to ask you too," he said.

"The answer is yes to everything and anything with you."

"Good, because I want you to come work for me as my assistant. When you're not working at the café, I mean." His hand rubbed down my back. " 'Cause I know you wanna do that."

"David . . ."

"Or you could just let me pay the college money back to your parents so that's not hanging over your head."

"No," I said, my voice determined. "Thank you. But I need to do that. And I think my parents are going to need to see me doing that."

"That's what I figured you'd say. But that's a lot of money for you to make, baby. If you take a second job we're never going to see each other."

"You're right. But do you think that's a wise idea, us working together?"

"Yeah," he told me, blue eyes serious. "You like organizing and that's what I need. It's a real job and I want you for it. If we find it starts to interfere with us, then we'll make a new plan. But I think mostly it'll just mean we spend more time together and have sex at work."

I laughed. "You promising to sexually harass me, Mr. Ferris?"

"Absolutely, Mrs. Ferris."

I kissed him soundly on the cheek. "Thank you for thinking of it. I'd love to work for you."

"If you decide to go back to college, then I'll get Adrian to find me a replacement. Not a big deal." He pulled me in against his chest. "But in the meantime, we're good."

"Best plan ever."

"Why, thank you. Coming from you, that means a lot."

David's gaze wandered over to the bar where Mal, Jimmy, and Ben were hanging out, keeping a low profile. I hadn't known they were joining us tonight. Jimmy had been steering clear of clubs and bars. "About time they got here," he murmured.

Next David turned to the band, rocking out in the corner. They were just in the process of winding up a solid rendition of a Pearl Jam classic.

"Wait here." David rose, taking me with him. He placed me back on the chair and signaled to his bandmates. Then he made his way toward the stage. His tall figure moved through the crowd with ease and the guys fell in behind him. En masse, they were pretty damn impressive. No matter how low-key they were trying to be. But I got the distinct feeling they were about to make their presence known. Once the band finished the song, David called the singer over. Holy shit. This was it. I bounced in my chair from excitement.

They talked for a moment, then the singer brought the

guitarist into it. Sure enough, the man gave his six-string over to David's waiting hands. I could see the look of surprise on both their faces as David's identity finally sank in. Jimmy gave the singer a nod and stepped up onto the platform. Behind him, Mal was already high-fiving the drummer and stealing his sticks. Even grim Ben smiled as he accepted the bass guitar from its original owner. The Divers took to the stage. Few in the bar seemed to realize quite what was going on yet.

"Hi. Sorry to interrupt, folks. My name's David Ferris and I'd like to play a song for my wife, Evelyn. Hope you don't mind."

Stunned silence broke out into thunderous applause. David stared at me across the sea of people as everyone swamped the dance floor to get closer.

"She's a Portland girl. So I guess that makes us in-laws. Be gentle with me, yeah?"

The crowd went batshit crazy in response. His hands moved over the strings, making the sweetest mix of rock and country music possible. Then he started to sing. Jimmy joined him for the chorus, their voices melding beautifully.

I thought I could let you go
I thought that you could leave and know
The time we took would fade
But I'm colder than the bed where we lay

You let go if you like, I'll hold on
Say no all you want, I'm not done
Baby, I promise you

Did you think I'd let you go?
That's never happening and now you know

Take your time, I'll wait
Regretting every last thing I said

The song was simple, sweet, and perfect. And the noise when they finished was deafening. People shouted and stamped their feet. It sounded like the roof was coming down on us. Security helped David and the guys move through the crush of people. More had arrived as they performed, alerted to the show by texts and calls and each and every sort of social media. A tidal wave of fans swamped them as they pressed through. A hand wrapped around my arm. I looked up to find Sam beside me with a grin on his face. We got our asses out of there pronto.

Sam and the security men cleared a path for us to the door and the waiting limousine outside. They were well prepared. We all bundled into the back of the limo. Immediately, David pulled me onto his lap. "Sam's going to make sure your friends are okay."

"Thank you. I think Portland knows you're here now."

"Yeah, I think you're right."

"Davie, you are a fucking show pony," Mal said, shaking his head. "I knew you were going to pull something like this. Guitarists are such a bunch of posers. If you had an ounce of sense, young lady, you'd have married a drummer."

I laughed and wiped the tears from my face.

"Why the fuck is she crying, what did you say to her?" David pulled me in closer. Outside people banged on the windows as the car slowly started moving forward.

"Are you okay?"

"I told her the truth, that she should have married a drummer. Impromptu fucking performances!" said Mal.

"Shut up."

"Like you've never gone all out to impress a girl," scoffed Ben.

"What happened in Tokyo?" asked Jimmy, reclining in the corner. "Remind me again about, ah . . . what was her name?"

"Oh shit, yeah. The chick from the restaurant," said Ben. "How much did they charge you for the damages, again?"

"I don't even know what you're talking about. Davie said to shut up," shouted Mal above the pair's raucous laughter. "Have some respect for his touching moment with Evelyn, you assholes."

"Ignore them." David cupped my face in the palm of his hand. "Why were you crying, hmm?"

"Because this is ten. If one was us being miserable and apart, then ten is your song. It's beautiful."

"You really liked it? 'Cause I can take it if you didn't, you don't have—"

I grabbed his face and kissed him, ignoring the noise and heckling around us. And I didn't stop kissing him until my lips were numb and swollen and so were his.

"Baby." He smiled, wiping away the last of my tears. "You say the best fucking things."

extracts reading groups
competitions books new
discounts extracts
competitions
books new
events books
new extracts titles reading groups
interviews
events extracts
discounts
new books events
events new
discounts extracts discounts
www.panmacmillan.com
extracts events reading groups
competitions books extracts new

SIX DAYS
OF THE
CONDOR

JAMES GRADY

NO EXIT PRESS

This edition published in 2015 by No Exit Press,
PO Box 394, Harpenden, Herts, AL5 1XJ, UK

Noexit.co.uk

2 4 6 8 10 9 7 5 3

Typeset by Avocet Typeset, Somerton, Somerset
in 13.5pt Bembo
Printed in Great Britain by Clays Ltd, St Ives plc

For more information about Crime Fiction go to @crimetimeuk

Six Days of the Condor was originally dedicated to Rick Applegate, Shirley Hodgson, and my parents – Tom and Donna Grady. Without their emotional support, the young man I was might never have created Condor. This volume merges past and present. Such a revision requires an addition to the original crew of dedicatees. Along with them, this one is for my wife Bonnie Goldstein, my children Rachel and Nathan.

Thanks for sharing my ride.

rhyme

rhyme

rhyme

by

James Grady

"History doesn't repeat itself, but it does rhyme."

Mark Twain

Every fiction is cradled by history – the history it portrays, the history into which it is born, the history during which it is subsequently discovered by each one of us.

This volume brings together two fictions created 30 years apart, and though they are linked by the obvious elements of author, plot, character, setting and theme, their defining link is captured by Mark Twain's observation that *history rhymes.*

Six Days of the Condor is my first novel, perhaps better known by the title of its adapted 1975 Robert Redford movie, *Three Days of the Condor.*

condor.net is the short story I wrote 30 years later after being ambushed by Mark Twain's "rhyme" of history.

But begin at the beginning.

I was 24 the year I wrote the novel *Six Days of the Condor* on a battered manual typewriter. It was 1973. Civilization swirled in the Cold War while Americans my age fought and died in an unpopular "conflict" chewing up thousands of lives in Southeast Asia. Assassins of political leaders proved that anybody could be murdered. Nixon was President, while a Texan named George Bush served Nixon as Ambassador to the United Nations, then head of Nixon's political party; that Bush later went on to

9

run the CIA and become President of the United States. Back in 1973, newspapers alleged wrongdoings launched from the White House. A massive U.S. internal security apparatus hunted illusive enemies while the CIA fought them overseas. The world declared itself in an energy crisis with oil being likened to blood.

Only the crazy did not feel fear.

Love and danger are the strongest intoxicants for a writer's imagination. Like most young men, I knew little about love. Luckily, I knew enough not to indulge my ignorance in my prose.

But danger … In those electric times, a young writer with a fevered imagination needed to know very little to snatch a tale out of the air around him.

I wrote *Six Days of the Condor* in four months, working a "day job" in the state of Montana and typing my heart out nights and weekends, approaching my first novel like the journalist I'd been schooled to be. I didn't know how ridiculous it was to dream that I could write a book that would be published. In truth, the long odds of reality didn't matter. I had no choice about being a writer, about writing. I'd dictated stories to my mother when I was four (she threw them away), and after half a dozen years of unsuccessfully bombarding magazines with poems and short stories, writing a novel seemed to be my next inevitable step.

Good fiction is an ambush for both reader and author.

I walked the battleground that begat Condor a little more than a year before I started pounding my keyboard: 1971. I was a college senior, one of twenty Woodstock warriors brought on a national fellowship from America's hinterland universities to the wonders of Washington,

D.C., there to work days on Congressional staffs and to be taught at night by a new genre of journalists called "investigative reporters."

I lived on A Street, Southeast, six blocks from the white icing Capitol dome that looked even grander than it had on my high school civics textbook. I rented a third floor garret in a massive row house. A seldom-seen man rented the other unit on my floor. We shared a bathroom. At night, through the thin walls, I heard him coughing and wheezing.

Every workday, I put on a cheap suit and a tan overcoat, walked through winter streets to my beloved job on the staff of populist U.S. Senator Lee Metcalf (D-Montana).

And every workday, I walked past a blockish, flat fronted, white stucco townhouse set back from the corner of A and Fourth Streets. A short, black-iron fence marked the border of the public sidewalk and that building's domain. Blinds obscured the windows. Then as now, a bronze plaque by the solid door proclaimed the building as the headquarters of the eminently respectable American Historical Association.

But I never saw anyone go in or out of that building.

Then, as I walked to work one gray day, a sniper's bullet cracked my skull: *Wouldn't it be great if that building were a CIA front?*

Wounded, reeling, I fell into the era's paranoia. *What if when I came back from lunch, everyone in my office had been murdered?*

It could happen to anyone.

But if it happened to a spy...

My fantasy about a covert CIA office on Congress's Capitol Hill was not without foundation in reality. In those days, a flat-faced, gray concrete building with an always-closed garage door and a windowless, locked entrance sat amidst colorful liquor stores, restaurants and bookstores along the strip of Pennsylvania Avenue that angled out from the Capitol and House office buildings. No sign identified that concrete edifice to the Congressional aides and tourists strolling past it every day, but several thousand of us *Washington insiders* shared the secret that the building belonged to J. Edgar Hoover's notorious *Big Brother*-like FBI. If you had enough official clout to ask "the Bureau" about the building, you were told that this Capitol Hill office was a translation center.

Sure, thousands of us thought, *but what do they really do in there?*

Conventional paranoia claimed the building was the center for the Bureau's bugging of Congressional offices and telephones – a democracy's nightmare that the FBI to this day vehemently denies.

The question of what the real spooks in the FBI were doing on Capitol Hill was quickly overshadowed in my fevered mind by the question of what my fantasized CIA employees stationed in my imagination's re-cast Capitol Hill townhouse were doing.

The reality of most espionage activity makes poor fiction. As U.S. President Lyndon B. Johnson noted when he swore in Richard Helms as head of the CIA years before that spy czar's questionable activities were exposed in the swirls from Watergate: "Most significant triumphs come not in the secrets passed in the dark, but in patient reading, hour after hour, of highly technical periodicals."

Such ordinary reality is not the meat of drama. Drama

occurs when reality breaks down. Or at the edge of the ordinary where determined people confront cause and effect with their consciences and wrestle fate.

Condor was conceived when Ian Fleming dominated the "spy" genre. Despite fine movies having been made from their excellent books, master authors of that era John Le Carre and Len Deighton were overshadowed by 007. Eric Ambler, Joseph Conrad, and Graham Greene could be found on library shelves, but at bookstores they were blanked out by the glitz of Sean Connery and Ursula Andress, sex and a Walther PPK.

As much as I loved "*Bond, James Bond*," I didn't want to write about a superhero. A superhero always triumphs. Is never in ultimate jeopardy.

And was someone who I'd never met. Apprentice journalist that I was, I wanted to keep one hand on facts while I shaped my fiction. So I knew that whoever my hero was in the fantasy that ambushed me on a Washington street, he was no superman.

But he did work for the CIA.

Then as now, the Central Intelligence Agency was America's best-known spy shop. In those post-McCarthy days, when our murdered President John Kennedy had publicly loved James Bond and been secretly engaged in covert intrigues that included assassination, the CIA was an invisible creature of mythic proportion.

These days, entire bookstores are devoted to tomes on the CIA, America's 21st Century minted brand name "Homeland Security" forces, spies, and terrorists. *B.C.* – *Before Condor* – the average bookstore carried *zero* books about the Agency. When I researched *Condor*, I found only three credible books on the CIA, two by David Wise and Thomas Ross and one by Andrew Tully.

Fictionally, the CIA was treated like a ghost everyone tiptoed around but no one touched. Its agents made appearances in hundreds of novels, but they were usually somber creatures of unquestioned monomania and solid competence. *What* and *how* and *why* they did what they did went unexamined. CIA agents were *ipso facto* on the right side: if not Yale superheroes, certainly dependable Boy Scouts tinged with romanticism.

A notable exception was the 1971 novel (that I hadn't read before writing *Condor*) called *The Rope Dancer*, written by Victor Marchetti, a CIA agent who in post-Condor 1974 co-authored *The Cia and the Cult of Intelligence*, a classic factual expose that the United States Supreme Court charged with protecting freedom of the press censored word-by-word. In his novel published before that, Marchetti followed a then-frequent and today absurd-sounding practice: he changed the name of the CIA to the non-existent NIA, further distancing fiction from reality.

Even Hollywood treated the CIA with a Tinkerbell touch: onscreen, the CIA meant impossible mission gadgets, trenchcoated knights in righteous pursuit of a Holy Grail. An engrossing exception that few people saw then (including me) was the 1972 movie *Scorpio*, starring Burt Lancaster as a CIA executive who may or may not deserve the assassin the Agency has forced to hunt him.

One truth about the espionage genre is that many "spy" stories are not about espionage. James Bond was called a spy, but his missions were more those of a global cop. Bond fought heroin dealers. In real life, spies are more likely to work with or at least try to co-opt fellow black marketers like drug dealers. In the tradition of Joseph Conrad and Somerset Maugham, Don Delillo and Robert Stone may write beautifully about men who use covert means to effect international policy, but such novels are relatively rare in "espionage" literature. Spies, intelligence officers, operatives, analysts and those who do the patient reading praised by LBJ are hard creatures to fictionalize – witness the fact that we have only one, perfect George Smiley.

So even though inspiration had ambushed me with two wonderful components for a novel, I still lacked what Alfred Hitchcock called the *MacGuffin*, the *why* that would trigger my novel's story.

Until the crusades of a muckraker, a Beat poet, and a brave historian lit the darkness of my imagination.

The last lecturer to my 1971 class of Congressional interns was Les Whitten, a novelist and partner to Jack Anderson, whose syndicated columns of original investigative reporting ran in almost a thousand U.S. newspapers.

The corrupt and powerful hated and feared Jack. Even after he was dead in 2006, the FBI stalked Anderson's ghost. Their probes to snatch up his "secret files" earned the anger of an investigating U.S. Senate committee and stirred up the hornets' nest of former Anderson reporters, of whom I was one. That night in 1971 when I met Les Whitten, I was a college kid. Four years later, we became colleagues working together for Anderson's investigative column.

After class that night in 1971, I persuaded Les to tell me the "CIA story" he told us wide-eyed college students that he would be breaking in the column after I left Washington for my isolated hometown of Shelby, Montana.

Allen Ginsberg is *the* Beat poet. By 1971, as America rolled toward a narcotics and law enforcement nightmare that none of us back then could imagine, he had already seen the best minds of his generation destroyed by madness, dragging themselves through America's streets in search of an *angry fix*. The horrors of heroin screamed too loudly for the man inside the poet to ignore. Cherubic, bald, bearded, homosexual, pot-smoking, mantra-changing Ginsberg did what few of his critics would ever dare to do. Ginsberg declared a personal war on heroin. Then backed his rhetoric with action. Les's story concerned Ginsberg's investigations into the CIA's allies in Southeast Asia and their ties to the heroin business.

Standing there in a night lit corridor of a U.S. Senate office building as Les whispered his news to me, I felt the invisible beast of the CIA shudder.

A year later, as I weighed my ability to sell a novel about the CIA in which not everyone was red-white-and-blue pure, I stumbled across a book by historian Alfred W. McCoy who braved the wrath of the U.S. government, French intelligence agencies, the Mafia, the *Union Corse* (the then major French criminal syndicate), the Chinese Triads and our exiled Kuomintang Chinese allies to write *The Politics of Heroin in Southeast Asia*, an analytical history of the 20th Century whose depth, accuracy and brilliance deserves all the prizes it never got. McCoy tramped the mountains of Laos, air-conditioned government corridors of Saigon, and along the *klongs* of Bangkok to gather evidence that showed how, in their Vietnam crusades, the governments of France and the United States had secretly *in the least* embraced ignorance about the gangsterism of those they called friends.

McCoy's book was the final ray of light I needed to see the path of my novel. *Condor* took wing, I naively sent the manuscript from nowhere Montana to New York publishers without the help of any kind of literary agent or personal contact, eventually – *astonishingly* – found a publishing roost.

Every novel is two books: the one the author writes, and the one that the publishers, editors, and the author carve for the reader. In the process of creating that second book, any author is both beef and butcher.

The novel *Six Days of the Condor* that I wrote differs from the novel my publishers printed. *Condor* originally was the tale of a bookish, mildly rebellious researcher who stumbles onto a heroin smuggling ring run by renegade operatives within the CIA. The renegades skim their drugs out of the product being sold by supposed U.S. "allies." As a CIA analyst, Condor is assigned to analyze novels for an obscure branch of the CIA – exposed by David Wise and Thomas Ross in their nonfiction. Condor's office is a discreet CIA townhouse on Washington, D.C.'s Capitol Hill falsely identified as the headquarters for the American Literary Historical Association.

Many of my "revelations" about the CIA came from Wise and Ross. The rest came from my assuming that the CIA, as a government bureaucracy, would function not too differently from other government bureaucracies. I

17

projected certain elements, like the existence of a "panic line" for agents in trouble that later days revealed to be real.

It was those projections along with the novel's attitude about the heretofore invisible beast called the CIA that gave *Condor* its unique spirit.

My protagonist was deliberately not a superhero; he was *anyman*, any reader, trapped by the paranoia of our times. I never let him do anything that I or someone I knew couldn't do. I chose "condor" for his codename because it elegantly implies a witness to death – "vulture" sounds gross.

Escaping lunchtime assassination by a fluke, Condor finds betrayal waiting within his colleagues when he calls for help. To survive, he must become the kind of field operative he'd only read about in novels and seen in movies. He prevails only because of a miscalculation of the hired assassin who'd originally tried to kill him. In true *noir* fashion, to reclaim his soul and revenge the murders of his colleagues and an innocent woman he'd dragooned into helping him, Condor becomes a cold blooded assassin.

And as first written, the novel had a prologue and epilogue set in Vietnam – where so much begins and ends for my generation.

Well. As a journalist and a first-time author, I was prepared for chain-saw editing of my manuscript. But my clipped and simple prose passed through my editor Starling Lawrence's hands with less surgery than I'd imagined possible. Decades later, Starling became a deservedly respected fiction author.

Still, the conglomerate of powers that published my first

book asked for three major changes: drop the Vietnam prologue and epilogue in favor of immediate story development, let the woman Condor dragoons into helping him live (*"Killing her is so dark and his believing she's dead is good enough."*), and change the heroin into something else: *"Could it be some kind of super drug? With THE FRENCH CONNECTION just out, there's a feeling that heroin has already been done."*

I reluctantly complied. Vietnam was excised, the woman was shot in the head but saved "off-screen" by the miracles of modern medicine, and the bags of heroin smuggled in book crates became morphine bricks – an intrinsically silly revision: nobody smuggles morphine bricks, they refine them into heroin.

I can argue that those three edits lessened the book. But such abstract judgments ignore an important truth of writing: prose consists of two decisive forces – an idea and its execution. Decades after the fact, I believe that my ideas were great, but can't swear that the writing skills of the young man I was then could execute those ideas well enough to merit their survival.

Some novels are three books: the author's original work, the edited published volume – and the story Hollywood projects on the silver screen.

No novelist has been better served by Hollywood than I.

Few stories adapted from novels to film have been more influenced by history's cradle than *Condor*. And perhaps that powerful influence creates a kind of logical prophetic power.

In August, 2006, former U.S. Senator and presidential candidate Gary Hart famously "blogged" about the

George W. Bush Administration's questionable and ruthless forays in the Middle East. Hart said:

It was all forecast years ago in the final scene of the movie Three Days of the Condor *when the CIA official Higgins explains to the naive CIA research character portrayed by Robert Redford: "Of course it's about the oil. Do you think the American people care how we get it? They just want us to get it."*

The movie based on a book eclipses any book; that's a 20th century marketing phenomenon, not an aesthetic judgment. More people go more often to movies than read books. Television and movies streaming into people's home and office computer terminals have mushroomed such facts into a cultural syndrome.

Hundreds of times, I have been introduced as "the author of that Robert Redford movie."

SIX DAYS became THREE DAYS, cinematic necessity (two hours film time chopped into six consecutive days of action would befuddle an audience) and great screen-writing by Lorenzo Semple, Jr., and David Rayfiel. In part to accommodate star Robert Redford's grueling schedule, the action moved from Washington, D.C. to New York: that there were CIA agents in NYC added to the paranoia.

And between my completion of the novel and the filming of the movie, history shifted, dramatically and powerfully. The screenwriters couldn't have conjured up such an inspiration: a global oil crisis.

What a MacGuffin! Unlike drugs, it had never *been done*.

Throw in Redford – and Faye Dunaway, Cliff Robertson, Max von Sydow, John Houseman, Tina Chen. Put Sidney Pollack in the director's chair.

Then come sit in the audience.

With me.

Awe is the only way to describe seeing fantasies you created out of thin air projected onto a movie screen in a theater full of strangers. Who like what they see almost as much as you love it. Awe, and a frightening kind of reverence, the insight of how lucky you are that it all happened in the first place, let alone happened so marvelously *well*.

The power of any novel or movie comes from more than the talents and skills of author and editor, of screenwriter and director and actors. Power for fiction comes from something deeper, from an alignment with the underlying forces of reality. *Credibility* is an incomplete expression of this alignment.

Credibility is beyond truth – it's *what could be*. No matter how strange, wonderful or terrifying, *what could be* is always cradled by *what is*.

History after Condor gained many benchmarks, from the tearing down of the Berlin Wall that symbolized the end of the Cold War to the Arctic's melting icebergs avalanching into the ocean because of Global Warming to jetliners hurtling out of the blue sky into a green field in Pennsylvania, the Pentagon, and New York's twin towers.

9/11 is the tattoo on our times.

The new cradle for history.

Now picture me driving our family car on the 8-laned New Jersey Turnpike that runs north from my Washington, D.C. home through industrial and suburban wastelands. My wife Bonnie sits beside me in the front seat. Adolescent son Nathan sprawls in the back seat. It's Autumn, 2003, a Tuesday afternoon. We're on our way to

New York City for a Thanksgiving holiday dinner being hosted for the first time by my documentary maker and future Academy Award nominee daughter Rachel.

Outside of our car, civilization swirled in what is coming to be called "the Long War." Americans not much older than my son fought and died in an unpopular "conflict" that's chewing up thousands of lives in Western Asia while a Texan named George Bush reigns as "the decider" President of the United States. Newspapers alleged wrongdoings launched from the White House. A U.S. internal security apparatus hunted illusive enemies while the CIA fought them overseas. The world declared itself in an energy crisis with oil being likened to blood.

And I stared out of my family car toward a New York City horizon scarred by sanctimonious hatred's horrific amputation of twin towers.

Only the crazy did not feel fear.

Our cell phone rang.

My wife answers. It's my movie agent.

Right away the whole day feels like a joke, because everyone who loves cinema knows that writers' agents never call them.

Truth is, he did. And said: There's mushrooming interest in a new *Three Days of the Condor* movie. You wrote the book, own some rights. Can I pursue this?

By now, we've exited the Turnpike and pulled into the parking lot of a faceless shopping mall that could be in Ohio or Bordeaux or outside London. I've stopped the car to deal with my agent's machinegun babble. Bonnie fishes a pen from her purse to scrawl words on a scrap of paper: "Just say *yes* and let's go!"

I did and we did. But Bonnie drove. I rode in the passenger seat.

Back on the Turnpike to New York in 2003. More than 100 miles to go. Behind me were decades when I'd gone from a *wanna be* writer to a novelist with more than a dozen books and almost as many published and often honored short stories to my credit, plus four years as an investigative reporter and a career in Hollywood working with some great actors, producers and directors, staffing a network TV show. I'd been honored by France with the *Grand Prix de Roman Noir* and in Italy with the Raymond Chandler medal. What I wanted was to build on that, be better, write more, go further.

I stared out of my cruising family car toward a New York City horizon, toward invisible twin scars, heard a ghost whisper:

"How would you do Condor *now?"*

Hollywood clamor echoed words like "re-make" and "sequel."

How could there be a remake? The world of my Condor had crumbled into history. More importantly, why should anyone "remake" a great movie that was an artistic triumph of its screenwriters, director, and actors?

The concept of a sequel seemed equally absurd. A sequel following the footsteps of the first movie would exist in Cold War morality an audience would find quaint. Plus, Robert Redford defined that Condor, a truth that had stopped my planned series of five Condor books after the second novel got lost in Redford's shadow. A "contemporary" sequel would either force Redford to be a "senior" spy in some age-appropriate drama or would require that from an actor faking Redford playing Condor.

But Condor isn't about an actor, it's about an ordinary person like all of us. Condor is about fear. Corruption. Conscience. Courage. Choice.

A ghost shot one bullet word into my skull: *re-imagining*.

Re-imagining. Other artists had done it. Alfred Hitchcock made *The Man Who Knew Too Much* in 1934 and in 1956 with his same MacGuffin set in two different eras of global menace. Roger Vadim's cinematic hands shaped two versions of *Et Dieu Crea La Femme*. John Fowles reworked his novel *The Magus*, Flaubert left us three different versions of *The Temptation of St. James*, and Henry James re-wrote much of his early fiction to etch richer colors into his youthful tattoos.

Condor was no virgin unknown to the world. Any "re-imagining" had to embrace yet "Judo" iconic techniques and moments of Condor's legend: the hero being a CIA agent who was not a trained spy, a menacing mailman, a massacre of Condor's co-workers, him being targeted for the wrong reasons by the right people, romance *"under the gun,"* and – because of the movie's boldness – a lady or the tiger ending. The re-imagining had to reflect my novel, honor the movie, *then* live on its own. Moreover, a re-imagined story had to breathe these times of its creation when our cyber synapses accelerate and compress art.

On the New Jersey Turnpike, my soul's wheels rumbled through whispers of ghosts. Our car tires rumbled over asphalt. The sunset horizon flowing outside my highway window shimmered those two invisible scars.

"OK," I told my wife after miles of silence. "I can do it."

"Good." She flicked the turn signal lever on for the *click*

click click announcing the direction we chose.

Over the next few weeks, the Hollywood interest that sparked my vision roared into a bonfire of film stars, a blaze lit with dreams of glory and gold, an inferno that vanished like smoke when establishing cinematic rights took a beat longer than the attention span of Tinsel Town. But as that smoke blew away, I created my re-imaging as a short story, the medium perfect for our cyber accelerated times, and one that from its heart to its action to its title portrays our wired new world: *condor.net*

I was so anxious to let the story fly that I published a rough draft of *condor.net* on my website. I also realized that the novel I was writing at the time *Mad Dogs* provided me the perfect chance to resolve the fate of my original *Condor* in a way that fits with both the Condor novels and the new *condor.net* story. A few months later, a U.S. magazine offered to let me polish and publish the storyA few months later, a U.S. magazine offered to let me polish and publish the story. Then, as part of celebrating 20 years of publishing, France's *Rivages Noir* publishing house and its editor/my friend Francois Guerif printed the polished story in a special French language *novella* edition.

This volume brings the novel, its history, its *re-imagining* as a short story together in one volume. Now as always, the air around us whispers the flapping of condor wings.

Listen.

James Grady
March, 2007 – Washington, D.C.

condor.net

condor.net
by
James Grady

"Do you know who you are?" said white-haired boss Richard Dray from behind his Washington, D.C. desk. Glasses hung from a shoelace looped around his neck.

The younger man on the other side of that desk that Monday morning smiled: "Aren't I the guy I see in my mirror?"

"No. You're Condor. In point of fact, our new Condor. A South American assassination consortium and two previous operatives for us had that code name."

"What happened to those other two guys?"

"One became a Watergate burglar. The other had … odd luck."

"I can imagine."

"That's not your job."

"Sure it is," said Condor. "I'm a cyber spy. I troll the worldwide web. If I find a hink, I zap a report into our secret network. Mark Twain said history doesn't repeat itself, though it might rhyme, so I try to imagine those rhymes."

"You *imagine* rhymes." Dray shook his head.

Condor shrugged: "It's a gift."

"You are a joke gift from the CIA. They detailed their open source cyber section to us at Homeland Security to avoid losing real turf in the 9/11 shuffle. Last week, they dumped you here. Now I'm getting complaints about you using your TOP SECRET clearance to track a Pentagon

Op called..." Dray consulted an e-mail on his monitor's screen: "Called RISING THUNDER.

"Why are you stepping outside your job description?" asked his boss.

"I see our guys' faces," said Condor, as his imagination ran a movie of 11 RISING THUNDER Delta Force commandos in a musty Pakistani barracks.

Condor became obsessed with the 11 American soldiers through video and photos in secret data streams he surfed. Eleven flesh and blood men, their destiny shaped by the CIA's discovery of an al Qaeda base masquerading as an Afghan village, a threat that with slam dunk certainty fit every prediction, every electronic intercept from terrorist-friendly Arab TV journalists to cell phone chatter in Malaysia. Condor knew every informant's whisper, every NSA satellite photo of bearded "villagers" carrying AK-47s.

RISING THUNDER was a Seize & Secure mission. The 11 American commandos would blitz the village via a stealth helicopter chopping through cold night air, seize the command hut, *wet work* authorized, *hold* until a cavalry wave of Rangers helicoptered over the dawn horizon to liberate the village and harvest fanatics from amidst the innocents.

"I know what's there," Condor told boss Richard Dray that Monday morning. "I know they're GO in 30 hours. But I don't know what's bothering me."

"Doesn't matter. RISING THUNDER is covered and you're not the blanket."

"If not me, who?"

"*Who?* You're Condor, not an owl. No more ... unauthorized imagining!'"

"I'll do my best," said Condor as he walked out of that sealed office ... and entered a second-floor cavern where CIA engineers had bricked over the windows above Washington streets, then built a cluster of six 'fishbowl' workstation cubicles. Jacobs Ladders built into each hearthigh green plastic partition rippled waves of blue electric bolts. Those electric blue lightning bolts zapped snooping microwaves and made this two-story spy factory crackle like Dr. Frankenstein's laboratory.

A blue ribbon zapped around Condor's fishbowl where pictures and printouts clung to his partition walls: clips from movies, the WTC smoking towers, a photo of him rappelling a cliff face. But instead of entering his cubicle, he walked to the coffee machine. Condor sneaked his cell phone out of his gray sports jacket.

The woman who answered his phone call said: "Yes?"

Condor whispered into his cell phone: "You've got to get me out of here."

"I pulled strings to get you *in* there. One week, and you already want to leave! There's no coming back across the river. Not now. The politics – are you in trouble?"

"Not exactly."

"Not again! That's why I blasted you out of – Tell me it's not the same thing!"

"Like I told you ten days ago, something about that Afghan op –"

"Bugs you. Your snooping on that triggered paranoids in our Firm. I had to promise you'd stop, that you were a smart loan to our Homeland detail, that –"

"Hey, this morning I almost figured out what's bothering me!" His nose wrinkled at the stench of burned coffee. "I just want to do my job."

"No: Do the job *they* want. And don't look to me. I'm not your boss anymore."

"But you know me. And I'm not going to stop, so ... Where are you now?"

"In my car by the White House."

"Meet me. Twenty minutes. Where I spilled on you."

He heard the hum of traffic. Angry honks. Her mental wheels whirling.

"Come on, Renee," said Condor. "Help me figure this out."

Renee Lake sighed. "Give me 25 minutes."

Condor put his cell phone away. Saw none of the other five analysts watching. The boss's steel door was closed. Condor dumped the hot mud in the coffee machine's glass pot down the drain. He switched the coffee machine off, swung it open. Pulled a red wire loose. Popped a blue wire free. Closed the machine. Flipped the power switch.

The power light stayed unlit.

He sighed guilt, but walked to an intercom on a wall, pushed the call button.

"Yes?" Boss Dray's voice boomed through speakers from beyond his steel door.

"The coffee machine's dead," Condor told the intercom box. "I'm making a Starbucks run. You like mocha?"

A voice yelled from the cluster of fishbowls: "Not fair!"

The other five analysts popped their head above their green fishbowl walls.

Juan loomed like a thoughtful NFL tackle: "We should all get to go."

The boss's disembodied voice boomed: "Non-task departures of personnel –"

"Staff motivation meeting!" ad-libbed Sarita. Officially, the Jacobs Ladder electric surges were "bio-benign," but Condor worried every time he saw static frame Sarita's beautiful Bombay face with a black fan of her electro-charged hair.

"No!" he yelled to the intercom box; to his colleagues: "I want to go alone!"

The disembodied voice boomed: "It is inappropriate for a supervisor to request personal favors from subordinate personnel. No whipped cream."

Los Beatles – two pale analysts with self-inflicted shaggy retro haircuts – high-fived through an electric blue bolt undulating up from the partition between their desks.

"I'll go on ahead!" yelled Condor, hurrying away from his five gathering colleagues. At the top of the stairs, his eyes filled with sunlight streaming into the first floor entryway through the glass door that could withstand a burst from an AK-47.

Clumping down the stairs, he fumbled for his cell phone to call Renee.

Saw the mailman walking up the outside stairs towards the glass door.

Saw the leather pouch the blue uniformed mailman clutched to his chest.

Condor opened the door.

"Thanks." The postal carrier stepped into the entryway. His nametag read BURT. The mailman put envelopes into the postal box that hid chemical sensors in its walls.

"And thanks again for pickin' me up Friday when I was

running in the rain. Most people never see us. It's like mailmen are invisible."

"Yeah, but guys like me see ghosts." Condor anxiously fingered his cell phone.

"True that," said the mailman. "Which reminds me ..."

Burt nodded toward the plaque mounted by the door buzzer.

"...Feenix Data Systems, Inc. What do you guys do?"

His fellow analysts maneuvered past Condor and the mailman – except for Juan, who stood still as a mountain, blocking the stairs up.

Condor diverted the mailman out to the sunny stoop: "Hey, I just work here."

"I hear that." The mailman walked to the next door in this D.C. neighborhood.

'Let's go,' said Juan, directing Condor to join their crew walking the other way.

'Nerds on parade,' said Sarita as the six co-workers strolled up the sidewalk.

Condor sighed. "Not what I planned."

'Life happens.' Sarita wrinkled her brow. "Is this about more than coffee?"

Sarita smelled like oranges and sunshine. She set her eyes on Condor as he walked beside her. Grinned. 'So what did you have in mind?'

'Dudes!' interrupted the chubby analyst named Hershel. He wore classic black & white sneakers. "You won't believe what I popped onto last Friday!"

Juan lowered his voice: "The first rule of our work is Do Not Talk About Work."

"What else can we talk about?" said Hershel as they

neared the neighborhood's Starbucks. "Movies? They make me nervous. Crowds. Popcorn."

"We're regular people," said the short Beatle as he held open the Starbucks door for his five colleagues. "We got a lot to say."

"Nobody listens," said the tall Beatle as the six secret agents entered Starbucks.

Condor scanned that coffee scented chamber they entered: *No Renee. Not yet.* An old man in the corner nursed a cup of decaf as he fed memories into a laptop. A *Mommy And Me* quartet devoured adult conversation while three of the Mommies rolled strollers with sleeping babies back and forth as Mom Four rocked her baby in a shoulder snuggly. Steam hissed as two green-aproned baristas behind the brown wooden counter prepared for a big order. The store's sound system played Muddy Waters growling the *Manish Boy* blues. The phone in Condor's pocket felt like a boulder.

'Order for me, OK?' he asked Juan. Condor hurried down a dead end hall.

"You're supposed to go *after* coffee!" Hershel told Condor and Sarita countered: "Grow up!" Condor entered the MENS ROOM where all he heard through the closed door was Muddy Waters thumping blues. Condor grabbed his phone. Punched re-dial.

One ring.

The bathroom sink glistened white. He saw himself in the mirror. Gray blazer, blue shirt, no tie, cell phone pressed to his ear as Muddy Waters proclaimed himself *"a full grown man."* Condor stared at his own mirrored reflection.

Two rings.

A stroller-rolling mom glanced at the bald man who entered the Starbucks. She noticed his right arm thrust under his sports jacket. *Hope he's not having a heart attack.* She turned back to her laughing friends as that man's surgeon-gloved left hand reached behind him to lock the door.

Three rings.

The bald man swung a silencer-equipped Uzi out from under his jacket. Shot the two baristas. *Caugh*, the woman barista wore a new red earring as she fell. *Caugh*, a heart shot knocked the male barista into the pastry case.

Four rings.

The bald man thumbed the Uzi to FULL AUTO and sprayed the huddle of chattering coworkers. Juan. Hershel. Sarita. *Los Beatles.* They all spun to a bloody heap. Ejected brass shell casings tinkled on the coffee shop's floor. The old man in the corner ducked behind his laptop's upraised screen – *caugh* one bullet punched a hole through that plastic and crimson flecked the keyboard.

In the bathroom, Condor heard weird noises. Condor frowned: *What the hell?*

The bald man *caugh*ed a bullet into a mother's screaming mouth. Babies wailed. Muddy Waters growled. One mom shoved her stroller away – *caugh* she sprawled across the table, knocking over paper cups of coffee to add to the liquid mess.

The third stroller mom sprang like a lioness towards the killer and he *caugh*ed a red line across her white blouse.

The mom with the snuggly cupped her hands over her baby's head. "Please no!"

In the bathroom, Condor heard the woman's plea as a warning of *threat! danger!* Dropped his phone in his pocket and grabbed the only loose item he could find.

Baldy zeroed his Uzi on snuggly Mom's forehead, pulled the trigger – *click.* A presumption of mercy flickered in her eyes. Then his left hand drew the 9mm Glock pistol holstered on his belt.

Motion erupted behind snuggly Mom.

Condor charged from the bathroom, his arm cocked to throw what he'd grabbed. He saw lumpy clothes heaped on the floor. Saw a bald man holding two guns. Saw *no chance/no choice* and leapt over the counter towards cover as he threw –

A toilet paper roll, its white paper chain unspooling towards the startled killer.

Off her funeral pyre rose Sarita. Shoulder shot. Rib shot. Refusing death. She charged the bald man who dared presume to be her assassin.

Three targets distracted the bald killer: the Mom, the Indian bitch who wouldn't just die, and the flying-through-the-air dork who'd thrown a fucking roll of toilet paper.

BAM! A bullet drilled through Sarita's chest missing her lungs, heart, aorta and spine as it ripped from her back. Stumbling, she kept going.

BAM! BAM! Bullets zinged past Condor as he fell behind the counter.

BAM! BAM! Snuggly Mom's eyes became flowing red fountains.

The crazy shot-to-hell CIA woman flopped towards the killer. He shoved her away with the empty Uzi, leveled his

Glock pistol at her face and BAM! A red dot blossomed right smack where *American born here* had refused to wear a caste mark.

Condor threw a giant cappuccino off the serving bar and hit the Glock.

Scalding liquid splashed the killer's face, burned his eyes. He screamed.

Condor vaulted the counter, wrestled the killer for the Uzi and Glock.

The killer let Condor have both guns, grabbed Condor's lapels, dropped towards the floor and windmilled him through the air with the foot-in-the-stomach judo throw.

Condor flew shoes-first into the Starbucks plate glass window. *Bustin' glass* exploded him outside, inertia tumbled him to his feet, bounced him off a parked car, his cell phone flipping from his pocket – skidding into the sewer slit. Condor held both guns. Looked through the shattered window. Saw the bald man clawing his pants leg up –

Ankle holster!

Condor threw the Uzi through the broken window and it bounced off the killer.

Got a pistol in my hand! BAM! Condor blasted a Glock slug into the crater. The bullet ripped through the Starbuck's bathroom wall and shattered the mirror.

Condor heard a voice behind him yell: "...shoot!"

Whirl aim at murder sound/man with gun – BAM!

Middle of the street, a blue shirted cop spun a pirouette/fell beside his cruiser.

BAM! A bullet zinged past Condor from inside the Starbucks and he ducked, ran the opposite direction of the

38

quickly parked police cruiser. Ran fast. Ran hard.

Ran knowing: *The killer's shooting at me!*

Ran knowing: *I shot a cop!*

He darted around the first corner – dress shop, card shop, blocks of houses –

"*Aaaah!*" screamed a woman with puffy dyed blonde hair at *man with a gun*.

Condor waved his arms: "No! I'm the good guy!"

But the woman screamed again and he ran.

Look back: nothing at the corner – *but the killer must be coming!* Condor stuck the pistol in his belt under his jacket, ran down an alley. Sirens wailed.

Four blocks later, he stood in the middle of a commercial strip. Sirens filled the blue sky cupping this upscale neighborhood. Pedestrians scanned the streets as Condor caught his breath, realized: *I don't need to run!* He grabbed for his cell phone – gone.

RETROVILLE read a pink neon sign over a store. A bell tinkled when Condor entered that jumble of disco jackets, lava lamps, Elvis busts, and rubber Halloween masks – JFK, Nixon, Reagan, Clinton, the first Bush. A shop chick with tattoos up her arm leaned against the glass counter.

He rushed to her: "Do you have a public phone?"

"Like, *what*?"

"A pay phone! Do you have a pay phone?"

"Hate to break it to you, but it's a world of cells."

"Where can I find one? A pay phone! A phone booth!"

"Like," she said, "that changing into Superman thing is *so* over."

Condor didn't even hear the bell ding as he hurried out.

39

Walk. Don't run. Cars and minivans slowed to a traffic jam in this neighborhood where expensive homes waited two blocks off the major street of shops. *Regular people* like he'd been just minutes ago frowned towards where the wailing sirens seemed to converge. An ambulance wooshed past, racing that way.

"*Go!*" whispered Condor. But he knew.

A lone pay phone clung to a drugstore's brick wall near an alley blocked by a delivery truck with blinking flashers. Condor grabbed the silver corded receiver – heard *dial tone.* Tapped in the toll-free CIA Panic Line number.

A woman's voice answered his call after the second ring: "Hello?"

"They're – we got – This is Condor. Section Gamma Six Seven. We got hit!"

"Say again."

"Condor! It's me! In Starbucks with a machinegun and all of them!"

"Stay calm. Report."

"We can't just talk on the damn phone!"

"It's OK. We'll take care of you. Where are you?"

"*What?*"

"What's your location? How can we help you if we don't know where you are?"

He frowned. "You popped my location on the first ring! Target on my back and you tell me to stay calm!"

Warning lights blinked on the truck in the nearby mouth of an alley.

"Condor, you called the right number. Now stay put."

"Out here in the open? With a killer loose? What sense does that make?"

"Are you're armed?"

"Yeah, but I'm – I'm not a real spy! I just imagine things!"

"Talk to me. Everything's –"

Car brakes squeal!

Condor whirled: a black sedan shuddered to a halt crossways in this side street. The driver ducked below the steering wheel, the passenger – *man, black leather jacket –*

Black Leather Jacket leapt out of the sedan, slammed his hands on its roof, his double-grip aiming a pistol.

At me! Condor dropped the phone, jerked the Glock from his belt and jumped towards the truck-filled alley.

BAM! A bullet splattered the brick wall beside Condor. Metal fragments sliced his sports jacket as he dodged down the alley alongside the delivery truck.

Behind him a man bellowed: "Fucker!"

Black Leather Jacket charged the alley. Hugged the edge of the drugstore wall. Sirens filled the city air. He crouched low – whirled into the gap between the drugstore bricks and the delivery truck. That narrow corridor showed him *empty alley*. Gun thrust in front of him, he scurried between the truck and the wall. Popped out: fifty steps of empty pavement led towards a gold SUV idling where the alley met the next main street.

The driver of the super-sized gold SUV never turned her face towards the gun-waving black-jacketed man as he flowed closer to her. A National Public Radio report on feminism in Africa vibrated her elephantine vehicle's rolled-up windows. Regular glasses saddled her head while prescription sunglasses covered her eyes. Her left hand pressed a cell phone to that ear. Her right hand held the steering wheel and a palm pilot she consulted as the traffic light two cars ahead of her turned green.

The SUV lurched forward as Black Leather Jacket ran from the alley. He saw only the driver's side. The SUV's departure cleared his view of the alley's continuing obstacle course of dumpsters and parked cars. The SUV lumbered through a left turn. Neither its multi-tasking driver nor Black Leather Jacket saw a desperate man clinging to the SUV'S door handles as he huddled on the vehicle's passenger side running board. The SUV slowed for the traffic jam. Condor flopped off the running board ...

And ran until he spotted a brown kiosk pole painted with a white "M" – Metro, Washington's subway. He stumbled down escalator stairs as they slid into a tunnel.

Underground in the enormous gray cavern, Condor caught his breath. Subway tracks bordered each side of the red tiled platform where he stood. A nursery school group trundled past him. A curly haired girl smiled at Condor: "Where are you going?"

An electronic sign above the platform glowed computer letters: **10:41 a.m. TERRORIST THREAT LEVEL BLUE. TWO TRAINS ARRIVING**.

A train roared into the station on the tracks behind him, its wind mussing his hair. Subway brakes squealed. Strangers' eyes shot bullets at him.

Ding-dong! chimed the train stopped behind Condor as its doors sprang open. People hurried out of the cars. The school kids lined up on the other edge of the platform.

Wait. Wait. He glanced at the computer letters sliding through the electric sign: **10:42 a.m. TERRORIST**

THREAT LEVEL ELEVATED TO LEVEL ORANGE.

Ding-dong! Condor jumped into the car a beat before the doors clunked shut. The train surged. Out the window, he saw that little girl wave *good-bye*.

Where are you going. Condor roared into a world of flashes. *Flash* and he's sitting on an orange plastic bench in a clattering subway train. *Flash* that man in the red jacket avoids his gaze. *Flash* and that woman putting on her makeup uses her mirror to watch him. *Flash* and a teenager nails him with hard eyes. *Flash* and Condor's changing trains once, twice, three times. *Flash* and he's standing, holding on to a subway car's bright silver pole that trapped his curved reflection. *Flash* and he's on an orange seat, shaking, soundlessly screaming for the whole world to see.

Who he saw coming toward him was Crazy Guy – wild hair above wilder eyes. He plopped on the seat beside Condor and filled the subway car with sour body odor.

Crazy Guy muttered: 'They're everywhere! They can see you!'

'Yeah,' said Condor and he believed it even as he meant *"go away."*

Crazy Guy bathed Condor with rancid breath, whispered: 'I'm invisible!'

'True that,' said Condor.

Then he blinked.

Gently, firmly, Condor worked his way up from the seat and past Crazy Guy, saying: "This is where I get off."

"But nothing's gone *ding-dong!*" said Crazy Guy.

"I hear things," said Condor as he walked to the doors of the hurtling train.

43

A slanting subway shaft telescoped into an ever bigger, ever brighter circle of sunlight as its escalator carried Condor up from underground darkness to the street of an ordinary high noon Monday in the capital of the new American empire.

He took a taxi to the huge postal service building he'd been to on Friday. Condor walked around to the parking yard of red, white and blue vehicles. He waved at the pensioner in the guard booth who didn't look up from his newspaper.

Condor hopped onto the loading dock, took the hall to the locker room, and when three mailmen in the corner spotted him, said: "You guys seen Burt?"

"Ain't he still out on his route?" The man checked his watch.

"Told him I'd have to wait," lied Condor, walking away. Two aisles over, he heard them resume 'back in the day' chatter, and knew to them, he was not even there.

He worked his way along the deserted aisle of green lockers. Stole a blue cap. The second mail carrier jacket he found hung loose on him but covered the Glock in his belt. Condor spotted a bin of leather mail pouches, grabbed one and join a group of off-shift personnel strolling past the pensioner security guard.

The metro bus he took rumbled through D.C. Reflections of the skull-like Capitol dome shimmered in the bus window glass. He covered his face as the bus rolled past swiveling video cameras perched on poles. He left the bus two blocks from an address he'd driven by a dozen times purely out of convenience or coincidence, not like some teen Romeo, went behind a green dumpster, changed into the postal jacket and cap, put his gray jacket in the pouch, and stepped out from behind the dumpster as a mailman.

Invisible.

The Cairo Arms is an 11-story apartment complex by a park. Condor took a deep breath, walked towards its glass front doors like he knew exactly what he was doing.

In the lobby, an old woman harangued the desk clerk about garbage. Neither of them noticed the mailman get in an elevator that whisked him up, up and away.

Seventh floor, on the side where apartment balconies faced the park. Condor stood in the empty hall outside the door labeled 722. Reached his hand up to knock – Stopped. Inspiration lit his face. He hurried to the elevator.

Standing outside Apartment 822 he heard a radio blaring 1970's "*classic*" rock.

Standing outside Apartment 922 he heard nothing. He pressed his ear against the wooden door. Still nothing. Knocked. No one responded. Condor pulled the Glock from his belt. Hands out for balance, he raised his right foot to kick in the door – froze. Put his foot down. Wrapped his hand around 922's doorknob, turned his wrist –

And the door swung open.

Condor scurried into the apartment, the unlocked door shutting behind him.

Like a SWAT warrior he'd never been, Condor darted from room to room: found no one in the barely furnished apartment with its jumble of law school books. In the bedroom, he stepped over a white bra and crumpled blue jeans, went to the balcony's sliding glass door and peered down to treetops of the park.

Muttered:"*Like*, that changing into Superman thing is *so* over."

He slid open the glass door. White curtains billowed around him.

Condor stood nine stories above the ground, way above the tallest trees in the park. Nobody else was on a balcony to admire his view or the long fall to earth.

"It's only a movie," Condor mumbled as he unsnapped the leather shoulder strap from the mailbag, clipped the bag onto his belt. Condor looped the strap around the black iron railing post at the balcony floor concrete. He swung his legs over the balcony, his toes pressing concrete, his heels resting on nine stories of empty air.

And lowered himself – *fell*, swinging, dangling above the long drop by holding the mail pouch strap with both hands. He swung back and forth until one swing put his shoes above the next balcony down – and he let go of the strap in his left hand.

Flew/crashed onto the concrete balcony below him. Because he still grasped the strap in one hand, it came with him. He bounced to his feet and pressed against the wall.

Saw no witnesses on the other eighth floor balconies.

The loud 1970's *classic* rock he'd heard in the hall outside door of 822 now vibrated the apartment balcony's glass door.

Condor edged along the glass door, peered around the apartment's open curtains. Saw a bedroom. Saw a vanity's mirror reflecting the living room. Into the mirror danced a woman old enough to be a grandmother, jeans and blouse and gray hair, rocking out barefoot in her apartment to 1970's radio *classics*. She danced out of view.

"You go, girl," whispered Condor.

He looped the pouch strap around the eighth floor railing post, swung to the balcony below. He glanced around the curtains over the seventh floor balcony's cracked-open glass door: Bedroom. Bureau. Bed. Door to the living room.

Condor left the mailbag and strap on the balcony's chaise lounge. Gripped the Glock, slid the glass door open and stepped into the bedroom. Glanced into the bathroom: shower tub, toilet, sink. He eased towards the angled-open bedroom door ...

Jumped into the living room, Glock aiming –

"Fuck you!"

Startled, Condor swung Glock to shoot or –

"Awack! Fuck you!" said the green parrot in a black cage.

Condor scanned the apartment living room beyond his gunsight: glass coffee table, black leather sofa and easy chair, TV, the front door, kitchen nook –

A red ON light glowed in an alarm box mounted by the front door.

He ran to the alarm box – read its LCD screen: MOTION DETECTOR OFF.

The parrot hopped in the black steel cage, so Condor believed the alarm.

Condor slumped into the black leather chair. He put the Glock on the glass coffee table. Books and good art filled the walls. A wine rack stood near the kitchen.

The TV stared at Condor. Its screen played muted visions: A bald man machinegunned a Starbucks ballet. A baby stroller rolled through a hail of bullets. The DVD clock read: 1:32. The TV showed him RT/Delta finishing breakfast in Pakistan.

"Awk! Fuck you!" cawed the parrot.

"Somebody beat you to it," whispered Condor.

The universe spun – he jerked alert: his watch read 2:25. In the TV, Condor saw RT/Delta cleaning assault rifles.

Condor left the black Glock on the glass coffee table.

The fridge held orange juice, carry out boxes, one apple. *How can I be hungry?* he wondered. But he was. He microwaved white cardboard boxes of Chinese food. Ate at the sink. Slumped in the leather chair. The VCR read 3:42. A mirage in the TV showed an RT/Delta intel officer use a knife as a pointer on a satellite photo of the al Qaeda village. The TV scene changed to Juan blocking the stairs that morning. Chubby Hershel told a story as he walked towards Starbucks. Sarita smiled above her partition wall as a blue lightning bolt crackled behind her face and floated her long black hair.

Click – door lock!

Condor whirled, saw the handle of the deadbolt on the apartment door turning ...

He grabbed the Glock and ran into the bedroom. The parrot cursed. Condor heard the front door swing open. Beeps shut off the alarm and a man's raspy voice said: "We're checking your place."

"Awwk! Fuck you!"

Condor scurried to the bedroom balcony's glass door.

"Nice pet," said a second man's voice.

Renee said: "He suits me."

"Take long to train him?" said a third man, a sneer in his voice.

"No longer than any other man."

Condor slipped out to the balcony, left the glass door

open an inch. The curtains blocked a view of him from anyone who didn't step onto the balcony.

Twenty heartbeats later, fingers gripped the glass door, slowly slid it open ...

"Look under the bed!" yelled a man's voice from deep in the apartment.

"Like I'd forget?" The man inside the bedroom saw a balcony only birds could get to and left the glass door open.

Condor counted to 30. Peered cautiously into the empty bedroom: empty. The door to the living room still gaped open. *Risk it*: he slipped inside the bedroom.

A giant black & white photo of wild horses running through a blizzard hung above the bed's brass poled headboard. The photo glass reflected Condor as he sneaked behind the angled-open bedroom door to listen to the voices in the living room.

Where Renee Lake sat on her couch. She wore a jacket and slacks, a chic brown shag cut above a bold face with eyes like comets and lips set in a grim line she gave the man in her leather chair and the five thugs fanned out behind him.

Renee said: "Don't bother bugging my place. I wired it with countermeasures."

"Are you that paranoid?" The man in the leather chair had the raspy voice.

"I'm that professional."

"We're all on the same team."

"You mean the team that just lost five dead plus *beacoup* collateral KIA's?"

"But not your Condor. Tell me about him."

"You're Homeland Security, not my CIA. I've done my de-brief."

"And I think you should be safety stashed with his boss Dray in the bowels of the Graylin, but I'm just a brick agent, not a suite star. Still, when I leave, there'll be a team on your door, one in the stairwell, one in the garage, one in the lobby."

"Leave my door and hallway clean. *Still*, I need to maintain cover. Buck me on this, you'll answer to my Deputy Director. He doesn't have my sense of humor."

"Is that what Condor likes? Word is, he has a monster crush on you."

"I don't know about that."

"He even hacked into your personnel file."

"So have you."

"I do my job. Condor's renegade snoop gave him this address."

"I've never seen him here."

"What are you to each other?"

"He's an intuitive savant. A dreamer. After 9/11, he had the *weird* desire to do something more than make money. Think you can understand that? He signed up, passed clearance, got attached to my section of the CIA Counter-Terrorism Center. I was his boss – only his boss. Nothing inappropriate materialized between us."

"Materialized is such a ... *careful* word."

"You want sloppy, interrogate somebody else."

"If the massacre was so sloppy that Condor survived, why is he still in the wind?"

"Beats me. Shock. Or good sense. When he called the Panic Line, two gunmen jumped him, and *of course* they *absolutely* identified themselves as undercover cops."

In the bedroom, Condor closed his eyes and silently swore: *Shit!*

The man in the living room said: "You think Condor just over-reacted?"

"I think he stayed alive in streets gone crazy with guns."

"So you trust him?"

Silence. Hesitation. Then Renee said: "As I know him, he's a good man."

"Just before we drove you over here, your people uncovered a Cayman Island bank account for him. With fifty grand in it. How did a good man earn that?"

"What ... What are you –?"

"Did you see the video tape from the jewelry store security camera? It caught your 'good' man shooting into the Starbucks. The analyst Sarita got hit by a bullet from a gun like he's shooting. His fingerprints are on the Uzi recovered at the scene – only his. And there's video of him wounding that uniformed cop."

"I can't figure that."

The man stood. "We've come up with three scenarios: Your Condor is crazy, confused, or crooked. When we figure out which, we might look hard at you."

"What you see is what you get."

The raspy voiced man said: "Really."

Hiding behind the bedroom door, Condor heard men leave the apartment. Heard the locks click. Heard Renee say: "Asshole."

"Bwack!"

Footsteps entered the bedroom beyond the door he hid behind. Shoes kicked off. Bare feet padded into the bathroom. A light switch clicked. The tinkle of urine. Toilet paper unspooled. Toilet flushed. Sink water ran, silenced. A jacket dropped onto the bed. Followed by a holstered gun.

Renee walked past his view. Didn't look at the door that hid Condor. Her pants were undone from the bathroom. She shut the drapes. Snapped on the bed table lamp. Her back stayed to him. Condor pushed the door away. Watched her work her slacks down, off sleek white thighs. She wore black bikini panties. Renee unbuttoned her blouse, tossed it to the bed. Condor's gun rose as she unhooked her black bra, let it fall.

He yelled: "Stop!"

And she whirled, hands up – *kung fu* fighter. Saw him in the mailman's jacket, gun locked on her. Her eyes flicked to the bed. To her holstered pistol.

"Freeze!" he said. "You were a field agent before you were a boss. I'm just an analyst, but don't make me show you I can shoot."

"How'd you get in here?"

"I rose to the occasion."

Her eyes focused on the uniform he wore: "Have you gone postal?"

"Yeah," he said, "and here's your mail: I didn't kill anybody!"

"Let's keep it that way."

Suddenly he realized Renee wore black panties and no bra. Her breasts were swollen teardrops. His gun trembled.

And she blushed. Pulled her hands from their martial pose to cover herself. She looked past the black bore of his gun to his eyes. Said: "What now?"

"You can put your shirt back on."

"Don't watch."

"We're not there yet."

He kept his gun on her as she grabbed the blouse, used her other arm to cover her breasts. She gave him her naked spine as she put on the blouse. She turned around –

And he'd clipped her gun on his belt. He sent her to the living room couch. He took the leather chair opposite her long bare legs and buttoned blouse.

The parrot hopped wildly in his cage.

"So," said Condor: "How was your day?"

"Same old same old." Renee glanced at the glass coffee table between them. An art deco ashtray with swooping naked beauties was out of plumb with the table edges. She casually leaned forward to adjust the heavy glass object.

"Stop!" She froze at Condor's order, flicked her gaze towards his alert pistol as he said: "You don't need to straighten anything."

Renee shrugged. "Whatever you want. You got the gun."

"Let me tell you about my day," and he did.

Sunset streamed through the windows when he finished.

She stared at him through the crimson light. Said: "Why?"

"Why what? Why kill us? *Why* equals *who*. Not an amateur nut, it was too – polished. But all the superpowers are gone, it's just us now."

"Plus a billion people who think we're the new evil empire."

"Yeah, but – al Qaeda, they ..." Condor blinked. Muttered: "*It's a world of cells. 'Cells' is what we call secret* teams of terrorists or spies. But even if CIA and FBI intell is right about al Qaeda cells operating inside our country, why all this?"

"Why come to me?" Renee shifted. Even distracted as he was, Condor's gun bore shifted with her like a watchful eye. The parrot squawked.

"You're who I've got left. I got shot at when I called the Panic Line. Plus somebody's framed me with an offshore account. Plus I put my fingerprints on the Uzi. Plus I shot a cop. Accidentally, but you're the pro, you add up my score."

Her eyes pulled him like gravity. "What do you really want me to do?"

"Believe me. Believe *in* me."

"You've got the gun."

"And if I put it down?" He shook his head.

"I believe you're in trouble."

"Hey, I *am* trouble." Wasn't a laugh he made. "And I'm not a trouble guy. Not a gunner like the Delta boys in – *RISING THUNDER!* Maybe, what I was doing, all this is linked to – Dray, my boss! He talked about getting complaints about me, but..."

Condor's blink keyed Renee to unfold and spread her legs, her black bikinied half moon facing him as her bare feet gripped the floor. Condor seemed not to care.

"But it was *all* of us who got killed," he said, his eyes floating back to the Starbucks. "Not just me. So if it wasn't about me, about RISING THUNDER ... *Hershel!*"

Condor's shout startled Renee, but she used that natural reaction to disguise her hands finding a grip on the edge of the leather couch.

"Hershel! He was wild about something he popped onto last Friday! He would have run straight to our boss Dray! But forget Hershel, the Agency will have my boss and everybody else focused on me because of the frame job and –"

Renee's bare thighs squeaked on the black leather couch.

Condor's Glock zeroed her heart: *"No!"*

"I was just –"

"No," he said. Saw the way her jaw set and knew he'd been right.

"Do you have any rope?" he said.

She blinked. "I've got twine in the utility drawer in the kitchen, I'll go get —"

"DON'T!" Condor rocketed out of the chair and away from her as she *naturally* started to rise with her suggestion. "You're not the helpful kind."

He made her kneel on the hard wooden floor. He backed into the kitchen, gun on her the whole time, aiming over the open counter. His free hand groped in the counter's utility drawer – lifted out a sheathed throwing knife.

"So much for your domestic side," he told her.

Renee watched his eyes float around her home while keeping her kneeling form in his gaze – and in the aim of his gun. His gaze locked on the P.C. in her corner. He ordered her to unplug and gather up all the P.C.'s cords, then march into the bedroom.

"What are you doing?" she said, as he made her sit in the middle of the bed.

"I have to get Dray to see everything, not just the frame

trapping me. Together we can focus the Agency on the truth. If nobody kills me first."

He made her tie one chord to her right wrist, tie the other end to the headboard's same side brass corner pole. Made her lay down, her arm lashed up behind her. He made a loop of a chord, cinched it around her left ankle.

"You can't get to Dray!" She raised her head off the bed while he lashed her left leg to that bottom corner pole. "They've got a team securing him at the Graylin hotel!"

"How's our CIA done with our security so far?" He shook his head. "I never thought I'd be standing here."

He pulled her right leg wide and apart from its mate, lashed it to the other corner post. Her spread-wide legs exposed her bikini panties' dark crescent.

"You can't get out of here! There're watchers on my exits! You won't make it!"

"I'll do my best to disappoint you," he told her.

And grabbed her left wrist. Tied her to the headboard.

"You can't leave me like this!" He went into the bathroom. Came out with a wide spool of white medical tape. "What if you don't come back?"

"Don't worry." He stared at her spread-eagled body. "Somebody will find you. You're the lucky kind."

Then he pressed a strip of white tape over her beautiful mouth, left.

The elevator dropped him down to the basement. He found a laundry room, storage bins, the furnace room jammed with a giant aluminum Christmas tree and a matching Star of David, strings of lights and ornaments. But no door out.

He rode the elevator up to LOBBY. The elevator door

slid open. He saw the reception desk, a man sitting in the lobby, watching the building entrance. The elevator door closed. Condor pushed the button marked ROOF.

Where he stood beneath the night sky of Washington, D.C. – not the artistic rooftops of Paris or the pigeon-cooped roofs of New York, but neither of those skylines held the glow of the Capitol dome, the blinking red light atop the Washington monument.

On the rear of Renee's building, the park side, Condor found steel rungs – and the plaque reading: WARNING – LADDER RUNGS END WITH FORTY FOOT DROP.

Pollution covered the stars. He spun in a frustrated circle under that lost light. The red eye atop the Washington monument winked at him, mocked him, winking …

Condor blinked.

He found it in the basement amidst the Christmas decorations: a snow-proof orange extension cord, had to be 100 feet long. The elevator took him back to the roof. He cinched one end of the cord around his chest, tied it to the other end. Dumped the orange loop off the roof by the steel rungs. Condor grabbed the steel rungs … and climbed down the back of the eleven story building.

He lost count of the rungs, his arms and legs aching, his heart pounding, his shoe – stepping down and finding nothing. Four stories of nothing.

Condor untied the ends of the extension cord, fed the long end over a rung until *woosh*: gravity sucked the long cord down into darkness.

"Bad idea," he whispered.

Hand-over-hand, gripping the thick rubber extension

cord, Condor lowered himself down four stories of brick wall. On the ground, he had to tie the cord loop on the rungs where it could be found by any midnight rambler. He ran into the park. Trees leapt out of the darkness. He swatted them away, got to a main street, caught a cab.

"You hear the news?" asked the cabby.

In the back seat, Condor found the cabby's eyes in the mirror. "What news?"

"Them massacre shootings. Like a dozen dead. But you know the good thing?"

"No."

"TV says it's them Russian mafias dusting each other off. Means they ain't gonna be locking up more black men."

The yellow cab rolled through the dark night.

"What am I doing here?" whispered Condor as the cab stopped near a cheap hotel.

'Where you told me to take you,' said the cabby.

Condor paid, sent the taxi on its way. Watched those twin red tail lights disappear in the night of the city street. Condor unbuttoned his filthy gray sports jacket.

'In the bowels of the Graylin.' A no-registration hole to hide a potential witness. Condor circled the block until he stared at the alley behind his target zone.

Coming up on midnight, his watch told him. A blue-black American city night.

In daylight Pakistan, RT/Delta would be fueling their helicopter.

He ran to the mouth of the Graylin alley. Nothing moved. He checked his back, his sides; saw only a laughing trio of club hoppers getting into a car a block away.

"Hell," muttered Condor. "I should have been dead this morning."

Face of stone, he walked into the alley, the Glock in his hand. He eased along the wall, eyes darting everywhere: Closed doors. Fire escapes overhead. Blue neon sign above a door just past a dumpster – GRA L N. A rat scurried past him.

Condor noticed that dumpster lid was wedged open – by a shoe.

He eased the dumpster lid up....

That shoe was worn by a dead man atop of another dead man.

The dumpster lid crashed down BANG!

Condor threw open the hotel's backdoor and jumped inside to a dank concrete maze of air ducts and cluttered corridors and throbbing machinery.

He thrust his Glock in front of him. Jumped around a corner: long corridor, service carts, overhead pipes – and a shaft of yellow light spilling out an open door.

Condor eased toward the light – stepped on a brass cartridge case. Stumbled into a serving cart piled high with dirty dishes. The cart slammed the wall. Plates crashed and exploded on the corridor floor.

A dead man flopped from behind the rolling cart.

Dead man! Face-shot corpse! Black man with a badge on his belt! Condor swung his Glock away from the corpse, aimed down the corridor. A dead white male lay by a metal cabinet 20 feet further up the hall. Condor knew in his guts: *partners*.

Condor leapt into the glowing yellow room.

Over the Glock sight, he saw a closet and a cot, TV, a

table against the far wall with a chair where his boss Dray slumped, the eyeglasses dangling from a shoelace around his neck getting smeared by blood streaming from his slashed throat.

Bleeding, he's still –

The closet burst open. The bald killer slammed a palm strike into Condor's back. The Glock flew from Condor's hand – hit a cinderblock wall, bounced back on the gray tiled floor as Condor's feet swept out from under him. Sprawled on the floor, Condor grabbed for his Glock. The bald killer kicked Condor's head. *White flash* burned his vision, but he saw a flutter near the bald killer, white paper scrap floating –

"Freeze!" yelled *someone else.*

Looking from the floor between the bald man's legs, Condor saw a *third man* in the hall – a third man aiming a pistol into this yellow room.

Third man jerked/crumpled, his gun stabbing towards the ceiling firing BANG! The bald killer ran from the room, stepped on the fallen third man.

As Condor scrambled to his feet. Grabbed the Glock. Stuffed the paper scrap in his pants pocket. Stepped into the hall.

The third man lay shoulder-shot, conscious, his eyes turning up to Condor –

"Halt!" yelled a voice from the corner of the corridor where Condor had come.

Condor ran the other way. A gun roared. A bullet splattered the wall near him. He ran through a yellow maze of pipes and locked doors.

Saw a giant open gap in the wall to his left. The sign above the gap read:

LAUNDRY BUNDLES ONLY!

Feet first, he plunged into that dark chute. Slid to the basement laundry room. A conveyer belt angled up to a barred door. Condor scrambled up the conveyer belt, threw the bar off the door, leapt outside, ran through the city night as sirens wailed.

Two taxis and a half mile walk later, he stood behind Renee's building. The orange extension cord dangled from the iron rungs four stories up. Condor envisioned RT/Delta training, those men using a rope to walk up an obstacle course wall. Knew he had to imagine himself into a Delta superman. Or die.

Renee heard her locks click. Her front door open and close. *"Squawk! Fuck you!"* She blinked and Condor stood staring down at her on the bed. He looked terrible. Smeared filthy. Flecked with red. Trembling. He tried to speak, shook his head. Left her tied to the bed and went into the bathroom. Shut the door.

He stood in the shower and let the water pound down on his nakedness. He didn't know if she could hear him gasping, sobbing in the steam. He dried off. Couldn't put his bloody shirt on again. Spotted a huge blue sweatshirt she slept in, pulled it on. Wore his modesty-protecting filthy trousers. Opened the bathroom door.

She stared at him with her brown eyes, hands and legs tied spread on the bed. Tape covered her mouth. He slumped beside her. The guns were on the bathroom floor.

He said: "I don't want any more killing."

Gently as he could, he pulled the tape off her mouth. She licked her lips, and he held her head so she could drink from the nightstand bottle of water.

Words flowed from him, babble summed up with: "They got there first."

"*They.* Who are '*they?*'" she said.

"Bald guy and his buddy who shot the man in the hall. Plus that shot man and his crew. So many *they's,* and I got trapped between them."

"The hit squad. And the good guys."

"How can you tell the difference?" asked Condor.

"That's your problem. How did bald guy know about the Graylin to hit your boss? Unless his cell is hooked into the good guys. Which means we can't trust anybody."

"You believe me?"

"The verdict on you is crazy, corrupt or confused. I've never seen a more confused man."

"Glad to oblige." He stared at her. "Why do you believe me?"

"Because you came back."

"That's all?"

"That's enough. For a start. For you."

"For me?" Condor shook his head. "I'm the guy running in the night. I don't even know who or what I'm running from."

"You're staying alive."

"Just staying alive isn't worth all that death." Condor stared at the woman he'd tied to the bed. "I have to trust you."

She shrugged her shoulders as much as she could. "Makes sense."

He untied her right hand. She lowered it to her side near him to let the blood flow back into it as he untied her left hand. She sat up, her legs still tied spread wide.

Exhausted, Condor told her: "You could beat the hell out of me tonight."

"I can beat the hell out of you tomorrow." She shrugged. "Might as well wait."

He untied first one of her legs, then the other. She flexed them. Stayed on the bed and didn't kill him or knock him down or go for the guns on the bathroom floor.

He blushed. "What that security guy told you. About me having a monster crush on you. I didn't … want you to find out like that."

"I already knew." She looked away. "Why do think I transferred you out of my section – beside your annoying tendency to poke around and make trouble."

"Sorry."

"I'm not. At least, I'm not sorry about your monster crush."

He blinked.

She said: "I didn't want you to die feeling sorry for liking me."

"You're too romantic."

"Yeah. That's my problem."

His hand floated up to her face. His thumb rubbed off tape adhesive stuck to her lower lip. Her face turned to be cupped by his clean hand. She saw his eyes close as he leaned in for a kiss. Mission accomplished, he pulled back, saw her staring at him.

Then her hands cupped his face. Her thumbs lay along his cheekbones. She whispered: "I could gouge out your eyes."

Condor blinked. Said: "Don't stop there."

She pulled him in to kiss. Put him on his back. Straddled him, long white legs and black bikini pinning him to the mattress. She stared down at him – ripped open her blouse and let it fall. Her naked back reflected in the glass of the picture above the bed, superimposed over a scene of wild horses in a blizzard as Renee picked up his tired hands, filled them with her teardrops of flesh.

Later. Under the covers of her bed. Laying face to face.

"What time is it?" he said.

"Right now." She smiled. Gave him the situational answer: "Near 3 a.m."

"Noon for RT/Delta. Nine hours and counting. Will you stop them?"

"How? And with what certainty? Besides, they – we – still have time."

Condor shook his head. "'Feels like I'm trapped in some net."

Her naked leg rose over him, her hand soothed his cheek. "You're here now."

He shook his head. "I was a regular guy, looking for real life."

"Congratulations, you found it." Her fingers brushed his lids. "But now close your eyes. Even if you can't sleep, there's nothing here to see."

She reached across him, snapped out the bed lamp.

Dawn found Condor standing in Renee's kitchen nook staring into the black coffee in his mug, smelling Starbucks and seeing Sarita and the slaughter cafe, dead men in the bowels of a hotel, RT/Delta gearing up for their raid. His coffee trembled.

He wore his pants – sponged to presentable. The sweatshirt was tight on him, but also presentable. He needed a shave.

The Glock waited on the counter. He pushed the button on the handle to release the ammo magazine. He thumbed two bullets free and it was empty.

"Plus one in the barrel," he muttered. Reloaded, set the Glock on the counter.

His eyes roamed around her home. He started out of the kitchen –

"Squawk! Fuck you!"

Startled, Condor jumped back behind the counter bordering the kitchen nook and living room. He grinned at the parrot in the cage: "What did I tell you about that?"

Condor found the sheathed throwing knife. He pushed the left sleeve of the sweatshirt up to his elbow, strapped the knife to his left arm, pulled the sweatshirt sleeve down, made sure his fingers could slide up the sleeve to unsnap and draw the knife. He hung his arms "naturally." Like a boy playing gunslinger, he checked his blurry reflection in the mirror of the aluminum refrigerator.

Shook his head, whispered to his reflection: "My name is Condor."

Renee walked out of the bedroom and tossed him a Steve McQueen green nylon jacket, saying: "See how you look in this."

She wore pants, a red bra that pulled at his eyes, her gun clipped on her belt.

He grinned: "Yeah, you'll get the stairwell guards to walk you to your car."

"After the Graylin, they'll want to make sure the base-

65

ment garage guards haven't been ambushed. That should let you to slip out the fire exit."

Renee pulled on a sweater, scrutinized him in the Steve McQueen jacket, said: "It fits, but you're lucky I like my things big."

She crossed to a desk, pulled out a cell phone with its number taped on it. Memorized the number, gave it to Condor and put a spare cell phone battery in her pocket. The paper scrap from the hotel crime scene was still in the plastic baggy where he'd sealed it. She put the baggy in her pocket, tossed him a set of car keys.

"Remember, it's a brown Ford, D.C. tags with a dented rear left door. Space 363. Just sign in as '*Parnell Jones*' and act like you have the right to be who you are."

"Who *I* am?" Condor smiled. "Spare cell phones, spare car stashed a few blocks away – *Parnell*: it could be a man or a woman, right? Are you always so … prepared?"

"A street dog keeps her bite," she told him. "Agency policies encourage that. But I'm going to violate the hell out of policy this morning to forensic that scrap of paper."

"Do you think –"

"Evidence like that paper is sacred to the Agency. Believe me, we know how to create a whole scenario from one scrap."

She slipped into her jacket, beckoned him to follow her to the door, saying: "Remember, I call you. Don't get stopped for a traffic ticket. Park at some mall and stay in the car. Shouldn't take more than four hours to get what's gettable."

"Then what?"

She nodded towards the counter: "Don't forget your gun."

Renee was wrong: she called him in four hours and twenty-one minutes, an eternity he agonized through in a mall parking lot on the fuzzy line between D.C. and Maryland.

"Took me this long to shake my 'security,'" she said in his new cell phone. "I'm in the car now, almost across the river."

The scrap of paper was a torn electric bill for a suburban house: "Easy Beltway access, quick shot to three airports, Amtrack, Capitol Hill and the White House."

He rendezvoused with her BMW at a rest stop. Electric signs on the road flashed Terrorist Threat Level ORANGE. No one followed them into an ordinary neighborhood.

She pulled to the curb. He parked behind her. No one moved on the sidewalks. No one watched out any house's windows. No cars rolled by them as she climbed in his car, nodded to a white frame dwelling set back from the street. The house was bordered, one neighbor's man-high hedge and another neighbor's tall wooden plank fence.

He looked at his watch: Sunset for RT/Delta. Last gear check before quarantine and their rendezvous with fate. Condor stared at the suspect house.

Renee said: "Want to knock?"

"Nah. Nobody's polite anymore."

"Remember: Don't shoot if you don't have to."

Renee kicked in the front door. Condor raced behind her through a living room with a TV and boxes of clothes, through to the tiny 'dining' room with two cots –

And a green stuffed chair that enthroned the bald man.

Who blinked at them, hands on his lap.

"Cover him!" yelled Renee.

She stepped out of Condor's way as he eased forward, gun leveled at the bald man. Renee backed towards Condor and the front room with its *what's-up-there* staircase. As she stepped beside Condor, the bald man ... smiled.

Fast, so fast Condor didn't know what was happening, Renee grabbed his gun hand in an *aikido* grasp, flipped him head over heels. His back slammed on the wooden floor. Breath blew out of him and he felt the Glock slide from his grasp to hers. Condor raised his head off the floor –

BAM! BAM!

The bald man in the green stuffed chair jerked with an astonished look on his face as two red flowers blossomed on his chest.

Condor gasped. On his back, he saw Renee with her arms spread like soaring wings, her smoking gun bore lined up on him as her left hand aimed Condor's Glock at the wall by the front door: BAM! BAM! BAM!

The Glock's slide blew back and locked from having fired its last round. She set the Glock on the floor, used a two handed grip on her own gun to zero Condor. "The irony is that *you* were supposed to die first."

Condor stared at the dead bald man in the green chair.

Renee said: "He was ex-Delta, on CIA contract. Found the al Qaeda cell based in this ordinary house. But instead of busting them, he sold himself. 'Course, I pulled all his strings, but I'm invisible. The terrorists don't know I exist: Baldy bought my strategy because al Qaeda won't deal with a woman.

"Now he can't demand his share." She smiled. "He was an easier hook than you, though neither of you were supposed to die until at least ..."

She checked her watch: "...an hour from now. After RISING THUNDER."

"You sold out the Delta team! They're heading into an ambush! It'll be worse than in Somalia! How much did you get out of al Qeada for killing our own guys?"

"Money makes the world go round. I want my turns."

"How much?"

She shrugged. "Five million. But don't worry: our guys won't die. Get up."

And he did, slowly, his back to her, saying: "But if our guys won't die..."

"Death is a commodity. If innocent Afghanistanis are slaughtered by an American raid caught on TV for the world ... That's a bonanza for our enemies."

As he faced Renee, Condor saw the TV behind her. Envisioned its dead green screen showing images of AK47-toting terrorists in a village. Saw those images blur, morph, mutate into a young girl, a frightened mother, an old man, a father and his baby.

"You're creating a My Lai massacre! You'll make our real terrorist war *rhyme* with the worst of Vietnam!

"You two and al Qaeda created perfect fake intelligence!" Excitement rang through Condor's fear. "That's what bugged me! Everything fit with absolute certainty!"

"People who are absolutely certain they're right are ripe to be made wrong."

Condor shook his head. "Won't work. Our Delta boys are the best gunners in the world. Savvy. Been there, done that. They won't massacre innocent civilians."

"They won't have to," said Renee. "Al Qaeda martyrs will kill every villager they can – using American guns. The

69

al Qaeda guys will fire on RT/Delta. Shoot at our guys, they shoot back. Imagine two, three minutes at full auto fire. TV cameras are camped close enough to arrive at the same time as the Rangers' helicopters. And in the glare of TV lights, who can prove it wasn't America that massacred that mother and child?

"No one will buy America's denials," she said. "How many times has the world found out we fibbed? But the Agency will look for a plot. Hunt for villains. Won't stop until they find something. So to cover my ass, I had to give them a fall guy.

"You. *Condor*. Framed as a traitor for al Qaeda. You 'spied' on RISING THUNDER because I kept steering you to it until you got hooked. I transferred you away from me to Homeland Security. I set up 'your' Cayman account. We were going to kill you after RISING THUNDER to make it look like al Qaeda was covering their tracks.

"But then yesterday morning, you called me. Said you were close to figuring out what was bugging you. We couldn't take a chance. Plus we didn't know what you'd told your co-workers. Thanks for bunching them all in the Starbucks kill zone."

"That's not my fault!"

"Maybe not, but here's how it looks in my frame, Version Three Point Zero: your Homeland Security team suspected you, so you had to kill them all – including your boss – before they could interfere with 'your' betrayal of RISING THUNDER.

"And here you are: caught *dead to rights* with Baldy who helped you betray America, kill your co-workers, and hunt down your boss. Al Qaeda fingerprints are everywhere in this safe house and at the Graylin where they backed up Baldy there. You checked their car out of the parking lot. A wounded Homeland Security guy even saw you at the Graylin. Me planting that electric bill in your car just now was a nice touch. It was going to be found *dropped* at the Graylin to lead the good guys here, but then you grabbed it, put your DNA on it. Thanks."

"You've been working me and the CIA, Baldy and al Qaeda for months!"

"I'm an industrious girl."

"Is that what you call it." Condor swallowed. "How am I supposed to die?"

"Resisting capture. I spotted you in my car mirrors. Maybe you were after me, too, who knows? I flipped your tail job. But *gosh*, my cell phone battery went dead. *Shit happens.* I couldn't call for back up.

"So I dogged you here. Exercised justifiable initiative. Kicked the door. You popped three rounds at me but I nailed you. Baldy went for his gun. I had to drill him. Trust me, the forensics will line up: it's not an exact science. While the CIA is busy sorting out this mess … RISING THUNDER explodes in global *primetime*."

"You think that will work?" said Condor.

"Sure. So do you. TV and computers create reality."

"Truth in a box." Condor shook his head. "Like a coffin."

"Pick up your empty gun," she told him. "Move over to the other side of Baldy."

"Why?"

She smiled. "So you can live longer."

Condor inhaled that dining room. A dead man slumped

in a green chair. The trash of an al Qaeda sleeper cell lay scattered everywhere. The woman he'd trusted in his bones stood behind him preparing his perfectly planned murder.

"Living is all I've got," muttered Condor. He dropped his eyes. Slumped.

She saw him bend towards the Glock to pick it up with both hands –

Blast towards her like an uncoiling wrestler. She clubbed his left elbow with her gun. He yelled, hooked his right hand at her and she snapped her left arm up to block –

Renee screamed as lightning ripped her forearm. *Knife, where did he get – oh!* She deflected his next stab, chopped his knife wrist. His weapon flew across the room.

But the knife surprise unbalanced her. Condor grabbed her gun hand, felt –

Renee thrust her gun arm straight up. Condor clung to her. His body pressed against hers as if they were ballet dancers. She pivoted into a hip throw. But as she curled into him, his free hand squeezed her bloody gash. Pain made her wince. That flinch meant throwing him flipped her, too. They spun through the air together –

Crashed with him on top of her, both of them face down.

She rolled him onto his back, her spine pressed his chest, her skull alongside his cheek. He grabbed her pistol. Pushed the bore of her gun into the notch under her jaw.

Renee lay on top of him. Her legs were outside of his, her shoes flat on the floor.

Condor lay under her. He pressed the gun under her chin.

They lay there.

Until she said: "*Gotchya.*"

"What?" yelled Condor.

Her hair floated on his left cheek. Smelled like coconut shampoo.

The gun under her jaw made Renee grimace her words: "You're not a killer."

"I almost got you with your knife! And … I'll shoot you now!"

"No. Self-defense, sure. Combat, if you're lucky. But *now* you'd have to do it stone cold, and that's not you. You're no executioner."

She flicked her left shoe off so that one bare foot kissed the wooden floor.

He pushed the gun barrel into her: "Don't!"

"OK," she said. "You're the one with the big hard gun."

"Yes I am! And you're going to … to …"

"To what?"

"I'm not going to stay trapped on this floor!"

"You're trapped on more than this floor," said Renee. "Officially, you're either corrupt, crazy, or confused. The Agency doesn't forgive any of those. So let me help you out. After all, we're in this together."

Condor said: "I didn't kill anybody. Or betray my country."

"Countries aren't what they used to be."

"There's freedom. There's justice."

"Justice. What is going to happen to '*just us*'?" Renee shifted –

Condor pushed the gun tighter under her jaw.

"You won't execute me. So it's my word against yours. The CIA won't know who to believe. They're already stuck with their cover story lies about the murders. They'll flush us *both* down some black hole. I'll be guilty, but you'll be a chump."

She maneuvered her knees higher so her hips rubbed his groin.

"Is that better for you?" she said.

"You don't care."

"Actually, I do. A girl should always respect a monster crush."

"You're the monster."

"But you're caught in the net."

"No!"

"Yes." He felt her smile. "Unless we become partners. We can stop the RISING THUNDER disaster. Pin all the sins on Baldy and al Qaeda. Bust this al Qaeda cell — they've got big, nasty plans. We'll come out of this as heroes — or at least free and clear. You won't want to ride off into the sunset with me, but we can share a goodbye kiss."

"Are you crazy?"

"Crazy doesn't mean much anymore."

"They'll get you!"

"Even if you convince them I'm guilty, only I can rat out this al Qaeda cell. Stop their next *kill-a-few-thousand-Americans* mission. Nobody can torture or drug it out of me, so your bosses will have to deal. Yesterday's gone and today is on its way out the door. I'm selling a safer tomorrow for a guarantee that takes me off the hook. So if you rebel against all that, then you become a new problem for national homeland security."

"They're better than that!"

"They? Who is 'they'? They are us, us is you, and look where you are."

"You can't win!" He felt his heart slamming under hers.

"I won't lose," said Renee. "How about you?"

He felt her smile. "Who are you going to be? A killer, a chump, or a survivor?"

They lay on their backs, her on top of him, his gun pressing under her jaw.

"Fuck your labels, I decide who I am," said Condor. "Put the gun in your mouth. Hold it tight. If you *kung fu*, I pull the trigger. We're getting off this floor."

He eased the pistol's bore up over her chin until it rested lightly on her lips.

She whispered into that black hole: "Then what?"

"Then I prove you wrong. The Agency won't buy your lies. They won't plea-bargain your treason and murders. All this, *us*: we're about more than *what works*. They'll give you what you deserve, and they'll let me be me."

Renee smiled. Said: *"Really?"*

And slowly, lovingly, slid her lips around the steel barrel of his gun.

The End

© *James Grady – 2005*

Six Days of the Condor

Preface

The events described in this novel are fictitious, at least to the author's best knowledge. Whether these events might take place is another question, for the structure and operations of the intelligence community are based on fact. Malcolm's branch of the CIA and the 54/12 Group do indeed exist, though perhaps no longer under the designations given to them here.

For the factual background to this story, the author is indebted to the following sources: Jack Anderson, *Washington Merry-Go-Round* (various dates); Alfred W. McCoy, *The Politics of Heroin in Southeast Asia* (1972); Andrew Tully, *CIA: The Inside Story* (1962); David Wise and Thomas B. Ross, *The Invisible Government* (1964) and *The Espionage Establishment* (1967).

James Grady, 1974

'... *most significant triumphs come not in the secrets passed in the dark, but in patient reading, hour after hour, of highly technical periodicals. In a real sense they [the 'patriotic and dedicated' CIA researchers] are America's professional students. They are unsung just as they are invaluable.'*

– *President Lyndon B. Johnson, on swearing in Richard M. Helms as CIA director, June 30, 1966*

Wednesday

Four blocks behind the Library of Congress, just past Southeast A and Fourth Street (one door from the corner), is a white stucco three-story building. Nestled in among the other town houses, it would be unnoticeable if not for its color. The clean brightness stands out among the fading reds, grays, greens, and occasional off-whites. Then, too, the short black iron picket fence and the small, neatly trimmed lawn lend an aura of quiet dignity the other buildings lack. However, few people notice the building. Residents of the area have long since blended it into the familiar neighborhood. The dozens of Capitol Hill and Library of Congress workers who pass it each day don't have time to notice it, and probably wouldn't even if they had time. Located where it is, almost off 'the Hill', most of the tourist hordes never come close to it. The few who do are usually looking for a policeman to direct them out of the notoriously rough neighborhood to the safety of national monuments.

If a passerby (for some strange reason) is attracted to the building and takes a closer look, his investigation would reveal very little out of the ordinary. As he stood outside the picket fence, he would probably first note a raised bronze plaque, about three feet by two feet, which proclaims the building to be the national headquarters of the American Literary Historical Society. In Washington, D.C., a city of hundreds of landmarks and headquarters of a multitude of organisations, such a building is not extraordinary. Should the passerby have an eye for architecture and design, he would be pleasantly intrigued by the ornate black wooden door flawed by a curiously large peephole. If our passerby's curiosity is not hampered by shyness, he might open the gate. He probably will not notice the slight click as the magnetic hinge moves from its resting place and breaks an electric circuit. A few short paces later, our passerby mounts the black iron steps to the stoop and rings the bell.

If, as is usually the case, Walter is drinking coffee in the small kitchen, arranging crates of books, or sweeping the floor, then the myth of security is not even flaunted. The visitor hears Mrs. Russell's harsh voice bellow 'Come in!' just before she punches the buzzer on her desk releasing the electronic lock.

The first thing a visitor to the Society's headquarters notices is its extreme tidiness. As he stands in the stairwell, his eyes are probably level with the top of Walter's desk, a scant four inches from the edge of the well. There are never any papers on Walter's desk, but then, with a steel reinforced front, it was never meant for paper. When the visitor turns to his right and climbs out of the stairwell, he sees Mrs. Russell. Unlike Walter's work area, her desk spawns paper. It covers the top, protrudes from drawers, and hides her ancient typewriter. Behind the processed forest sits Mrs. Russell. Her gray hair is thin and usually disheveled. In any case, it is too short to be of much help to her face. A horseshoe-shaped brooch dated 1932 adorns what was once a left breast. She smokes constantly.

Strangers who get this far into the Society's headquarters (other than mailmen and delivery boys) are few in number. Those few, after being screened by Walter's stare (if he is there), deal with Mrs. Russell. If the stranger comes for business, she directs him to the proper person, provided she accepts his clearance. If the stranger is merely one of the brave and curious, she delivers a five-minute, inordinately dull lecture on the Society's background of foundation funding, its purpose of literary analysis, advancement, and achievement (referred to as 'the 3 A's'), shoves pamphlets into usually less-than-eager hands, states that there is no one present who can answer further questions, suggests writing to an unspecified address for further information, and then bids a brisk 'Good day'. Visitors are universally stunned by this onslaught and leave meekly, probably without noticing the box on Walter's desk which took their picture or the red light and buzzer above the door which announces the opening of the gate. The visitor's disappointment would dissolve into fantasy should he learn that he had just visited a section branch office of a department of the Central Intelligence Agency's Intelligence Division.

The National Security Act of 1947 created the Central Intelligence Agency, a result of the World War II experience of being caught flat-footed at Pearl Harbor. The Agency, or the Company, as many of its employees call it, is the largest and most active entity in the far-flung American intelligence network, a network composed of eleven major agencies, around two hundred thousand persons, and annually budgeted in the billions of dollars. The C.I.A.'s activities, like those of its major counterparts – Britain's M.I.6., Russia's K.G.B., and Red China's Social Affairs Department – range through a spectrum of covert espionage, technical research, the funding of loosely linked political action groups, support to friendly governments, and direct paramilitary operations. The wide variety of activities of these agencies, coupled with their basic mission of national security in a troubled world, has made the intelligence agency one of the most important branches of government. In America, former C.I.A. Director Allen Dulles once said, 'The National Security Act of 1947 ... has given Intelligence a more influential position in our government than Intelligence enjoys in any other government in the world.'

The main activity of the C.I.A. is simple, painstaking research. Hundreds of researchers daily scour technical journals, domestic and foreign periodicals of all kinds, speeches, and media broadcasts. This research is divided between two of the four divisions of the C.I.A. The Research Division (R.D.) is in charge of technical intelligence, and its experts provide detailed reports of the latest scientific advances in all countries, including the United States and its allies. The Intelligence Division (I.D.) engages in a highly specialized form of scholastic research. About 80 per cent of the information I.D. handles comes from 'open' sources: public magazines, broadcasts, journals, and books. I.D. digests its data and from this fare produces three major types of reports: one type makes long-range projections dealing with areas of interest, a second is a daily review of the current world situation, and the third tries to detect gaps in C.I.A. activities. The research gathered by both I.D. and R.D. is used by the other two divisions: Support (the administrative arm which deals with logistics, equipment, security, and communications) and Plans (all covert activities, the actual spying divisions).

The American Literary Historical Society, with head-quarters in Washington and a small receiving office in Seattle, is a section branch of one of the smaller depart-ments in the C.I.A. Because of the inexact nature of the data the department deals with, it is only loosely allied to I.D., and, indeed, to C.I.A. as a whole. The department (officially designated as Department 17, C.I.A.I.D.) reports are not consistently incorporated in any one of the three major research report areas. Indeed, Dr. Lappe, the very serious, very nervous head of the Society (officially titled Section 9, Department 17, C.I.A.I.D.), slaves over weekly, monthly, and annual reports which may not even make the corresponding report of mother Department 17. In turn, Department 17 reports often will not impress major group co-ordinators on the division level and thus will fail to be incorporated into any of the I.D. reports. *C'est la vie.*

The function of the Society and of Department 17 is to keep track of all espionage and related acts recorded in literature. In other words, the Department reads spy thrillers and murder mysteries. The antics and situations of thousands of volumes of mystery and mayhem are carefully detailed, and analysed in Department 17 files. Volumes dating as far back as James Fenimore Cooper have been scrutinised. Most of the company-owned volumes are kept at the Langley, Virginia, C.I.A. central complex, but the Society headquarters maintains a library of almost three thousand volumes. At one time the Department was housed in the Christian Heurich Brewery near the State Department, but in the fall of 1961, when C.I.A. moved to its Langley complex, the Department transferred to the Virginia suburbs. In 1970 the ever-increasing volume of pertinent literature began to create logistic and expense problems for the Department. Additionally, the Deputy Director of I.D. questioned the need for highly screened and, therefore, highly paid analysts. Consequently, the Department re-opened its branch section in metropolitan Washington, this time conveniently close to the Library of Congress. Because the employees were not in the central complex, they needed only to pass a cursory Secret clearance rather than the exacting Top Secret clearance required for employment at the complex. Naturally, their salaries paralleled their rating.

The analysts for the Department keep abreast of the literary field and divide their work basically by mutual consent. Each analyst has areas of expertise, areas usually defined by author. In addition to summarising plots and methods of all the books, the analysts daily receive a series of specially 'sanitised' reports from the Langley complex. The reports contain capsule descriptions of actual events with all names deleted and as few necessary details as possible. Fact and fiction are compared, and if major correlations occur, the analyst begins a further investigation with a more detailed but still sanitised report. If the correlation still appears strong, the information and reports are passed on for review to a higher classified section of the Department. Somewhere after that the decision is made as to whether the author was guessing and lucky or whether he knew more than he should. If the latter is the case, the author is definitely unlucky, for then a report is filed with the Plans Division for action. The analysts are also expected to compile lists of helpful tips for agents. These lists are forwarded to Plans Division instructors, who are always looking for new tricks.

Ronald Malcolm was supposed to be working on one of those lists that morning, but instead he sat reversed on a wooden chair, his chin resting on the scratched walnut back. It was fourteen minutes until nine o'clock, and he had been sitting there since he climbed the spiral staircase to his second-story office at 8.30, spilling hot coffee and swearing loudly all the way. The coffee was long gone and Malcolm badly wanted a second cup, but he didn't dare take his eyes off his window.

Barring illness, every morning between 8.40 and 9.00 an incredibly beautiful girl walked up Southeast A, past Malcolm's window, and into the Library of Congress. And every morning, barring illness or unavoidable work, Malcolm watched her for the brief interval it took her to pass out of view. It became a ritual, one that helped Malcolm rationalise getting out of a perfectly comfortable bed to shave and walk to work. At first lust dominated Malcolm's attitude, but this had gradually been replaced by a sense of awe that was beyond his definition. In February he gave up even trying to think about it, and now, two months later, he merely waited and watched.

It was the first real day of spring. Early in the year there had been intervals of sunshine scattered through generally rainy days, but no real spring. Today dawned bright and stayed bright. An aroma promising cherry blossoms crept through the morning smog. Out of the corner of his eye Malcolm saw her coming, and he tipped his chair closer to the window.

The girl didn't walk up the street, she strode, moving with purpose and the pride born of modest yet firm, knowledgeable confidence. Her shiny brown hair lay across her back, sweeping past her broad shoulders to fall halfway to her slender waist. She wore no make-up, and when she wasn't wearing sunglasses one could see how her eyes, large and well-spaced, perfectly matched her straight nose, her wide mouth, her full face, her square chin. The tight brown sweater hugged her large breasts and even without a bra there was no sag. The plaid skirt revealed full thighs, almost too muscular. Her calves flowed to her ankles. Three more firm steps and she vanished from sight.

Malcolm sighed and settled back in his chair. His typewriter had a half-used sheet of paper in the carriage. He rationalised that this represented an adequate start on his morning's work. He belched loudly, picked up his empty cup, and left his little red and blue room.

When he got to the stairs, Malcolm paused. There were two coffeepots in the building, one on the main floor in the little kitchen area behind Mrs. Russell's desk and one on the third floor on the wrapping table at the back of the open stacks. Each pot had its advantages and disadvantages. The first-floor pot was larger and served the most people.

Besides Mrs. Russell and ex-drill instructor Walter ('Sergeant Jennings, if you please!'), Dr. Lappe and the new accountant-librarian Heidegger had their offices down-stairs, and thus in the great logistical scheme of things used that pot. The coffee was, of course, made by Mrs. Russell, whose many faults did not include poor cooking. There were two disadvantages to the first-floor pot. If Malcolm or Ray Thomas, the other analyst on the second floor, used that pot, they ran the risk of meeting Dr. Lappe. Those meetings were uncomfortable. The other disadvantage was Mrs. Russell and her smell, or, as Ray was wont to call her, Perfume Polly.

Use of the third-floor pot was minimal, as only Harold Martin and Tamatha Reynolds, the other two analysts, were permanently assigned that pot. Sometimes Ray or Malcolm exercised their option. As often as he dared, Walter wandered by for refreshments and a glance at Tamatha's frail form. Tamatha was a nice girl, but she hadn't a clue about making coffee. In addition to subjecting himself to a culinary atrocity by using the third-floor pot, Malcolm risked being cornered by Harold Martin and bombarded with the latest statistics, scores, and opinions from the world of sports, followed by nostalgic stories of high-school prowess. He decided to go downstairs.

Mrs. Russell greeted Malcolm with the usual disdainful grunt as he walked by her desk. Sometimes, just to see if she had changed, Malcolm stopped to 'chat' with her. She would shuffle papers, and no matter what Malcolm talked about she rambled through a disjointed monologue dealing with how hard she worked, how sick she was, and how little she was appreciated. This morning Malcolm went no further than a sardonic grin and an exaggerated nod.

Malcolm heard the click of an office door opening just as he started back upstairs with his cup of coffee, and braced himself for a lecture from Dr. Lappe.

'Oh, ah, Mr. Malcolm, may I ... may I talk to you for a moment?'

Relief. The speaker was Heidegger and not Dr. Lappe. With a smile and a sigh, Malcolm turned to face a slight man so florid that even his bald spot glowed. The inevitable tabcollar white shirt and narrow black tie squeezed the large head from the body.

'Hi, Rich,' said Malcolm, 'how are you?'

'I'm fine ... Ron. Fine.' Heidegger tittered. Despite six months of total abstinence and hard work, his nerves were still shot. Any inquiry into Heidegger's condition, however polite, brought back the days where he fearfully sneaked drinks in C.I.A. bathrooms, frantically chewing gum to hide the security risk on his breath. After he 'volunteered' for cold turkey, traveled through the hell of withdrawal, and began to pick up pieces of his sanity, the doctors told him he had been turned in by the security section in charge of monitoring the rest rooms. 'Would you, I mean, could you come in for a second?'

Any distraction was welcome. 'Sure, Rich.'

They entered the small office reserved for the accountant-librarian and sat, Heidegger behind his desk, Malcolm on the old stuffed chair left by the building's former tenant. For several seconds they sat silent.

Poor little man, thought Malcolm. Scared shitless, still hoping you can work your way back into favor. Still hoping for return to your Top Secret rating so you can move from this dusty green bureaucratic office to another dusty but more Secret office. Maybe, Malcolm thought, if you are lucky, your next office will be one of the other three colors intended to 'maximise an efficient office environment', maybe you'll get a nice blue room the same soothing shade as three of my walls and hundreds of other government offices.

'Right!' Heidegger's shout echoed through the room. Suddenly conscious of his volume, he leaned back in his chair and began again.'I ... I hate to bother you like this ...'

'Oh, no trouble at all.'

'Right. Well, Ron – you don't mind if I call you Ron, do you? Well, as you know, I'm new to this section. I decided to go over the records for the last few years to acquaint myself with the operation.' He chuckled nervously. 'Dr. Lappe's briefing was, shall we say, less than complete.'

Malcolm joined in his chuckle. Anybody who laughed at Dr. Lappe had something on the ball. Malcolm decided he might like Heidegger after all.

He continued, 'Right. Well. You've been here two years, haven't you? Ever since the move from Langley?'

Right, thought Malcolm as he nodded. Two years, two months, and some odd days.

'Right. Well, I've found some ... discrepancies I think need clearing up, and I thought maybe you could help me.' Heidegger paused and received a willing but questioning shrug from Malcolm. 'Well, I found two funny things – or rather, funny things in two areas.

'The first one had to do with accounts, you know,

money payed in and out for expenses, salaries, what have you. You probably don't know anything about that, it's something I'll have to figure out. But the other thing has to do with the books, and I'm checking with you and the other research analysts to see if I can find out anything before I go to Dr. Lappe with my written report.' He paused for another encouraging nod. Malcolm didn't disappoint him.

'Have you ever, well, have you ever noticed any missing books? No, wait,' he said, seeing the confused look on Malcolm's face, 'let me say that again. Do you ever know of an instance where we haven't got books we ordered or books we should have?'

'No, not that I know of,' said Malcolm, beginning to get bored. 'If you could tell me which ones are missing, or might be missing ...' He let his sentence trail off, and Heidegger took the cue.

'Well, that's just it, I don't really know. I mean, I'm not really sure if any are, and if they are, what they are or even why they are missing. It's all very confusing.' Silently, Malcolm agreed.

'You see,' Heidegger continued, 'some time in 1968 we received a shipment of books from our Seattle purchasing branch. We received all the volumes they sent, but just by chance I happened to notice that the receiving clerk signed for *five* crates of books. But the billing order – which, I might add, bears both the check marks and signatures of our agent in Seattle *and* the trucking firm – says there were *seven* crates. That means we're missing two crates of books without really missing any books. Do you understand what I mean?'

Lying slightly, Malcolm said, 'Yeah, I understand what you're saying, though I think it's probably just a mistake. Somebody, probably the clerk, couldn't count. Anyway, you say we're not missing any books. Why not just let it go?'

'You don't understand!' exclaimed Heidegger, leaning forward and shocking Malcolm with the intensity in his voice. 'I'm responsible for these records! When I take over I have to certify I receive everything true and proper. I did that, and this mistake is botching up the records! It looks bad, and if it's ever found I'll get the blame. Me!' By the time he finished, he was leaning across the desk and his volume was again causing echoes.

Malcolm was thoroughly bored. The prospect of listening to Heidegger ramble on about inventory discrepancies did not interest him in the least. Malcolm also didn't like the way Heidegger's eyes burned behind those thick glasses when he got excited. It was time to leave. He leaned toward Heidegger.

'Look, Rich,' he said, 'I know this mess causes problems for you, but I'm afraid I can't help you out. Maybe one of the other analysts knows something I don't, but I doubt it. If you want my advice, you'll forget the whole thing and cover it up. In case you haven't guessed, that's what your predecessor Johnson always did. If you want to press things, I suggest you don't go to Dr. Lappe. He'll get upset, muddy the whole mess beyond belief, blow it out of proportion, and everybody will be unhappy.'

Malcolm stood up and walked to the door. Looking back, he saw a small, trembling man sitting behind an open ledger and a draftsman's light.

Malcolm walked as far as Mrs. Russell's desk before he let

out a sigh of relief. He threw what was left of the cold coffee down the sink, and went upstairs to his room, sat down, put his feet up on his desk, farted, and closed his eyes.

When he opened them a minute later he was staring at his Picasso print of Don Quixote. The print appropriately hung on his half-painted red wall. Don Quixote was responsible for Ronald Leonard Malcolm's exciting position as a Central Intelligence agent. Two years.

In September of 1970, Malcolm took his long delayed Master's written examination. Everything went beautifully for the first two hours: he wrote a stirring explanation of Plato's allegory of the cave, analysed the condition of two of the travelers in Chaucer's *Canterbury Tales*, discussed the significance of rats in Carnus's *The Plague*, and faked his way through Holden Caulfield's struggle against homosexuality in *Catcher in the Rye*. Then he turned to the last page and ran into a brick wall that demanded, 'Discuss in depth at least three significant incidents in Cervantes' *Don Quixote*, including in the discussion the symbolic meaning of each incident, its relation to the other two incidents and the plot as a whole, and show how Cervantes used these incidents to characterise Don Quixote and Sancho Panza.'

Malcolm had never read *Don Quixote*. For five precious minutes he stared at the test. Then, very carefully, he opened a fresh examination book and began to write:

'I have never read *Don Quixote*, but I think he was defeated by a windmill. I am not sure what happened to Sancho Panza.

'The adventures of Don Quixote and Sancho Panza, a team generally regarded as seeking justice, can be compared to the adventures of Rex Stout's two most famous characters, Nero Wolfe and Archie Goodwin. For example, in the classic Wolfe adventure *The Black Mountain* ...'

After finishing a lengthy discussion of Nero Wolfe, using *The Black Mountain* as a focal point, Malcolm turned in his completed examination, went home to his apartment, and contemplated his bare feet.

Two days later he was called to the office of the professor of Spanish Literature. To his surprise, Malcolm was not chastised for his examination answer. Instead, the professor asked Malcolm if he was interested in 'murder mysteries'. Startled, Malcolm told the truth: reading such books helped him maintain some semblance of sanity in college. Smiling, the professor asked if he would like to 'so maintain your sanity for money?' Naturally, Malcolm said, he would. The professor made a phone call, and that day Malcolm lunched with his first C.I.A. agent.

It is not unusual for college professors, deans, and other academic personnel to act as C.I.A. recruiters. In the early 1950s a Yale coach recruited a student who was later caught infiltrating Red China.

Two months later Malcolm was finally 'cleared for limited employment', as are 17 per cent of all C.I.A. applicants. After a special, cursory training period, Malcolm walked up the short flight of iron stairs of the American Literary Historical Society to Mrs. Russell, Dr. Lappe, and his first day as a full-fledged intelligence agent.

Malcolm sighed at the wall, his calculated victory over Dr. Lappe. His third day at work, Malcolm quit wearing a suit and tie. One week of gentle hints passed before Dr. Lappe called him in for a little chat about etiquette. While the good Doctor agreed that bureaucracies tended to be a little stifling, he implied that one really should find a method other than 'unconventional' dress for letting in the sun. Malcolm said nothing, but the next day he showed up for work early, properly dressed in suit and tie and carrying a large box. By the time Walter reported to Dr Lappe at ten, Malcolm had almost finished painting one of his walls fire-engine red. Dr. Lappe sat in stunned silence while Malcolm innocently explained his newest method for letting in the sun. When two other analysts began to pop into the office to exclaim their approval, the good Doctor quietly stated that perhaps Malcolm had been right to brighten the individual rather than the institution. Malcolm sincerely and quickly agreed. The red paint and painting equipment moved to the third-floor storage room. Malcolm's suit and tie once more vanished. Dr. Lappe chose individual rebellion rather than inspired collective revolution against government property.

Malcolm sighed to nostalgia before he resumed describing a classic John Dickson Carr method for creating 'locked-door' situations.

Meanwhile Heidegger had been busy. He took Malcolm's advice concerning Dr. Lappe, but he was too frightened to try and hide a mistake from the Company. If they could catch you in the bathroom, no place was safe. He also knew that if he could pull a coup, rectify a malfunctioning situation, or at least show he could responsibly recognise problems, his chances of being reinstated in grace would greatly increase. So through ambition and paranoia (always a bad combination) Richard Heidegger made his fatal mistake.

He wrote a short memo to the chief of mother Department 17. In carefully chosen, obscure, but leading terms, he described what he had told Malcolm. All memos were usually cleared through Dr. Lappe, but exceptions were not unknown. Had Heidegger followed the normal course of procedure, everything would have been fine, for Dr. Lappe knew better than to let a memo critical of his section move up the chain of command. Heidegger guessed this, so he personally put the envelope in the delivery bag.

Twice a day, once in the morning and once in the evening, two cars of heavily armed men pick up and deliver intra-agency communications from all C.I.A. sub-stations in the Washington area. The communications are driven the eight miles to Langley, where they are sorted for distribution. Rich's memo went out in the afternoon pickup.

A strange, and unorthodox thing happened to Rich's memo. Like all communications to and from the Society, the memo disappeared from the delivery room before the sorting officially began. The memo appeared on the desk of a wheezing man in a spacious east-wing office. The man read it twice, once quickly, then again, very, very slowly. He left the room and arranged for all files pertaining to the Society to disappear and reappear at a Washington location. He then came back and telephoned to arrange a date at a current art exhibit. Next he reported in sick and caught a bus for the city. Within an hour he was engaged in earnest conversation with a distinguished-looking gentleman who might have been a banker. They talked as they strolled up Pennsylvania Avenue.

That night the distinguished-looking gentleman met yet another man, this time in Clyde's, a noisy, crowded Georgetown bar frequented by the Capitol Hill crowd. They too took a walk, stopping occasionally to gaze at reflections in the numerous shopwindows. The second man was also distinguished-looking. Striking is a more correct adjective. Something about his eyes told you he definitely was not a banker. He listened while the first man talked.

'I am afraid we have a slight problem.'

'Really?'

'Yes. Weatherby intercepted this today.' He handed the second man Heidegger's memo.

The second man had to read it only once. 'I see what you mean.'

'I knew you would. We really must take care of this, now.'

'I will see to it.'

'Of course.'

'You realise that there may be other complications besides this,' the second man said as he gestured with Heidegger's memo, 'which may have to be taken care of.'

'Yes. Well, that is regrettable, but unavoidable.' The second man nodded and waited for the first man to continue. 'We must be very sure, completely sure about those complications.' Again the second man nodded, waiting. 'And there is one other element. Speed. Time is of the absolute essence. Do what you must to follow that assumption.'

The second man thought for a moment and then said, 'Maximum speed may necessitate ... cumbersome and sloppy activity.'

The first man handed him a portfolio containing all the 'disappeared' files and said, 'Do what you must.'

The two men parted after a brief nod of farewell. The first man walked four blocks and turned the corner before he caught a taxi. He was glad the meeting was over. The second man watched him go, waited a few minutes scanning the passing crowds, then headed for a bar and a telephone.

That morning at 3.15 Heidegger unlocked his door to the knock of police officers. When he opened the door he found two men in ordinary clothes smiling at him. One was very tall and painfully thin. The other was quite distinguished, but if you looked in his eyes you could tell he wasn't a banker.

The two men shut the door behind them.

'These activities have their own rules and methods of concealment which seek to mislead and obscure.'

— President Dwight D. Eisenhower, 1960

Thursday, Morning to Early Afternoon

The rain came back Thursday. Malcolm woke with the start of a cold — congested, tender throat and a slightly woozy feeling. In addition to waking up sick, he woke up late. He thought for several minutes before deciding to go to work. Why waste sick time on a cold? He cut himself shaving, couldn't make the hair over his ears stay down, had trouble putting in his right contact lens, and found that his raincoat had disappeared. As he ran the eight blocks to work it dawned on him that he might be too late to see The Girl. When he hit Southeast A, he looked up the block just in time to see her disappear into the Library of Congress. He watched her so intently he didn't look where he was going and he stepped in a deep puddle. He was more embarrassed than angry, but the man he saw in the blue sedan parked just up from the Society didn't seem to notice the blunder. Mrs. Russell greeted Malcolm with a curt 'Bout time'. On the way to his room, he spilled his coffee and burned his hand. Some days you just can't win.

Shortly after ten there was a soft knock on his door, and

Tamatha entered his room. She stared at him for a few seconds through her thick glasses, a timid smile on her lips. Her hair was so thin Malcolm thought he could see each individual strand.

'Ron,' she whispered, 'do you know if Rich is sick?'

'No!' Malcolm yelled, and then loudly blew his nose.

'Well, you don't need to bellow! I'm worried about him. He's not here and he hasn't called in.'

'That's too fuckin' bad.' Malcolm drew the words out, knowing that swearing made Tamatha nervous.

'What's eating *you*, for heaven's sake?' she said.

'I've got a cold.'

'I'll get you an aspirin.'

'Don't bother,' he said ungraciously. 'It wouldn't help.'

'Oh, you're impossible! Goodbye!' She left, closing the door smartly behind her.

Sweet Jesus, Malcolm thought, then went back to Agatha Christie.

At 11.15 the phone rang. Malcolm picked it up and heard the cool voice of Dr. Lappe.

'Malcolm, I have an errand for you, and it's your turn to go for lunch. I assume everyone will wish to stay in the building.' Malcolm looked out the window at the pouring rain and came to the same conclusion. Dr. Lappe continued. 'Consequently, you might as well kill two birds with one stone and pick up lunch on the way back from the errand. Walter is already taking food orders. Since you have to drop a package at the Old Senate Office Building, I suggest you pick up the food at Jimmy's. You may leave now.'

Five minutes later a sneezing Malcolm trudged through

the basement to the coalbin exit at the rear of the building. No one had known the coalbin exit existed, as it hadn't been shown on the original building plans. It stayed hidden until Walter moved a chest of drawers while chasing a rat and found the small, dusty door that opened behind the lilac bushes. The door can't be seen from the outside, but there is enough room to squeeze between the bushes and the wall. The door only opens from the inside.

Malcolm muttered to himself all the way to the Old Senate Office Building. He sniffled between mutters. The rain continued. By the time he reached the building, the rain had changed his suede jacket from a light tan to a black brown. The blond receptionist in the Senator's office took pity on him and gave him a cup of coffee while he dried out. She said he was 'officially' waiting for the Senator to confirm delivery of the package. She coincidentally finished counting the books just as Malcolm finished his coffee. The girl smiled nicely, and Malcolm decided delivering murder mysteries to a senator might not be a complete waste.

Normally, it's a five-minute walk from the Old Senate Office Building to Hap's on Pennsylvania Avenue, but the rain had become a torrent, so Malcolm made the trip in three minutes. Jimmy's is a favorite of Capitol Hill employees because it's quick, tasty, and has its own brand of class. The restaurant is run by ex-convicts. It is a cross between a small Jewish delicatessen and a Montana bar. Malcolm gave his carry-out list to a waitress, ordered a meatball sandwich and milk for himself, and engaged in his usual Jimmy's pursuit of matching crimes with restaurant employees.

While Malcolm had been sipping coffee in the Senator's office, a gentleman in a raincoat with his hat hiding much of his face turned the corner from First Street and walked up Southeast A to the blue sedan. The custom-cut raincoat matched the man's striking appearance, but there was no one on the street to notice. He casually but completely scanned the street and buildings, then gracefully climbed in the front seat of the sedan. As he firmly shut the door, he looked at the driver and said, 'Well?'

Without taking his eyes off the building, the driver wheezed, 'All present or accounted for, sir.'

'Excellent. I watch while you phone. Tell them to wait ten minutes, then hit it.'

'Yes, sir.' The driver began to climb out of the car, but a sharp voice stopped him.

'Weatherby,' the man said, pausing for effect, 'there will be no mistakes.'

Weatherby swallowed. 'Yes, sir.'

Weatherby walked to the open phone next to the grocery store on the corner of Southeast A and Sixth. In Mr. Henry's, a bar five blocks away on Pennsylvania Avenue, a tall, frightfully thin man answered the bartender's page for 'Mr. Wazburn'. The man called Wazburn listened to the curt instructions, nodding his assent into the phone. He hung up and returned to his table, where two friends waited. They paid the bill (three brandy coffees), and walked up First Street to an alley just behind Southeast A. At the street light they passed a young, long-haired man in a rain-soaked suede jacket hurrying in the opposite direction. An empty yellow van stood between the two buildings on the edge of the alley. The men climbed in the back and prepared for their morning's work.

Malcolm had just ordered his meatball sandwich when a mailman with his pouch slung in front of him turned the corner at First Street to walk down Southeast A. A stocky man in bulging raincoat walked stiffly a few paces behind the mailman. Five blocks farther up the street a tall, thin man walked toward the other two. He also wore a bulging raincoat, though on him the coat only reached his knees.

As soon as Weatherby saw the mailman turn on to Southeast A, he pulled out of his parking place and drove away. Neither the men in the car nor the men on the street acknowledged the others' presence. Weatherby sighed relief in between wheezes. He was overjoyed to be through with his part of the assignment. Tough as he was, when he looked at the silent man next to him he was thankful he had made no mistakes.

But Weatherby was wrong. He had made one small, commonplace mistake, a mistake he could have easily avoided. A mistake he should have avoided.

If anyone had been watching, he would have seen three men, two businessmen and a mailman, coincidentally arrive at the Society's gate at the same time. The two businessmen politely let the mailman lead the way to the door and push the button. As usual, Walter was away from his desk (though it probably wouldn't have made any difference if he had been there). Just as Malcolm finished his sandwich at Hap's, Mrs. Russell heard the buzzer and rasped, 'Come in.'

And with the mailman leading the way, they did.

★

Malcolm dawdled over his lunch, polishing off his meatball sandwich with the specialty of the house, chocolate rum cake. After his second cup of coffee, his conscience forced him back into the rain. The torrent had subsided into a drizzle. Lunch had improved Malcolm's spirits and his health. He took his time, both because he enjoyed the walk and because he didn't want to drop the three bags of sandwiches. In order to break the routine, he walked down Southeast A on the side opposite the Society. His decision gave him a better view of the building as he approached, and consequently he knew something was wrong much earlier than he normally would have.

It was a little thing that made Malcolm wonder. A small detail quite out of place yet so insignificant it appeared meaningless. But Malcolm noticed little things, like the open window on the third floor. The Society's windows are rolled out rather than pushed up, so the open window jutted out from the building. When Malcolm first saw the window the significance didn't register, but when he was a block and a half away it struck him and he stopped.

It is not unusual for windows in the capital to be open, even on a rainy day. Washington is usually warm, even during spring rains. But since the Society building is air-conditioned, the only reason to open a window is for fresh air. Malcolm knew the fresh-air explanation was absurd because of the particular window that stood open. Tamatha's window.

Tamatha – as everyone in the section knew – lived in terror of open windows. When she was nine, her two teenage brothers had fought over a picture the three of them had found while exploring the attic. The older brother had slipped on a rug and had plunged out the attic window to the street below, breaking his neck and becoming paralyzed for life. Tamatha had once confided in Malcolm that only a fire, rape, or murder would make her go near any open window. Yet her office window stood wide open.

Malcolm tried to quell his uneasiness. Your damn over-active imagination, he thought. It's probably open for a perfectly good reason. Maybe somebody is playing a joke on her. But no staff member played practical jokes, and he knew no one would tease Tamatha in that manner. He walked slowly down the street, past the building, and to the corner. Everything else seemed in order. He heard no noise in the building, but then they were all probably reading.

This is silly, he thought. He crossed the street and quickly walked to the gate, up the steps, and, after a moment's hesitation, rang the bell. Nothing. He heard the bell ring inside the building, but Mrs. Russell didn't answer. He rang again. Still nothing. Malcolm's spine began to tingle and his neck felt cold.

Walter is shifting books, he thought, and Perfume Polly is taking a shit. They must be. Slowly he reached in his pocket for the key. When anything is inserted in the keyhole during the day, buzzers ring and lights flash all over the building. At night they also ring in Washington police headquarters, the Langley complex, and a special security house in downtown Washington. Malcolm heard the soft buzz of the bells as he turned the lock. He swung the door open and quickly stepped inside.

From the bottom of the stairwell Malcolm could only

see that the room appeared to be empty. Mrs. Russell wasn't at her desk. Out of the corner of his eye he noticed that Dr. Lappe's door was partially open. There was a peculiar odor in the room. Malcolm tossed the sandwich bags on top of Walter's desk and slowly mounted the stairs.

He found the sources of the odor. As usual, Mrs. Russell had been standing behind her desk when they entered. The blast from the machine gun in the mailman's pouch had knocked her almost as far back as the coffee-pot. Her cigarette had dropped on her neck, singeing her flesh until the last millimeter of tobacco and paper had oxidized. A strange dullness came over Malcolm as he stared at the huddled flesh in the pool of blood. An automaton, he slowly turned and walked into Dr. Lappe's office.

Walter and Dr. Lappe had been going over invoices when they heard strange coughing noises and the thump of Mrs. Russell's body hitting the floor. Walter opened the door to help her pick up the dropped delivery (he heard the buzzer and Mrs. Russell say, 'What have you got for us today?'). The last thing he saw was a tall, thin man holding an L-shaped device. The postmortem revealed that Walter took a short burst, five rounds in the stomach. Dr. Lappe saw the whole thing, but there was nowhere to run. His body slumped against the far wall beneath a row of bloody diagonal holes.

Two of the men moved quietly upstairs, leaving the mailman to guard the door. None of the other staff had heard a thing. Otto Skorzeny, Hitler's chief commando, once demonstrated the effectiveness of a silenced British sten gun by firing a clip behind a batch of touring generals. The German officers never heard a thing, but they refused to copy the British weapon, as the Third Reich naturally made better devices. These men were satisfied with the sten. The tall man flung open Malcolm's door and found an empty office. Ray Thomas was behind his desk on his knees picking up a dropped pencil when the stocky man found him. Ray had time to scream, 'Oh, my God, no …' before his brain exploded.

Tamatha and Harold Martin heard Ray scream, but they had no idea why. Almost simultaneously they opened their doors and ran to the head of the stairs. All was quiet for a moment; then they heard the soft shuffle of feet climbing the stairs. The steps stopped, then a very faint metallic *click*, *snap*, *twang* jarred them from their lethargy. They couldn't have known the exact source of the sound (a new ammunition clip being inserted and the weapon being armed), but they instinctively knew what it meant. They both ran into their rooms, slamming the doors behind them.

Harold showed the most presence of mind. He locked his door and dialed three digits before the stocky man kicked the door open and cut him down.

Tamatha reacted on a different instinct. For years she thought only a major emergency could get her to open a window. Now she knew such an emergency was on her. She frantically rolled the window open, looking for escape, looking for help, looking for anything. Dizzied by the height, she took her glasses off and laid them on her desk. She heard Harold's door splinter, a rattling cough, the thump, and fled again to the window. Her door slowly opened.

For a long time nothing happened, then slowly Tamatha turned to face the thin man. He hadn't fired for fear a slug would fly out the window, hit something, and draw attention to the building. He would risk that only if she screamed. She didn't. She saw only a blur, but she knew the blur was motioning her away from the window. She moved slowly toward her desk. If I'm going to die, she thought, I want to see. Her hand reached out for her glasses, and she raised them to her eyes. The tall man waited until they were in place and comprehension registered on her face. Then he squeezed the trigger, holding it tight until the last shell from the full clip exploded, ejecting the spent casing out of the side of the gun. The bullets kept Tamatha dancing, bouncing between the wall and the filing cabinet, knocking her glasses off, disheveling her hair. The thin man watched her riddled body slowly slide to the floor, then he turned to join his stocky companion, who had just finished checking the rest of the floor. They took their time going downstairs.

While the mailman maintained his vigil on the door, the stocky man searched the basement. He found the coalbin door but thought nothing of it. He should have, but then his error was partially due to Weatherby's mistake. The stocky man did find and destroy the telephone switchbox. An inoperative phone causes less alarm than a phone unanswered. The tall man searched Heidegger's desk. The material he sought should have been in the third drawer, left-hand side, and it was. He also took a manila envelope. He dumped a handful of shell casings in the envelope with a small piece of paper he took from his jacket pocket. He sealed the envelope and wrote on the outside. His gloves made writing difficult, but he wanted to disguise his hand-writing anyway. The scrawl designated the envelope as a personal package for 'Lockenvar, Langley headquarters'. The stocky man opened the camera and exposed the film. The tall man contemptuously tossed the envelope on Mrs. Russell's desk. He and his companions hung their guns from the straps inside their coats, opened the door, and left as inconspicuously as they had come, just as Malcolm finished his piece of cake.

Malcolm moved slowly from office to office, floor to floor. Although his eyes saw, his mind didn't register. When he found the mangled body that had once been Tamatha, the knowledge hit him. He stared for minutes, trembling. Fear grabbed him, and he thought, I've got to get out of here. He started running. He went all the way to the first floor before his mind took over and brought him to a halt.

Obviously they've gone, he thought, or I'd be dead now. Who 'they' were never entered his mind. He suddenly realised his vulnerability. My God, he thought, I have no gun, I couldn't even fight them if they came back. Malcolm looked at Walter's body and the heavy automatic strapped to the dead man's belt. Blood covered the gun. Malcolm couldn't bring himself to touch it. He ran to Walter's desk. Walter kept a very special weapon clipped in the leg space of his desk, a sawed-off 20-gauge shotgun. The weapon held only one shell, but Walter often bragged how it saved his life at Chosen Reservoir. Malcolm grabbed it by its pistol-like butt. He kept it pointed at the closed door as he slowly sidestepped towards Mrs. Russsell's desk. Walter kept a revolver in her drawer, 'just in case'. Mrs. Russell, a widow, had called it her 'rape gun'. 'Not to fight them off,' she would say, 'but to encourage them.' Malcolm stuck the gun in his belt, then picked up the phone.

Dead. He punched all the lines. Nothing.

I have to leave, he thought, I have to get help. He tried to shove the shotgun under his jacket. Even sawed off, the gun was too long: the barrel stuck out through the collar and bumped his throat. Reluctantly, he put the shotgun back under Walter's desk, thinking he should try to leave everything as he found it. After a hard swallow, he went to the door and looked out the wide-angled peephole. The street was empty. The rain had stopped. Slowly, standing well behind the wall, he opened the door. Nothing happened. He stepped out on the stoop. Silence. With a bang he closed the door, quickly walked through the gate and down the street, his eyes darting, hunting for anything unusual. Nothing.

Malcolm headed straight for the phone corner. Each of the four divisions of the C.I.A. has an unlisted 'panic number', a phone number to be used only in the event of a major catastrophe, only if all other channels of communication are unavailable. Penalty for misuse of the number can be as stiff as expulsion from the service with loss of pay. Their panic number is the one top secret every C.I.A. employee from the highest cleared director to the lowest cleared janitor knows and remembers.

The Panic Line is always manned by highly experienced agents. They have to be sharp even though they seldom do anything. When a panic call comes through, decisions must be made, quickly and correctly.

Stephen Mitchell was officer of the day manning I.D.'s Panic phone when Malcolm's call came through. Mitchell had been one of the best traveling (as opposed to resident) agents in the C.I.A. For thirteen years he moved from trouble spot to trouble spot, mainly in South America. Then in 1967 a double agent in Buenos Aires planted a plastic bomb under the driver's seat in Mitchell's Simca. The double agent made an error: the explosion only blew off Mitchell's legs. The error caught the double agent in the form of a wire loop tightened in Rio. The Agency, not wanting to waste a good man, shifted Mitchell to the Panic Section.

Mitchell answered the phone after the first ring. When he picked up the receiver a tape recorder came on and a trace automatically began.

'493-7282.' All C.I.A. telephones are answered by their numbers.

'This is ...' For a horrible second Malcolm forgot his code name. He knew he had to give his department and section number (to distinguish himself from other agents who might have the same code name), but he couldn't remember his code name. He knew better than to use his real name. Then he remembered. 'This is Condor, Section 9, Department 17. We've been hit.'

'Are you on an Agency line?'

'I'm calling from an open phone booth a little ways from ... base. Our phones aren't working.'

Shit, thought Mitchell, we have to use double talk. With his free hand he punched the Alert button. At five different locations, three in Washington, two in Langley, heavily armed men scurried to cars, turned on their engines, and waited for instructions. 'How bad?'

111

'Maximum, total. I'm the only one who …'

Mitchell cut him off. 'Right. Do any civilians in the area know?'

'I don't think so. Somehow it was done quietly.'

'Are you damaged?'

'No.'

'Are you armed?'

'Yes.'

'Are there any hostiles in the area?'

Malcolm looked around. He remembered how ordinary the morning had seemed. 'I don't think so, but I can't be sure.'

'Listen very closely. Leave the area, slowly, but get your ass away from there, someplace safe. Wait an hour. After you're sure you're clean, call again. That will be at 1.45. Do you understand?'

'Yes.'

'O.K., hang up now, and remember, don't lose your head.'

Mitchell broke the connection before Malcolm had taken the phone from his ear.

After Malcolm hung up, he stood on the corner for a few seconds, trying to formulate a plan. He knew he had to find someplace safe where he could hide unnoticed for an hour, someplace close. Slowly, very slowly, he turned and walked up the street. Fifteen minutes later he joined the Iowa City Jaycees on their tour of the nation's Capitol building.

Even as Malcolm spoke to Mitchell, one of the largest and most intricate government machines in the world began to grind. Assistants monitoring Malcolm's call dispatched four cars from Washington security posts and one car from Langley with a mobile medical team, all bound for Section 9, Department 17. The squad leaders were briefed and established procedure via radio as they homed in on the target. The proper Washington police precinct was alerted to the possibility of an assistance request by 'federal enforcement officials'. By the time Malcolm hung up, all D.C. area C.I.A. bases had received a hostile-action report. They activated special security plans. Within three minutes of the call all deputy directors were notified, and within six minutes the director, who had been in conference with the Vice-President, was personally briefed over a scrambled phone by Mitchell. Within eight minutes all the other main organs of America's intelligence community received news of a possible hostile action.

In the meantime Mitchell ordered all files pertaining to the Society sent to his office. During a panic situation, the Panic officer of the day automatically assumes awesome power. He virtually runs much of the entire Agency until personally relieved by a deputy director. Only seconds after Mitchell ordered the files, Records called him back.

'Sir, the computer check shows all primary files on Section 9, Department 17, are missing.'

'They're *what*?'

'Missing, sir.'

'Then send me the secondary set, and God damn it, send it under guard!' Mitchell slammed the phone down before the startled clerk could reply. Mitchell grabbed another phone and connected immediately. 'Freeze the base,' he ordered. Within seconds all exits from the compound were sealed. Anyone attempting to leave or enter the area would have been shot. Red lights flashed throughout the buildings. Special security teams began clearing the corridors, ordering all those not engaged in Panic or Red priority business to return to their base offices. Reluctance or even hesitance to comply with the order meant a gun barrel in the stomach and handcuffs on the wrists.

The door to the Panic Room opened just after Mitchell froze the base. A large man strode firmly past the security guard without bothering to return the cursory salute. Mitchell was still on the phone, so the man settled down in a chair next to the second in command.

'What the hell is going on?' The man would normally have been answered without question, but right now Mitchell was God. The second looked at his chief. Mitchell, though still barking orders into the phone, heard the demand. He nodded to his second, who in turn gave the big man a complete synopsis of what had happened and what had been done. By the time the second had finished, Mitchell was off the phone, using a soiled handkerchief to wipe his brow.

The big man stirred in his chair. 'Mitchell,' he said, 'if it's all right with you, I think I'll stay around and give you a hand. After all, I am head of Department 17.'

'Thank you, sir,' Mitchell replied, 'I'll be glad of any help you can give us.'

The big man grunted and settled down to wait.

If you had been walking down Southeast A just behind the Library of Congress, at 1.09 on that cloudy Thursday afternoon, you would have been startled by a sudden flurry of activity. Half a dozen men sprang out of nowhere and converged on a three-storey white building. Just before they reached the door, two cars, one on each side of the road, double-parked almost in front of the building. A man sat in the back seat of each car, peering intently at the building and cradling something in his arms. The six men on foot went through the gate together, but only one climbed the steps. He fiddled with a large ring of keys and the lock. When the door clicked he nodded to the others. After throwing the door wide open and hesitating for an instant, the six men poured inside, slamming the door behind them. A man got out of each car. They slowly began to pace up and down in front of the building. As the cars pulled away to park, the drivers both nodded at men standing on the corners.

Three minutes later the door opened. A man left the building and walked slowly towards the closest parked car. Once inside, he picked up a phone. Within seconds he was talking to Mitchell.

'They were hit all right, hard!' The man speaking was Allan Newbury. He had seen combat in Vietnam, at the Bay of Pigs, in the mountains of Turkey, dozens of alleys, dark buildings, and basements all over the world, yet Mitchell could feel uneasy sickness in the clipped voice.

'How and how bad?' Mitchell was just beginning to believe.

'Probably a two- to five-man team, no sign of forcible entry. They must have used silenced machine guns of some sort or the whole town would have heard. Six dead in the building, four men, two women. Most of them probably didn't know what hit them. No signs of an extensive search, security camera and film destroyed. Phones are dead, probably cut somewhere. A couple of bodies will have to be worked on before identity can be definitely established. Neat, clean, and quick. They knew what they were doing down to the last detail, and they knew how to do it.'

Mitchell waited until he was sure Newberry had finished. 'O.K. This is beyond me. I'm going to hold definite action until somebody upstairs orders it. Meantime you and your men sit tight. Nothing is to be moved. I want that place frozen and sealed but good. Use whatever means you must.'

Mitchell paused, both to emphasise his meaning and to hope he wasn't making a mistake. He had just authorised Newberry's team to do anything, including premeditated, non-defensive kills, Stateside action without prior clearance. Murder by whim, if they thought the whim might mean something. The consequences of such a rare order could be very grave for all concerned. Mitchell continued. 'I'm sending out more men to cover the neighborhood as additional security. I'll also send out a crime lab team, but they can only do things that won't disturb the scene. They'll bring a communications setup, too. Understand?'

'I understand. Oh, there's something a little peculiar we've found.'

Mitchell said, 'Yes?'

'Our radio briefing said there was only one door. We found two. Make any sense to you?'

'None,' said Mitchell, 'but nothing about this whole thing makes sense. Is there anything else?'

'Just one thing.' The voice grew colder. 'Some son of a

bitch butchered a little girl on the third floor. He didn't hit her, he butchered her.' Newberry signed off.

'What now?' asked the big man.

'We wait,' said Mitchell, leaning back in his wheelchair. 'We sit and wait for Condor to call.'

At 1.40 Malcolm found a phone booth in the Capitol. With change acquired from a bubbly teen-age girl he dialed the panic number. It didn't even finish one complete ring.

'493-7282.' The voice on the phone was tense.

'This is Condor, Section 9, Department 17. I'm in a public phone booth, I don't think I was followed, and I'm pretty sure I can't be heard.'

'You've been confirmed. We've got to get you to Langley, but we're afraid to let you come in solo. Do you know the Circus 3 theaters in the Georgetown district?'

'Yes.'

'Could you be there in an hour?'

'Yes.'

'O.K. Now, who do you know at least by sight who's stationed at Langley?'

Malcolm thought for a moment. 'I had an instructor codenamed Sparrow IV.'

'Hold on.' Through priority use of the computer and communications facilities, Mitchell verified Sparrow IV's existence and determined that he was in the building. Two minutes later he said, 'O.K., this is what is going to happen. Half an hour from now Sparrow IV and one other man will park in a small alley behind the theaters. They'll wait exactly one hour. That gives you thirty minutes leeway either direction. There are three entrances to the alley you can take on foot. All three allow you to see anybody in front of you before they see you. When you're sure you're clean, go down the alley. If you see anything or anybody suspicious, if Sparrow IV and his partner aren't there or somebody is with them, if a God damn pigeon is at their feet, get your ass out of there, find someplace safe, and call in. Do the same if you can't make it. O.K.?'

'OKahahaachoo!'

Mitchell almost shot out of his wheelchair. 'What the hell was that? Are you O.K.?'

Malcolm wiped the phone off. 'Yes, sir, I'm fine. Sorry, I have a cold. I know what to do.'

'For the love of Christ.' Mitchell hung up. He leaned back in his chair. Before he could say anything, the big man spoke.

'Look here, Mitchell. If you have no objection, I'll accompany Sparrow IV. The Department is my responsibility, and there's no young tough around here who can carry off what might be a tricky situation any better, tired old man as I may be.'

Mitchell looked at the big, confident man across from him, then smiled. 'O.K. Pick up Sparrow IV at the gate. Use your car. Have you ever met Condor?'

The big man shook his head. 'No, but I think I've seen him. Can you supply a photo?'

Mitchell nodded and said, 'Sparrow IV has one. Ordnance will give you anything you want, though I suggest a hand gun. Any preference?'

The big man walked towards the door. 'Yes,' he said, looking back, 'a .38 Special with silencer just in case we have to move quietly.'

'It'll be waiting in the car, complete with ammo. Oh,' said Mitchell, stopping the big man as he was halfway out the door, 'thanks again, Colonel Weatherby.'

The big man turned and smiled. 'Think nothing of it, Mitchell. After all, it's my job.' He closed the door behind him and walked towards his car. After a few steps he began to wheeze very softly.

> *'Faulty execution of a winning combination has lost many a game on the very brink of victory. In such cases a player sees the winning idea, plays the winning sacrifice and then inverts the order of his follow-up moves or misses the really clinching point of his combination.'*
>
> – Fred Reinfeld, *The Complete Chess Course*

Thursday Afternoon

Malcolm had little trouble finding a taxi, considering the weather. Twenty minutes later he paid the driver two blocks from the Circus theaters. Again he knew it was all-important that he stay out of sight. A few minutes later he sat at a table in the darkest corner of a bar crowded with men. The bar Malcolm chose is the most active male homosexual hangout in Washington. Starting with the early lunch hour at eleven and running until well after midnight, men of all ages, usually middle to upper middle class, fill the bar to find a small degree of relaxation among their own kind. It's a happy as well as a 'gay' bar. Rock music blares, laughter drifts into the street. The levity is strained, heavy with irony, but it's there.

Malcolm hoped he looked inconspicuous, one man in a bar crowded with men. He nursed his tequila Collins, drinking it as slowly as he dared, watching faces in the crowd for signs of recognition. Some of the faces in the crowd watched him too.

No one in the bar noticed that only Malcolm's left hand rested on the small table. Under the table his right hand held a gun, a gun he pointed at anyone coming near him.

At 2.40 Malcolm jumped from his table to join a large group leaving the bar. Once outside, he quickly walked away from the group. For several minutes he crossed and recrossed Georgetown's narrow streets, carefully watching the people around him. At three o'clock, satisfied he was clean, he headed towards the Circus theaters.

Sparrow IV turned out to be a shaky, spectacled instructor of governmental procedure. He had been given no choice concerning his role in the adventure. He made it quite clear that this was not what he was hired for, he most definitely objected, and he was very concerned about his wife and four children. Mostly to shut him up, Ordnance dressed him in a bulletproof vest. He wore the hot and heavy armor under his shirt. The canvas frustrated his scratching attempts. He had no recollection of anyone called Condor or Malcolm; he lectured Junior Officer Training classes by the dozen. The people at Ordnance didn't care, but they listened anyway.

Weatherby briefed the drivers of the crash cars as they walked towards the parking lot. He checked the short gun with the sausage-shaped device and nodded his approval to the somber man from Ordnance. Ordinarily Weatherby would have had to sign for the gun, but Mitchell's authority rendered such procedures unnecessary. The Ordnance man helped Weatherby adjust a special shoulder holster, handed him twenty-five extra rounds, and wished him luck. Weatherby grunted as he climbed into his light blue sedan.

The three cars rolled out of Langley in close formation with Weatherby's blue sedan in the middle position. Just as they exited from the Beltway turnpike to enter Washington, the rear car 'blew' a tire. The driver 'lost control' of his vehicle, and the car ended up across two lanes of traffic. No one was hurt, but the accident blocked traffic for ten minutes. Weatherby closely followed the other crash car as it turned and twisted its way through the maze of Washington traffic. On a quiet residential street in the city's southwest quadrant the crash car made a complete U-turn and started back in the opposite direction. As it passed the blue sedan, the driver flashed Weatherby the O.K. sign, then sped out of sight. Weatherby headed towards Georgetown, checking for tails all the way.

Weatherby figured out his mistake. When he dispatched the assassination team, he ordered them to kill everyone in the building. He had said everyone, but he hadn't specified how many that was. His men had followed orders, but the orders hadn't been complete enough to let them know one man was missing. Why the man wasn't there Weatherby didn't know and he didn't care. If he had known about the missing man, this Condor, he could have arranged a satisfactory solution. He had made the mistake, so now he had to rectify it.

There was a chance Condor was harmless, that he wouldn't remember his conversation with the Heidegger man, but Weatherby couldn't take that chance. Heidegger questioned all the staff except Dr. Lappe. Those questions could not be allowed to exist. Now one man knew about those questions, so, like the others, that man must die even if he didn't realise what he knew.

Weatherby's plan was simple, but extremely dangerous. As soon as Condor appeared he would shoot him. Self-defense. Weatherby glanced at the trembling Sparrow IV. An unavoidable side product. The big man had no qualms concerning the instructor's pending death. The plan was fraught with risks: Condor might be better with his weapon than anticipated, the scene might be witnessed and later reported, the Agency might not believe his story and use a guaranteed form of interrogation, Condor might turn himself in some other way. A hundred things could go wrong. But no matter how high the risks, Weatherby knew they were not the certainty that faced him should he fail. He might be able to escape the Agency and the rest of the American intelligence network. There are several ways, ways that have been successfully used before. Such things were Weatherby's forte. But he knew he would never escape the striking-looking man with strange eyes. That man never failed when he acted directly. Never. He would act directly against Weatherby the dangerous bungler, Weatherby the threat. This Weatherby knew, and it made him wheeze painfully. It was this knowledge that made any thought of escape or betrayal absurd. Weatherby had to account for his error. Condor had to die.

Weatherby drove through the alley slowly, then turned around and came back, parking the car next to some garbage cans behind the theaters. The alley was empty just as Mitchell said it would be. Weatherby doubted if anyone would enter it while they were there: Washingtonians tend to avoid alleys. He knew Mitchell would arrange for the area to be free of police so that uniforms wouldn't frighten

Condor. That was fine with Weatherby. He motioned for Sparrow IV to get out. They leaned against the car, prominent and visibly alone. Then, like any good hunter staging an ambush, Weatherby blanked his mind to let his senses concentrate.

Malcolm saw them standing there before they knew he was in the alley. He watched them very carefully from a distance of about sixty paces. He had a hard time controlling sneezes, but he managed to stay silent. After he was certain they were alone, he stepped from behind the telephone pole and began to walk towards them. His relief built with every step.

Weatherby spotted Malcolm immediately. He stepped away from the car, ready. He wanted to be very, very sure, and sixty paces is only a fair shot for a silenced pistol. He also wanted to be out of Sparrow IV's reach. Take them one at a time, he thought.

Recognition sprang on Malcolm twenty-five paces from the two men, five paces sooner than Weatherby anticipated any action. A picture of a man in a blue sedan parked just up from the Society in the morning rain flashed through Malcolm's mind. The man in that car and one of the men now standing in front of him were the same. Something was wrong, something was very wrong. Malcolm stopped, then slowly backed up. Almost unconsciously he tugged at the gun in his belt.

Weatherby knew something was wrong, too. His quarry had quite unexpectedly stopped short of the trap, was now fleeing, and was probably preparing an aggressive defense. Malcolm's unexpected actions forced Weatherby to abandon his original plan and react to a new situation.

While he quickly drew his own weapon, Weatherby briefly noted Sparrow IV, frozen with fright and bewilderment. The timid instructor still posed no threat.

Weatherby was a veteran of many situations requiring rapid action. Malcolm's pistol barrel had just cleared his belt when Weatherby fired.

A pistol, while effective, can be a difficult weapon to use under field conditions, even for an experienced veteran. A pistol equipped with a silencer increases this difficulty, for while the silencer allows the handler to operate quietly, it cuts down on his efficiency. The bulk at the end of the barrel is an unaccustomed weight requiring aim compensation by the user. Ballistically, a silencer cuts down on the bullet's velocity. The silencer may affect the bullet's trajectory. A silencer-equipped pistol is cumbersome, difficult to draw and fire quickly.

All these factors worked against Weatherby. Had he not been using a silenced pistol – even though his quarry's retreat forced him to take time to revise his plans – there would have been no contest. As it was, the pistol's bulk slowed his draw. He lost accuracy attempting to regain speed. The veteran killer tried for the difficult but definite head shot, but he overcompensated. Milliseconds after the soft *plop!*, a heavy chunk of lead cut through the hair hanging over Malcolm's left ear and whined off to sink in the Potomac.

Malcolm had only fired one pistol in his life, a friend's .22 target model. All five shots missed the running gopher. He fired Mrs. Russell's gun from the waist, and a deafening roar echoed down the alley before he knew he had pulled the trigger.

When a man is shot with a .357 magnum he doesn't grab a neat little red hole in his body and slide slowly to the ground. He goes down hard. At twenty-five paces the effect is akin to being hit by a truck. Malcolm's bullet smashed through Weatherby's left thigh. The force of the blast splattered a large portion of Weatherby's leg over the alley; it flipped him into the air and slammed him face down in the road.

Sparrow IV looked incredulously at Malcolm. Slowly Malcolm turned towards the little instructor, bringing the gun into line with the man's quivering stomach.

'He was one of them!' Malcolm was panting though he hadn't exerted himself. 'He was one of them!' Malcolm slowly backed away from the speechless instructor. When he reached the edge of the alley, Malcolm turned and ran.

Weatherby groaned, fighting off the shock of the wound. The pain hadn't set in. He was a very tough man, but it took everything he had to raise his arm. He had somehow held on to the gun. Miraculously, his mind stayed clear. Very carefully he aimed and fired. Another *plop!*, and a bullet shattered on the theater wall, but not before it tore through the throat of Sparrow IV, instructor of governmental procedure, husband, father of four. As the body crumpled against the car, Weatherby felt a strange sense of elation. He wasn't dead yet, Condor had vanished again, and there would be no bullets for Ballistics to use in determining who shot whom. There was still hope. He passed out.

A police car found the two men. It took them a long time to respond to the frightened shopkeeper's call, because all the Georgetown units had been sent to check out a sniper report. The report turned out to be from a crank.

Malcolm ran four blocks before he realised how conspicuous he was. He slowed down, turned several corners, then hailed a passing taxi to downtown Washington.

Sweet Jesus, Malcolm thought, he was one of them. He was one of them. The Agency must not have known. He had to get to a phone. He had to call ... Fear set in. Suppose, just suppose the man in the alley wasn't the only double. Suppose he had been sent there by a man who knew what he was. Suppose the man at the other end of the Panic Line was also a double.

Malcolm quit his suppositions to deal with the immediate problem of survival. Until he thought it out he wouldn't dare call in. And they would be looking for him. They would have looked for him even before the shooting, the only survivor of the section, they ... But he wasn't! The thought raced through his mind. He wasn't the only survivor of the section. Heidegger! Heidegger was sick, home in bed, sick! Malcolm searched his brain. Address, what did Heidegger say his address was? Malcolm had heard Heidegger tell Dr. Lappe his address was ... Mount Royal Arms!

Malcolm explained his problem to the cabby. He was on his way to pick up a blind date, but he had forgotten the address. All he knew was she lived in the Mount Royal Arms. The cabby, always eager to help young love, called his dispatcher, who gave him the address in the northwest quadrant. When the cabby let him out in front of the aging building, Malcolm gave him a dollar tip.

Heidegger's name tape was stuck next to 413. Malcolm buzzed. No return buzz, no query over the call box. While he buzzed again, an uneasy but logical assumption grew in his mind. Finally, he pushed three other buzzers. No answer came, so he punched a whole row. When the jammed call box squealed, he yelled, 'Special delivery!' The door buzzer rang and he ran inside.

No one answered his knock at Apartment 413, but by then he didn't really expect an answer. He got on his knees and looked at the lock. If he was right, only a simple spring night lock was on. In dozens of books he'd read and in countless movies, the hero uses a small piece of stiff plastic and in a few seconds a locked door springs open. Plastic – where could he find a piece of stiff plastic? After several moments of frantic pocket slapping, he opened his wallet and removed his laminated C.I.A. identification card. The card certified he was an employee of Tentrex Industries, Inc., giving relevant information regarding his appearance and identity. Malcolm had always liked the two photos of himself, one profile, one full face.

For twenty minutes Malcolm sneezed, grunted, pushed, pulled, jiggled, pleaded, threatened, shook, and finally hacked at the door with his card. The plastic lamination finally split, shooting his I.D. card through the crack and into the locked room.

Frustration turned to anger. Malcolm relieved his cramped knees by standing. If nobody has bothered me up till now, he thought, a little more noise won't make much difference. Backed with the fury, fear, and frustration of the day, Malcolm smashed his foot against the door. Locks and doors in the Mount Royal Arms are not of the finest quality. The management leans towards cheap rent, and the building construction is similarly inclined. The door of 413 flew inward, bounced off its doorstop, and was caught on the return swing by Malcolm. He shut the door a good deal more quietly than he had opened it. He picked his I.D. card out of the splinters, then crossed the room to the bed and what lay on it.

Since time forestalled any pretense, they hadn't bothered to be gentle with Heidegger. If Malcolm had lifted the pajama top, he would have seen the mark a low-line punch leaves if the victim's natural tendency to bruise is arrested by death. The corpse's face was blackish blue, a state induced by, among other things, strangulation. The room stank from the corpe's involuntary discharge.

Malcolm looked at the beginning-to-bloat body. He knew very little about organic medicine, but he knew that this state of decomposition is not reached in a couple of hours. Therefore Heidegger had been killed before the others. 'They' hadn't come here after they discovered him missing from work but before they hit the building. Malcolm didn't understand.

Heidegger's right pajama sleeve lay on the floor. Malcolm didn't think that type of tear would be made in a fight. He flipped the covers back to look at Heidegger's arm. On the underside of the forearm he found a small bruise, the kind a tiny bug would make. Or, thought Malcolm, remembering his trips to the student health service, a clumsily inserted hypodermic. They shot him full of something, probably to make him talk. About what? Malcolm had no idea. He began to search the room when he remembered about fingerprints. Taking his handkerchief from his pocket, he wiped everything he remembered touching, including the outside of the door. He found a pair of dusty handball gloves on the cluttered dresser. Too small, but they covered his fingers.

After the bureau drawers he searched the closet. On the top shelf he found an envelope full of money, fifty- and one-hundred-dollar bills. He didn't take the time to count it, but he estimated that there must be at least ten thousand dollars.

He sat on the clothes-covered chair. It didn't make sense. An ex-alcoholic, an accountant who lectured on the merits of mutual funds, a man frightened of muggers, keeping all that cash stashed in his closet. It didn't make sense. He looked at the corpse. At any rate, he thought, Heidegger won't need it now. Malcolm put the envelope inside his shorts. After a last quick look around, he cautiously opened the door, walked down the stairs, and caught a downtown bus at the corner.

Malcolm knew his first problem would be evading his pursuers. By now there would be at least two 'they's after him: the Agency and whatever group hit the Society. They all knew what he looked like, so his first move would have to be to change his appearance.

The sign in the barbershop said 'No Waiting', and for once advertising accurately reflected its product. Malcolm took off his jacket facing the wall. He slipped the gun inside the bundle before he sat down. His eyes never left the jacket during the whole haircut.

'What do you want, young fellow?' The graying barber snipped his scissors gleefully.

Malcolm felt no regrets. He knew how much the

haircut might mean. 'A short butch, just a little longer than a crew cut, long enough so it will lay down.'

'Say, that'll be quite a change.' The barber plugged in an electric clipper.

'Yeah.'

'Say, young man, are you interested in baseball? I sure am. I read an article in the *Post* today about the Orioles and spring training, and the way this fellow figures it...'

After the haircut Malcolm looked in the mirror. He hadn't seen that person for five years.

His next stop was Sunny Surplus. Malcolm knew a good disguise starts with the right attitude, but he also knew good props were invaluable. He searched through the entire stock until he found a used field jacket with the patches intact that fitted reasonably well. The name patch above the left pocket read 'Evans'. On the left shoulder was a tricolored eagle patch with the word 'Airborne' in gold letters on a black background. Malcolm knew he had just become a veteran of the 101st Airborne Division. He bought and changed into a pair of blue stretch jeans and an outrageously priced set of used jump boots ('$15, guaranteed to have seen action in Vietnam'). He also bought underwear, a cheap pullover, black driving gloves, socks, a safety razor, and a toothbrush. When he left the store with the bundle under his arm, he pretended he had a spike rammed up his ass. His steps were firm and well measured. He looked cockily at every girl he passed. After five blocks he needed a rest, so he entered one of Washington's countless Hot Shoppe restaurants.

'Can Ah have a cup of caufee?' The waitress didn't bat an eye at Malcolm's newly acquired southern accent. She brought him his coffee. Malcolm tried to relax and think.

Two girls were in the booth behind Malcolm. A lifetime habit made him listen to their conversation.

'So you're not going anywhere for your vacation?'

'No, I'm just going to stay home. For two weeks I'll shut the world out.'

'You'll go crazy.'

'Maybe, but don't try calling me for a progress report, because I probably won't even answer the phone.'

The other girl laughed. 'What if it's a hunk of man who's just pining for companionship?'

The other girl snorted. 'Then he'll just have to wait for two weeks. I'm going to relax.'

'Well, it's your life. Sure you won't have dinner tonight?'

'No, really, thanks, Anne. I'm just going to finish my coffee and then drive home, and starting right now I won't have to hurry for another two weeks.'

'Well, Wendy, have fun.' Thighs squeaked across plastic. The girl called Anne walked towards the door, right past Malcolm. He caught a glimpse of a tremendous pair of legs, blond hair, and a firm profile vanishing in the crowd. He sat very still, sniffling occasionally, nervous as hell, for he had found the answer to his shelter problem.

It took the girl called Wendy five minutes to finish her coffee. When she left she didn't even look at the man sitting behind her. She couldn't have seen much anyway, as his face was hidden behind a menu. Malcolm followed her as soon as she paid and started out the door. He threw his money on the counter as he left.

All he could tell from behind was that she was tall, thin but not painfully skinny like Tamatha, had short hair, and only medium legs. Christ, he thought, why couldn't she have been the blond? Malcolm's luck held, for the girl's car was in the back section of a crowded parking lot. He casually followed her past the fat attendant leering from behind a battered felt hat. Just as the girl unlocked the door of a battered Corvair, Malcolm yelled, 'Wendy! My God, what are you doing here?'

Startled, but not alarmed, the girl looked up at the smiling figure in the army jacket walking towards her.

'Are you talking to me?' She had narrow-set brown eyes, a wide mouth, a little nose, and high cheekbones. A perfectly ordinary face. She wore little or no makeup.

'I shore am. Don't you remember me, Wendy?' He was only three steps from her now.

'I ... I don't think so.' She noticed that his one hand held a package and his other was inside his jacket.

Malcolm stood beside her now. He set the package on the roof of her car and casually placed his left hand behind her head. He tightly grabbed her neck, bending her head down until she saw the gun in his other hand.

'Don't scream or make any quick moves or I'll splatter you all over the street. Understand?' Malcolm felt the girl shiver, but she nodded quickly. 'Now get in the car and unlock the other door. This thing shoots through windows and I won't even hesitate.' The girl quickly climbed into the driver's seat, leaned over, and unlocked the other door. Malcolm slammed her door shut, picked up his package, slowly walked around the car, and got in.

'Please don't hurt me.' Her voice was much softer than in the restaurant.

'Look at me.' Malcolm had to clear his throat. 'I'm not

133

going to hurt you, not if you do exactly as I say. I don't want your money, I don't want to rape you. But you must do exactly as I say. Where do you live?'

'In Alexandria.'

'We're going to your apartment. You'll drive. If you have any ideas about signaling for help, forget them. If you try, I'll shoot. I might get hurt, but you'll be dead. It's not worth it. O.K.?' The girl nodded. 'Let's go.'

The drive to Virginia was tense. Malcolm never took his eyes off the girl. She never took her eyes off the road. Just after the Alexandria exit she pulled into a small courtyard surrounded by apartment units.

'Which one is yours?'

'The first one. I have the top two floors. A man lives in the basement.'

'You're doing just fine. Now, when we go up the walk, just pretend you're taking a friend to your place. Remember, I'm right behind you.'

They got out and walked the few steps to the building. The girl shook and had trouble unlocking the door, but she finally made it. Malcolm followed her in, gently closing the door behind him.

'I have treated this game in great detail because I think it is important for the student to see what he's up against, and how he ought to go about solving the problems of practical play. You may not be able to play the defense and counterattack this well, but the game sets a worthwhile goal for you to achieve: how to fight back in a position where your opponent has greater mobility and better prospects.'

– Fred Reinfeld, *The Complete Chess Course*

Thursday Evening – Friday Morning

'I don't believe you.' The girl sat on the couch, her eyes glued to Malcolm. She was not as frightened as she had been, but her heart felt as if it was breaking ribs.

Malcolm sighed. He had been sitting across from the girl for an hour. From what he found in her purse, he knew she was Wendy Ross, twenty-seven years old, had lived and driven in Carbondale, Illinois, distributed 135 pounds on her five-foot-ten frame (he was sure that was an overestimated lie), regularly gave Type O Positive blood to the Red Cross, was a card-carrying user of the Alexandria Public Library and a member of the University of Southern Illinois Alumni Association, and was certified to receive and deliver summonses for her employers, Bechtel, Barber, Sievers, Holloron, and Muckleston. From what he read on her face, he knew she was frightened and telling

135

the truth when she said she didn't believe him. Malcolm didn't blame her, as he really didn't believe his story either, and he knew it was true.

'Look,' he said, 'if what I said wasn't true, why would I try to convince you it was?'

'I don't know.'

'Oh, Jesus!' Malcolm paced the room. He could tie her up and still use her place, but that was risky. Besides, she could be invaluable. He had an inspiration in the middle of a sneeze.

'Look,' he said, wiping his upper lip, 'suppose I could at least prove to you I was with the C.I.A. Then would you believe me?'

'I might.' A new look crossed the girl's face.

'O.K., look at this.' Malcolm sat down beside her. He felt her body tense, but she took the mutilated pieces of paper.

'What's this?'

'It's my C.I.A. identification card. See, that's me with long hair.'

Her voice was cold. 'It says Tentrex Industries, not C.I.A. I can read, you know.' He could see she regretted her inflection after she said it, but she didn't apologise.

'I know what it says!' Malcolm grew more impatient and nervous. His plan might not work. 'Do you have a D.C. phone book?'

The girl nodded toward an end table. Malcolm crossed the room, picked up the huge book, and flung it at the girl. Her reactions were so keyed she caught it without any trouble. Malcolm shouted at her, 'Look in there for Tentrex Industries. Anywhere! White pages, yellow pages, anywhere. The card gives a phone number and an address on Wisconsin Avenue, so it should be in the book. Look!'

The girl looked, then she looked again. She closed the book and stared at Malcolm. 'So you've got an I.D. card for a place that doesn't exist. What does that prove?'

'Right!' Malcolm crossed the room excitedly, bringing the phone with him. The cord barely reached. 'Now,' he said, very secretively, 'look up the Washington number for the Central Intelligence Agency. The numbers are the same.'

The girl opened the book again and turned the pages. For a long time she sat puzzled, then with a new look and a questioning voice she said, 'Maybe you checked this out before you made the card, just for times like this.'

Shit, thought Malcolm. He let all the air out of his lungs, took a deep breath, and started again. 'O.K., maybe I did, but there's one way to find out. Call that number.'

'It's after five,' said the girl. 'If no one answers am I supposed to believe you until morning?'

Patiently, calmly, Malcolm explained to her. 'You're right. If Tentrex is a real company, it's closed for the day. But C.I.A. doesn't close. Call that number and ask for Tentrex.' He handed her the phone. 'One thing. I'll be listening, so don't do anything wrong. Hang up when I tell you.'

The girl nodded and made the call. Three rings.

'W.E.4-3926.'

'May I have Tentrex Industries, please?' The girl's voice was very dry.

'I'm sorry,' said a soft voice. A faint click came over the line. 'Everyone at Tentrex has gone for the day. They'll be back in the morning. May I ask who is calling and what the nature of your business ...'

Malcolm broke the connection before the trace had a chance to even get a general fix. The girl slowly replaced the receiver. For the first time she looked directly at Malcolm. 'I don't know if I believe everything you say,' she said, 'but I think I believe some of it.'

'One final piece of proof.' Malcolm took the gun out of his pants and laid it carefully in her lap. He walked across the room and sat in the beanbag chair. His palms were damp, but it was better to take the risk now than later. 'You've got the gun. You could shoot me at least once before I got to you. There's the phone. I believe in you enough to think you believe me. Call anybody you want. Police, C.I.A., F.B.I., I don't care. Tell them you've got me. But I want you to know what might happen if you do. The wrong people might get the call. They might get here first. If they do, we're both dead.'

For a long time the girl sat still, looking at the heavy gun in her lap. Then, in a soft voice Malcolm had to strain to hear, she said, 'I believe you.'

She suddenly burst into activity. She stood up, laid the gun on the table and paced the room. 'I ... I don't know what I can do to help you, but I'll try. You can stay here in the extra bedroom. Umm.' She looked towards the small kitchen and meekly said, 'I could make something to eat.'

Malcolm grinned, a genuine smile he thought he had lost. 'That would be wonderful. Could you do one thing for me?'

'Anything, anything, I'll do anything.' Wendy's nerves unwound as she realised she might live.

'Could I use your shower? The hair down my back is killing me.'

She grinned at him and they both laughed. She showed him the bathroom upstairs and provided him with soap, shampoo, and towels. She didn't say a word when he took the gun with him. As soon as she left him he tiptoed to the top of the stairs. No sound of a door opening, no telephone dialing. When he heard drawers opening and closing, silverware rattling, he went back to the bathroom, undressed, and climbed into the shower.

Malcolm stayed in the shower for thirty minutes, letting the soft pellets of water drive freshness through his body. The steam cleared his sinuses, and by the time he shut off the water he felt almost human. He changed into his new pullover and fresh underwear. He automatically looked in the mirror to straighten his hair. It was so short he did it with two strokes of his hand.

The stereo was playing as he came down the stairs. He recognised the album as Vince Guaraldi's score for *Black Orpheus*. The song was 'Cast Your Fate to the Wind'. He had the album too, and told her so as they sat down to eat.

During green salad she told Malcolm about smalltown life in Illinois. Between bites of frozen German beans he heard about life at Southern Illinois University. Mashed potatoes were mixed with a story concerning an almost fiancé. Between chunks of the jiffy-cooked Swiss steak he learned how drab it is to be a legal secretary for a stodgy corporate law firm in Washington. There was a lull for Sara Lee cherry covered cheesecake. As she poured coffee she summed it all up with, 'It's really been pretty dull. Up till now, of course.'

During dishes he told her why he hated his first name.

She promised never to use it. She threw a handful of suds at him, but quickly wiped them off.

After dishes he said good night and trudged up the stairs to the bathroom. He put his contact lenses in his portable carrying case (what I wouldn't give for my glasses and soaking case, he thought). He brushed his teeth, crossed the hall to a freshly made bed, stuck a precautionary handkerchief under his pillow, laid the gun on the night stand, and went to sleep.

She came to him shortly after midnight. At first he thought he was dreaming, but her heavy breathing and the heat of her body were too real. His first fully awake thought noted that she had just showered. He could faintly smell bath powder mingling with the sweet odor of sex. He rolled on his side, pulling her eager body against him. They found each other's mouth. Her tongue pushed through his lips, searching. She was tremendously excited. He had a hard time untangling himself from her arms so he could strip off his underwear. By now their faces were wet from each other. Naked at last, he rolled her over on her back, pulling his hand slowly up the inside of her thigh, delicately trailing his fingers across rhythmically flowing hips, up across her flat, heaving stomach to her large, erect nipples. His fingers closed on one small breast, easily gathering the mound of flesh into his hand. From out of nowhere he thought of the girl who walked past the Society's building: she had such fine, large breasts. He softly squeezed his hand. Wendy groaned loudly and pulled his head to her chest, his lips to her straining nipples. As his mouth slowly caressed her breasts, he ran his hand down, down to the wet fire between her legs. When he touched her she sucked in air, softly but firmly arching her back. She found him, and a second later softly moaned, 'Now, please now!' He mounted her, clumsily as first-time lovers do. They pressed together. She tried to cover every inch of her body with him. His hard thrusts spread fire through her body. She ran her hands down his back, and just before they exploded he felt her fingernails digging into his buttocks, pulling him ever deeper.

They lay quietly together for half an hour, then they began again, slowly and more carefully, but with a greater intensity. Afterwards, as she lay cradled on his chest, she spoke. 'You don't have to love me. I don't love you, I don't think so anyway. But I want you, and I need you.'

Malcolm said nothing, but he drew her closer. They slept.

Other people didn't get to bed that night. When Langley heard the reports of the Weatherby shooting, already frazzled nerves frazzled more. Crash cars full of very determined men beat the ambulance to the alley. Washington police complained to their superiors about 'unidentified men claiming to be federal officers' questioning witnesses. A clash between two branches of government was averted by the entrance of a third. Three more official-looking cars pulled into the neighborhood. Two very serious men in pressed white shirts and dark suits pushed their way through the milling crowd to inform commanders of the other departments that the F.B.I. was now officially in charge. The 'unidentified federal officers' and the Washington police checked with their headquarters and both were told not to push the issue.

The F.B.I. entered the case when the powers-that-were

141

adopted a working assumption of espionage. The National Security Act of 1947 states, 'The agency [C.I.A.] shall have no police, subpoena, law-enforcement powers, or internal security functions.' The events of the day most definitely fell under the heading of internal subversive activities, activities that are the domain of the F.B.I. Mitchell held off informing the sister agency of details for as long as he dared, but eventually a deputy director yielded to pressure.

But the C.I.A. would not be denied the right to investigate assaults on its agents, no matter where the assaults occurred. The Agency has a loophole through which many questionable activities funnel. The loophole, Section 5 of the Act, allows the Agency to perform 'such other functions and duties related to intelligence affecting the national security as the National Security Council may from time to time direct.' The Act also grants the Agency the power to question people inside the country. The directors of the Agency concluded that the extreme nature of the situation warranted direct action by the Agency. This action could and would continue until halted by a direct order from the National Security Council. In a very polite but pointed note they so informed the F.B.I., thanking them, of course, for their co-operation and expressing gratitude for any future help.

The Washington police were left with one corpse and a gunshot victim who had disappeared to an undisclosed hospital in Virginia, condition serious, prognosis uncertain. They were not pleased or placated by assurances from various federal officers, but they were unable to pursue 'their' case.

The jurisdictional mishmash tended to work itself out in

the field, where departmental rivalry meant very little compared to dead men. The agents in charge of operations for each department agreed to co-ordinate their efforts. By evening one of the most extensive man hunts in Washington's history began to unfold, with Malcolm as the object of activity. By morning the hunters had turned up a good deal, but they had no clues to Malcolm's whereabouts.

This did little to brighten a bleak morning after for the men who sat around a table in a central Washington office. Most of them had been up until very late the night before, and most of them were far from happy. The liaison group included all of the C.I.A. deputy directors and representatives from every intelligence group in the country. The man at the head of the table was the deputy director in charge of Intelligence Division. Since the crisis occurred in his division, he had been placed in charge of the investigation. He summed up the facts for the grim men he faced.

'Eight Agency people dead, one wounded, and one, a probable double, missing. Again, we have only a tentative – and I must say doubtful – explanation of why.'

'What makes you think the note the killers left is a fake?' The man who spoke wore the uniform of the United States Navy.

The Deputy Director sighed. The Captain always had to have things repeated. 'We're not saying it's a fake, we only think so. We think it's a ruse, an attempt to blame the Czechs for the killings. Sure, we hit one of their bases in Prague, but for tangible, valuable intelligence. We only killed one man. Now, they go in for many things, but melodramatic revenge isn't one of them. Nor is leaving notes on the scene neatly explaining everything. Especially when it gains them nothing. Nothing.'

'Ah, may I ask a question or two, Deputy?'

The Deputy leaned forward, immediately intent. 'Of course, sir.'

'Thank you.' The man who spoke was small and delicately old. To strangers he inevitably appeared to be a kindly old uncle with a twinkle in his eye. 'Just to refresh my memory – stop me if I'm wrong – the one in the apartment, Heidegger, had sodium pentothal in his blood?'

'That's correct, sir.' The Deputy strained, trying to remember if he had forgotten any detail in the briefing.

'Yet none of the others were 'questioned', as far as we can tell. Very strange. They came for him in the night, before the others. Killed shortly before dawn. Yet your investigation puts our boy Malcolm at his apartment that afternoon after Weatherby was shot. You say there is nothing to indicate Heidegger was a double agent? No expenditures beyond his income, no signs of outside wealth, no reported tainted contacts, no blackmail vulnerability?'

'Nothing, sir.'

'Any signs of mental instability?' C.I.A. personnel are among the highest groups in the nation for incidence of mental illness.

'None, sir. Excepting his former alcoholism, he appeared to be normal, though somewhat reclusive.'

'Yes, so I read. Investigation of the others reveal anything out of the ordinary?'

'Nothing, sir.'

'Would you do me a favor and read what Weatherby said to the doctors? By the way, how is he?'

'He's doing better, sir. The doctors say he'll live, but they are taking his leg off this morning.' The Deputy shuffled papers until he found the one he sought. 'Here it is. Now, you must remember he has been unconscious most of the time, but once he woke up, looked at the doctors, and said, "Malcolm shot me. He shot both of us. Get him, hit him".'

There was a stir at the end of the table and the Navy captain leaned forward in his chair. In his heavy, slurred voice he said, 'I say we find that son of a bitch and blast him out of whatever rat hole he ran into!'

The old man chuckled. 'Yes. Well, I quite agree we must find our wayward Condor. But I do think it would be a pity if we "blasted" him before he told us why he shot poor Weatherby. Indeed, why anybody was shot. Do you have anything else for us, Deputy?'

'No, sir,' said the Deputy, stuffing papers into his brief-case. 'I think we've covered everything. You have all the information we do. Thank you all for coming.'

As the men stood to leave, the old man turned to a colleague and said quietly, 'I wonder why.' Then with a smile and a shake of his head he left the room.

Malcolm woke up only when Wendy's caresses became impossible for even a sick man to ignore. Her hands and mouth moved all over his body, and almost before he knew what was happening she mounted him and again he felt her fluttering warmth turn to fire. Afterwards, she looked at him for a long time, lightly touching his body as if exploring an unseen land. She touched his forehead and frowned.

'Malcolm, do you feel O.K.?'

Malcolm had no intention of being brave. He shook his head and forced a raspy 'No' from his throat. The one word seemed to fuel the hot vise closing around his throat. Talking was out for the day.

'You're sick!' Wendy grabbed his lower jaw. 'Let me see!' she ordered, and forced his mouth open. 'My God, it's red down there!' She let go of Malcolm and started to climb out of bed. 'I'm going to call a doctor.'

Malcolm caught her arm. She turned to him with a fearful look, then smiled. 'It's O.K. I have a friend whose husband is a doctor. He drives by here every day on his way to a clinic in D.C. I don't think he's left yet. If he hasn't, I'll ask him to stop by to see my sick friend.' She giggled. 'You don't have to worry. He won't tell a soul because he'll think he's keeping another kind of secret. O.K.?'

Malcolm looked at her for a second, then let go of her arm and nodded. He didn't care if the doctor brought Sparrow IV's friend with him. All he wanted was relief.

The doctor turned out to be a paunchy middle-aged man who spoke little. He poked and prodded Malcolm, took his temperature, and looked down his throat so long Malcolm thought he would throw up. The doctor finally looked up and said, 'You've got a mild case of strep throat, my boy.' He looked at an anxious Wendy hovering nearby. 'Nothing to worry about, really. We'll fix him up.' Malcolm watched the doctor fiddle with something in his bag. When he turned towards Malcolm there was a hypodermic needle in his hand. 'Roll over and puff your shorts down.'

A picture of a limp, cold arm with a tiny puncture

flashed through Malcolm's mind. He froze.

'For Christ's sake, it won't hurt that much. It's only penicillin.'

After giving Malcolm his shot, the doctor turned to Wendy. 'Here,' he said, handing her a slip of paper. 'Get this filled and see that he takes them. He'll need at least a day's rest.' The doctor smiled as he leaned close to Wendy. He whispered, 'And Wendy, I do mean total rest.' He laughed all the way to the door. On the porch, he turned to her and slyly said, 'Whom do I bill?'

Wendy smiled shyly and handed him twenty dollars. The doctor started to speak, but Wendy cut his protest short. 'He can afford it. He – we – really appreciate you coming over.'

'Hmph,' snorted the doctor sarcastically, 'he should. I'm late for my coffee break.' He paused to look at her. 'You know he's the kind of prescription I've thought you needed for a long time.' With a wave of his hand he was gone.

By the time Wendy got upstairs, Malcolm was asleep. She quietly left the apartment. She spent the morning shopping with the list Malcolm and she had composed while waiting for the doctor. Besides filling the prescription, she bought Malcolm several pairs of underwear, socks, some shirts and pants, a jacket, and four different paperbacks, since she didn't know what he liked to read. She carted her bundles home in time to make lunch. She spent a quiet afternoon and evening, occasionally checking on her charge. She smiled all day long.

Supervision of America's large and sometimes cumbersome intelligence community has classically posed the problem of *sed quis custodiet ipsos Custodes:* who guards the guardians? In addition to the internal checks existing independently in each agency, the National Security Act of 1947 created the National Security Council, a group whose composition varies with each change of presidential administration. The Council always includes the President and Vice-President and usually includes major cabinet members. The Council's basic duty is to oversee the activities of the intelligence agencies and to make policy decisions guiding those activities.

But the members of the National Security Council are very busy men with demanding duties besides overseeing a huge intelligence network. Council members by and large do not have the time to devote to intelligence matters, so most decisions about the intelligence community are made by a smaller Council 'sub-committee' known as the Special Group. Insiders often refer to the Special Group as the '54/12 Group', so called because it was created by Secret Order 54/12 early in the Eisenhower years. The 54/12 Group is virtually unknown outside the intelligence, community, and there only a handful of men are aware of its existence.

Composition of the 54/12 Group also varies with each administration. Its membership generally includes the director of the C.I.A., the Under Secretary of State for Political Affairs or his deputy, and the Secretary and Deputy Secretary of Defense. In the Kennedy and early Johnson administrations the presidential representative and key man on the 54/12 Group was McGregor Bundy. The other members were McCone, McNamara, Roswell Gilpatric (Deputy Secretary of Defense), and U. Alexis

Johnson (Deputy Under Secretary of State for Political Affairs).

Overseeing the American intelligence community poses problems for even a small, full-time group of professionals. One is that the overseers must depend on those they oversee for much of the information necessary for regulation. Such a situation is naturally a delicate perplexity.

There is also the problem of fragmented authority. For example, if an American scientist spies on the country while employed by N.A.S.A., then defects to Russia and continues his spying but does it from France, which American agency is responsible for his neutralisation? The F.B.I., since he began his activities under their jurisdiction, or the C.I.A., since he shifted to activities under their purview? With the possibility of bureaucratic jealousies escalating into open rivalry, such questions take on major import.

Shortly after it was formed, the 54/12 Group tried to solve the problems of internal information and fragmented authority. The 54/12 Group established a small special security section, a section with no identity save that of staff for the 54/12 Group. The special section's duties included liaison work. The head of the special section serves on a board composed of leading staff members from all intelligence agencies. He has the power to arbitrate jurisdictional disputes. The special section also has the responsibility of independently evaluating all the information given to the 54/12 Group by the intelligence community. But most important, the special section is given the power to perform 'such necessary security functions as extraordinary circumstances might dictate, subject to Group [the 54/12 Group] regulation'.

To help the special section perform its duties, the 54/12 Group assigned a small staff to the section chief and allowed him to draw on other major security and intelligence groups for needed staff and authority.

The 54/12 Group knows it has created a potential problem. The special section could follow the natural tendency of most government organisations and grow in size and awkwardness, thereby becoming a part of the problem it was created to solve. The special section, small though it is, has tremendous power as well as tremendous potential. A small mistake by the section could be a lever of great magnitude. The 54/12 Group supervises its creation cautiously. They keep a firm check on any bureaucratic growth potentials in the section, they carefully review its activities, keeping the operational work of the section at a bare minimum, and they place only extraordinary men in charge of the section.

While Malcolm and Wendy waited for the doctor, a large, competent-looking man sat in an outer office on Pennsylvania Avenue, waiting to answer a very special summons. His name was Kevin Powell. He waited patiently but eagerly: he did not receive such a summons every day. Finally a secretary beckoned, and he entered the inner office of a man who looked like a kindly, delicate old uncle. The old man motioned Powell to a chair.

'Ah, Kevin, how wonderful to see you.'

'Good to see you, sir. You're looking fit.'

'As do you, my boy, as do you. Here.' The old man tossed Powell a file folder. 'Read this.' As Powell read, the old man examined him closely. The plastic surgeons had done a marvelous job on his ear, and it took an experienced eye to detect the slight bulge close to his left armpit. When Powell raised his eyes, the old man said, 'What do you think, my boy?'

Powell chose his words carefully. 'Very strange, sir. I'm not sure what it means, though it must mean a great deal.'

'Exactly my thoughts, my boy, exactly mine. Both the Agency and the Bureau [F.B.I.] have squads of men scouring the city, watching the airports, buses, trains, the usual routine, only expanded to quite a staggering level. As you know, it's these routine operations that make or break most endeavors, and I must say they are doing fairly well. Or they were up until now.'

He paused for breath and an encouraging look of interest from Powell. 'They've found a barber who remembers giving our boy a haircut – rather predictable yet commendable action on his part – some time after Weatherby was shot. By the way, he is coming along splendidly. They hope to question him late this evening. Where was I … Oh, yes. They canvassed the area and found where he bought some clothes, but then they lost him. They have no idea where to look next. I have one or two ideas about that myself, but I'll save them for later. There are some points I want you to check me on. See if you can answer them for me, or maybe find some questions I can't find.

'Why? Why the whole thing? If it was Czechoslovakia, why that particular branch, a do-nothing bunch of analysts? If it wasn't, we're back to our original question.

'Look at the method. Why so blatant? Why was the man Heidegger hit the night before? What did he know that the others didn't? If he was special, why kill the others too?

If Malcolm works for them, they didn't need to question Heidegger about much. Malcolm could have told them.

'Then we have our boy Malcolm, Malcolm with the many "why's". If he is a double, why did he use the Panic procedure? If he is a double, why did he set up a meeting – to kill Sparrow IV, whom he could have picked off at his leisure had he worked at establishing the poor fellow's identity? If he isn't a double, why did he shoot the two men he called to take him to safety? Why did he go to Heidegger's apartment after the shooting? And, of course, where, why, and how is he now?

'There are a lot of other questions that grow from these, but I think these are the main ones. Do you agree?'

Powell nodded and said, 'I do. Where do I fit in?'

The old man smiled. 'You, my dear boy, have the good fortune to be on loan to my section. As you know, we were created to sort out the mishmashes of bureaucracy. I imagine some of those paper pushers who shuffled my poor old soul here assumed I would be stuck processing paper until I died or retired. Neither of those alternatives appeal to me, so I have redefined liaison work to mean a minimum of paper and a maximum of action, pirated a very good set of operatives, and set up my own little shop, just like in the old days. With the official maze of the intelligence community, I have a good deal of confusion to play with. A dramatist I once knew said the best way to create chaos is to flood the scene with actors. I've managed to capitalise on the chaos of others.

'I think some of my efforts,' he added in a modest tone, 'small though they may be, have been of some value to the country.

'Now we come to this little affair. It isn't really much of my business, but the damn thing intrigues me. Besides, I think there is something wrong with the way the Agency and the Bureau are handling the whole thing. First of all, this is a very extraordinary situation, and they are using fairly ordinary means. Second, they're tripping over each other, both hot to make the pinch, as they say. Then there's the one thing I can't really express. Something about this whole affair bothers me. It should never have happened. Both the idea behind the event and the way in which the event manifested itself are so ... wrong, so out of place. I think it's beyond the parameters of the Agency. Not that they're incompetent – though I think they have missed one or two small points – but they're just not viewing it from the right place. Do you understand, my boy?'

Powell nodded. 'And you are in the right place, right?'

The old man smiled. 'Well, let's just say one foot is in the door. Now here's what I want you to do. Did you notice our boy's medical record? Don't bother looking, I'll tell you. He has many times the number of colds and respiratory problems he should. He often needs medical attention. Now, if you remember the transcript of the second panic call, he sneezed and said he had a cold. I'm playing a long shot that his cold is much worse, and that wherever he is, he'll come out to get help. What do you think?'

Powell shrugged. 'Might be worth a try.'

The old man was gleeful. 'I think so, too. Neither the Agency nor the Bureau has tumbled to this yet, so we have a clear field. Now, I've arranged for you to head a special team of D.C. detectives – never mind how I managed it, I did. Start with the general practitioners in the metropolitan area. Find out if any of them have treated anyone like our boy – use his new description. If they haven't, tell them to report to us if they do. Make up some plausible story so they'll open up to you. One other thing. Don't let the others find out we're looking too. The last time they had a chance, two men got shot.'

Powell stood to go. 'I'll do what I can, sir.'

'Fine, fine, my boy. I knew I could count on you. I'm still thinking on this. If I come up with anything else, I'll let you know. Good luck.'

Powell left the room. When the door was shut, the old man smiled.

While Kevin Powell began his painstakingly dull check of the Washington medical community, a very striking man with strange eyes climbed out of a taxi in front of Sunny's Surplus. The man had spent the morning reading a Xeroxed file identical with the one Powell had just examined. He had received the file from a very distinguished-looking gentleman. The man with the strange eyes had a plan for finding Malcolm. He spent an hour driving around the neighborhood, and now he began to walk it. At bars, newspaper stands, public offices, private buildings, anywhere a man could stop for a few minutes, he would stop and show an artist's projected sketch of Malcolm with short hair. When people seemed reluctant to talk to him, the man flashed one of five sets of credentials the distinguished man had obtained. By 3.30 that afternoon he was tired, but it didn't show. He was more resolute than ever. He stopped at a Hot Shoppe for coffee. On the way out he flashed the picture and a badge at the cashier in a by now automatic manner. Almost anyone else would have registered the shock he felt when the clerk said she recognised the man.

'Yeah, I saw the son of a bitch. He threw his money at me he was in such a hurry to leave. Ripped a nylon crawling after a rolling nickel.'

'Was he alone?'

'Yeah, who would want to be with a creep like that?'

'Did you see which way he went?'

'Sure I saw. If I'd have had a gun I'd have shot him. He went that way.'

The man carefully paid his bill, leaving a dollar tip for the cashier. He walked in the direction she had pointed. Nothing, no reason to make a man looking for safety hurry that particular way. Then again ... He turned into the parking lot and became a D.C. detective for the fat man in the felt hat.

'Sure, I seen him. He got into the car with the chick.'

The striking man's eyes narrowed. 'What chick?'

'The one that works in them lawyers. The firm rents space for all the people that work there. She ain't so great to look at, but she's got class, if you know what I mean."

'I think so,' said the fake detective, 'I think so. Who is she?'

'Just a minute.' The man in the hat waddled into a small shack. He returned carrying a ledger. 'Let's see, lot 63 ... lot 63. Yeah, here it is. Ross, Wendy Ross. This here is her Alexandria address.'

The narrow eyes glanced briefly at the offered book and recorded what they saw. They turned back to the man in the felt hat. 'Thanks.' The striking man began to walk away.

'Don't mention it. Say, what's this guy done?'

The man stopped and turned back. 'Nothing, really. We're just looking for him. He ... he's been exposed to something – it couldn't hurt you – and we just want to make sure he's all right.'

Ten minutes later the striking man was in a phone booth. Across the city a distinguished-looking gentlemen picked up a private phone that seldom rang. 'Yes,' he said, then recognised the voice.

'I have a firm lead.'

'I knew you would. Have someone check it out, but don't let him act on it unless absolutely unavoidable circumstances arise. I want you to handle it personally so there will be no more mistakes. Right now I have a more pressing matter for your expert attention.

'Our sick mutual friend?'

'Yes. I'm afraid he has to take a turn for the worse. Meet me at place four as soon as you can.' The line went dead.

The man stayed in the phone booth long enough to make another short call. Then he hailed a taxi and rode away into the fading light.

A small car parked across and up the street from Wendy's apartment just as she brought a tray of stew to Malcolm. The driver could see Wendy's door very clearly, even though he had to bend his tall, thin body into a very strange position. He watched the apartment, waiting.

> 'Overconfidence breeds error when we take for granted that the game will continue on its normal course; when we fail to provide for an unusually powerful resource – a check, a sacrifice, a stalemate. Afterwards the victim may wail, "But who could have dreamt of such an idiotic–looking move?"'
>
> – Fred Reinfeld, The Complete Chess Course

Saturday

'Are you feeling any better?'

Malcolm looked up at Wendy and had to admit that he was. The pain in his throat had subsided to a dull ache and almost twenty-four hours of sleep had restored a good deal of his strength. His nose still ran most of the time and talking brought pain, but even these discomforts were slowly fading.

As the discomforts of his body decreased, the discomforts of his mind increased. He knew it was Saturday, two days after his co-workers had been killed and he had shot a man. By now several very resourceful, very determined groups of people would be turning Washington upside down. At least one group wanted him dead. The others probably had little affection for him. In a dresser across the room lay $9,382 stolen from a dead man, or at least removed from his apartment. Here he was, lying sick in bed without the foggiest notion about what had happened or what he was to do. On top of all that, here on his bed sat a funny-looking girl wearing a T shirt and a smile.

'You know, I really don't understand it,' he rasped. He didn't. In all the hours he had devoted to the problem he could find only four tentative assumptions that held water: that the Agency had been penetrated by somebody; that somebody had hit his section; that somebody had tried to frame Heidegger as a double by leaving the 'hidden' money; and that somebody wanted him dead.

'Do you know what you're going to do yet?' Wendy used her forefinger to trace the outline of Malcolm's thigh under the sheet.

'No.' He said exasperatedly, 'I might try the panic number later tonight, if you'll take me to a phone booth.'

She leaned forward and lightly kissed his forehead. 'I'll take you anywhere.' She smiled and lightly kissed him, his eyes, his cheek, down to his mouth, down to his neck. Flipping back the sheet, she kissed his chest, down to his stomach, down.

Afterwards they showered and he put in his contacts. He went back to bed. When Wendy came back into his room, she was fully dressed. She tossed him four paperbacks. 'I didn't know what you liked, but these should keep you busy while I'm gone.'

'Where are –' Malcolm had to pause and swallow. It still hurt. 'Where are you going?'

She smiled. 'Silly boy, I've got to shop. We're low on food and there are still some things you need. If you're very good – and you're not bad – I might bring you a surprise.' She walked away but turned back at the door. 'If the phone rings, don't answer unless it rings twice, stops, then rings again. That'll be me. Aren't I learning how to be a good spy? I'm not expecting anybody. If you're quiet, no one will know you're here.' Her voice took on a more serious tone. 'Now, don't worry, O.K.? You're perfectly safe here.' She turned and left.

Malcolm had just picked up one book when her head popped round the doorjamb. 'Hey,' she said, 'I just thought of something. If I get strep throat, will it classify as venereal disease?' Malcolm missed when he threw the book at her.

When Wendy opened her door and walked to her car, she didn't notice the man in the van parked across the street stirring out of lethargy. He was a plain-looking man. He wore a bulky raincoat even though spring sunshine ruled the morning. It was almost as if he knew the good weather couldn't last. The man watched Wendy pull out of the parking lot and drive away. He looked at his watch. He would wait three minutes.

Saturday is a day off for most government employees, but not for all. This particular Saturday saw a large number of civil servants from various government levels busily and glumly drawing overtime. One of these was Kevin Powell. He and his men had talked to 216 doctors, receiving nurses, interns, and other assorted members of the medical profession. Over half the general practitioners and throat specialists in the Washington area had been questioned. It was now eleven o'clock on a fine Saturday morning. All Powell had to report to the old man behind the mahogany desk could be summed up in one word: nothing.

The old man's spirits weren't dimmed by the news. 'Well, my boy, just keep on trying, that's all I can say, just keep on trying. If it's any consolation, let me say we're in the same position as the others, only they have run out of things to do except watch. But one thing has happened: Weatherby is dead.'

Powell was puzzled. 'I thought you said his condition was improving.'

The old man spread his hands. 'It was. They planned to question him late last night or early this morning. When the interrogation team arrived shortly after one a.m., they found him dead.'

'How?' Powell's voice held more than a little suspicion.

'How indeed? The guard on the door swears only medical personnel went in and out. Since he was in the Langley hospital, I'm sure security must have been tight. His doctors say that, given the shock and the loss of blood, it is entirely possible he died from the wound. They were sure he was doing marvelously. Right now they're doing a complete autopsy.'

'It's very strange.'

'Yes it is, isn't it? But because it's strange, it should have been almost predictable. The whole case is strange. Ah, well, we've been over this ground before. I have something new for you.'

Powell leaned closer to the desk. He was tired. The old man continued, 'I told you I wasn't satisfied with the way the Agency and the Bureau were handling the case. They've run into a blind wall. I'm sure part of the reason is that their method led them there. They've been looking for Malcolm the way a hunter looks for any game. While they're skilled hunters, they're missing a thing or two. I want you to start looking for him as though you were the prey. You've read all the information we have on him, you've been to his apartment. You must have some sense of the man. Put yourself in his shoes and see where you end up.

'I have a few helpful tidbits for you. We know he needed transportation to get wherever he is. If nothing else, a man on foot is visible, and our boy wants to avoid that. The Bureau is fairly certain he didn't take a cab. I see no reason to fault their investigation along those lines. I don't think he would ride a bus, not with the package the man at the store sold him. Besides, one never knows who one might meet on a bus.

'So there's your problem. Take a man or two, men who can put themselves in the right frame of mind. Start from where he was last seen. Then, my boy, get yourself hidden the way he has.'

Just before Powell opened the door, he looked at the smiling old man and said, 'There's one other thing that's strange about this whole business, sir. Malcolm was never trained as a field agent. He's a researcher, yet look how well he's made out.'

'Yes, that is rather strange,' answered the old man. He smiled and said, 'You know, I'm getting rather keen to meet our boy Malcolm. Find him for me, Kevin, find him for me quickly.'

Malcolm needed a cup of coffee. The hot liquid would make his throat feel better and the caffeine would pep him up. He grinned slowly, being careful not to stretch tender neck muscles. With Wendy, a man needed a lot of pep. He went downstairs to the kitchen. He had just put a pot on to boil when the doorbell rang.

Malcolm froze. The gun was upstairs, right next to his bed where he could reach it in a hurry, provided, of course, that he was in bed. Quietly, Malcolm tiptoed to the door. The bell rang again. He sighed with relief when he saw through the one-way glass peephole that it was only a bored-looking mailman, his bag slung over one shoulder, a package in one hand. Then he became annoyed. If he didn't answer the door, the mailman might keep coming back until he delivered his package. Malcolm looked down at his body. He only had on jockey shorts and a T shirt. Oh well, he thought, the mailman's probably seen it all before. He opened the door.

'Good morning, sir, how are you today?'

The mailman's cheer seemed to infect Malcolm. He smiled back, and said hoarsely, 'Got a little cold. What can I do for you?'

'Got a package here for a Miss ...' The mailman paused and slyly smiled at Malcolm. 'A Miss Wendy Ross. Special delivery, return receipt requested.'

'She's not here right now. Could you come back later?'

The mailman scratched his head. 'Well, could, but it would sure be easier if you signed for it. Hell, government don't care who signs, long as it's signed.'

'O.K.,' said Malcolm. 'Do you have a pen?'

The mailman slapped his pockets unsuccessfully.

'Come on in,' Malcolm said. 'I'll get one.'

The mailman smiled as he entered the room. He closed the door behind him. 'You're making my day a lot easier by going to all this trouble,' he said.

Malcolm shrugged. 'Think nothing of it.' He turned and went into the kitchen to find a pen. As he walked through the door, his mind abstractedly noted that the mailman had put the package down and was unslinging his pouch.

The mailman was very happy. His orders had been to determine whether Malcolm was in the apartment, to reconnoiter the building, and to make a hit only if it could be done with absolute safety and certainty. He knew a bonus would follow his successful display of initiative in hitting Malcolm. The girl would come later. He pulled the silenced sten gun out of his pouch.

Just before Malcolm came around the corner from the kitchen he heard the click when the mailman armed the sten gun. Malcolm hadn't found a pen. In one hand he carried the coffeepot and in the other an empty cup. He thought the nice mailman might like some refreshment. That Malcolm didn't die then may be credited to the fact that when he turned the corner and saw the gun swinging toward him he didn't stop to think. He threw the pot of boiling coffee and the empty cup straight at the mailman.

The mailman hadn't heard Malcolm coming. His first thought centered on the objects flying towards his face. He threw up his arms, covering his head with the gun. The coffeepot bounced off the gun, but the lid flew off and hot coffee splashed down on bare arms and an upturned face.

Screaming, the mailman threw the gun away from him. It skidded across the floor, stopping under the table holding Wendy's stereo. Malcolm made a desperate dive for it, only to be tripped by a black loafer. He fell to his hands and staggered up. He quickly looked over his shoulder and ducked. The mailman flew over Malcolm's head. Had the flying side kick connected, the back of Malcolm's head would have shattered and in all probability his neck would have snapped.

Even though he hadn't practiced in a dojo for six months, the mailman executed the difficult landing perfectly. However, he landed on the scatter rug Wendy's grandmother had given her as a birthday present. The rug slid along the waxed floor and the mailman fell to his hands. He bounced up twice as fast as Malcolm.

The two men stared at each other. Malcolm had at least ten feet to travel before he could reach the gun on his right. He could probably beat the mailman to the table, but before he could pull the gun out the man would be all over his back. Malcolm was closest to the door, but it was closed. He knew he wouldn't have the precious seconds it would take to open it.

The mailman looked at Malcolm and smiled. With the toe of his shoe he tested the hardwood floor. Stick. With deft, practiced movements he slipped his feet out of the loafers. He wore slipperlike socks. These too came off when he rubbed his feet on the floor. The mailman came prepared to walk quietly, barefoot, and his preparations served him in an unexpected manner. His bare feet hugged the floor.

Malcolm looked at his smiling opponent and began to accept death. He had no way of knowing the man's brown belt proficiency, but he knew he didn't stand a chance. Malcolm's knowledge of martial arts was almost negligible. He had read fight scenes in numerous books and seen them in movies. He had had two fights as a child, won one, lost one. His physical education instructor in college had spent three hours teaching the class some cute tricks he had learned in the Marines. Reason made Malcolm try to copy the man's stance, legs bent, fists clenched, left arm in front and bent perpendicular to the floor, right arm held close to the waist.

Very slowly the mailman began to shuffle across the fifteen feet that separated him from his prey. Malcolm began to circle towards his right, vaguely wondering why he bothered. When the mailman was six feet from Malcolm he made his move. He yelled and with his left arm feinted a backhand snap at Malcolm's face. As the mailman anticipated, Malcolm ducked quickly to his right side. When the mailman brought his left hand back, he dropped his left shoulder and whirled to his right on the ball of his left foot. At the end of the three-quarters circle his right leg shot to meet Malcolm's ducking head.

But six months is too long to be out of practice and expect perfect results, even when fighting an untrained amateur. The kick missed Malcolm's face, but thudded into his left shoulder. The blow knocked Malcolm into the wall. When he bounced off he barely dodged the swinging hand chop follow-through blow.

The mailman was very angry with himself. He had missed twice. True, his opponent was injured, but he should have been dead. The mailman knew he must get back into practice before he met an opponent who knew what to do.

A good karate instructor will emphasise that karate is three-quarters mental. The mailman knew this, so he devoted his entire mind to the death of his opponent. He concentrated so deeply he failed to hear Wendy as she opened and shut the door, quietly so as not to disturb

Malcolm's sleeping. She had forgotten her checkbook.

Wendy was dreaming. It wasn't real, these two men standing in her living room. One her Malcolm, his left arm twitching to life at his side. The other a short, stocky stranger standing so strangely, his back towards her. Then she heard the stranger very softly say, 'You've caused enough trouble!' and she knew it was all frighteningly real. As the stranger began to shuffle towards Malcolm, she carefully reached around the kitchen corner, and took a long carving knife from a sparkling set held on the wall by a magnet. She walked towards the stranger.

The mailman beard the click of heels on the hardwood floor. He quickly feinted towards Malcolm and whirled to face the new challenge. When he saw the frightened girl standing with a knife clutched awkwardly in her right hand, the worry that had been building in his brain ceased. He quickly shuffled towards her, dodging and dipping as she backed away trembling. He let her back up until she was about to run into the couch, then he made his move. His left foot snapped forward in a roundhouse kick and the knife flew from her numbed hand. His left knuckles split the skin just beneath her left cheekbone in a vicious backhand strike. Wendy sank, stunned, to the couch.

But the mailman had forgotten an important maxim of multiple-attackers situations. A man being attacked by two or more opponents must keep moving, delivering quick, alternate attacks to each of his opponents. If he stops to concentrate on one before all of his opponents have been neutralised, he leaves himself exposed. The mailman should have whirled to attack Malcolm immediately after the kick. Instead he went for the *coupe de grâce* on Wendy.

By the time the mailman had delivered his backhand blow to Wendy, Malcolm had the sten gun in his hand. He could use his left arm only to prop the barrel up, but he lined the gun up just as the mailman raised his left hand for the final downward chop.

'Don't!'

The mailman whirled towards his other opponent just as Malcolm pulled the trigger. The coughing sounds hadn't stopped before the mailman's chest blossomed with a red, spurting row. The body flew over the couch and thudded on the floor.

Malcolm picked Wendy up. Her left eye began to puff shut and a trickle of blood ran down her cheek. She sobbed quietly, 'My God, my God, my God.'

It took Malcolm five minutes to calm her down. He peered cautiously through the blinds. No one was in sight. The yellow van across the street looked empty. He left Wendy downstairs with the machine gun huddled in her arms pointed at the door. He told her to shoot anything that came through. He quickly dressed, and packed his money, his clothes, and the items Wendy had bought him in one of her spare suitcases. When he came downstairs., she was more rational. He sent her upstairs to pack. While she was gone, he searched the corpse and found nothing. When she came down ten minutes later, her face had been washed and she carried a suitcase.

Malcolm took a deep breath and opened the door. He had a coat draped over his revolver. He couldn't bring himself to take the sten gun. He knew what it had done. No one shot him. He walked to the car. Still no bullets. No one was even visible. He nodded to Wendy. She ran to the car dragging their bags. They got in and he quietly drove away.

Powell was tired. He and two other Washington detectives were covering covered ground, walking along all the streets in the area where Malcolm had last been sighted. They questioned people at every building. All they found were people who had been questioned before. Powell was leaning against a light pole, trying to find a new idea, when he saw one of his men hurrying towards him.

The man was Detective Andrew Walsh, Homicide. He grabbed Powell's arm to steady himself. 'I think I've found something, sir.' Walsh paused to catch his breath. 'You know how we've found a lot of people who were questioned before? Well, I found one, a parking-lot attendant, who told the cop who questioned him something that isn't in the official reports.'

'For Christ's sake, *what?*' Powell was no longer tired.

'He made Malcolm, off a picture this cop showed him. More than that, he told him he saw Malcolm get into a car with this girl. Here's the girl's name and address.'

'When did all this happen?' Powell began to feel cold and uneasy.

'Yesterday afternoon.'

'Come on!' Powell ran down the street to the car, a panting policeman in his wake.

They had driven three blocks when the phone on the dash buzzed. Powell answered. 'Yes?'

'Sir, the medical survey team reports a Dr. Robert Knudsen identified Condor's picture as the man he treated for strep throat yesterday. He treated the suspect at the apartment of a Wendy Ross, R-o…'

Powell cut the dispatcher short. 'We're on our way to her apartment now. I want all units to converge on the area, but do not approach the house until I get there. Tell them to get there as quickly but as quietly as they can. Now give me the chief.'

A full minute passed before Powell heard the light voice come over the phone. 'Yes, Kevin, what do you have?'

'We're on our way to Malcolm's hideout. Both groups hit on it at about the same time. I'll give you details later. There's one other thing: somebody with official credentials has been looking for Malcolm and not reporting what he finds.'

There was a long pause, then the old man said, 'This could explain many things, my boy. Many things. Be very careful. I hope you're in time.' The line went dead. Powell hung up, and resigned himself to the conclusion that he was probably much too late.

Ten minutes later Powell and three detectives rang Wendy's doorbell. They waited a minute, then the biggest man kicked the door in. Five minutes later Powell summed up what he found to the old man.

'The stranger is unidentifiable from here. His postman's uniform is a fake. The silenced sten gun was probably used during the hit on the Society. The way I see it, he and someone else, probably our boy Malcolm, were fighting. Malcolm beat him to the gun. I'm sure it's the mailman's because his pouch is rigged to carry it. Our boy's luck seems to be holding very well. We've found a picture of the girl, and we've got her car license number. How do you want to handle it?'

'Have the police put out an A.P.B. on her for … murder. That'll throw our friend who's monitoring us and using our credentials. Right now, I want to know who the dead man is, and I want to know fast. Send his photo and prints to every agency with a priority rush order. Do not include any other information. Start your teams looking for Malcolm and the girl. Then I guess we have to wait.'

A dark sedan drove by the apartment as Powell and the others walked towards their cars. The driver was tall and painfully thin. His passenger, a man with striking eyes hidden behind sunglasses, waved him on. No one noticed them drive past.

Malcolm drove around Alexandria until he found a small, dumpy used-car lot. He parked two blocks away and sent Wendy to make the purchase. Ten minutes later, after having sworn she was Mrs. A. Edgerton for the purpose of registration and paid an extra hundred dollars cash, she drove off in a slightly used Dodge. Malcolm followed her to a park. They transferred the luggage and removed the license plates from the Corvair. Then they loaded the Dodge and slowly drove away.

Malcolm drove for five hours. Wendy never spoke during the whole trip. When they stopped at the Parisburg, Virginia, motel, Malcolm registered as Mr. and Mrs. Evans. He parked the car behind the motel 'so it won't get dirty from the traffic passing by'. The old lady running the motel merely shrugged and went back to her T.V. She had seen it before.

Wendy lay very still on the bed. Malcolm slowly undressed. He took his medicine and removed his contacts before he sat down next to her.

'Why don't you undress and get some sleep, honey?'

She turned and looked at him slowly. 'It's real, isn't it.' Her voice was softly matter-of-fact. 'The whole thing is real. And you killed that man. In my apartment, you killed a man.'

'It was either him or us. You know that. You tried, too.'

She turned away. 'I know.' She got up and slowly undressed. She turned off the light and climbed into bed. Unlike before, she didn't snuggle close. When Malcolm went to sleep an hour later, he was sure she was still awake.

> *'Where there is much light there is also much shadow.'*
>
> *— Goethe*

Sunday

'Ah, Kevin, we seem to be making progress.'

The old man's crisp, bright words did little to ease the numbness gripping Powell's mind. His body ached, but the discomfort was minimal. He had been conditioned for much more severe strains than one missed rest period. But during three months of rest and recuperation, Powell had become accustomed to sleeping late on Sunday mornings. Additionally, the frustration of his present assignment irritated him. So far his involvement had been *post facto*. His two years of training and ten years' experience were being used to run errands and gather information. Any cop could do that, and many cops were. Powell didn't share the old man's optimism.

'How, sir?' Frustrated as he was, Powell spoke respectfully. 'Some trace of Condor and the girl?'

'No, not yet.' Despite a very long night, the old man sparkled. 'There's still a chance she bought that car, but it hasn't been seen. No, our progress is from another angle. We've identified the dead man.'

Powell's mind cleared. The old man continued.

'Our friend was once Calvin Lloyd, sergeant, United States Marine Corps. In 1959 he left that group rather suddenly while stationed in Korea as an adviser to a South Korean Marine unit. There is a good chance he was mixed up in the murder of a Seoul madam and one of her girls. The Navy could never find any direct evidence, but they think the madam and he were running a base commuter service and had a falling out over rebates. Shortly after the bodies were found, Lloyd went A.W.O.L. The Marines didn't look for him very hard. In 1961 Navy Intelligence received a report indicating he had died rather suddenly in Tokyo. Then in 1963 he was identified as one of several arms dealers in Laos. Evidently his job was technical advice. At the time, he was linked to a man called Vincent Dale Maronick. More on Maronick later. Lloyd dropped out of sight in 1965, and until yesterday he was again believed dead.'

The old man paused. Powell cleared his throat, signaling that he wanted to speak. After receiving a courteous nod, Powell said, 'Well, at least we know that much. Besides telling us a small who, how does it help?'

The old man held up his left forefinger. 'Be patient, my boy, be patient. Let's take our steps slowly and see what paths cross where.

'The autopsy on Weatherby yielded only a probability, but based on what has happened, I'm inclined to rate it very high. There is a chance his death may be due to an air bubble in the blood, but the pathologists won't swear to it. His doctors insist the cause must be external – and there-fore not their fault. I'm inclined to agree with them. It's a pity for us Weatherby isn't around for questioning, but for someone it's a very lucky break. Far too lucky, if you ask me.

'I'm convinced Weatherby was a double agent, though for whom I have no idea. The files that keep turning up missing, our friend with credentials covering the town just ahead of us, the setup of the hit on the Society. They all smell of inside information. With Weatherby eliminated, it follows he could have been the leak that became too dangerous for someone. Then there's that whole shooting scene behind the theaters. We've been over that before, but something new occurred to me.

'I had both Sparrow IV's and Weatherby's bodies examined by our Ballistics men. Whoever shot Weatherby almost amputated his leg with the bullet. According to our man it was at least a .357 magnum with soft lead slugs. But Sparrow IV had only a neat round hole in his throat. Our Ballistics man doesn't think they were shot with the same gun. That, plus the fact Weatherby wasn't killed, makes the whole thing look fishy. I think our boy Malcolm, for some reason or other, shot Weatherby and then ran. Weatherby was hurt, but not hurt so bad he couldn't eliminate witness Sparrow IV. But that's not the interesting piece of news.

'From 1958 until late 1969, Weatherby was stationed in Asia, primarily out of Hong Kong, but with stints in Korea, Japan, Taiwan, Laos, Thailand, Cambodia, and Vietnam. He worked his way up the structure from special field agent to station head. You'll note he was there during the same period as our dead mailman. Now for a slight but very interesting digression. What do you know about the man called Maronick?'

Powell furrowed his brow. 'I think he was some sort of special agent. A freelancer, as I recall.'

The old man smiled, pleased. 'Very good, though I'm

not sure if I understand what you mean by "special". If you mean extremely competent, thorough, careful, and highly successful, then you're correct. If you mean dedicated and loyal to one side, then you are very wrong. Vincent Maronick was – or is, if I'm not mistaken – the best free-lance agent in years, maybe the best of this century for his specialty. For a short-term operation requiring cunning, ruthlessness, and a good deal of caution, he was the best money could buy. The man was tremendously skilled. We're not sure where he received his training, though it's clear he was American. His individual abilities were not so outstanding that they couldn't be matched. There were and are better planners, better shots, better pilots, better sabo-teurs, better everything in particular. But the man had a persevering drive, a toughness that pushed his capabilities far beyond those of his competitors. He's a very dangerous man, one of the men I could fear.

'In the early sixties he surfaced working for the French, mainly in Algeria, but, please note, also taking care of some of their remaining interests in Southeast Asia. Starting in 1963, he came to the attention of those in our business. At various times he worked for Britain, Communist China, Italy, South Africa, the Congo, Canada, and he even did two stints for the Agency. He also did a type of consulting service for the I.R.A. and the O.A.S. (against his former French employers). He always gave satisfaction, and there are no reports of any failures. He was very expensive. Rumor has it he was looking for a big score. Exactly why he was in the business isn't clear, but my guess is it was the one field that allowed him to use his talents to the fullest and reap rewards quasi-legally. Now here's the interesting part.

'In 1964 Maronick was employed by the Generalissimo on Taiwan. Ostensibly he was used for actions against mainland China, but at the time the General was having trouble with the native Taiwanese and some dissidents among his own immigrant group. Marionick was employed to help preserve order. Washington wasn't pleased with some of the Nationalist government's internal policies. They were afraid the General's methods might be a little too heavy-handed for our good. The General refused to agree, and began to go his own merry way. At the same time, we began to worry about Maronick. He was just too good and too available. He had never been employed against us, but it was just a matter of time. The Agency decided to terminate Maronick, as both a preventive measure and as a subtle hint to the General. Now, who do you suppose was station agent out of Taiwan when the Maronick termination order came through?'

Powell was 90 per cent sure, so he ventured, 'Weatherby?'

'Right you are. Weatherby was in charge of the termination operation. He reported it successful, but with a hitch. The method was a bomb in Maronick's billet. Both the Chinese agent who planted the bomb and Maronick were killed. Naturally, the explosion obliterated both bodies. Weatherby verified the hit as an eyewitness.

'Now let's back up a little. Whom do you suppose Maronick employed as an aide on at least five different missions?

It wasn't a guess. Powell said, 'Our dead mailman, Sergeant Calvin Lloyd.'

'Right again. Now here's yet another clincher. We never

had much on Maronick, but we did have a few foggy pictures, sketchy descriptions, whatnot. Guess whose file is missing?' The old man didn't even give Powell a chance to speak before he answered his own question. 'Maronick's. Also, we have no records of Sergeant Lloyd. Neat, yes?'

'Yes indeed.' Powell was still puzzled. 'What makes you think Maronick is involved?'

The old man smiled. 'Just playing an inductive hunch. I racked my brain for a man who could and would pull a hit like the one on the Society. When, out of a dozen men, Maronick's file turned up missing, my curiosity rose. Navy Intelligence sent over the identification of Lloyd, and his file noted he had worked with Maronick. Wheels began to turn. When they both linked up with Weatherby, lights flashed and a band played. I spent a very productive morning making my poor old brain work when I should have been feeding pigeons and smelling cherry blossoms.'

The room was silent while the old man rested and Powell thought. Powell said, 'So you figure Maronick is running some kind of action against us and Weatherby was doubling for him, probably for some time.'

'No,' said the old man softly, 'I don't think so.'

The old man's reply surprised Powell. He could only stare and wait for the soft voice to continue.

'The first and most obvious question is why. Given all that has happened and the way in which it has happened, I don't think the question can practically and logically be approached. If it can't be approached logically, then we are starting from an erroneous assumption, the assumption that the C.I.A. is the central object of an action. Then there's the next question of who. Who would pay – and I imagine pay dearly – for Maronick with Weatherby's duplicity and at least Lloyd's help to have us hit in the way we have been hit? Even given that phony Czech revenge note, I can think of no one. That, of course, brings us back to the why question, and we're spinning our wheels in a circle going nowhere. No, I think the proper and necessary question to ask and answer is not who or why, but what. What is going on? If we can answer that, then the other questions and their answers will flow. Right now, there is only one key to that what, our boy Malcolm.'

Powell sighed wearily. 'So we're back to where we started from, looking for our lost Condor.'

'Not exactly where we started from. I have some of my men digging rather extensively in Asia, looking for whatever it is that ties Weatherby, Maronick, and Lloyd together. They may find nothing, but no one can tell. We also have a better idea of the opposition, and I have some men looking for Maronick.'

'With all the machinery you have at your disposal we should be able to flush one of the two, Malcolm or Maronick – sounds like a vaudeville team, doesn't it?'

'We're not using the machinery, Kevin. We're using us, plus what we can scrounge from the D.C. police.'

Powell choked. 'What the hell! You control maybe fifty men, and the cops can't give you much. The Agency has hundreds of people working on this thing now, not counting the Bureau and the N.S.A. and the others. If you give them what you have given me, they could ...'

Quietly but firmly the old man interrupted. 'Kevin, think a moment. Weatherby was the double in the Agency, possibly with some lower-echelon footmen. He, we assume, acquired the false credentials, passed along the needed information, and even went into the field himself. But if he was the double, then who arranged for his execution, who knew the closely guarded secret of where he was and enough about the security setup to get the executioner (probably the competent Maronick) in and out again?' He paused for the flicker of understanding on Powell's face. 'That's right, another double. If my hunch is correct, a very highly placed double. We can't risk any more leaks. Since we can't trust anyone, we'll have to do it ourselves.'

Powell frowned and hesitated before he spoke. 'May I make a suggestion, sir?'

The old man deliberately registered surprise. 'Why, of course you may, my dear boy! You are supposed to use your fine mind, even if you are afraid of offending your superior.'

Powell smiled slightly. 'We know, or at least we are assuming, there is a leak, a fairly highly placed leak. Why don't we keep after Malcolm but concentrate on stopping the leak from the top? We can figure out what group of people the leak could be in and work on them. Our surveillance should catch them even if so far they haven't left a trail. The pressure of this thing will force them to do something. At the very least, they must keep in touch with Maronick.'

'Kevin,' the old man replied quietly, 'your logic is sound, but the conditions of your assumptions invalidate your plan. You assume we can identify the group of people who could be the source of the leak. One of the troubles with our intelligence community – indeed, one of the reasons for my own section – is that things are so big and so complicated such a group easily numbers over fifty, probably numbers over a hundred, and may run as high as two hundred persons. That's if the leak is conscious on their part. Our leak may be sloppy around his secretary, or his communications man may be a double.

'Even if the leak is not of a secondary nature, through a secretary or a technician, such surveillance would be massive, though not impossible. You've already pointed out my logistical limitations. In order to carry out your suggestion, we would need the permission and assistance of some of the people in the suspect group. That would never do.

'We also have a problem inherent in the group of people with whom we would be dealing. They are professionals in the intelligence business. Don't you think they might tumble to our surveillance? And even if *they* didn't, each one of their departments has its own security system we would have to avoid. For example, officers in Air Force Intelligence are subject to unscheduled spot checks, including surveillance and phone traps. It's done both to see if the officers are honest and to see if someone else is watching them. We would have to avoid security teams *and* a wary, experienced suspect.

'What we have,' the old man said, placing the tips of his fingers together, 'is a classic intelligence problem. We have possibly the world's largest security and intelligence organisation, an entity ironically dedicated to both stopping the flow of information from and increasing the flow to this country. At a moment's notice we can assign a hundred trained men to dissect a fact as minuscule as a misplaced luggage sticker. We can turn the same horde loose on any given small group and within a few days we would know everything the group did. We can bring tremendous pressure to bear on any point we can find. There lies the problem: on this case we can't find the point. We know there's a leak in our machine, but until we can isolate the area it's in, we can't dissect the machine to try to pinpoint the leak. Such activity would be almost certainly futile, and possibly dangerous, to say nothing of awkward. Besides, the moment we start looking, the opposition will know we know there's a leak.

'The key to this whole problem is Malcolm. He might be able to pinpoint the leak for us, or at least steer us in a particular direction. If he does, or if we turn up any links between Maronick's operation and someone in the intelligence community, we will, of course, latch on to the suspect. But until we have a firm link, such an operation would be sloppy, hit-and-miss work. I don't like that kind of job. It's inefficient and usually not productive.'

Powell covered his embarrassment with a formal tone. 'Sorry, sir. I guess I wasn't thinking.'

The old man shook his head. 'On the contrary, my boy,' he exclaimed, 'you were thinking, and that's very good. It's the one thing we've never been able to train our people to do, and it's one thing these massive organisations tend to discourage. It's far better to have you thinking and proposing schemes which, shall we say, are hastily considered and poorly conceived, here in the office, than it is for you to be a robot in the street reacting blindly. That gets every one into trouble, and it's a good way to wind up dead. Keep thinking, Kevin, but be a little more thorough.'

'So the plan is still to find Malcolm and bring him home safe, right?'

The old man smiled. 'Not exactly. I've done a lot of thinking about our boy Malcolm. He is our key. They, whoever they are, want our boy dead, and want him dead badly. If we can keep him alive, *and* if we can make him troublesome enough to them so that they center their activities on his demise, then we have turned Condor into a key. Maronick and company, by concentrating on Malcolm, make themselves into their own lock. If we are careful and just a shade lucky, we can use the key to open the lock. Oh, we still have to find our Condor, and quickly, before anyone else does. I'm making some additional arrangements to aid us along that line too. But when we find him, we prime him.

'After you've had some rest, my assistant will bring you instructions and any further information we receive.'

As Powell got up to go, he said, 'Can you give me anything on Maronick?'

The old man said, 'I'm having a friend in the French secret service send over a copy of their file on the flight from Paris. It won't arrive until tomorrow. I could have had it quicker, but I didn't want to alert the opposition. Outside of what you already know, I can only tell you that physically Maronick is reportedly a very striking man.'

Malcolm began to wake just as Powell left the old man's office. For a few seconds he lay still, remembering all that had happened. Then a soft voice whispered in his ear, 'Are you awake?'

Malcolm rolled over. Wendy rested on one elbow, shyly looking at him. His throat felt better and he sounded almost normal when he said, 'Good morning.'

Wendy blushed. 'I'm ... I'm sorry about yesterday, I mean how mean I was. I just ... I just have never seen or done anything like that and the shock ...'

Malcolm shut her up with a kiss. 'It's O.K. It was pretty horrible.'

'What are we going to do now?' she asked.

'I don't know for sure. I think we should hole up here for at least a day or two.' He looked around the sparsely furnished room. 'It may be a little dull.'

Wendy looked up at him and grinned. 'Well, not too dull.' She kissed him lightly, then again. She pulled his mouth down to her small breast.

Half an hour later they still hadn't decided anything.

'We can't do that *all* the time,' Malcolm said at last.

Wendy made a sour face and said, 'Why not?' But she sighed acceptance. 'I know what we can do!' She leaned half out of the bed and groped on the floor. Malcolm grabbed her arm to keep her from falling.

'What the hell are you doing?' he asked.

'I'm looking for my purse. I brought some books we can read out loud. You said you liked Yeats.' She rummaged under the bed. 'Malcolm, I can't find them, they aren't here. Everything else is in my purse, but the books are missing. I must have ... Owww!' Wendy jerked back on the bed and pried herself loose from Malcolm's suddenly tightened grip. 'Malcolm, what are you doing? That hurt ...'

'The books. The missing books.' Malcolm turned and looked at her. 'There is something about those missing books that's important! That has to be the reason!'

Wendy was puzzled. 'But they're only poetry books. You

can get them almost anywhere. I probably just forgot to bring them.'

'Not those books, the Society's books, the ones Heidegger found missing!' He told her the story.

Malcolm felt the excitement growing. 'If I can tell them about the missing books, it'll give them something to start on. The reason my section was hit must have been the books. They found out Heidegger was digging up old records. They had to hit everybody in case someone else knew. If I can give the Agency those pieces, maybe they can put the puzzle together. At least I'll have something more to give them than my story about how people get shot wherever I go. They frown on that.'

'But how will you tell the Agency? Remember what happened the last time you called them?'

Malcolm frowned. 'Yes, I see what you mean. But the last time they set up a meeting. Even if the opposition has penetrated the Agency, even if they know what goes over the Panic Line, I still think we're O.K. With all that has gone on, I imagine dozens of people must be involved. At least some of them will be clean. They'll pass on what I phone in. It should ring some right bells somewhere.' He paused for a moment. 'Come on, we have to go back to Washington.'

'Hey, wait a minute!' Wendy's outstretched hand missed its grasp on Malcolm's arm as he bounded out of bed and into the bathroom. 'Why are we going back there?'

The shower turned on. 'Have to. A long-distance phone call can be traced in seconds, a local one takes longer.' The tempo of falling water on metal walls increased.

'But we might get killed!'

'What?'

Wendy yelled, but she tried to be as quiet as possible. 'I said we might be killed.'

'Might get killed here too. You scrub my back and I'll scrub yours.'

'I'm very disappointed, Maronick.' The sharp words cut through the strained air between the two men. The distinguished-looking speaker knew he had made a mistake when he saw the look in his companion's eyes.

'My name is Levine. You will remember that. I suggest you do not make a slip like that again.' The striking man's crisp words undercut the other man's confidence, but the distinguished-looking gentleman tried to hide his discomposure.

'My slip is minor compared to the others that have been happening,' he said.

The man who wished to be called Levine showed no emotion to the average eye. An acute observer who had known him for some time *might* have detected the slight flush of frustrated anger and embarrassment.

'The operation is not yet over. There have been setbacks, but there has been no failure. Had there been failure, neither of us would be here.' As if to emphasise his point, he gestured towards the crowds milling around them. Sunday is a busy day for tourists at the Capitol building.

The distinguished-looking man regained his confidence. In a firm whisper he said, 'Nevertheless there have been setbacks. As you so astutely pointed out, the operation is not yet over. I need not remind you that it was scheduled for completion three days ago. Three days. A good deal can happen in three days. For all our bumbling we have been very lucky. The longer the operation continues, the greater the risk that certain things will come to the fore. We both know how disastrous that could be.'

'Everything possible is being done. We must wait for another chance.'

'And if we don't get another chance? What then, my fine friend, what then?'

The man called Levine turned and looked at him. Once again the other man felt nervous. Levine said, 'Then we make our chance.'

'Well, I certainly hope there will be no more ... setbacks.'

'I anticipate none.'

'Good. I shall keep you informed of all the developments in the Agency. I expect you to do the same with me. I think there is nothing further to say.'

'There is one other thing,' Levine said calmly. 'Operations such as this sometimes suffer certain kinds of internal setbacks. Usually these ... setbacks happen to certain personnel. These setbacks are planned by operation directors, such as yourself, and they are meant to be permanent. The common term for such a setback is double cross. If I were my director, I would be most careful to avoid any such setback, don't you agree?' The pallor crossing the other man's face told Levine there was no disagreement. Levine smiled politely, nodded farewell, and walked away. The distinguished man watched him stalk down the marble corridors and out of sight. The gentleman shuddered slightly, then went home to Sunday brunch with his wife, son, and a fidgety new daughter-in-law.

While Malcolm and Wendy dressed and the two men left the Capitol grounds, a telephone truck pulled up to the outer gates at Langley. After the occupants and their mission were cleared, they proceeded to the communications center. The two telephone repairmen were accompanied by a special security officer on loan from another branch. Most of the Agency men were looking for a man called Condor. The security officer had papers identifying him as Major David Burros. His real name was Kevin Powell, and the two telephone repairmen, ostensibly there to check the telephone tracing device, were highly trained Air Force electronics experts flown in from Colorado less than four hours before. After their mission was completed, they would be quarantined for three weeks. In addition to checking the tracing device, they installed some new equipment and made some complicated adjustments in the wiring of the old. Both men tried to keep calm while they worked from wiring diagrams labeled Top Secret. Fifteen minutes after they began work, they electronically signaled a third man in a phone booth four miles away. He called a number, let it ring until he received another signal, then hung up and walked quickly away. One of the experts nodded at Powell. The three men gathered their tools and left as unobtrusively as they had come.

An hour later Powell sat in a small room in downtown Washington. Two plainclothes policemen sat outside the door. Three of his fellow agents lounged in chairs scattered around the room. There were two chairs at the desk where

Powell sat, but one was unoccupied. Powell talked into one of the two telephones on the desk.

'We're hooked up and ready to go, sir. We've tested the device twice. It checked out from our end and our man in the Panic Room said everything was clear there. From now on, all calls made to Condor's panic number will ring here. If it's our boy, we'll have him. If it's not ... Well, let's hope we can fake it. Of course, we can also nullify the bypass and just listen in.'

The old man's voice told his delight. 'Excellent, my boy, excellent. How's everything else working out?'

'Marian says the arrangements with the *Post* should be complete within the hour. I hope you realise how much our ass is in the fire on this. Someday we'll have to tell the Agency we tapped their Panic Line, and they won't appreciate that at all.'

The old man chuckled. 'Don't worry about that, Kevin. It's been in the fire before and it will be there again. Besides, theirs is roasting too, and I imagine they won't feel too bad if we pull it out for them. Any reports from the field?'

'Negative. Nobody reports a sign of Malcolm or the girl. When our boy goes to ground, he goes to ground.'

'Yes, I was thinking much the same thing myself. I don't think the opposition has got him. I'm rather proud of his efforts so far. Do you have my itinerary?'

'Yes, sir. We'll call you if anything happens.' The old man hung up, and Powell settled down for what he hoped would be a short wait.

Wendy and Malcolm arrived in Washington just as the sun was setting. Malcolm drove to the center of the city. He

188

parked the car at the Lincoln Memorial, removed their luggage, and locked the vehicle securely. They came into Washington via Bethesda, Maryland. In Bethesda they purchased some toiletries, clothes, a blond wig, and a large padded 'visual disguise and diversionary' bra for Wendy, a roll of electrical tape, some tools, and a box of .357 magnum shells.

Malcolm took a carefully calculated risk. Using Poe's 'Purloined Letter' principle that the most obvious hiding place is often the safest, he and Wendy boarded a bus for Capitol Hill. They rented a tourist room on East Capitol Street less than a quarter of a mile from the Society. The proprietress of the dingy hostel welcomed the Ohio honeymooners. Most of her customers had checked out and headed home after a weekend of sightseeing. She didn't even care if they had no rings and the girl had a black eye. In order to create a believable image of loving young marrieds (or so Malcolm whispered), the young couple retired early.

'In war it is not men, but the man who counts.'

– Napoleon

Monday, Morning
to Midafternoon

The shrill scream from the red phone jarred Powell from his fitful nap. He grabbed the receiver before a second ring. The other agents in the room began to trace and record the call. Concentrating on listening, Powell only half saw their scurrying figures in the morning light. He took a deep breath and said, '493-7282.'

The muffled voice on the other end seemed far away. 'This is Condor.'

Powell began the carefully prepared dialogue. 'I read you, Condor. Listen closely. The Agency has been penetrated. We're not sure who, but we're pretty sure it's not you.' Powell cut the beginning of a protest short. 'Don't waste time protesting your innocence. We accept it as a working assumption. Now, why did you shoot Weatherby when they came to pick you up?'

The voice on the other end was incredulous. 'Didn't Sparrow IV tell you? That man – Weatherby? – shot at me! He was parked outside the Society Thursday morning. In the same car.'

'Sparrow IV is dead, shot in the alley.'

'I didn't …'

'We know. We think Weatherby did. We know about you and the girl.' Powell paused to let this sink in. 'We traced you to her apartment and found the corpse. Did you hit him?'

'Barely. He almost got us.'

'Are you injured?'

'No, just a little stiff and woozy.'

'Are you safe?'

'For the time being, fairly.'

Powell leaned forward tensely and asked the hopeless and all-important question. 'Do you have any idea why your group was hit?'

'Yes.' Powell's sweaty hand tightened on the receiver as Malcolm quickly told of the missing books and financial discrepancies Heidegger had discovered.

When Malcolm paused, Powell asked in a puzzled voice, 'But you have no idea what it all means?'

'None. Now, what are you going to do about getting us to safety?'

Powell took the plunge. 'Well, that's that going to be a little problem. Not just because we don't want you set up and hit, but because you're not talking to the Agency.'

Five miles away, in a phone booth at a Holiday Inn, Malcolm's stomach began to chum. Before he could say anything, Powell spoke again.

'I can't go into the details. You will simply have to trust us. Because of the penetration of the Agency at what is probably a very high level, we've taken over. We plugged into the Panic Line and intercepted your call. Please don't hang up. We've got to blow the double in the Agency and find out what this was all about. You're our only way, and we want you to help us. You have no choice.'

'Bullshit, man! You might be another security agency, and then again you might not. Even if you are O.K., why the hell should I help you? This isn't my kind of work! I read about this stuff, not do it.'

'Consider the alternatives.' Powell's voice was cold. 'Your luck can't hold forever, and some very determined and competent people besides us are looking for you. As you said, this isn't your line of work. Someone will find you. Without us, all you can do is hope that the right someone does find you. If we're the right someone, then everything is already O.K. If we're not, then at least you know what we want you to do. It's better than running blind. Any time you don't like our instructions, don't follow them. There's one final clincher. We control your communication link with the Agency. We even have a man on the listed line.' (This was a lie.) 'The only other way you can go home is to show up at Langley in person. Do you like the idea of going in there cold?'

Powell paused and got no answer. 'I thought not. It won't be too dangerous. All we basically want is for you to stay hidden and keep rattling the opposition's cage. Now, here's what we know so far.' Powell gave Malcolm a concise rundown of all the information he had. Just as he finished, his man in charge of tracing the call came to him and shrugged his shoulders. Puzzled, Powell continued. 'Now, there's another way we can communicate with you. Do you know how to work a book code?'

'Well ... You better go over it again.'

'O.K. First of all pick up a paperback copy of *The*

Feminine Mystique. There is only one edition. Got that? O.K. Now, whenever we want to communicate with you, we will run an ad in the *Post.* It will appear in the first section, and the heading will read, "Today's Lucky Sweepstakes Winning Numbers Are:" followed by a series of hyphenated numbers. The first number of each series is the page number, the second is the line number, and the third is the word number. When we can't find a corresponding word in the book, we'll use a simple number–alphabet code. A is number one, B is number two, and so on. When we code such a word, the first number will be thirteen. The *Post* will forward any communication you want to send us if you address it to yourself, care of Lucky Sweepstakes, Box 1, *Washington Post.* Got it?'

'Fine. Can we still use the Panic Line?'

'We'd rather not. It's very chancy.'

Powell could see the trace man across the room whispering furiously into another phone. Powell said, 'Do you need anything?'

'No. Now, what is it you want me to do?'

'Can you call the Agency back on your phone?'

'For a conversation as long as this?'

'Definitely not. It should only take a minute or so.'

'I can, but I'll want to shift to another phone. Not for at least half an hour.'

'O.K. Call back and we will let the call go through. Now, here's what we want you to say.' Powell told him the plan. When both men were satisfied, Powell said, 'One more thing. Pick a neighborhood you won't have to be in.'

Malcolm thought for a moment. 'Chevy Chase.'

'O.K.,' Kevin said. 'You will be reported in the Chevy

Chase area in exactly one hour. Thirty minutes later a
Chevy Chase cop will be wounded while chasing a man
and a woman answering your descriptions. That should
make everyone concentrate their forces in Chevy Chase,
giving you room to move. Is that enough time?'

'Make it an hour later, O.K.?'

'O.K.'

'One more thing. Who am I talking to, I mean personally?'

'Call me Rogers, Malcolm.' The connection went dead.
No sooner had Powell placed the phone in the cradle than
his trace man ran to him.

'Do you know what that little son of a bitch did? Do you
know what he did?' Powell could only shake his head. 'I'll
tell you what he did, that little son of a bitch. He drove all
over town and wired pay phones together, then called and
hooked them all up so they transmitted one call through
the lines, but each phone routed the call back through the
terminal. We traced the first one in a little over a minute.
Our surveillance team got there right away. They found an
empty phone booth with homemade Out of Order signs
and his wiring job. They had to call back for a trace on the
other phone. We've gone through three traces already and
there are probably more hookups to go, that son of a bitch!'

Powell leaned back and laughed for the first time in
days. When he found the part in Malcolm's dossier that
mentioned his summer employment with the telephone
company, he laughed again.

Malcolm left the phone booth and walked to the parking
lot. In a rented U-Haul pickup with Florida plates a chesty

blonde wearing sunglasses sat chewing gum. Malcolm stood in the shade for a few moments while he checked the lot. Then he walked over and climbed in the truck. He gave Wendy the thumbs-up sign, then began to chuckle.

'Hey,' she said, 'what is it? What's so funny?'

'You are, you dummy.'

'Well, the wig and the falsies were your idea! I can't help it if …' His protesting hand cut her short.

'That's only part of it,' he said, still laughing. 'If you could only see yourself.'

'Well, I can't help it if I'm good.' She slumped in the seat. 'What did they say?'

As they drove to another phone booth, Malcolm told her.

Mitchell had been manning the Panic phone since the first call. His cot lay a few feet from his desk. He hadn't seen the sun since Thursday. He hadn't showered. When he went to the bathroom the phone followed. The head of the Panic Section was debating whether to give him pep shots. The Deputy Director had decided to keep Mitchell on the phone, as he stood a better chance than a new man of recognising Malcolm should he call again. Mitchell was tired, but he was still a tough man. Right now he was a tough *determined* man. He was raising his ten-o'clock coffee to his lips when the phone rang. He spilled the coffee as he grabbed the receiver.

'493-7282.'

'This is Condor.'

'Where the hell …'

'Shut up. I know you're tracing this call, so there isn't

much time. I would stay on your line, but the Agency has been penetrated.'

'What!'

'Somebody out there is a double. The man in the alley' – Malcolm almost slipped and said 'Weatherby' – 'shot at me first. I recognised him from when he was parked in front of the Society Thursday morning. The other man in the alley must have told you that, though, so ...' Malcolm slowed, anticipating interruption. He got it.

'Sparrow IV was shot. You ...'

'I didn't do it! Why would I want to do it? Then you didn't know?'

'All we know is we have two more dead people than when you first called.'

'I might have killed the man who shot at me, but I didn't kill Maronick.'

'Who?'

'Maronick, the man called Sparrow IV.'

'That wasn't Sparrow IV's name.'

'It wasn't? The man I shot yelled for Maronick after he hit the ground. I figured Maronick was Sparrow IV.' (Easy, thought Malcolm, don't overdo it.) 'Never mind that now, time is running short. Whoever hit us was after something Heidegger knew. He told all of us about something strange he found in the records. He said he was going to tell somebody out at Langley. That's why I figure there is a double. Heidegger told the wrong man.

'Listen, I've stumbled onto something. I think I might be able to figure some more out. I found something at Heidegger's place. I think I can work it out if you give me time. I know you must be looking for me. I'm afraid to come in or let you find me. Can you pull the heat off me until I figure out what I know that makes the opposition want me dead?'

Mitchell paused for a moment. The trace man frantically signaled him to keep Malcolm talking. 'I don't know if we can or not. Maybe if ...'

'There's no more time. I'll call you back when I find out some more.' The line went dead. Mitchell looked at his trace man and got a negative shake of the head.

'How the hell do you figure that?'

Mitchell looked at the speaker, a security guard. The man in the wheelchair shook his head. 'I don't, but it's not my job to figure it. Not this one.' Mitchell looked around the room. His glance stopped when it came to a man he recognised as a veteran agent. 'Jason, does the name Maronick mean anything to you?'

The nondescript man called Jason slowly nodded his head. 'It rings a bell.'

'Me too,' said Mitchell. He picked up a phone. 'Records? I want everything you got on people called Maronick, any spelling you can think of. We'll probably want several copies before the day is out, so hop to it.' He broke the connection, then dialed the number of the Deputy Director.

While Mitchell waited to be connected with the Deputy Director, Powell connected with the old man. 'Our boy did fine, sir.'

'I'm delighted to hear that, Kevin, delighted.'

In a lighter voice Powell said, 'Just enough truth mingled with some teasing tidbits. It'll start the Agency rolling the

197

right way, but hopefully they won't catch up to us. If you're right, our friend Maronick may begin to feel nervous. They'll be more anxious than ever to find our Condor. Anything new on your end?'

'Nothing. Our people are still digging into the past of all concerned. Outside of us, only the police know about the connection between Malcolm and the man killed in the girl's apartment. The police are officially listing it and her disappearance as parts of a normal murder case. When the time is right, that little tidbit will fall into appropriate hands. As far as I can tell, everything is going exactly according to plan. Now I suppose I'll have to go to another dreary meeting with a straight face, gently prodding our friends in the right direction. I think it best if you stay on the line, monitoring, not intercepting, but be ready to move any time.'

'Right, sir.' Powell hung up. He looked at the grinning men in the room and settled back to enjoy a cup of coffee.

'I'll be damned if I can make head or tail of it!' The Navy captain thumped his hand on the table to emphasise his point, then leaned back in his spacious padded chair. The room was stuffy. Sweat stains grew under the Captain's armpits. Of all the times for the air conditioning to break down, he thought.

The Deputy Director said patiently, 'None of us are really too sure what it means, either, Captain.' He cleared his throat to take up where he had been cut off. 'As I was saying, except for the information we received from Condor – however accurate it may be – we are really no further than at our last meeting.'

The Captain leaned to his right and embarrassed the man from the F.B.I. sitting next to him by whispering, 'Then why call the God damn meeting?' The withering glance from the Deputy Director had no effect on the Captain.

The Deputy continued. 'As you know, Maronick's file is missing. We've requested copies of England's files. An Air Force jet should have them here in three hours. I would like any comments you gentlemen might have.'

The man from the F.B.I. spoke immediately. 'I think Condor is partially right. The C.I.A. has been penetrated.' His colleague from the Agency squirmed. 'However, I think we should put it in the past tense and say "had" been penetrated. Obviously Weatherby was the double. He probably used the Society as some sort of courier system and Heidegger stumbled onto it. When Weatherby found out, the Society had to be hit. Condor was a loose end that had to be tied up. Weatherby goofed. There are probably some members of his cell still running around, but I think fate has sealed the leak. As I see it, the important thing for us to do now is bring in Condor. With the information he can give us, we can try to pick up those few remaining men – including this Maronick, if he exists – and find out how much information we've lost.'

The Deputy Director looked around the room. Just as he was about to close the meeting, the old man caught his eye.

'Might I make an observation or two, Deputy?'

'Of course, sir. Your comments are always welcome.'

The men in the room shifted slightly to pay better attention. The Captain shifted too, though obviously out of frustrated politeness.

Before he spoke, the old man looked curiously at the representative from the F.B.I. 'I must say I disagree with our colleague from the Bureau. His explanation is very plausible, but there are one or two discrepancies I find disturbing. If Weatherby was the top agent, then how and why did he die? I know it's a debatable question, at least until the lab men finish those exhaustive tests they've been making. I'm sure they will find he was killed. That kind of order would have to come down from a high source. Besides, I feel there is something wrong with the whole double agent–courier explanation. Nothing for sure, just a hunch. I think we should continue pretty much as we have been, with two slight changes.

'One, pry into the background of all concerned and look for crossing paths. Who knows what we may find? Two, let's give the Condor a chance to fly. He may find something yet. Loosen up the hunt for him, and concentrate on the background search. I have some other ideas I would like to work on for your next meeting, if you don't mind. That's all I have now. Thank you, Deputy.'

'Thank you, sir. Of course, gentlemen, the ultimate decision lies with the director of the Agency. However, I've been assured our recommendations will carry weight. Until we have a definite decision, I plan to continue as we have been.'

The old man looked at the Deputy Director and said, 'You may be sure we shall give you whatever assistance we can.'

Immediately the F.B.I. man snapped, 'That goes for us too!' He glared at the old man and received a curious smile in reply.

'Gentlemen,' said the Deputy Director, 'I would like to thank all of you for the assistance you have given us, now as well as in the past. Thank you all for coming. You'll be notified of the next meeting. Good day.'

As the men were leaving, the F.B.I. man glanced at the old man. He found himself staring into a pair of bright, curious eyes. He quickly left the room. On the way out, the Navy captain turned to mutter to a representative from the Treasury Department, 'Jesus, I wish I had stayed on line duty! These dull meetings wear me out.' He snorted, put on his naval cap, and strode from the room. The Deputy was the last to leave.

'I don't like this at all.'

The two men strolled along the Capitol grounds just on the edges of the shifting crowds. The afternoon tourist rush was waning, and some government workers were leaving work early. Monday is a slow day for Congress.
j205

'I think he shouldn't be the only one.' The rare Washington wind carried the striking man's voice to his companion, who shivered in spite of the warm weather.

'What do you mean?'

The reply was tinged with disgust. 'It doesn't make sense. Weatherby was a tough, experienced agent. Even though he was shot, he managed to kill Sparrow IV. Do you really believe a man like that would yell out my name? Even if he made a slip, why would he yell for me? It doesn't make sense.'

'Pray tell, then, what does make sense?'

'I can't say for sure. But there's something we don't know going on. Or at least something I don't know.'

Nervous shock trembled in the distinguished man's voice. 'Surely you're not suggesting I'm withholding information from you?'

The wind filled the long pause. Slowly, Levine-Maronick answered. 'I don't know. I doubt it, but the possibility exists. Don't bother to protest. I'm not moving on the possibility. But I want you to remember our last conversation.'

The men walked in silence for several minutes. They left the Capitol grounds and began to stroll leisurely past the Supreme Court Building on East Capitol Street. Finally the older man broke the silence. 'Do your men have anything new?'

'Nothing. We've been monitoring all the police calls and communications between the Agency and Bureau teams. With only three of us, we can't do much field work. My plan is to intercept the group that picks Condor up before they get him to a safe house. Can you arrange for him to be brought to a certain one, or at least find out what advance plans they've made? It will cut down on the odds quite a bit.' The older man nodded, and Maronick continued.

'Another thing that strikes me wrong is Lloyd. The police haven't linked him with this thing yet, as far as I can tell. Condor's prints must have been all over that place, yet the police either haven't lifted them – which I doubt – or reported them on the A.P.B. I don't like that at all. It doesn't fit. Could you check on that in such a way that you don't stir them into activity?'

The older man nodded again. The two continued their

stroll, apparently headed home from work. By now they were three blocks from the Capitol, well into the residential area. Two blocks down the street a city bus pulled over to the side, belched diesel smoke, and deposited a small group of commuters on the sidewalk. As the bus pulled away, two of the commuters detached themselves from the group and headed towards the Capitol.

Malcolm had debated about turning in the rented pickup. It gave them relatively private transportation, but it was conspicuous. Pickups are not common in Washington, especially pickups emblazoned with 'Alfonso's U-Haul, Miami Beach'. The truck also ran up a bill, and Malcolm wanted to keep as much of his money in reserve as he could. He decided public transportation would suffice for the few movements he planned. Wendy halfheartedly agreed. She liked driving the pickup.

It happened when they were almost abreast of the two men walking towards them on the other side of the street. The gust of wind proved too strong for the bobby pin holding Wendy's loose wig. It jerked the blond mass of hair from her head, throwing it into the street. The wig skidded to a stop and lay in an ignoble heap almost in the center of the road.

Excited and shocked, Wendy cried out, 'Malcolm, my wig! Get it, get it!' Her shrill voice carried above the wind and the slight traffic. Across the street Levine-Maronick pulled his companion to an abrupt halt.

Malcolm knew Wendy had made a mistake by calling out his name. He silenced her with a gesture as he stepped between the parked cars and into the street on a retrieval mission. He noticed the two men across the street watching him, so he tried to appear nonchalant, perhaps embarrassed for his wife.

Levine-Maronick moved slowly but deliberately, his keen eyes straining at the couple across the street, his mind making point-to-point comparisons. He was experienced enough to ignore the shock of fantastic coincidence and concentrate on the moment. His left hand unbuttoned his suit coat. Out of the corner of his eye and in the back of his mind Malcolm saw and registered all this, but his attention centered on the lump of hair at his feet. Wendy reached him just as he straightened up with the wig in his hands.

'Oh, shit, the damned thing is probably ruined.' Wendy grabbed the tangled mass from Malcolm. 'I'm glad we don't have far to go. Next time I'll use two ...'

Maronick's companion had been out of the field too long. He stood on the sidewalk, staring at the couple across the street. His intent gaze attracted Malcolm's attention just as the man incredulously mouthed a word. Malcolm wasn't sure of what the man said, but he knew something was wrong. He shifted his attention to the man's companion, who had emerged from behind a parked car and begun to cross the street. Malcolm noticed the unbuttoned coat, the waiting hand flat against the stomach.

'Run!' He pushed Wendy away from him and dove over the parked sports car. As he hit the sidewalk, he hoped he was making a fool of himself.

Maronick knew better than to run across an open area charging a probably armed man hiding behind bulletproof cover. He wanted to flush his quarry for a clear shot. He also knew part of his quarry was escaping. That had to be prevented. When his arm stopped moving, his body had snapped into the classic shooting stance, rigid, balanced. The stubby revolver in his right hand barked once.

Wendy had taken four very quick steps when it occurred to her she didn't know why she was running. This is silly, she thought, but she slowed only slightly. She dodged between two parked cars and slowed to a jog. Four feet from the shelter of a row of tour buses she turned her head, looking over her left shoulder for Malcolm.

The steel-jacketed bullet caught her at the base of the skull. It spun her up and around, slowly, like a marionette ballerina turning on one tiny foot.

Malcolm knew what the shot meant, but he still had to look. He forced his head to the left and saw the strange, crumpled form on the sidewalk twenty feet away. She was dead. He knew she was dead. He had seen too many dead people in the last few days to miss that look. A stream of blood trickled downhill towards him. The wig was still clutched in her hand.

Malcolm had his gun out. He raised his head and Maronick's revolver cracked again. The bullet screeched across the car's hood. Malcolm ducked. Maronick quickly began to angle across the street. He had four rounds left, and he allowed two of them for further harassing fire.

Capitol Hill in Washington has two ironic qualities: it has both one of the highest crime rates and one of the highest concentrations of policemen in the city. Maronick's shots and the screams of frightened tourists brought one of the traffic policemen on the run. He was a short, portly man named Arthur Stebbins. In five more years he planned to retire. He lurched towards the scene of a possible crime with full confidence that a score of fellow officers were only seconds behind him. The first thing he saw was a man edging across the street, a gun in his hand. This was also the last thing he saw, for Maronick's bullet caught him square in the chest.

Maronick knew he was in trouble. He had hoped for another minute before the police arrived. By that time Condor would have been dead, and he could be far away. Now he saw two more blue forms a block away. They were tugging at their belts. Maronick swiftly calculated the odds, then turned, looking for a way out.

At this instant a rather bored congressional aide heading home from the Rayburn House Office Building drove up the side street just behind Maronick. The aide stopped his red Volkswagen beetle to check for traffic on the main artery. Like many motorists, he paid little attention to the areas he passed through. He barely realised what happened when Maronick jerked his door open, pulled him from the car, whipped the pistol across his face, and then sped away in the beetle.

Maronick's companion stood stiff through the whole episode. When he saw Maronick make his getaway, he too took flight. He ran up East Capitol Street. Less than fifty feet from the scene he climbed into his black Mercedes Benz and sped away. Malcolm raised his head in time to see the license plate of the car.

Malcolm looked down the street to the policemen. They huddled around the body of their comrade. One of them spoke into his belt radio, calling in the description of Maronick and the red Volkswagen and asking for rein-forcements and an ambulance. It dawned on Malcolm that they hadn't seen him yet, or that if they had, they thought of him as only a passerby-witness to a police killing. He looked around him. The people huddled behind parked cars and along the clipped grass were too frightened to yell until he was out of sight. He quickly walked away in the direction the Volkswagen had come. Just before he turned the corner he looked back at the crumpled form on the sidewalk. A policeman was bending over Wendy's still body. Malcolm swallowed and turned away. Three blocks later he caught a cab and headed downtown. As he sat in the back seat, his body shook slightly, but his mind burned.

'The first step toward becoming a skilful defensive player, then, is to handle the defense in an aggressive spirit. If you do that, you can find subtle defensive resources that other players would not dream of. By seeking active counterplay, you will often upset clever attacking lines. Better yet, you will upset your opponent.'

– Fred Reinfeld, *The Complete Chess Course*

Late Monday

'All hell has broken loose, sir.' Powell's voice reflected the futility he felt.

'What do you mean?' On the other end of the telephone line the old man strained to catch every word.

'The girl has been shot on Capitol Hill. Two witnesses tentatively identified that old photo of Maronick. They also identified the girl's companion who fled as Malcolm. As far as we can tell, Malcolm wasn't injured. Maronick got a cop, too.'

'Killing two people in one day makes Maronick rather busy.'

'I didn't say she was dead, sir.'

After an almost imperceptible pause the tight voice said, 'Maronick is not known for missing. She is dead, isn't she?'

'No, sir, although Maronick didn't miss by much. Another fraction of an inch and he would have splattered her brain all over the sidewalk. As it is, she has a fairly serious head wound. She's in the Agency hospital now. They had to do a little surgery. This time I made the security arrangements. We don't want another Weatherby. She's unconscious. The doctors say that she'll probably stay that way for a few days, but they think she'll eventually be O.K.'

The old man's voice had an eager edge as he asked, 'Was she able to tell anyone anything, anything at all?'

'No, sir,' Powell replied disappointedly. 'She's been unconscious since she was shot. I've got two of my men in her room. Besides double-checking everyone who comes in, they're waiting in case she wakes up.

'We've got another problem. The police are mad. They want to go after Maronick with everything they've got. A dead cop and a wounded girl on Capitol Hill mean more to them than our spy chase. I've been able to hold them back, but I don't think I can for long. If they start looking using the tie-ins they know, the Agency is bound to find out. What should I do?'

After a pause, the old man said, 'Let them. Give them a slightly sanitised report of everything we know, enough to give them some leads on Maronick. Tell them to go after him with everything they can muster, and tell them they'll have lots of help. The only thing we must insist on is first questioning rights once they get him. Insist on that, and tell them I can get authority to back up our claim. Tell them to find Malcolm too. Does it look like Maronick was waiting for them?'

'Not really. We found the boarding house used by Malcolm and the girl. I think Maronick was in the neighborhood and just happened to spot them. If it hadn't been for the police, he probably would have nailed Condor. There's one other thing. One witness swears Maronick wasn't alone. He didn't get a good look at the other man, but he says the guy was older than Maronick. The older man disappeared.'

'Any confirmation from other witnesses?'

'None, but I tend to believe him. The other man is probably the main double we are after. The Hill is an excellent rendezvous. That could explain Maronick stumbling onto Malcolm and the girl.'

'Yes. Well, send me everything you can on Maronick's friend. Can the witness make an I.D. sketch or a license-plate number? Anything?'

'No, nothing definite. Maybe we'll get lucky and the girl can help us with that if she wakes up soon.'

'Yes,' the old man said softly, 'that would be lucky.'

'Do you have any instructions?'

The old man was silent for a few moments, then said, 'Put an ad – no, better make it two ads – in the *Post*. Our boy, wherever he is, will expect to hear from us. But he's probably not too organised, so put a simple, uncoded ad to run on the same page as the coded one. Tell him to get in touch with us. In the coded ad tell him the girl is alive, the original plan is off, and we're trying to find some way to bring him in safe. We'll have to take the chance that he either has or can get a copy of the code book. We can't say anything important in the uncoded ad because we don't know who else besides our boy might be reading the *Post*.'

'Our colleagues will guess something is up when they see the uncoded ad.'

'That's an unpleasant fact, but we knew we would have to face them eventually. However, I think I can manage them.'

'What do you think Malcolm will do?'

There was another short pause before the old man replied. 'I'm not sure,' he said. 'A lot depends on what he knows. I'm sure he thinks the girl is dead. He would have responded differently to the situation if he thought she was alive. We may be able to use her somehow, as bait for either Malcolm or the opposition. But we'll have to wait and see on that.'

'Anything else you want me to do?'

'A good deal, but nothing I can give you instructions for. Keep looking for Malcolm, Maronick, and company, anything which might explain this mess. And keep in touch with me, Kevin. After the meeting with our colleagues, I'll be at my son's house for dinner.'

'I think it's disgusting!' The man from the F.B.I. leaned across the table to glare at the old man. 'You knew all along that the murder in Alexandria was connected with this case, yet you didn't tell us. What's worse, you kept the police from reporting it and handling it according to form. Disgusting! Why, by now we could have traced Malcolm and the girl down. They would both be safe. We would be hot after the others, provided, of course, that we didn't already have them. I've heard of petty pride, but this is national security! I can assure you, we at the Bureau would not behave in such a manner!'

The old man smiled. He had told them only about the link between Maronick and the murder in Alexandria. Imagine their anger if they realised how much more he knew! He glanced at the puzzled faces. Time to mend fences, or at least to rationalise. 'Gentlemen, gentlemen, I can understand your anger. But of course you realise I had a reason for my actions.

'As you all know, I believe there is a leak in the Agency. A substantial leak, I might add. It was and is my opinion that this leak would thwart our efforts on this matter. After all, the end goal – whether we admit it or not – is to plug that very leak. Now, how was I to know that the leak was not in this very group? We are not immune from such dangers.' He paused. The men around the table were too experienced to glance at each other, but the old man could feel the tension rising. He congratulated himself.

'Now then,' he continued, 'perhaps I was wrong to conceal so much from the group, but I think not. Not that I'm accusing anyone – or, by the way, that I have abandoned the possibility of the leak's being here. I still think my move prudent. I also believe it wouldn't have made much difference, despite what our friend from the F.B.I. says. I think we would still be where we are today. But that is not the question, at least not now. The question is, Where do we go from here and how?'

The Deputy Director looked around the room. No one seemed eager to respond to the old man's question. Of course, such a situation meant he should pick up the ball. The Deputy dreaded such moments. One always had to be so careful about stepping on toes and offending people. The Deputy felt far more at ease on his field missions when he only had to worry about the enemy. He cleared his throat and used a ploy he hoped the old man expected. 'What are your suggestions, sir?'

The old man smiled. Good old Darnsworth. He played the game fairly well, but not very well. In a way he hated to do this to him. He looked away from his old friend and stared into space. 'Quite frankly, Deputy, I'm at a loss for suggestions. I really couldn't say. Of course, I think we should keep, on trying to do something.'

Inwardly the Deputy winced. He had the ball again. He looked around the table at a group of men now suddenly not so competent and eager-looking. They looked everywhere but at him, yet he knew they were watching his every move. The Deputy cleared his throat again. He resolved to end the agony as quickly as possible. 'As I see it, then, no one has any new ideas. Consequently, I have decided that we will continue to operate in the manner we have been.' (Whatever that means, he thought.) 'If there is nothing further ...' He paused only momentarily. '... I suggest we adjourn.' The Deputy shuffled his papers, stuffed them into his briefcase, and quickly left the room.

As the others rose to leave, the Army Intelligence representative leaned over to the Navy captain and said, 'I feel like the nearsighted virgin on his honeymoon who couldn't get hard: I can't see what to do and I can't do it either.'

The Navy captain looked at his counterpart and said, 'I never have that problem.'

Malcolm changed taxis three times before he finally headed for northeast Washington. He left the cab on the fringes of the downtown area and walked around the neighborhood. During his ride around town he formed a plan, rough and vague, but a plan. His first step was to find all-important shelter from the hunters.

It took only twenty minutes. He saw her spot him and discreetly move in a path parallel to his. She crossed the street at the corner. As she stepped up to the sidewalk she 'tripped' and fell against him, her body pressed close to his.

Her arms ran quickly up and down his sides. He felt her body tense when her hands passed over the gun in his belt. She jerked away and a pair of extraordinarily bright brown eyes darted over his face.

'Cop?' From her voice she couldn't have been more than eighteen. Malcolm looked down at her stringy dyed blond hair and pale skin. She smelled from the perfume sampler at the corner drugstore.

'No.' Malcolm looked at the frightened face. 'Let's say I'm involved in a high-risk business.' He could see the fear on her face, and he knew she would take a chance.

She leaned against him again, pushing her hips and her chest forward. 'What are you doing around here?'

Malcolm smiled. 'I want a lay. I'm willing to pay for it. Now, if I'm a cop, the bust is no good, cause I entrapped you. O.K.?'

She smiled. 'Sure, tiger. I understand. What kind of party are we going to have?'

Malcolm looked down at her. Italian, he thought, or maybe Central European. 'What do you charge?'

The girl looked at him, judging possibilities. It had been a slow day. 'Twenty dollars for a straight lay?' She made it clear she was asking, not demanding.

Malcolm knew he had to get off the streets soon. He looked at the girl. 'I'm in no hurry,' he said. 'I'll give you ... seventy-five for the whole night. I'll throw in breakfast if we can use your place.'

The girl tensed. It might take her a whole day and half the night to make that kind of money. She decided to gamble. Slowly she moved her hand into Malcolm's crotch, covering her action by leaning into him, pushing her breast against his arm. 'Hey, honey, that sounds great, but ...' She almost lost her nerve. 'Could you make it a hundred? Please? I'll be extraspecial good to you.'

Malcolm looked down and nodded. 'A hundred dollars. For the full night at your place.' He reached in his pocket and handed her a fifty-dollar bill. 'Half now, half afterwards. And don't think about any kind of setup.'

The girl snatched the money from his hand. 'No setup. Just me. And I'll be real good – real good. My place isn't far.' She linked her arms in his to guide him down the street.

When they reached the next corner, she whispered, 'Just a second, honey, I have to talk to that man.' She released his arm before he could think and hurried to the blind pencil hawker on the corner. Malcolm backed against the wall. His hand shot inside his coat. The gun butt was sweaty.

Malcolm saw the girl slip the man the fifty dollars. He mumbled a few words. She walked quickly to a nearby phone booth, almost oblivious of a boy who jostled her and grinned as her breasts bounced. The sign said Out of Order, but she opened the door anyway. She looked through the book, or so Malcolm thought. He couldn't see too well, as her back was towards him. She shut the door and quickly returned.

'Sorry to keep you waiting, honey. Just a little business deal. You don't mind, do you?'

When they came abreast of the blind man, Malcolm stopped and pushed the girl away. He snatched the thick sunglasses off the man's face. Carefully watching the astonished girl, he looked at the pencil seller. The two empty sockets made him push the glasses back quicker than he had taken them off. He staffed a ten-dollar bill into the man's cup. 'Forget it, old man.'

The hoarse voice laughed. 'It's done forgotten, mister.'

As they walked away, the girl looked at him. 'What did you do that for?'

Malcolm looked down at the puzzled, dull face. 'Just checking.'

Her place turned out to be one room with a kitchen-bath area. As soon as they were safely inside, she bolted and locked the door. Malcolm fastened the chain. 'Be right with you, honey. Take off your clothes. I'll fix you up real good right away.' She darted into the curtained-off bathroom area.

Malcolm looked out the window. Three stories up. No one could climb in. Fine. The door was solid and double-locked. He didn't think anyone had followed them, or even really noticed them. He slowly took off his clothes. He put the gun on the small table next to the bed and covered it with an old *Reader's Digest*. The bed squeaked when he lay down. Both his mind and his body ached, but he knew he had to act as normal as possible.

The curtains parted and she came to him, her eyes shining. She wore a long-sleeved black nightgown. The front hung open. Her breasts dangled – long, skinny, pencils. The rest of her body matched her breasts, skinny, almost emaciated. Her voice was distant. 'Sorry I took so long, sugar. Let's get down to business.'

She climbed on the bed and pulled his head to her breasts. 'There, baby, there you go.' For a few minutes she ran her hands over him, then she said, 'Now I'll take real good care of you.' She moved to the base of the bed and buried her head in his crotch. Minutes later she coaxed his body into a response. She got up and went to the bathroom. She returned holding a jar of Vaseline. 'Oh, baby, you were real good, real good, sugar.' She lay down on the bed to apply the lubricant to herself. 'There, sugar, all ready for you. All ready for you whenever you want.'

For a long time they lay there. Malcolm finally looked at her. Her body moved slowly, carefully, almost laboriously. She was asleep. He went to the bathroom. On the back of the stained toilet he found the spoon, rubber hose, matches, and homemade syringe. The small plastic bag was still three-quarters full of the white powder. Now he knew why the nightgown had long sleeves.

Malcolm searched the apartment. He found four changes of underwear, three blouses, two skirts, two dresses, a pair of jeans,, and a red sweater to match the purple one laying on the floor. A torn raincoat hung in the closet. In a shot box in the kitchen be found six of the possession return receipts issued upon release from a Washington jail. He also found a two-year-old high-school identification card. Mary Ruth Rosen. Her synagogue address was neatly typed on the back. There was nothing to eat except five Hersheys, some coconut, and a little grapefruit juice. He ate everything. Under the bed he found an empty Mogen David 20/20 wine bottle. He propped it against the door. If his theory worked, it would crash loudly should the door open. He picked up her inert form. She barely stirred. He put her on the torn armchair and threw a blanket over the limp bundle. It wouldn't make any difference if her body wasn't comfortable in the night. Malcolm took out his lenses and lay down on the bed. He was asleep in five minutes.

'In almost every game of chess there comes a crisis that must be recognized. In one way or another a player risks something – if he knows what he's doing, we call it a "calculated risk".

'If you understand the nature of this crisis; if you perceive how you've committed yourself to a certain line of play; if you can foresee the nature of your coming task and its accompanying difficulties, all's well. But if this awareness is absent, then the game will be lost for you, and fighting back will do no good.'

– Fred Reinfeld, *The Complete Chess Course*

Tuesday, Morning through Early Evening

Malcolm woke shortly after seven. He lay quietly until just before eight, his mind going over all the possibilities. In the end he still decided to carry it through. He glanced at the chair. The girl had slid onto the floor during the night. The blanket was wrapped over her head and she was breathing hard.

Malcolm got up. With a good deal of clumsy effort he put her on the bed. She didn't stir through the whole process.

The bathroom had a leaky hose and nozzle hooked up to the tub, so Malcolm took a tepid shower. He successfully shaved with the slightly-used safety razor. He desperately wanted to brush his teeth, but he couldn't bring himself to use the girl's toothbrush.

Malcolm looked at the sleeping form before he left the

apartment. Their agreement had been for a hundred dollars, and he had only paid her fifty. He knew where that money went. Reluctantly, he laid the other fifty dollars on the dresser. It wasn't his money anyway.

Three blocks away he found a Hot Shoppe where he breakfasted in the boisterous company of neighbors on their way to work. After he left the restaurant he went to a drugstore. In the privacy of a Gulf station rest room he brushed his teeth. It was 9.38.

He found a phone booth. With change from the Gulf station he made his calls. The first one was to Information and the second one connected him with a small office in Baltimore.

'Bureau of Motor Vehicle Registration. May I help you?'

'Yes,' Malcolm replied. 'My name is Winthrop Estes, of Alexandria. I was wondering if you could help me pay back a favor.'

'I'm not sure what you mean.'

'You see, yesterday as I was driving home from work, my battery tipped over right in the middle of the street. I got it hooked up again, but there wasn't enough charge to fire the engine. Just as I was about to give up and try to push the thing out of the way, this man in a Mercedes Benz pulled up behind me. At great risk to his own car, he gave me the push necessary to get mine started. Before I had a chance to even thank him, he drove away. All I got was his license number. Now, I would at least like to send him a thank-you note or buy him a drink or something. Neighborly things like that don't happen very often in D.C.'

The man on the other end of the line was touched.

'They certainly don't. With his Mercedes! Phew, that's some nice guy! Let me guess. He had Maryland plates and you want me to check and see who he is, right?'

'Right. Can you do it?'

'Well … Technically no, but for something like this, what's a little technicality? Do you have the number?'

'Maryland 6E-49387.'

'6E-49387. Right. Hold on just one second and I'll have it.' Malcolm heard the receiver clunk on a hard surface. In the background, footsteps faded into a low office murmur of typewriters and obscure voices, then grew stronger. 'Mr. Estes? We've got it. Black Mercedes sedan, registered to a Robert T. Atwood, 42 Elwood – that's E-l-w-o-o-d – Lane, Chevy Chase. Those people must really be loaded. That's *the* country-squire suburb. He could probably afford a scratch or two on his car. Funny, those people usually don't give a damn, if you know what I mean.'

'I know what you mean. Listen, thanks a lot.'

'Hey, don't thank me. For something like this, glad to do it. Only don't let it get around, know what I mean? Might tell Atwood the same thing, O.K.?'

'O.K.!'

'You sure you got it? Robert Atwood, 42 Elwood Lane, Chevy Chase?'

'I've got it. Thanks again.' Malcolm hung up and stuffed the piece of paper with the address on it into his pocket. He wouldn't need it to remember Mr. Atwood. For no real reason, he strolled back to the Hot Shoppe for coffee. As far as his watchful eyes could tell, no one noticed him.

The morning *Post* lay on the counter. On impulse he began to thumb through it. It was on page twelve. They hadn't taken any chances. The three-inch ad. was set in bold type and read, 'Condor call home.'

Malcolm smiled, hardly glancing at the coded sweepstakes ad. If he called in, they would tell him to come home or at least lie low. That wasn't what he intended. There was nothing they could say in the coded message that could make any difference to him. Not now. Their instructions had lost all value yesterday on Capitol Hill.

Malcolm frowned. If his plan went wrong, the whole thing might end unsatisfactorily. Undoubtedly that end would also mean Malcolm's death, but that didn't bother him too much. What bothered him was the horrible waste factor that failure would mean. He had to tell someone, somehow, just in case. But he couldn't let anyone know, not until he had tried. That meant delay. He had to find a way of delayed communication.

The sign flashing across the street gave him the inspiration. With the materials he had at hand he began to write. Twenty minutes later he stuffed curt synopses of the last five days and a prognosis for the future into three small envelopes begged from the waitress. The napkins were to the F.B.I. The pieces of junk paper from his wallet filled the envelope addressed to the C.I.A. The map of D.C. he had picked up at the Gulf station went to the *Post*. These three envelopes went into a large manila envelope he bought at the drugstore. Malcolm stuck the big envelope in a mailbox. Pickup was scheduled for 2.00 p.m. The big envelope was addressed to Malcolm's bank, which for some reason closed at 2.00 p.m. on Tuesdays. Malcolm reckoned it would take the bank until at least tomorrow to find and mail the letters. He had a minimum of twenty-four hours to operate in, and he had passed on what he knew. He considered himself free of obligations.

While Malcolm spent the rest of the day standing in the perpetually long line at the Washington Monument, security and law-enforcement agencies all over the city were quietly going bananas. Detectives and agents tripped over each other and false reports of Malcolm. Three separate carloads of officials from three separate agencies arrived simultaneously at the same boarding house to check out three separate leads, all of which were false. The proprietress of the boarding house still had no idea what happened after the officials angrily drove away. A congressional intern who vaguely resembled Malcolm's description was picked up and detained by an F.B.I. patrol. Thirty minutes after the intern was identified and released from federal custody, he was arrested by Washington police and again detained. Reporters harassed already nervous officials about the exciting Capitol Hill shootout. Congressmen, senators, and political hacks of every shade kept calling the agencies and each other, inquiring about the rumored security leak. Of course, everyone refused to discuss it over the phone, but the senator-congressman-department chief wanted to be personally briefed. Kevin Powell was trying once again to play Condor and retrace Malcolm. As he walked along East Capitol Street, puzzling, perturbing questions kept disturbing the lovely spring day. He received no answers from the trees and buildings, and at 11.00 he gave up the chase to meet the director of the hunt.

Powell was late, but when he walked quickly into the room he did not receive a reproachful glance from the old man. Indeed, the old man's congeniality seemed at a new height. At first Powell thought the warmth was contrived for the benefit of the stranger who sat with them at the small table, but he gradually decided it was genuine.

The stranger was one of the biggest men Powell had ever seen. It was hard to judge his height while he sat, but Powell guessed he was at least six feet seven. The man had a massive frame, with at least three hundred pounds of flesh supplying extra padding beneath the expensively tailored suit. The, thick black hair was neatly greased down. Powell noticed the man's little piggy eyes quietly, carefully taking stock of him.

'Ah, Kevin,' said the old man, 'how good of you to join us. I don't believe you know Dr. Lofts.'

Powell didn't know Dr. Lofts personally, but he knew the man's work. Dr. Crawford Lofts was probably the foremost psychological diagnostician in the world, yet his reputation was known only in very tightly controlled circles. Dr. Lofts headed the Psychiatric Evaluation Team for the Agency. P.E.T. came into its own when its evaluation of the Soviet Premier convinced President Kennedy that he should go ahead with the Cuban blockade. Ever since then, P.E.T. had been given unlimited resources to compile its evaluation of major world leaders and selected individuals.

After ordering coffee for Powell, the old man turned and said, 'Dr. Lofts has been working on our Condor. For the last few days he has talked to people, reviewed our boy's work and dossiers, even lived in his apartment. Trying to build an action profile, I believe they call it. You can explain it better, Doctor.'

The softness of Loft's voice surprised Powell. 'I think

you've about said it, old friend. Basically, I'm trying to find out what Malcolm would do, given the background he has. About all I can say is that he will improvise fantastically and ignore whatever you tell him unless it fits into what he wants.' Dr. Lofts did not babble about his work at every opportunity. This too surprised Powell, and he was unprepared when Lofts stopped talking.

'Uh, what are you doing about it?' Powell stammered, feeling very foolish when he heard his improvised thoughts expressed out loud.

The Doctor rose to go. At least six-seven. 'I've got field workers scattered at points throughout the city where Malcolm might turn up. If you'll excuse me, I want to get back to supervising them.' With a curt, polite nod to the old man and Powell, Dr. Lofts lumbered from the room.

Powell looked at the old man. 'Do you think he has much of a chance?'

'No, no more than anyone else. That's what he thinks, too. Too many variables for him to do much more than guess. The realisation of that limitation is what makes him good.

'Then why bring him in? We can get all the manpower we want without having to pull in P.E.T.'

The old man's eyes twinkled, but there was coldness in his voice. 'Because, my dear boy, it never hurts to have a lot of hunters if the hunters are hunting in different ways. I want Malcolm very badly, and I don't want to miss a trick. Now, how are you coming from your end.'

Powell told him, and the answer was the same as it had been from the beginning: no progress.

★

At 4.30 Malcolm decided it was time to steal a car. He had considered many other ways of obtaining transportation, but crossed them off his list as too risky. Providence combined with the American Legion and a Kentucky distillery to solve Malcolm's problem.

If it hadn't been for the American Legion and their National Conference on Youth and Drugs, Alvin Phillips would never have been in Washington, let alone at the Washington Monument. He was chosen by the Indiana state commander to attend the expense-paid national conference to learn all he could about the evils of drug abuse among the young. While at the conference, he had been given a pass which would enable him to avoid the lines at the Monument and go straight to the top. He lost his pass the night before, but he felt obligated to at least see the Monument for the folks back home.

If it hadn't been for a certain Kentucky distillery, Alvin would not have been in his present state of intoxication. The distillery kindly provided all conference participants with a complimentary fifth of their best whiskey. Alvin had become so upset by the previous day's film describing how drugs often led to illicit sex among nubile teen-age girls that the night before he drank the entire bottle by himself in his Holiday Inn room. He liked the whiskey so much that he bought another fifth to help him through the conference and 'kill the dog that bit him'. He finished most of that fifth by the time the meetings broke up and he managed to navigate to the Monument.

Malcolm didn't find Alvin, Alvin found the line. Once there, he made it plain to all who could hear that he was standing in this hot God damn sun out of patriotic duty.

He didn't have to be here, he could have gone right to the God damn top, except for that God damn hustling floozy who lifted his wallet and the God damn pass. He sure fooled her God damn ass with those traveler's checks – best God damn things you could buy. She sure had God damn big jugs, though. God damn it, all he wanted to do was take her for a ride in his new car.

When Malcolm heard the word 'car', he immediately developed a dislike for cheap God damn floozies and a strong affection for the American Legion, Indiana, Kentucky whiskey, and Alvin's band-new Chrysler. After a few short introductory comments, he let Alvin know he was talking to a fellow veteran of American wars, one whose hobby just happened to be automobiles. Have another drink, Alvin, old buddy.

'S'at right? You really dig cars?' The mention of important matters pulled Alvin part way out of the bottle. It didn't take a lot of effort for bosom companionship to slide him back down. 'You wanna see a real good 'un? Got me bran'-new one. Jus' drove 't here from Indiana. Ever been to Indiana? Gotta come, come see me. An' the old lady. She ain't much to look at – we're forry-four, you know. I don't look forry-four, do I? Where was I? Oh yeah, ol' lady. Good woman. A li'l fat, but what the hell, I always say …'

By this time Malcolm had manoeuvered Alvin away from the crowd and into a parking lot. He had also shared half a dozen swigs from the bottle Alvin carefully kept hidden under his soggy suit coat. Malcolm would raise the bottle to his closed lips and move his Adam's apple, in appreciation. He didn't want alcohol slowing him down for the night. When Alvin took his turn, he more than made up for Malcolm's abstention. By the time they reached the parking lot, only two inches remained in the bottle.

Malcolm and Alvin talked about those God damn kids and their God damn drugs. Especially the girls, the teen-age girls, just like the cheerleaders in Indiana, hooked on that marijuana and ready to do anything, 'anything', for that God damn drug. Anything. Malcolm casually mentioned that he knew where two such girls were hanging around, just waiting to do anything for that God damn marijuana. Alvin stopped him and plaintively said, 'Really?' Alvin thought very, hard when Malcolm ('John') assured him that such was the case. Malcolm let the discussion lag, then he helped Alvin suggest meeting these two girls so Alvin could tell the folks back in Indiana what it was really like. Really like. Since the girls were in kind of a public place, it probably would be best if 'John' went and picked them up and brought them back here. Then they could all go to Alvin's room and talk. Better to talk to them there than here. Find out why they'd do anything, *anything*, for that God damn marijuana. Alvin gave Malcolm the keys just as they reached the shiny new car.

'Got lotsa gas, lotsa gas. Sure ya don't need any money?' Alvin fumbled with his clothes and extracted a weather-beaten wallet. 'Take watcha need, bitch last night only got traveler's checks.' Malcolm took the wallet. While Alvin shakily tipped the bottle to his lips, his new friend removed all identification papers from the wallet, including a card with his car license number. He gave the wallet back to Alvin.

'Here,' he said. 'I don't think they'll want any money.

227

Not now.' He smiled briefly, secretively. When Alvin saw the smile his heart beat a shade faster. He was too far gone to show much facial expression.

Malcolm unlocked the car. A crumpled blue cap lay on the front seat. On the floor was a six-pack of beer Alvin had brought to help ease the heat. Malcolm put the cap on his friend's head and exchanged the now empty whiskey bottle for the six-pack of beer. He looked at the flushed face and blurred eyes. Two hours in the sun and Alvin should pass out. Malcolm smiled and pointed to a grassy mall.

'When I come back with the girls, we'll meet you over there, then go to your room. You'll recognise us because they both have big jugs. I'll be back with them just after you finish the six-pack. Don't worry about a thing.' With a kindly push he sent Alvin staggering off to the park and the tender mercies of the city. When he pulled out of the parking lot, he glanced at the rearview mirror in time to see Alvin lurch to a sitting position on a portion of grass well away from anyone else. Malcolm turned the corner as Alvin opened a beer can and took a long, slow swig.

The car had almost a full tank of gas. Malcolm drove to the expressway circling the city. He stopped briefly at a drive-in restaurant in Chevy Chase for a cheeseburger and use of the rest room. In addition to relieving himself, he checked his gun.

Number 42 Elwood Lane was indeed a country estate. The house was barely visible from the road. Direct access to it was through a private lane closed off by a stout iron gate. The closest neighboring house was at least a mile away. Dense woods surrounded the house on three sides.

The land between the house and the road was partially cleared. From Malcolm's brief glance he could tell that the house was large, but he didn't stop for a closer look. That would be foolish.

From a small gas station just up the road he obtained a map of the area. The woods behind the house were uninhabited hills. When he told the gas-station attendant he was a vacationing ornithologist and that he might have seen a very rare thrush, the attendant helped him by describing some unmapped country roads which might lead to the bird's nesting area. One such road ran behind 42 Elwood Lane.

Because of the attendant's anxious help, Malcolm found the proper road. Bumpy, unpaved, and with only traces of gravel, the road wound around hills, through gullies, and over ancient cowpaths. The woods were so dense that at times Malcolm could see only twenty feet from the road. His luck held, though, and when he topped a hill he saw the house above the trees to his left, at least a mile away. Malcolm pulled the car off the road, bouncing and lurching into a small clearing.

The woods were quiet, the sky was just turning pink. Malcolm quickly pushed his way through the trees. He knew he had to get close to the house before all light faded or he would never find it.

It took him half an hour of hard work. As the day shifted from sunset to twilight, he reached the top of a small hill. The house was just below him, three hundred yards away. Malcolm dropped to the ground, trying to catch his breath in the crisp, fresh air. He wanted to memorise all he could see in the fading light. Through the windows of the house he caught fleeting glimpses of moving figures. The yard was big, surrounded by a rock wall. There was a small shed behind the house.

He would wait until dark.

Inside the house Robert Atwood sat back in his favorite easy chair. While his body relaxed, his mind worked. He did not want to meet with Maronick and his men tonight, especially not here. He knew the pressure was on them, and he knew they would press him for some sort of alternate solution. At present Atwood didn't have one. The latest series of events had changed the picture considerably. So much depended on the girl. If she regained consciousness and was able to identify him ... well, that would be unfortunate. It was too risky to send Maronick after her, the security precautions were too tight. Atwood smiled. On the other hand, the girl's survival might pose some interesting and favorable developments, especially in dealing with Maronick. Atwood's smile broadened. The infallible Maronick had missed. True, not by much, but he had missed. Perhaps the girl, a living witness, might be useful against Maronick. Just *how* Atwood wasn't sure, but he decided it might be best if Maronick continued thinking the girl was dead. She could be played later in the game. For the time being Maronick must concentrate on finding Malcolm.

Atwood knew Maronick had insisted on meeting him at his home in order to commit him even further. Maronick would make it a point to be seen by someone in the neighborhood whom the police might later question should things go wrong. In this way Maronick sought to further ensure Atwood's loyalty. Atwood smiled. There were ways around that one. Perhaps the girl might prove a useful lever there. If ...

'I'm going now, dear.' Atwood turned towards the speaker, a stocky gray-haired woman in an expensively-cut suit. He rose and walked with his wife to the door. When he was close to his wife, his eyes invariably traveled to the tiny scars on her neck and the edge of her hairline where the plastic surgeon had stretched and lifted years from her skin. He smiled, wondering if the surgery and all her hours at an exclusive figure salon made her lover's task any more agreeable.

Elaine Atwood was fifty, five years younger than her husband and twenty-four years older than her lover. She knew the man who had driven her wild and brought back her youth as Adrian Queens, a British graduate student at American University. Her husband knew all about her lover, but he knew that Adrian Queens was really Alexy Ivan Podgovich, an aspiring K.G.B. agent who hoped to milk the wife of a prominent American intelligence officer for information necessary to advance his career. The 'affair' between Podgovich and his wife amused him and served his purposes very well. It kept Elaine busy and distracted and provided him with an opportunity to make an intelligence coup of his own. Such things never hurt a man's career, if he knows how to take advantage of opportunity.

'I may just stay over at Jane's after the concert, darling. Do you want me to call?'

'No, dear, I'll assume you are with her if you aren't home by midnight. Don't worry about me. Give Jane my love.'

The couple emerged from the house. Atwood delivered a perfunctory kiss to his wife's powdered cheek. Before she reached the car in the driveway (a sporty American car, not the Mercedes) her mind was on her lover and the long night ahead. Before Atwood closed the front door his mind was back on Maronick.

Malcolm saw the scene in the doorway, although he couldn't discern features at that distance. The wife's departure made his confidence surge. He would wait thirty minutes.

Fifteen of that thirty minutes had elapsed when Malcolm realised there were two men walking up the driveway towards the house. Their figures barely stood out from the shadows. If it hadn't been for their motion, Malcolm would never have seen them. The only thing he could distinguish from his distant perch was the tall leanness of one of the men. Something about the tall man triggered Malcolm's subconscious, but he couldn't pull it to the surface. The men, after ringing the bell, vanished inside the house.

With binoculars, Malcolm might have seen the men's car. They had parked it just off the road inside the gate and walked the rest of the way. Although he wanted to leave traces of his visit to Atwood's house, Maronick saw no point in letting Atwood get a look at their car.

Malcolm counted to fifty, then began to pick his way towards the house. Three hundred yards. In the darkness it was hard to see tree limbs and creepers reaching to trip him and bring him noisily down. He moved slowly, ignoring the scratches from thornbushes. Halfway to the house, Malcolm stumbled over a stump, tearing his pants and wrenching his knee, but somehow he kept from crying out. One hundred yards. A quick, limping dash through brush stubble and long grass before he crouched behind the stone wall. Malcolm eased the heavy magnum into his hand while he fought to regain his breath. His knee throbbed, but he tried not to think about it. Over the stone wall lay the house yard. In the yard to the right was the crumbling tool shed. A few scattered evergreens stood between him and the house. To his left was blackness.

Malcolm looked at the sky. The moon hadn't risen yet. There were few clouds and the stars shone brightly. He waited, catching his breath and assuring himself his ears heard nothing unusual in the darkness. He vaulted the low wall and ran to the nearest evergreen. Fifty yards.

A shadow quietly detached itself from the tool shed to swiftly merge with an evergreen. Malcolm should have noticed. He didn't.

Another short dash brought Malcolm to within twenty-five yards of the house. Glow from inside the building lit up all but a thin strip of grass separating him and the next evergreen. The windows were low. Malcolm didn't want to chance a fleeting glance to the outside catching him running across the lawn. He sprawled to his belly and squirmed across the thin shadowed strip. Ten yards. Through open windows he could hear voices. He convinced himself different noises were his imagination playing on Mother Nature.

Malcolm took a deep breath and made a dash for the bush beneath the open window. As he was taking his second step, he heard a huffing, rushing noise. The back of his neck exploded into reverberating fire.

> '*The truth, the whole truth, and nothing but the truth.*
>
> — *Traditional oath*

Late Tuesday Night, Early Wednesday Morning

Consciousness returned abruptly to Malcolm. He felt a dim awareness around his eyes, then suddenly his body telegraphed a desperate message to his brain: he had to vomit. He lurched forward, up and had his head thrust into a thoughtfully provided bucket. When he stopped retching, he opened his aching eyes to take in his plight.

Malcolm blinked to clear his contacts. He was sitting on the floor of a very plush living room. In the opposite wall was a small fireplace. Two men sat in easy chairs between him and that wall. The man who shot Wendy and his companion. Malcolm blinked again. He saw the outline of a man on his right. The man was very tall and thin. As he turned to take a closer look, the man behind him jerked Malcolm's head so he again faced the two seated men. Malcolm tried to move his hands, but they were tied behind his back with a silk tie that would leave no marks.

The older of the two men smiled, obviously very pleased with himself. 'Well, Condor,' he said, 'welcome to my nest.'

The other man was almost impassive, but Malcolm thought he saw curious amusement in the cold eyes.

The older man continued. 'It has taken us a long time to find you, dear Malcolm, but now that you are here, I'm really rather glad our friend Maronick didn't shoot you too. I have some questions to ask you. Some questions I already know the answers to, some I don't. This is the perfect time to get those answers. Don't you agree?'

Malcolm's mouth was dry. The thin man held a glass of water to his lips. When Malcolm finished, he looked at the two men and rasped, 'I have some questions too. I'll trade you answers.'

The older man smiled as he spoke. 'My dear boy. You don't understand. I'm not interested in your questions. We won't even waste our time with them. Why should I tell you anything? It would be so futile. No, you shall talk to us. Is he ready yet, Cutler, or did you swing that rifle a little too hard?'

The man holding Malcolm had a deep voice. 'His head should be clear by now.' With a quick flick of his powerful wrists the man pulled Malcolm down to the floor. The thin man pinned Malcolm's feet, and Maronick pulled down Malcolm's pants. He inserted a hypodermic needle into Malcolm's tensed thigh, sending the clear liquid into the main artery. It would work quicker that way, and the odds that a coroner would notice a small injection on the inside of a thigh are slim.

Malcolm knew what was happening. He tried to resist the inevitable. He forced his mind to picture a brick wall, to feel a brick wall, smell a brick wall, become a brick wall. He lost all sense of time, but the bricks stood out. He heard the voices questioning him, but he turned their sounds to bricks for his wall.

Then slowly, piece by piece, the truth serum chiseled away at the wall. His interrogators carefully swung their hammers. Who are you? How old are you? What is your mother's name? Small, fundamental pieces of mortar chipped away. Then bigger hunks. Where do you work? What do you do? One by one bricks pried loose. What happened last Thursday? How much do you know? What have you done about it? Why have you done it?

Little by little, piece by piece, Malcolm felt his wall crumble. While he felt regret, he couldn't will the wreckage to stop. Finally his tired brain began to wander. The questions stopped and he drifted into a void. He felt a slight prick on his thigh and the void filled with numbness.

Maronick made a slight miscalculation. The mistake was understandable, as he was dealing with milligrams of drugs to obtain results from an unknown variable, but he should have erred on the side of caution. When he secretly squirted out half the dosage in the syringe Atwood gave him, Maronick thought he had still used enough to produce unconsciousness. He was a little short. The drug combined with the sodium pentothal as predicted, but it was only strong enough to cause stupor, not unconsciousness.

Malcolm was in a dream. His eyelids hung low over his contacts, but they wouldn't shut. Sounds came to him through a stereo echo box. His mind couldn't connect, but it could record.

– Shall we kill him now? (The deep voice.)

– No, on the scene.

– Who?

– I'll let Charles do it, he likes blood. Give him your knife.

– Here, you give it to him. I'll check this again.

Receding footsteps. A door opens, closes. Hands running over his body. Something brushes his face.

– Damn.

A pink slip of paper on the floor by his shoulder. The tears fogging his contacts, but on the paper, '# 27, T.W.A., National, 6 a.m.'

The door opens, closes. Footsteps approaching.

– Where are Atwood and Charles?

– Checking the grounds in case he dropped anything.

– Oh. By the way, here's that reservation I made for you. James Cooper.

Paper rustles.

– Fine, let's go.

Malcolm felt his body lift off the floor. Through rooms. Outside to the cooling night air. Sweet smells, lilacs blooming. A car, into the back seat. His mind began to record more details, close gaps. His body was still lost, lying on the floor with a pair of heavy shoes pressed in his back. A long, bumpy ride. Stop. Engine dies and car doors open.

– Charles, can you carry him into the woods, up that way, maybe fifty yards. I'll bring the shovel in a few minutes. Wait until I get there. I want it done a certain way.

A low laugh. – No trouble.

Up into the air, jammed onto a tall, bony shoulder, bouncing over a rough trail, pain jarring life back into the body.

By the time the tall man dropped Malcolm on the ground, consciousness had returned. His body was still numb, but his mind was working and his eyes were bright. He could see the tall man smile in the dimly lit night. His eyes found the source of the series of clicks and snaps cutting through the humid air. The man was opening and closing the switchblade in eager anticipation.

Twigs snapped and dead leaves crunched under a light foot. The striking man appeared at the edge of the small clearing. His left hand held a flashlight. The beam fell on Malcolm as he tried to rise. The man's right hand hung close to his side. His clear voice froze Malcolm's actions. 'Is our Condor all right?'

The tall man broke in impatiently. 'He's fine, Maronick, as if it mattered. He sure came out of that drug quickly.' The thin man paused to lick his lips. 'Are you ready now?'

The flashlight beam moved to the tall man's eager face. Maronick's voice came softly through the night air. 'Yes, I am.' He raised his right arm and with a soft plop! from the silencer shot the tall man through the solar plexus.

The bullet buried itself in Charles's spine. The concussion knocked him back on his heels, but he slumped forward to his knees, then to his face. Maronick walked over to the long, limp form. To be very sure, he fired one bullet through the head.

Malcolm's mind reeled. He knew what he saw, but he didn't believe it. The man called Maronick walked slowly towards him. He bent over and checked the bonds that held Malcolm's feet and hands. Satisfied, he sat on a handily-placed log, turned off the flashlight, and said, 'Shall we talk?

'You stumbled into something and you blundered your way through it. I must say I've developed a sort of professional admiration for you during the last five days. However, that has nothing to do with my decision to give you a chance to come out of this alive – indeed, a hero.

'In 1968, as part of their aid to a beleaguered, anti-communist government, the C.I.A. assisted certain Meo tribes in Laos with the main commercial activity of that area, narcotics production. Mixed among all the fighting going on in that area there was a war between competing commercial factions. Our people assisted one faction by using transport planes to move the unprocessed opiate product along its commercial route. The whole thing was very orthodox from a C.I.A. point of view, though I imagine there are many who frown on the U.S. government pushing dope.

'As you know, such enterprises are immensely profitable. A group of us, most of whom you have met, decided that the opportunity for individual economic advancement was not to be overlooked. We diverted a sizable quantity of unprocessed, high-quality morphine bricks from the official market and channeled them into another source. We were well rewarded for our labor.

'I disagreed with Atwood's handling of the matter from the start. Instead of unloading the stuff in Thailand to local processing labs and taking a reasonable profit, he insisted on exporting the morphine bricks directly to the States and selling them to a U.S. group who wanted to avoid as many middlemen as possible. To do that, we needed to use the Agency more than was wise.

'We used your section for two purposes. We compromised a bursar – not your old accountant – to juggle and later rejuggle the books and get us seed money. We then shipped the morphine Stateside in classified book cases. They fitted quite nicely into those boxes, and since they were shipped as classified materials, we didn't have to worry about customs inspection. Our agent in Seattle intercepted the shipment and delivered it to the buyers. But this background has little to do with your being here.

'Your friend Heidegger started it all. He had to get curious. In order to eliminate the possibility that someone might find something fishy, we had to eliminate Heidegger. To cover his death and just in case he told someone else, we had to hit the whole section. But you botched our operation through blind luck.'

Malcolm cleared his throat. 'Why are you letting me live?'

Maronick smiled. 'Because I know Atwood. He won't feel safe until my associates and I are dead. We're the only ones who can link him to the whole mess. Except you. Consequently, we have to die. He is probably thinking of a way to get rid of us. We are supposed to pick up those envelopes at the bank tomorrow. I'm quite sure we would be shot in a holdup attempt, killed in a car wreck, or just "disappear". Atwood plays dumb, but he's not.'

Malcolm looked at the dark shape on the ground. 'I still don't understand. Why did you kill that man Charles?'

'I like to cover my tracks too. He was dangerous dead weight. It will make no difference to me who reads the letters. The powers-that-be already know I'm involved. I shall quietly disappear to the Middle East, where a man of my talents can always find suitable employment.

'But I don't want to turn a corner someday and find American agents waiting for me, so I'm giving the country a little present in hopes it will regard me as a sheep gone astray but not worth chasing. My farewell present – Robert Atwood. I'm letting you live for somewhat the same reason. You also have the chance to deliver Mr. Atwood. He has caused you a lot of grief. After all, it was he who necessitated all those deaths. I am merely a technician like yourself. Sorry about the girl, but I had no option. *C'est la guerre.*'

Malcolm sat for a long time. Finally he said, 'What's the immediate plan?'

Maronick stood. He threw the switchblade at Malcolm's feet. Then he gave him still another injection. His voice was impassive. 'This is an extremely strong stimulant. It would put a dead man on his feet for half a day. It should give you enough oomph to handle Atwood. He's old, but he's still very dangerous. When you cut yourself free, get back to the clearing where we parked the car. In case you didn't notice, it's the same one you used. There are one or two things that might help you in the back seat. I would park just outside his gate, then work my way to the rear of the house. Climb the tree and go in through the window on the second floor. It somehow got unlocked. Do what you like with him. If he kills you, there are still the letters and several corpses for him to explain.'

Maronick looked down at the figure by his feet. 'Goodbye, Condor. One last word of advice. Stick to research. You've used up all your luck. When it comes right down to it, you're not very good.' He vanished in the woods.

After a few minutes of silence, Malcolm heard a car start and drive away. He wormed his way towards the knife.

It took him half an hour. Twice he cut his wrists, but each time it was only minor and the bleeding stopped as soon as he quit using his hands.

He found the car. There was a note taped to the window. The body of the man called Cutler sprawled by the door. He had been shot in the back. The note had been written while the tall man carried Malcolm into the woods. It was short, to the point: 'Your gun jammed with mud. Rifle in back has 10 rds. Hope you can use automatic.'

The rifle in back was an ordinary .22 varmint rifle. Cutler had used it for target practice. Maronick left it for Malcolm, as he figured any amateur could handle so light a weapon. He left the automatic pistol with silencer just in case. Malcolm ripped the note off and drove away.

By the time he coasted the car to a stop outside Atwood's gate, Malcolm felt the drug taking effect. The pounding in the back of his neck and head, the little pains in his body, all had vanished. In their place was a surging, confident energy. He knew he would have to fight the overestimation and over-confidence the drug brought.

The oak tree proved simple to climb and the window was unlocked. Malcolm unslung the rifle. He worked the bolt to arm the weapon. Slowly, quietly, he tiptoed to the dark hall, down the carpeted hallway to the head of the stairs. He heard Tchaikovsky's '1812' Overture booming from the room where he had been questioned. Every now and then a triumphant hum would come from a familiar voice. Slowly Malcolm went down the stairs.

Atwood had his back to the door when Malcolm entered the room. He was choosing another record from the rack in the wall. His hand paused on Beethoven's Fifth.

Malcolm very calmly raised the rifle, clicked off the safety, took aim, and fired. Hours of practice on gophers, rabbits, and tin cans guided the bullet home. It shattered Atwood's right knee, bringing him screaming to the floor.

Terror and pain filled the old man's eyes. He rolled over in time to see Malcolm work the action again. He screamed as Malcolm's second bullet shattered his other knee. His mouth framed the question, 'Why?'

'Your question is futile. Let's just say I didn't want you going anywhere for a while.'

Malcolm worked in a frenzy of activity. He tied towels around the moaning man's knees to slow the bleeding; then he tied his hands to an end table. He ran upstairs and aimlessly rifled rooms, burning up the energy coursing through his blood. He fought hard and was able to control his mind. Maronick chose his drugs well, he thought. Atwood the planner, the director, the thinker was downstairs, Malcolm thought, in pain and harmless. The secondary members of the cell were all dead. Maronick was the only one left, Maronick the enforcer, Maronick the killer. Malcolm thought briefly of the voices on the other end of the Panic Line, the professionals, professionals like Maronick. No, he thought, so far it has been me. Them against me. Maronick had made it even more personal when he killed Wendy. To the professionals it was just a job. They didn't care. Hazy details of a plan formed around his ideas and wants. He ran to Atwood's bedroom, where he exchanged his tattered clothes for one of several suits. Then he visited the kitchen and devoured some cold chicken and pie. He went back to the room where Atwood lay, took a quick look around, then dashed to his car for the long drive.

Atwood lay very still for some time after Malcolm had left. Slowly, weakly, he tried to pull himself and the table across the floor. He was too weak. All he succeeded in doing was knocking a picture off the table. It fell face up. The glass didn't break into shreds he could use to cut his bonds. He resigned himself to *his* fate. He slumped prone, resting for whatever might lie ahead. He looked briefly at the Picture and sighed. It was of him. In his uniform of a captain in the United States Navy.

Wednesday Morning

Mitchell had reached what Agency psychiatrists call the Crisis Acclimatisation Level, or Zombie Stage 4. For six days he had been stretched as tight as any spring could be stretched. He adjusted to this state and now accepted the hypertension and hyperactivity as normal. In this state he would be extremely competent and extremely effective as long as any challenge fell within the context of the conditions causing the state. Any foreign stimulus would shatter his tensed composure and tear him apart at the seams. One of the symptoms of this state is the ignorance of the subject. Mitchell merely felt a little nervous. His rational process told him he must have overcome the exhaustion and tension with a sort of second wind. That was why he was still awake at 4.20 in the morning. Disheveled and smelly from six days without bathing, he sat behind his desk going over reports for the hundredth time. He hummed softly. He had no idea that the two additional security men standing by the coffee urn were for him. One was his backup and the other was a psychiatrist protégé of Dr. Lofts. The psychiatrist was there to watch Mitchell as well as monitor any of Malcolm's calls.

Brrring!

The call jerked all the men in the room out of relaxation. Mitchell calmly held up one hand to reassure them While he used the other hand to pick up the receiver. His easy movements had the quiet quickness of a natural athlete or a well-oiled machine.

'493-7282.'

'This is Condor. It's almost over.'

'I see. Then why don't you ...'

'I said almost. Now listen, and get it right. Maronick, Weatherby, and their gang were working under a man called Atwood. They were trying to cover their tracks from a smuggling operation they pulled off in 1968. They used Agency facilities and Heidegger found out. The rest just sort of came naturally.

'I've got one chore left. If I don't succeed, you'll know about it. At any rate, I've mailed some stuff to my bank. You better pick it up. It will be there this morning.

'You better send a pretty good team to Atwood's right away. He lives at 42 Elwood Lane, Chevy Chase.' (Mitchell's second picked up a red phone and began to speak softly. In another part of the building men raced toward waiting cars. A second group raced towards a Cobra combat helicopter kept perpetually ready on the building roof.) 'Send a doctor with them. Two of Maronick's men are in the woods behind the house, but they're dead. Wish me luck.'

The phone clicked before Mitchell could speak. He looked at his trace man and got a negative shake of the head.

The room burst into activity. Phones were lifted and all through Washington people woke to the shrill ring of a special bell. Typewriters clicked, messengers ran from the room. These who could find nothing definite to do paced. The excitement around him did not touch Mitchell. He sat at his desk, calmly running through the developed procedure. His forehead and palms were dry, but deep in his eyes a curious light burned.

Malcolm depressed the phone hook and inserted another dime. The buzzer only sounded twice.

The girl had been selected for her soft, cheery voice. 'Good morning. T.W.A. May I help you?'

'Yes, my name is Henry Cooper. My brother is flying out today for an overdue vacation. Getting away from it all, you understand. He didn't tell anyone where he was going for sure because he hadn't made up his mind. What we want to do is give him a last-minute going-away present. He's already left his apartment, but we think he's on Flight 27, leaving at six. Could you tell me if he has a reservation?'

There was a slight pause, then, 'Yes, Mr. Cooper, your brother has booked a reservation on that flight for ... Chicago. He hasn't picked up his ticket yet.'

'Fine, I really appreciate this. Could you do me another favor and not tell him we called? The surprise is named Wendy, and there's a chance she'll be either flying with him or taking the next plane.'

'Of course, Mr. Cooper. Shall I make a reservation for the lady?'

'No, thank you. I think we better wait and see how it works out at the airport. The plane leaves at six, right?'

'Right.'

'Fine, we'll be there. Thank you.'

'Thank you, sir, for thinking of T.W.A.'

Malcolm stepped out of the phone booth. He brushed some lint off his sleeve. Atwood's uniform fitted him fairly well, though it was somewhat bulky. The shoes were a loose fit and his feet tended to slip in them. The highly polished leather creaked as he walked from the parking lot into the main lobby of National Airport. He carried the raincoat draped over his arm and pulled the hat low over his forehead.

Malcolm dropped an unstamped envelope addressed to the C.I.A. in a mailbox. The letter contained all he knew, including Maronick's alias and flight number. The Condor hoped he wouldn't have to rely on the U.S. postal system.

The terminal was beginning to fill with the bustling people who would pass through it during the day. A wheezing janitor swept cigarette butts off the red rug. A mother tried to coax a bored infant into submission. A nervous coed sat wondering if her roommate's half-fare card would work. Three young Marines headed home to Michigan wondering if she would work. A retired wealthy executive and a penniless wino slept in adjoining chairs, both waiting for daughters to fly in from Detroit. A Fuller Brush executive sat perfectly still, bracing himself for the effects of a jet flight on a gin hangover. The programmer for the piped-in music had decided to jazz up the early-morning hours, and a nameless orchestra played watered-down Beatle music.

Malcolm strode to a set of chairs within hearing range of the T.W.A. desk. He sat next to the three Marines, who respectfully ignored his existence. He held a magazine so it obscured most of his face. His eyes never left the T.W.A.

desk. His right hand slipped inside the Navy jacket to bring the silenced automatic out. He slipped his gun-heavy hand under the raincoat and settled back to wait.

At precisely 5.30 Maronick walked confidently through the main doors. The striking gentleman had developed a slight limp, the kind observers invariably try to avoid looking at and the kind they always watch. The limp dominates their impression and their mind blurs the other details their eyes record. A uniform often accomplishes the same thing.

Maronick had grown a mustache with the help of a theatrical supply house, and when he stopped at the T.W.A. desk Malcolm did not recognise him. But Maronick's soft voice drew his attention, and he strained to hear the conversation.

'My name is James Cooper. I believe you have a reservation for me.'

The desk clerk flipped her head slightly to place the wandering auburn lock where it belonged. 'Yes, Mr. Cooper, Flight 27 to Chicago. You have about fifteen minutes until boarding time.'

'Fine.' Maronick paid for his ticket, checked his one bag, and walked aimlessly away from the counter. Almost empty, he thought. Good. A few servicemen, everything normal; mother and baby, normal; old drunks, normal; college girl, normal. No large preponderance of men standing around busily doing nothing. No one scurrying to phones, including the girl behind the desk. Everything normal. He relaxed even more and began to stroll, checking the terminal and giving his legs the exercise they would miss on the long flight. He didn't notice the Navy captain who slowly joined him at a distance of twenty paces.

Malcolm almost changed his mind when he saw Maronick looking so confident and capable. But it was too late for that. Help might not arrive in time and Maronick might get away. Besides, this was something Malcolm had to do himself. He fought down the drug-edged nervousness. He would get only one chance.

National Airport, while not breath-takingly beautiful, is attractive. Maronick allowed himself to admire the symmetry of the corridors he passed through. Fine colors, smooth lines.

Suddenly he stopped. Malcolm barely had time to dodge behind a rack of comic books. The proprietress gave him a withering glance but said nothing. Maronick checked his watch and held a quick debate with himself. He would just have time. He began to move again, substituting a brisk walk for his leisurely stroll. Malcolm followed his example, carefully avoiding loud footsteps on the marble stretches. Maronick took a sudden right and passed through a door, which swung shut behind him.

Malcolm trotted to the door. His hand holding the gun under the raincoat was sweating from the heat, the drug, and his nerves. He stopped outside the brown door. Gentlemen. He looked around him. No one. Now or never. Being careful to keep the gun between his body and the door, he pulled the weapon out from under the coat. He tossed the heavy raincoat to a nearby chair. Finally, his heart beating against his chest, he leaned on the door.

It opened easily and quietly. One inch. Malcolm could

see the glistening white brightness of the room. Mirrors sparkled on the wall to his far left. He opened the door a foot. The wall with the door had a line of three shiny sinks. He could see four urinals on the opposite wall, and he could make out the corner of one stall. No one stood at the sinks or the urinals. Lemony disinfectant tingled his nose. He pushed the door open and stepped in. It closed behind him with a soft *woosh* and he leaned heavily against it.

The room was brighter than the spring day outside the building. The piped-in music found no material capable of absorbing its volume, so the sound echoed off the tile walls – cold, crisp, blaring notes. There were three stalls opposite Malcolm. In the one on the far left he could see shoes, toes pointed towards him. Their polish added to the brightness of the room. The flute in the little box on the ceiling posed a gay musical question and the piano answered. Malcolm slowly raised the gun. The sound of toilet paper turning a spindle cued the band. The flute piped a more melancholy note, as it inquired once more. A tiny click from the gun's safety preceded the sound of tearing paper and the piano's soft reply.

The gun jumped in Malcolm's hand. A hole tore through the thin metal stall door. Inside the stall the legs jerked, then pushed upward. Maronick, slightly wounded in the neck, desperately reached for the gun in his back pocket, but his pants were around his ankles. Maronick normally carried his gun holstered either at his belt or under his arm, but he had planned to ditch the weapon before passing through the security screening at the airport. There would probably be no need of a gun at this stage of the plan, especially at a large, crowded airport, but the cautious Maronick put his gun in his back pocket, unobtrusive but sometimes awkward to reach, just in case.

Malcolm fired again. Another bullet tore through screeching metal to bury itself in Maronick's chest and fling his body against the wall. Malcolm fired again, and again and again and again. The gun spat the spent cartridge cases in to the tile floor. Bitter cordite mixed with the lemony smell. Malcolm's third bullet ripped a hole through Maronick's stomach. Maronick sobbed softly, and fell down along the right side of the metal cage. His weakening arm depressed the plunger. The *woosh* of water and waste momentarily drowned out his sobs and the coughs from the gun. As Malcolm fired the fourth time, a passing stewardess hearing the muffled cough remembered it was cold season. She vowed to buy some vitamins. That bullet missed Maronick's sinking form. The lead shattered on the tile wall, sending little pieces of shrapnel into the metal walls and tile roof. A few hit Maronick's back, but they made no difference. Malcolm's fifth bullet buried itself in Maronick's left hip, positioning the dying man on the stool.

Malcolm could see the arms and feet of a man slumped on a toilet. A few red flecks stained the tile pattern. Slowly, almost deliberately, Maronick's body began to slide off the toilet. Malcolm had to be sure before he confronted the man's face, so he squeezed the trigger for the last two rounds. An awkward knee on a naked and surprisingly hairless leg jammed against a stall post. The body shifted slightly as it settled to the floor. Malcolm could see enough of the pale face. Death replaced Maronick's striking appearance with a rather common, glassy dullness. Malcolm dropped the gun to the floor. It skidded to a stop near the body.

It took Malcolm a few minutes to find a phone booth. Finally a pretty oriental stewardess helped the rather dazed naval officer. He even had to borrow a dime from her.

'493-7282.' Mitchell's voice wavered slightly.

Malcolm took his time. In a very tired voice he said, 'This is Malcolm. It's over. Maronick is dead. Why don't you send somebody to pick me up? I'm at National Airport. So is Maronick. I'm the guy in the Navy uniform by the Northwest terminal.'

Three carloads of agents arrived two minutes ahead of the squad car summoned by the janitor who had found more than dirty toilets in his rest room.

'The whole is equal to the sum of its parts.'

— *Traditional mathematical concept*

Wednesday Afternoon

'It was like shooting birds in a cage.' The three men sipped their coffee. Powell looked at the smiling old man and Dr. Lofts. 'Maronick didn't stand a chance.'

The old man looked at the doctor. 'Do you have any explanation for Malcolm's actions?'

The large man considered his answer, then said, 'Without having talked to him at great length, no. Given his experiences of the last few days, especially the deaths of his friends and his belief that the girl was dead, his upbringing, training, and the general situation he found himself in, to say nothing of the drug's possible effect, I think his reaction was logical.'

Powell nodded. He turned to his superior and said, 'How's Atwood?'

'Oh, he will live, for a while at least. I always wondered about his oafishness. He did too well to be the idiot he played. He can be replaced. How are we handling Maronick's death?'

Powell grinned. 'Very carefully. The police don't like it, but we've pressured them into accepting the idea that the Capitol Hill Killer committed suicide in the men's room of National Airport. Of course, we had to bribe the janitor

254

to forget what he saw. No real problems, however!

A phone by the old man's elbow rang. He listened for a few moments, then hung up. He pushed the button next to the phone and the door opened.

Malcolm was coming down from the drug. He had spent three hours bordering on hysteria, and during that time he had talked continually. Powell, Dr. Lofts, and the old man heard six days compressed into three hours. They told him Wendy was alive after he finished, and when they took him to see her he was dazed by exhaustion. He stared at the peacefully sleeping form in the bright, antiseptic room and seemed not to be aware of the nurse standing beside him. 'Everything will be fine.' She said it twice but got no reaction. All Malcolm could see of Wendy was a small head swathed in bandages and a sheet-covered form connected by wires and plastic tubing to a complicated machine. 'My God,' he whispered with mixed relief and regret, 'my God.' They let him stand there in silence for several minutes before they sent him out to be cleaned up. Now he had on clothes from his apartment, but he looked strange even in them.

'Ah, Malcolm, dear boy, sit down. We won't keep you long.' The old man was at his charming best, but he failed to affect Malcolm.

'Now, we don't want you to worry about a thing. Everything is taken care of. After you've had a nice long rest, we want you to come back and talk to us. You will do that, won't you, my boy?'

Malcolm slowly looked at the three men. To them his voice seemed very old, very tired. To him it seemed new. 'I don't have much choice, do I?'

The old man smiled, patted him on the back, and,

mbling platitudes, led him to the door. When he
returned to his seat, Powell looked at him and said, 'Well,
sir, that's the end of our Condor.'

The old man's eyes twinkled. 'Don't be so sure, Kevin,
my boy, don't be so sure.'